Why Seagulls Roost in Paris

KATHLEEN CURTIN

Published by Kathleen Curtin
spleodrach
Email: kurtin@orange.fr
Twitter: Kathleen curtin@kitybern
Facebook: Why Seagulls Roost in Paris-Kathleen Curtin

Editors: Ellen M. Curtin and Majella Flynn
Design: www.emmagraves.co.uk
Formatter: Yvonne Betancourt - www.ebook-format.com

ISBN: 979-10-96434-03-9

ACKNOWLEDGEMENTS

To Huguette Jarrosson who has always unconditionally motivated and encouraged me to reach for my dreams. Your endless wisdom and strength has given me wonderful example to follow. Merci to you and your husband, Andre.

Majella, you have once again done a phenomenal job – there are no words for the unfailing patience and support that you have given, together with your husband, Paul.

Bruce Wertz, your work, advice and invaluable contribution on so many fronts have been vital.

Family, near and far, Go raibh maith agat!

To those special friends: knowing I can count on you means everything; Eilis O'Mahony, Joan Cahill, Breda Crowley, Mary and Ian Stoyle, Mary and Dan Kelleher, Kevin and Anne Long, Tim Flynn, Maggie and Philip Mohally, Eddy and Triona Fitzgerald - and all your children, spouses and partners.

A number of friends, students and acquaintances in France have given in countless ways – by keeping my head above water and being willing listeners; the list is exhaustive, but for this book a salute to Carmela Barloy, Sylvie Brunet, Kristel Fleureau, Marie-Pol Lecorvec, Francois Mauduit, Agnes Quelin…

To all the readers and book people: every story of mine that you have ever bought, read, or spoken about has given me great pleasure and makes it all worthwhile. You are now happily too many to mention, but know that you are in my heart.

And just as in every book, I must return to my beginnings and acknowledge the two people to whom I owe everything. Although they both have passed on, my mother and father have never left my side. They were my first teachers and story book – and the best.

TO MY SISTER, AILEEN – THANK YOU!
You have shared my childhood memories and grown up dreams.
You have been a branch to lean on in rough weather and a light helping
me through the tunnel in darker times – never judging, but always giving.

1

"Yes – or – No?" Madame Misere glared at me.

"I–I have to think it over." 'Don't take it,' a voice warned in my head, 'you will go mad here.'

"Think – It – Over!" each word was enunciated and churned out in disbelief by my potential new landlady. "This is Neuilly-sur-Seine! Do you not realise how many people are interested in this room – it will not be here tomorrow?"

Mme Misere was middle aged, of average height and slightly built. There was nothing extraordinary about her, but with her dark flashing eyes and hawk-like nose, she seemed big and powerful. Her platinum blond hair was swept back into a French knot, a style that older Parisian women showed off with elegance. Her makeup was minimal and she wore what at first glance appeared to be a plain skirt, blouse and shoes – but there was nothing plain about any of those items. Her ivory blouse was silk and without a wrinkle; her grey well-cut skirt showed off long legs, and a pair of expensive, black leather shoes sported a heel high enough to add femininity, but low enough for practicality. A pink and orange silk scarf draped casually over one shoulder, pearl earrings, a matching pearl ring and a silver watch that she kept glancing at, completed the look. It was what French people called BCBG, 'bon chic bon genre' – basically, style with attitude.

It was a hot day and the little room where we were standing was stuffy, but Mme Misere, smelling of lily perfume, looked fresh and cool. I had on a black T-shirt and a pair of blue jeans that I thought flattered my figure – but now compared with this chic lady just seemed like faded jeans on a skinny body. A pair of cheap runners did not add to my 5 foot 5 inches, and under her scrutiny as she towered over me, I felt more like a school girl than a woman.

I was twenty-four, that delicate age category when we still think we can get away with looking like teenagers, but shy away from the full responsibility of adulthood. Until now, I had au-paired for a French family in the 17th district of Paris, and in addition I'd had the good fortune to give English conversation classes to Madame Defoe, a wealthy businessman's wife, who lived in this very suburb of Neuilly-sur-Seine. Mme Misere had agreed to meet me on Mme Defoe's excellent recommendation. The job of teaching Mme Defoe happened by chance. An acquaintance of an acquaintance who was returning to Ireland sought out a replacement – and due to my inability to say no to people, I accepted to teach Mme Defoe, albeit with little enthusiasm. But in the end, that little weekly hour and a half class in her Neuilly home was my good fortune. Mme Defoe was a practical, resourceful lady and a great support to somebody like me as she had already gone through some of life's knocks. Until meeting her, I'd been at a personal low and experiencing the depths of depression. Today, I barely pulled myself out of bed and desperately needed something to hope for. Leaving my au-pair job and moving out on my own was part of that hope and change – but renting this room might not encourage the optimistic side of my nature.

I could feel the perspiration on my pale skin and knew my makeup-free face was shining. I was sure my long tawny hair must look limp and my green eyes, my strongest feature, would appear dull and tired due to a sleepless night.

"Yes, Mme Misere," my voice squeaked, "I do realise that there's demand for rooms such as yours." In truth, it was the most wretched, dismal place I'd seen in my life. The old hen house on the farm near where I'd grown up in Ireland had more appeal than this squat. How could anyone be expected to live in such a cheerless chicken coop?

"Well, what is it to be?" Once more, Mme Misere looked impatiently at her watch, then folded her arms and leaned towards me, making me feel hounded and intimidated.

"How much is the rent?" I asked, annoyed that my voice squeaked even more.

She swung her arm abruptly and I ducked, "This is a fine room in a building of standing and you will not find better – at two thousand six hundred Francs a month, it is very reasonable."

"Two thousand six hundred Francs!" I worked hard to stop my eyebrows from lifting.

She gave another edgy wave with her hands, making it clear to me there was no negotiating this price. "This is Neuilly-sur-Seine," she repeated.

With its wealthy select residential neighbourhoods, gated entrances and cul-de-sacs, Neuilly-sur-Seine was described as the ghetto of the rich. In addition, it was home to many corporate headquarters. While as a suburb it was excluded from the 20 administrative districts of Paris, Neuilly was unofficially known as the 21st district and served by Metro Line 1, a central artery of the city. It had all the advantages of living in Paris: boutiques, restaurants, theatres, cinemas, hospitals and clinics – but none of the disadvantages, such as being overrun with tourists and beggars. There were wonderful wide and straight tree-lined avenues and boulevards whose buildings displayed the architecture of the mid-nineteenth century, known as the Haussmann period. Many of these buildings were five or six storeys high. Their distinguishing features included elevated ceilings at ground level, perfectly adapted for shops and businesses, and elaborate first floor balconies, called Noble Balconies. The name 'Noble' hailed from former times when there were no lifts and naturally the first floor was the choice of the privileged; thus, the lower levels sported more elaborate architectural details. Neuilly-sur-Seine also had lots of fountains, squares, playgrounds, gardens and parks. It incorporated part of the great Bois de Boulogne, a natural unwinding public park for Parisians as well as Neuilléens with its lakes, walkways, equestrian centre and the renowned Longchamp Racecourse.

So yes, the address of what might be my future residence was Neuilly-sur-Seine, but this building, situated close to the Porte Maillot roundabout that separated us from Paris proper, was not the best section of the suburb. On top, with its eight storeys, it lacked some of the architectural qualities of the Haussmann period. Certainly on entering the building, I was at first impressed by the black and white marbled hallway and great marble winding staircase lined with a luxurious red carpet runner and gold fittings. There was also a quaint old-fashioned wooden lift with a wrought-iron gate at the front of the building. But I quickly discovered that the lift served the residents of the main apartments and that the seventh floor attic rooms, where I was now, could only be accessed by a narrow wooden stairway at the back of the courtyard. And yet, that Neuilly address commanded such a high rent. Fair enough, things didn't come cheap in 1998, but I was close to broke. I was also useless at bargaining.

'Take it,' my common sense inner voice took over. 'You've been flat hunting for weeks and you haven't come up with anything else. You have to start somewhere.'

Mme Misere moved away from the doorway and I squeezed my way farther inside. She claimed the room was ten and a half metres squared, emphasising the half, but in my opinion it was barely ten metres squared – and her definition of fully furnished was minimalist at best.

"You will find the kitchen well equipped," Mme Misere gushed.

'You mean a space with a few plugs and switches,' I said to myself, but simply nodded.

"And you have a good bed."

It was difficult to get around the bed, for although small, it left little space for anything else. In fact, it was not unlike what I imagined a prison bed would look like.

"You see here the washbasin," she pointed a well manicured, clear-polished nail towards the window.

"Yes indeed." I looked in dismay at a very shallow, worse-for-wear, chipped, ceramic sink beneath the window.

I sat wearily on the only chair and rested my arms on a wobbly wooden table between the foot of the bed and sink.

Madame Misere was anxious to point out that there was an immersion to heat the water and a rail to hang my clothes from. The rail, an ordinary clothes horse that could be bought at any supermarket, was stored in a narrow built-in wooden wardrobe. Other so-called rented accommodation of similar size didn't supply those extras, she said. The room was crammed and didn't have much space for walking or moving about without risk of bumping and bruising. But a room it was and mine to rent if I wanted it. French people called rooms like this a 'chambre de bonne,' roughly translated as a maid's room, because in the old days it served exactly as that. Apartments often came not just with a cellar, but also a 'chamber de bonne' on the attic floor.

I heard Mme Misere's impatient huff and didn't dare look at her face. I needed air, the heat was stifling and perspiration trickled down my back. I wiped my damp brow, stood up from the little table and took one step to the only window. Something about the glass panes reminded me of what I'd been told about war-glass from the 1940s – basically, the quality was thinner and cheaper. I opened it, noting that the shutters were made from old, rotting timber, stiff and reluctant to yield. They had recently been freshened up with a coat of white paint which was already scaly and flaking.

Mme Misere brushed past me and stuck her head all the way out the window, putting a hand to her ear in an exaggerated gesture. "Listen, Mademoiselle, listen. You are not too disturbed by the noise – you can hardly hear a thing."

'Well no,' I mocked silently. The room was, after all, just under the roof. From my limited Parisian experience, I knew that apparently quiet areas burst into life at the most unexpected times of the day and night. When deciding on a suitable place to live, one would be advised to do a twenty-four/seven sit-in to discover all the potential sources of noise pollution and every other problem that was likely to crop up.

Seeing some doubt on my face, Mme Misere emphasised her point, "Listen, there is no noise."

'Okay, okay, I get the message,' I continued my personal discussion. It annoyed me that the lady insisted on speaking in broken English, especially as I did speak French fluently.

"What about my neighbours, are they noisy?" I finally dared to ask a question.

"Noisy?" Mme Misere looked at me in puzzlement, "not at all, they are very calm."

"Really, who's next door?"

She made a tut-tutting sound, "You mean just next door, Room 1?"

"Yes, next door." My question seemed to be giving her some bother and I waited curiously for her answer.

"Why, Monsieur – Monsieur," the name escaped her somehow, "why, that man is in no condition to make noise."

"I'm not sure I understand – what condition is he in?"

"Now – look out there, isn't that nice?" Mme Misere seemed determined to move the conversation on. "You see, the visa-via is perfect and the street is wide. Oh look, you can just see the tip of the Eiffel Tower."

I didn't think the street was that wide and as for the Eiffel Tower – I looked and looked, I goggled until my eyes almost popped out of my head, but I couldn't glimpse it. I grimaced – Mme Misere wouldn't lie about that, would she? 'Liz Downey, you're too much of a doubter,' I chastised myself. I could, however, capture the sight and sound of the endless traffic snaking its way around the Porte Maillot roundabout in a most undisciplined manner.

"And le Bois de Boulogne," Mme Misere gestured at a slightly different angle.

Once again, I struggled to bring the famous wood into my line of vision. I turned my head to the right and to the left. Ah, I suppose she meant those few branches reflected off that ugly, blue mirrored building on the Paris side of the traffic roundabout.

"And greenery right outside your window," Mme Misere bestowed a benevolent smile that appeared to take in the length and breadth of Rue Montrosier.

That was true. I couldn't deny having the privilege of looking down on the crowns of some horse chestnut trees. There was, however, one great view that I was sure of – if I just walked around the corner onto Avenue Charles de Gaulle, I would be able to see L'Arc de Triomphe at the top of the Champs Elysées on the east and La Grande Arche de la Défense on the west. But even that priceless view was temporarily spoilt by the fact that L'Arc de Triomphe was currently under renovation and completely covered with scaffolding. I would have to wait until next year to examine the details of that early 19th-century arch, first requested by Napoleon Bonaparte and today honouring those who died for France during the Revolution and other wars.

I took one more peek out the window and told myself, 'Liz Downey, you had better be sure, because this is what you will be seeing for a long time to come.' I heard a shriek. 'Could those be seagulls swooping onto that roof-top across the street?' I asked myself. 'Nah, couldn't be, they should be on a wing over the Atlantic. They must be pigeons' –from this distance, I couldn't tell the difference between seagulls and pigeons.

I focused on making up my mind. The biggest difficulty I saw was that apart from one chipped basin, there were no other washing facilities – there was neither bath nor shower. The only toilet was a 'Turkish Loo' down the corridor which was shared by everyone on this side of the landing. The logic of a Turkish toilet was that a hole in the ground over which one was supposed to squat was more hygienic than an actual sit on toilet. Another drawback was the fact that the room was hot and if we had a real heat wave, I'd surely fry here. I tried to be positive – we were approaching September and I wouldn't need to worry about heat waves until summer came around next year.

Although I tried to gain time by requesting a few days to think over my decision, Mme Misere wasn't having any of it. She told me that I had to give my answer today and get Mme Defoe, my guarantor, to sign all the documents if I wanted to secure the lease.

Everything went into motion once Mme Defoe decided to help me. When I told her of my wish to leave my au-pairing job and find a place on my own, she understood my need for independence and at the same time my lack of funds. Mme Defoe, though rich, had earned her money through hard work and patience, making her a resourceful woman. Unfortunately, her own attic rooms were already let out, but she was kind and could see that I needed help. A 'chambre de bonne' to rent wasn't something one saw advertised in the usual magazines and newspapers, but having lived during the same war as the glass, Mme Defoe had her own idea of what social networking was – if you wanted something, you went after it in the old-fashioned way. She personally inquired and got information from her own concierge about the availability of a room in the neighbourhood – concierges and caretakers were usually the first to know about such things. She also encouraged me to check in all the local cafés, bakers, dry-cleaners... I followed her helpful advice – and here I was, knowing I was fortunate to find this room, but wishing it was a little bigger with a toilet, and accessed by a lift.

"Okay," I said, "I'll take it – if you're sure the floor is quiet."

"I promise you, the floor is very, very calm." Mme Misere smiled and shook my hand to seal the deal and in so doing sealing my fate for the next twelve months.

****

In the days that followed, finalising the terms and conditions of the lease fell smoothly into place. A quick checklist was drawn up of the room's contents, together with a basic contract and Mme Defoe's signature as guarantor. It was a very simple contract, as 10.5m squared was barely inside the legal limit of what could be called rented accommodation. I signed on the dotted line, rather begrudgingly paid a month's rent in advance, together with a deposit – and 'voila,' it was mine for the next year.

Looking on the bright side, I now had a place to call my own. I wouldn't have to do babysitting anymore, except if I wanted to, and there would be no more ironing clothes for extra money. I'd no longer be living in the shadow of another family, even if the Soudier family for whom I had au-paired for the past year were very kind. I was lucky to now have this little room where I could be really independent. I'd gained a new freedom and while I didn't exactly flap my wings or flutter about in delight, I did afford myself a little smile. "I am now living in Room Number 2, at 9 Rue Montrosier, Neuilly-sur-Seine," I liked the sound of the address rolling off my tongue.

"Par ici, Messieurs – par ici," a high pitched voice drifted from the street through my open window.

What was all that commotion? I asked myself. I hung my upper body out the window and saw that Madame Gomes, the concierge, was standing out on the street next to the 'Sapeurs Pompiers,' and their distinctive red fire-truck. Something must be amiss somewhere to bring the fire brigade; perhaps there had been an accident. Mme Misere had introduced me briefly to Mme Gomes on my first visit – it was comforting to know that somebody took care of the building and was on duty to deal with general services.

"C'EST ICI," this time Mme Gomes shouted her words.

I withdrew inside my window again, but sniffed the air a little, keeping my ears open in case of an emergency.

Less than a minute later, 'Thump – Thump – Thump –' sounded loudly on the stairs. It seemed that the hullabaloo had entered my part of building. I opened my door and walked down the narrow corridor to the landing in time to see a breathless concierge making her way up the wooden steps and simultaneously dishing out directions to two firemen.

"What's going on?" I asked.

"Oh, Mon Dieu!" Madame Gomes gulped for air on the landing. The pint-sized woman raised her flushed face towards me, "Oh heavens above, Monsieur Charteau died in Room 1. The poor man was worn to nothing, he was recovering from cancer, but he didn't recover. Now, procedure has to take place – we can't avoid procedure. When someone's been dead for a day or so, we have to deal with it the right way."

"A day or so – a dead man has been in that room for a more than a day?"

"He wasn't dead when he arrived here," the concierge assured me, "but he is now, dead as dead can be."

"Are they taking his body away?"

"Can't do that yet – there's a procedure to follow. They have to locate his relatives – so nobody can touch the room, not until the authorities give permission."

Mme Gomes seemed willing to share a good chunk of her knowledge on the situation with me. I strained my ears and concentrated hard to pick up what the woman was saying as it came spluttering out in a jumble of Portuguese and French.

"It was the closed window and smell really that alerted us. When M. Charteau was in form and active, he'd go out during the day, but when he was feeling poorly, he wouldn't walk outside and hated being disturbed. That's why we didn't notice or pay heed until a short time ago. Then I used the spare key to check in on him and – "

"But they will remove his body today, won't they?" I didn't relish the thought of spending my first night next door to a dead man.

"I suppose, it depends on procedure," the concierge tilted her elf-like face and patted her short brown curls.

I shuddered, thinking that maybe I'd end up like M. Charteau – alone, forgotten and pushing daisies up the floor boards. I hadn't thought about the smell until the concierge drew my attention to it, that dead smell, and now I was sure it was filling my nostrils. But it wasn't the only scent – what was that other distinctive spicy odour forcing its way through?

"Who else is living on this floor?" I asked.

Mme Gomes waved her hand to indicate the corridor on the other side of the landing, "Monsieur and Madame Bjania live there – they have two children, and they have friends, many, many friends. Then, there's Monsieur Jacques next door to them. He's special, very special," she gave me a look as if I should know what that meant.

I understood from her wandering description that he was some sort of rag and bone man who as well as being on social welfare, made his living from collecting scrap and reselling it.

"There's Monsieur Brosse," Mme Gomes continued.

I gathered that he was a handy man who kept to himself.

"There's my son, Demetrio, on this side – and two students will be arriving – and then – "

I'd lost track, it was a whole village.

We looked on as one of the firemen stuck red tape across the doorway of my dead neighbour. He'd be nothing more than that, a dead neighbour and a complete stranger to me. This was a morose beginning to my new life.

"No luck in that room," Mme Gomes shook her head while making the sign of the cross.

"Why do you say that?" I was annoyed with myself for even asking.

"Murder!"

My heart sank – more macabre news.

"There was a terrible murder in that very room," the concierge lowered her voice, although she didn't make a great effort or persist very long at keeping it that way. Sensationalism was infectious after all and the firemen were now included among her audience in this titbit of information.

I held on to my patience and listened while trying to piece together the story from the fragments Mme Gomes gave us. Apparently, Room 1, at 9 Rue Montrosier, had a sordid history. But the concierge was vague on the particulars of when and who and how. She was, however, clear on one thing: the front pages of newspapers in the past carried the headline – 'MONTROSIER SLAUGHTER.'

'Shit,' I didn't like the sound of that.

I pressed her for more details, but from what I could glean, it was certainly more than one hundred years before and the supposed news headline was a case of 'somebody who told somebody who told somebody…' Nothing to be worried about, I tried to dismiss the whole thing to myself. Stories like that were to be found everywhere – there wasn't a place that didn't have its tales of grief, sorrow and tragedy.

"Happens all the time," said one of the firemen.

I wasn't sure if he were joking or not.

"Not a grain of luck there," repeated Mme Gomes, "that room's better off empty. Every time people come to live there, they are struck down by misfortune; if it isn't murders, it's mysterious disappearances and horrible illnesses. Nobody ever lasts for long in Room 1 – look at M. Charteau and his sad end."

"He was suffering from cancer, you can't really blame the room for that," I decided to put a stop to her fear-mongering and negative prophesies.

But the concierge wasn't interested in rational reasoning, "Room 1 attracts troubled people and people with trouble," she grasped the banister and began her descent.

I turned to one of the firemen for more information and he assured me that the Coroner would be arriving shortly and that my neighbour's body would be removed before nightfall. Feeling slightly better, I went back to my own room, refusing to let Mme Gomes's talk and stories from the past dampen my spirits.

I sat on the edge of my bed, picked up and began leafing through the only book I'd brought with me from Ireland, one that had been passed down through generations in my family. I treasured this tattered copy of *Twenty Years A-Growing*, by Maurice O'Sullivan, 1933. I'd done the growing bit and the next twenty was supposed to be 'twenty years a-flowering.' Well, I'd made small inroads to that period of my life, but I hadn't done much flowering or blooming yet. According to the old proverb, that period would be followed by 'twenty years a-fading,' and finally 'twenty years when it doesn't matter whether you're here or gone.' I'd better hurry up or I'd soon be 'a-fading.'

I pressed the book to my cheek and thought of my mother. My father died when I was just a one-year-old, so Mum and I were always very close. The book was one of her gifts to me for my thirteenth birthday. That was when she'd been proud of me. That was before I'd dropped out of my secure secondary school teacher's job after a mere few months and hiked off to France with the man of my dreams, Marc-Antoine, a visiting French teacher. Apart from one telephone call when Mum told me that I had broken her heart, we didn't have a chance to speak again before her untimely death. I often thought about that – could a broken heart kill someone? People said shock triggered many things and my actions certainly shocked my mother. Who could say? The only certainty was that next time I saw Mum it was too late to tell her that she'd been right about Marc-Antoine, and too late for her to tell me, 'I told you so.'

11

It took Marc-Antoine three months to show his true colours and dump me. Pride had kept me from going back to Ireland sooner. I'd already swallowed a good portion of it by working as an au-pair and trying to live somehow in France rather than running home and crying for help. Besides, Mum hadn't understood that I hated secondary school teaching. What a disaster that had been. I'd been hopeless with unruly adolescents and my classroom had been without discipline or control. I'd only gone into teaching to please Mum in the first place.

Eventually, I had gone back home, but by then it was too late. Mum suffered a stroke – when I got to the hospital, a nurse informed me that she had already slipped into a coma. I will never forget walking into the hospital room where she lay, a room so different to the one I stood in now, with other sounds and smells. Everything was still vivid in my mind, especially Mum's face as pale as the white pillow her head rested on. I did tell her then how much I loved her. I don't know if she understood, but I repeated it over and over. The nurses and medical staff were kind, but I didn't want kindness, I just wanted Mum to open her eyes and to say that everything was all right. She never regained consciousness. I felt so useless, I hadn't been there when she needed me most. If only I could turn back the clock.

'It's for the best' were the words I heard most often from people commiserating with me at the funeral. How I hate it when people tell me things like that and I hate it even more when people tell me how I should feel. There were words like, 'You are young, you'll get over it in time.' Sure, I thought, we get over everything, sometimes faster than we should. 'Your whole life is before you, do something with it' was the advice of one of Mum's well-meaning friends. I hadn't made much of a go of my life so far.

Only eighteen months had passed since Mum's death, and yet it seemed like another time and another world. The rented cottage was all she had in life, but compared to the room I was renting, it was a mansion. I recalled standing on the cliff and hearing the cries of the seagulls the day I removed all her belongings and locked the door for the last time. The Atlantic Ocean had never seemed harsher or colder and I'd never been lonelier. I knew then that I was alone, truly alone. There was nobody to approve or disapprove of my choices. My life was mine to live and my mistakes were my own to make.

I'd come back to Paris and tried to continue as before. But it became harder and harder to function normally. One day, while babysitting the children of the Soudier family, I was overcome with sadness and had the sensation of sliding into a dark hole. I somehow managed to get through the evening, but went to bed that night feeling total emptiness and in despair. The next morning, the feeling was still with me and it continued for many weeks. It was as if a shadow had fallen on me and the depression that had been creeping up on me was taking over my life. That had been my lowest point. Fortunately for me, I was already teaching Mme Defoe and it was her astuteness and emotional sensitivity that probably saved my life. She recognised that I needed help and directed me to a good doctor. With his assistance and medication, I managed to drag myself out of that black hole and gradually recover my confidence. That personal experience humbled me and made me understand the delicateness of human nature and how frail the thread of life really is.

I put down the book and wiped my tears. "There now, do you feel better?" I had the same bad habit as Mum of talking out loud to myself. There was nothing like a good dose of guilt and self-pity to comfort oneself. I decided that was enough of that, I wasn't going to sit on the bed wallowing all day, I would do something useful.

Action was a great cure and always helped to lift my soul. I needed to stock up my reserves of food. I checked my shopping list: rice, pasta, tuna, sauces, and cheap chocolate wafers, simply because I liked them. Coffee was essential, I couldn't move without pots of it. I'd get a few cans of beer; I justified the beer by telling myself that I was entitled to some luxuries in life. I decided I didn't need bottled water and would make do with tap water. It would avoid me hauling bottles up seven floors and save a little money. When I sampled the water from the tap, I found it passable enough. If I didn't let it sit too long, I could hardly taste the chlorine. I didn't give myself time to examine the logic of my conclusions too closely.

"Right," I slapped my thigh, "get going – to the supermarket."

I hopped down the stairs and met a policeman and a serious dark suited man in discussion with Mme Gomes in the main hallway. I didn't linger and went outside, noting that an ambulance had already arrived. I walked onto Avenue Charles de Gaulle, taking a moment to admire a scaffolding-covered Arc de Triomphe to the east and the Arch of La Défense to the west. I had to admit that I couldn't have found a more convenient location: my room was a few minutes from the Metro Line 1, a hop, skip and a jump from stores and airport buses, and I could practically spit from my window into Paris. I'd arrived in Neuilly-sur-Seine, home to traditional Catholic and Jewish populations and to numerous lovely churches and synagogues. But the vulgarity of 'Nouveau Riche,' tanned faces, big cars and 'bling bling' were also on display in this traditional suburb. While Neuilly-sur-Seine was beautiful, it did have some ugliness and undesirable spots. I had heard that prostitutes hovered on the margins of this exclusive suburb. The ring road at the Porte Maillot roundabout and the woodlands of Boulogne converted to zones of prostitution at night for all sorts of loveless trade.

I didn't delay in my local Monoprix supermarket, a popular chain in France. I found supermarkets in Paris different to Ireland. They were small and poky – service was slow and grumpy and customers specialised in jumping the queue.

Afterwards, I counted my change and decided I could afford one Espresso on the terrace of Café du Marché in the market square. I was told that an open street market took place three mornings a week and I looked forward to experiencing that and meandering leisurely through the stalls. The waiter looked glum and just greeted me with a nod. He returned, swished a cloth across the table, planted my coffee – and was gone. Café du Marché was basic and the iron chairs made loud scraping noises on the tiled floors. The round plastic-top tables with wrought iron legs were solid but small, and could not accommodate too many items. There were just a few customers inside at the counter and the main business seemed to be a steady stream of people to the Tabac section from where cigarettes, lottery tickets and such were sold. Cigarette butts were strewn here and there on the terrace. I had already noted that in many cafés, ash trays got emptied onto the pavement and from there brushed into the gutter. The main clientele included early morning tradesmen and builders coming to and from construction sites, taxi drivers, delivery people, and alcoholics buying their next fix. Popular cafés usually served a basic French breakfast of fresh crispy baguette and viennoiserie-pastry such as croissant, pain au raisin or pain au chocolat. Customers could also buy a hard boiled egg from a stand set up on the counter. Such cafés were often preferred by the local population, drifting in and out before or after walking a dog, sitting with the morning newspaper, or simply taking a five-minute break, just as I was doing. They were appreciated for their basic simplicity and lower prices compared to some of the more fashionable places. After a while, I took an abandoned Le Parisien newspaper from a nearby table, resigning myself to a forced break while my neighbour's remains were hopefully being removed.

I gave it a good half hour before taking up my bags again and returning to my building in time to see an ambulance being driven away. I made my way slowly back up to my room. The stairs were steep and I paused several times to take a breath. The place suddenly seemed to have lost the last vestiges of any quaint, friendly feel. The aroma of various cooking smells from other rooms hung in the air – spicy chicken mingled with steak and onion. I didn't know if I'd grow to like those smells and once again started doubting my decision to rent the room. I wasn't convinced that I'd be glad to come up here alone, late at night. Mme Gomes had mentioned to me that a couple of students would be moving in soon – hopefully their arrival might help to lighten the atmosphere.

I reached the bend before the last flight of steps. The landing floor boards creaked – I paused and waited, expecting somebody descending the stairs to appear. But nobody came – instead I heard footsteps padding softly on the corridor. I listened carefully and caught the slight noise of a door opening and closing. 'Stop being so jumpy,' I cautioned myself, 'it's just a curious person and they slipped away because they didn't want to meet or talk to anyone.' I turned down the corridor, my shopping bags crinkling and crackling. On passing the late M. Charteau's door, I saw that the red tape had been removed and took it as a signal that his remains were no longer there. The room was empty again and waiting for its next tenant, or victim as Mme Gomes believed.

The gloom crept in to my little room. I lay on top of the bed in the fading light, listening to Radio Classique on my little clock radio. Pretty soon, the shadows turned to darkness and I had to switch on the only light. The naked bulb hanging from the ceiling added to the stark surrounds. I tried to see the funny side of things. In my room, I'd certainly taken a step back in terms of material comfort and a step forward in humility, patience, lung reinforcement and calf strengthening. The stairs promised to be a constant endurance test.

I got off the bed, cracked open a can of beer and went to the window thinking that the Eiffel Tower might be more visible at night when illuminated. Huh, there was no sign of the elusive tower. Maybe I needed more faith and to work harder at believing. I looked with greater fervour, but there were still no lights outlining anything that resembled a tower. However, the Paris side of the ring road was glowing with slow moving lines of traffic and Avenue de la Grande Armée was lit up all the way towards L'Arc de Triomphe.

I gave myself a quick superficial sponge cold wash and got into bed, deciding it was too hot for any clothes. Sufficiently buoyed up by alcohol, I felt more confident about having made the right choice. If I wanted to stay in Paris and prove that I could stand on my own two feet, I'd have to make the most of this place. One thing was certain – it would be the single life for me from now on. I wasn't going to depend on anyone, least of all, a man. On that point, I was sure – I would be strong and make it on my own.

"Oh, God blast that beer," I found myself grumbling one hour later.

It'd been difficult to get through the evening without a few cans. I had persuaded myself that I should drink all three of them, as they'd get warm quickly without a fridge. But now I was paying the price. I put my hands on a T-shirt and pair of shorts – it wasn't possible to venture out undressed. I took pains to unlock the door as noiselessly as possible, opening it in millimetre measures. Then I made a dash for the toilet.

I did my business quickly managing a delicate balancing feat. The cistern resounded like an articulated truck in the stillness of the night and I could only begin to imagine what it would sound like around here when all the rooms were occupied and it was in constant use.

I got back out on the corridor and froze for a second on hearing a wailing sound. I glanced warily in the direction of the cursed Room 1 – had the noise come from there or did I imagine it? Had the dead man come back, or was it the murdered woman of years before? 'Don't be an idiot,' I rebuked, 'it's just a draught creating that whistling effect.' One could persuade themselves of anything in the middle of the night. I went as quickly as my legs could carry me back to my room. I decided that nightly trips on the corridor were not a good idea and in future I was either going to have to give up the beer or get a chamber pot. The choice wasn't hard to make.

I tossed and turned, while my ears tuned into all the different sounds inside and outside the building. I heard someone come slowly up the stairs and someone else rustling a plastic bag go down. A door opened and closed and somebody thudded around their room – it was probably Mme Gomes's sixteen-year-old son. He seemed very restless and moved around for a long time. Finally, I heard the plumping of a mattress and the groaning of springs. The concierge's lodge on the ground floor wasn't big enough for all her family of four. I felt sorry for her son having to sleep up here, but I felt better knowing I wasn't alone on this side of the corridor.

The clock radio flashed one o'clock. I turned on my side – a cough, the distant hum of traffic, and a host of vibrations and movements coming from the different floors fed my nervous ravings and imaginings. Everything in the building was heaving and breathing, rising and falling. It was never totally still. Some doubts came knocking at my mind. 'Go away, go away,' I hunted them off vehemently, but they came back. 'Where to now, what next?' I asked myself. My failure with Marc-Antoine was well and truly behind me. That had been a hard earned experience. But I was a good pupil and I'd learnt my lesson: trust few was the new rule I'd resolved to live by. Falling back on au-pairing hadn't been a choice, but it had helped me get by. However, I couldn't have done that forever and I now needed to figure out what my next move was. People were often surprised that my steady, serious outward appearance disguised an impulsive nature. Twenty-four was still young, but it was time to find a proper job. It didn't take much stretch of the imagination to divine what I was most likely to try first. I could speak English, couldn't I? Surely it was a small step from giving Mme Defoe conversation classes to getting more official hours in an English language school. The city was brimming over with language schools. My financial reserves were low and I knew that I'd have to get my hands on money fast. Teaching? God, I couldn't bear the thought of it. "Not teaching, no please," I begged nobody in particular. A wave of panic hit me, followed by a wave of loneliness, and sleep finally enveloped me.

2

A scream tore through the morning air. It was tinged with horror, disgust and a splash of other emotions. The scream was my own.

That wasn't a good sign, not a good sign at all. I knew they would have been lurking around somewhere, the odds were strongly in favour of their presence. I didn't mind as long as I couldn't see them. But now I'd seen the creatures – I was being forced to watch them in action and could no longer deny their existence. The one I'd seen scurrying had been taking pleasure in an open packet of chocolate wafers which I had left sitting on the single portable hot-plate on top of the wobbly table at the foot of my bed. The dark creature stood out against the white enamel.

"God, I should have known it," I groaned, "cockroaches."

That was it – I jumped out of bed, didn't take time to brush my hair or wash my face, but pulled on the nearest pair of jeans I could find. I zipped up a light jacket and got my bare feet into a pair of runners. I didn't care how hot it was or what I looked like, I needed a solution immediately. I ran down the stairs and kept running until I got to the supermarket. I bought a bunch of cockroach poison traps and ran back.

Mme Gomes was brushing the marble tiles of the main hallway, but took the time to give me a speculative glance and then to scrutinise through the thin plastic of the bag in my hand. She shook her head, "That Bjania family, we had no cockroaches until they arrived in the building."

I didn't stay to discuss the issue with her and kept going through the hall, across the courtyard and up the back stairs. Once in my room, I placed the traps everywhere. I then put every open food package in a rubbish bag and only dared to nibble a croissant I had bought on the way back.

It was better not to dwell on the cockroaches and instead to sort out how I was going to support myself. As far as I was concerned, there was no time to waste. I had a class planned with Mme Defoe and she had a computer that she didn't know how to use, but I did and intended to utilise it in my search for a future job.

A few hours later, I had procured my first interview. Egged on by Mme Defoe and driven with the knowledge that I had no choice, it hadn't taken me long to find offers. I'd sifted through the recommended sites and bibles for English language teachers. It was clear that Teachers of English as a Foreign Language (TEFL) were in great demand. Finally, a small ad appealed because it seemed so straightforward – 'TEFL TEACHERS WANTED – Call William Whyte's School of English and Foreign Languages immediately.' The manager, Judith Harding, told me over the phone to come in to see her as soon as possible – they were urgently seeking TEFL teachers.

****

It was a strange sensation, the Alice in Wonderland effect. I had left the banks of the Seine and some fine linden and honey locust trees and made my way to Boulevard Saint Michel, crossed Place Saint Michel with its Baroque fountain of St. Michel killing a demon and entered the narrower streets of the Latin Quarter. The district was teaming with tourists and restaurants. I wished I could lounge on a sunny terrace and watch people go by, while inhaling the smells of cooking and brewing. Instead, I took the quieter, meandering Rue des Soeurs which had fewer cafés and restaurants, but many jewellery, antique and old book shops. There were also some small artists' galleries and residential buildings. I felt something wet on my face and looked up – somebody was watering their balcony flower boxes. I reached building number 30, pressed a button, then pushed in a heavy, giant-sized, varnished wooden door that was beautifully crafted with ornamental panels and a great brass handle. I found myself standing on a cobble-stoned courtyard and looking around at six-storey buildings. The door swung slowly closed and clicked softly after me. I examined my hands and was surprised not to see the dustings of history coming off. I could definitely feel like I was transported to the Middle Ages. The Latin Quarter's historical significance was palpable to me and transcended the 20th century.

At the opposite end of the yard was a much more disappointing structure squashed gracelessly in to a corner. Its structural design didn't fit in with the period and looked like a mistake. Part of it was old and in line with the rest of the architecture, but stuck on to that was a badly constructed shed-like extension with a corrugated roof that seemed like an afterthought. The gold plaque near the courtyard door on Rue des Soeurs had falsely announced grandeur: WILLIAM WHYTE'S SCHOOL Of ENGLISH & FOREIGN LANGUAGES.

One barred window and a heavy iron door beckoned me back to professional life. I heard a cry over my head and recognising the shriek, looked up – there they were again, seagulls in Paris. Seeing them and hearing their call reminded me of the Atlantic Ocean and immediately encouraged me. I walked across the cobbles, my best pair of shoes tapping out tentative steps. I slipped inside the half-open door and just like Alice in Wonderland everything started downsizing once I entered the building.

The ceilings were low and I kept wanting to crouch or to bend my head, even if I wasn't that tall and it wasn't necessary. The corridors were narrow – some doors were closed and from the voices inside, it was clear that classes were being conducted. Other doors were open and I saw that the rooms were quite small and furnished with miniature tables and chairs that looked more suitable for children. Apart from at the front, there seemed to be no other windows. All the rooms had names such as 'London, Oxford, Cambridge, St. Alban's, Exeter, Durham' – I felt that I had arrived in Little Britain. 'Lindisfarne' was a coffee space, and 'Stratford-Upon-Avon' looked like a library. 'St. Thomas's Tower' was no more than cupboard size, I noted as I peeped around the door, and 'St. Cuthbert's' whose door had swung open a little was definitely a cupboard. What an unusual hotchpotch for a school, I thought.

"W–W–S–O–E and F–L Bonjour – " a woman's voice croaked, drawing my attention to a door near the entrance that I must have missed coming in. The voice repeated the letters, delivering them at a slow, painstaking speed, in a partly French, partly American accent. It was proof if anything that the school's name which was so difficult to pronounce wasn't its strongest selling point to potential English students. I listened to the droning words as the voice conducted a conversation and I was momentarily lulled into a quiet meditation.

Suddenly, I realised the phone call had ended and the words were being directed at me, "You want a guided tour, or are you just looking for information?" The voice was now speaking English and the distinctly American accent came from the office with a glass door that was ajar. I couldn't see the woman directly, but I could make out the shadow of a hunched figure with longish hair, sitting behind a desk.

"I'm here for an interview, I have an appointment with Judith Harding," I said.

"Yeah," said the gravely voice, "you have an appointment with both of us."

I approached the door and understood that there wasn't one but in fact two adjoining offices. The woman behind the desk was easily over sixty. She was wearing thick black-framed reading glasses and her bleached blond hair hung limply around a face framing a prominent hooked nose.

"I'm Lena Kedrova, just call me Lena," she introduced herself in a friendlier manner, "I just help around here, you know, testing and admin. Judith is out visiting a client and should be back soon. You can sit here and wai–wai–" Lena gave a chesty cough, "wait for her to come back."

I sat on the chair across from her desk, catching a strong whiff of musky perfume and cigarettes. I opened my bag and took out a file containing my résumé and pretended to read it.

Lena took a pencil and leaned over a hard-backed journal on the desk – she seemed intent on ticking off lines, before transferring details on to the computer in slow, clumsy, one-fingered typing. She then pressed her face closely to the screen to read what she'd typed. Technology was obviously not her forte, I surmised.

"So, are you coming or going, just passing through Paris, or running off somewhere else from something or someone?"

I looked up – Lena's glare clearly communicated the question was intended for me.

I sat up straight in my chair, "I'm not running at all, from anything or anyone. I came to Paris to – to – broaden my horizons."

"Ah," Lena began paring her pencil, "they all say that. Many teachers pass through here and a lot of them are running, or hiding and avoiding. It ain't hard to tuck yourself away for a while here in this city."

"Surely not," I said.

"Surely yes," Lena shook the parings from a page into a dustbin and tapped a few more letters, "They fly in here – some don't last that long and fly off again. Others fly back home."

"Not everyone?"

"No, the rest stay roosting – broken wings, misfits, can't seem to find the right branch. They perch here and the years go by. That's the thing about living in Paris, you either love it or hate it – and that's the thing about teaching, makes you or breaks you. It's a vocation I say and there ain't many people with the true calling."

I wondered if this were some sort of preliminary interview Lena was conducting to test my mettle.

"How long have you been here?" I asked, trying to deflect attention away from me.

She inhaled noisily through her nose, "Long enough. I came to Europe when I was twenty, came on a boat and I never went back. I'm scared to death of flying."

Speaking about birds, if what she said were true, then Lena wasn't the return-migratory species. I now understood better the subtle twang to her accent. I felt that I'd switched to an old American movie channel.

There was a grunt and for the first time I noticed an unusual looking dog sprawled under the table. It looked like a Rat-Terrier, leaning more towards the rat than anything else, and some other mongrel mix that gave it longer hair than usual. What a decrepit creature, I thought – it huddled into a pitiful ball, as my disapproving look took in the brown and white lacklustre hair on its back.

"That's Hamilton," Lena smiled, showing a rather large set of teeth. "He don't like to be alone in the apartment and barks so much that it bothers the neighbours. Judith lets me keep him here. You wanna have a look around our residence, it ain't Hotel California, and it sure ain't a five-star?" she laughed at her own joke.

"Yes of course," I said, even though I had already taken a tour. I decided her laugh was closer to a cackle and I was also beginning to wonder if she exaggerated her accent for effect.

She closed the journal. Hamilton staggered to a vertical position, shaking and jingling the harness attached to his body.

"No, Hamilton," Lena waved her finger, "no walkies yet."

The dog dropped his head and crouched down again.

I followed the bony, slightly stooped Lena, as she shuffled down the corridor in flat blue runners that matched her blue pullover and loose-fitting navy trousers.

"Don't know if Judith will hire you, but no harm in looking and I don't think she has much choice." Lena got chattier, "A teacher ran out on us. They often do that – run – and leave us high and dry. Judith was livid."

If Lena was trying to dissuade me from working for Whyte's, she was doing a good job of it. I kept a few steps behind – the corridor was so narrow, it had to be taken in single file. I noted the false ceilings, revealing brown patches where rain water had clearly leaked in. The floor tiles must get dangerous and slippery on damp days, I thought. I marvelled once again at the kindergarten-sized desks and chairs. Could adults really sit there and look serious learning English? The French weren't usually tall, but sitting on childlike furniture must be uncomfortable. I also noticed that the furniture was blue, red or white, and perhaps meant to represent the colours of the Union Jack or the French flag. Who knows what the décor was supposed to represent.

I re-focused on my objective of securing a job and tried to show a general interest. I racked my brains, "Were you there at the beginning when Mr. Whyte founded the school?"

"Nope."

"It's been open a long time, I saw in the brochure, more than twenty years, hasn't it?"

"Yup."

So much for trying, Lena had lost her skills of communication and Mr. Whyte was a no-go subject for now.

The phone rang and Lena turned, "Gotta go. Why don't you fetch yourself a coffee from 'Lindisfarne' and I'll give you a holler when Judith gets back," she tottered off.

I went into 'Lindisfarne' which was furnished with a small plastic white table surrounded by a few red plastic chairs, in addition to a sink, an electric kettle and cupboards. I found a large jar of instant coffee and a spoon and made a bitter-tasting beverage. I suddenly felt dejected and down – I'd been hoping for something more inspiring. The idea of teaching was already hard for me to accept, but these premises were doing nothing to motivate me back to the classroom.

Just then, the door swung open generating a gush of air and a young man entered, "Oh, hi there." The cheeriness of his greeting, together with a head of overgrown dark curls and cheeky grin, lifted my mood. I liked him immediately.

"Are you new here?" he asked.

"I'm here for an interview."

"No worries, I'm sure you'll get it," he gave me an unmistakably appreciative look. "I'm Michael."

"I'm Liz."

Michael emptied several sachets of sugar into his coffee, "Going to need this. Hope to see you again – I'm off to 'St. Thomas's Tower,'" he winked as he walked out the door.

I found myself responding with a giggle. It was a silly school girl reaction, but he had cheered me up no end.

Ten minutes later, Lena returned, her shuffling gait unmistakable, "We're more or less ready now."

I followed her back to the reception area.

Judith marched directly to me. She looked like she belonged in this unusual school, more so because she was very small and the furniture was perfect-sized for her. Judith was definitely English, no mistaking the nasal, tonic accent.

"You're Elizabeth," the quick handshake from a no-nonsense, short-raven-haired woman told me all I needed to know: let's get down to business and waste no time was her approach to life.

"Yes, just call me Liz."

The woman, who looked like she was in her early forties, gave me a thorough scanning through tinted glasses, indicating she seemed to like what she saw in me. "Great, I hope you can teach, we need someone 'normal' urgently, Monday in fact." She signalled with her hand that I was to enter her side of the office, which showed off a more managerial desk and adult-sized chairs.

I was still trying to work out what 'normal' was intended to mean when a phone rang. "Will you take that, Lena?" Judith turned to me, "Would you like a cup of tea or coffee?"

"No, thank you," I wanted to get the interview over with.

"W–W–S–O–E and F–L," Lena drawled, "Bonjour."

Lena finished her explanations on the phone and Judith launched the interview. It was the first time I'd performed an interview in such a noisy environment. I could see Judith and hear Lena, when we weren't interrupted by phones, or teachers sticking their heads in the door, or students entering and exiting. Some of the classes seemed to be on a coffee break. I reworked my first sketch of the school and changed it from a maze to a beehive. It was the perfect honeycomb design with teachers and students like drones full of intent and purpose buzzing around the place.

"So, what's your experience," Judith got to the point, "can you teach?"

"Well, I did the TEFL course," I didn't specify that it had lasted half a day. "I have experience of secondary school teaching in Ireland, as you can see on my résumé." There was no need to mention the brevity of the experience and the disaster it had been. "I've been doing private teaching up to now, some business people." That 'business people' was a little lie, it was just Mme Defoe, which was more like gentile English conversational exchanges in return for cash, advice and practical gifts, hardly teaching at all.

Judith then asked me a few questions in French to check out my language skills. She said it was useful to have French basics as some students might need to discuss problems outside the class in their native language.

My French was good – that was one thing I was proud of.

"If Liz has French, she can stand in for me sometimes, here at reception," Lena put her head around the door.

I didn't want to encourage that 'stand in for me' business. I was here to teach, not to do office administration. "Teaching is my main skill," I clarified. "Of course, if the school is stuck for someone in the office, I don't mind helping out occasionally." So much for my being firm.

"You know I had an Irish nanny when I was a kid. I just loved Nora," Lena looked at me fondly.

"Is that right," I said. At least, it was a point in my favour.

"You aren't planning to leave Paris in the near future, are you?" Judith brought the conversation back to essentials.

"I've no intention of it."

"Can you guarantee me that you aren't going to quit like some teachers and leave us understaffed?" Judith needed reassurance and a firm commitment.

"I give you my word," I promised, "I have no plans to leave." That was the most honest information I'd given in the interview. In fact, I'd no plans at all.

Some sort of nod of agreement must have passed between Lena and Judith, based more on 'what choice do we have, let's try her out,' because Judith then proceeded to explain school policy to me and started filling out my contract.

Footsteps resounded clearly on the courtyard and the main door swung open causing the atmosphere to change abruptly in the office. Judith's posture seemed to stiffen.

"Good morning, ladies – you are all gainfully occupied I see," said a man in a posh and snooty tone.

Judith nodded and Lena said, "Good morning, Mr. Whyte."

I didn't turn around, but could tell from Judith's forced smile that Mr. Whyte wasn't her favourite person.

"Judith," his voice sounding like cut-glass, "what happened to M. Chevalier's class, it's not marked up on the board?"

"He cancelled because he has a problem with the teacher," Judith's reply was sharp, matching his in tone.

"Not again! I want to see that teacher immediately, right this minute, do you hear me?"

I made myself as small as possible, mimicking Lena's immediate mouse-like demeanour.

"You can't," Judith said shrilly.

"Why?"

"John quit," her eyes flashed.

"Judith, I must absolutely talk to you in my office right away."

"As you can see, I'm busy. I'll see you after this interview."

There was a long silence. If I hadn't been there, I was sure one of them would have erupted.

"In that case, as soon as you have finished," he stormed off down the corridor.

Judith continued finalising the paperwork as if nothing had happened. She went quickly through the contract details and then gave me general instructions about the classes.

I heard low crackling like the sound of electronic interference – a second later, there was a hooting noise similar to a fog horn. Judith took a chunky mobile phone out of her bag and glanced at it impatiently before answering. "Yes?"

Her exchange was short and clipped, revealing no information. Judith finished the call, dropped the phone brusquely into her bag and turned back to me. She kept her timbre soft and even, but her anger simmered.

"That was Mr. Whyte – he wants to have a word with the new teacher assigned to P.A.F.I., Pecquet Associés de Finance International," she clarified as she pinned her eyes directly on mine. "That's now you. He's in 'St. Alban's' and waiting for you," she stressed the last three words.

I knocked on 'St. Alban's' door.

"Come in."

Mr. Whyte stood in front of his desk. His office was quite bare, except for a large empty bookcase, a desk and two chairs. His three-piece suit along with a watch chain appeared like a scene from a Charles Dickens' novel. Still, I reasoned that while it wasn't a current fashion trend, his look was plausible if he was marketing himself as the quintessential English gentleman to promote his school as authentically English. Deep down, I had a strange hunch that he wasn't all that interested in marketing.

"Welcome to Whyte's," he shook my hand.

"Thank you," I resisted wiping my hand as his clammy clasp made me feel uneasy.

He sat down, rested his elbows on the table and pressed his sweaty palms together, "Please take a seat – am?"

"Elizabeth, my name's Elizabeth Downey," I volunteered, preferring to keep my distance by giving the official version of my name.

A few painfully long seconds passed before he spoke again. "I understand, Miss Downey, that you'll be taking over some classes at P.A.F.I?"

"Yes."

"Good, good. I just wanted to fill you in on one or two things."

I observed his eyes were too pale; they were predominately white with tiny dark specks, making him appear shifty to me.

"P.A.F.I. is our most important client to date. While we are always trying to enlarge our client base, P.A.F.I. is our main income source for now. Do you understand what I'm saying?"

I felt like answering that I wasn't stupid, but instead uttered a timid "Yes."

"I set up that contract a long time ago. The company's top people know this school and count on us to uphold our good tradition of teaching English to their executives." He then got to his major point, "At the end of each week, I want a detailed report on every student. You will put the files in my mail box in the main office and let me know everything."

I knew this was an order and not a request.

His authoritative tone niggled and spurred me to say, "Judith explained the process to me, but she told me the reports were monthly."

He gave me a long, hard stare, "Yes, but P.A.F.I. reports are different and they need more detail, a little insight as to how you feel students are progressing in their job and such, relating to English of course." He took a key, opened a drawer and took out a bundle of papers. "You must fill in this questionnaire on each of your students weekly."

"Okay," I mumbled, just wanting to get out of there as fast as possible. I'd no idea if I would do what he had demanded and commanded in military style, all I knew for certain is that I had taken an instant dislike to him. What had I got myself in to? This place was really odd, there must be more conventional schools to work for. Still it was a job, I argued with myself – I had to get experience somewhere and this weird school would have to do for now

Mr. Whyte stood up, "I wish you well at William Whyte's School of English and Foreign Languages." He opened the door for me as I fled his overbearing presence.

I left the school, laden down with two heavy shopping bags full of files and my head bursting with instructions. I had inherited the former teacher's timetable. Most of my teaching would be at La Defence where P.A.F.I. was located. That was, at least, positive for me because I could get a bus or the Metro train there easily from Neuilly. However, I would have to go farther into the western suburbs of Nanterre for some of my other classes. My timetable was topsy-turvy as I had to juggle evening exam classes in the school on the same day I had very early morning classes in the suburbs.

I also had a Saturday morning class which meant I only had Sundays off. I couldn't help feeling taken advantage of, but had little choice for now. I would be paid by the hour and, all going well, my contract would be updated from temporary to permanent in three months.

I would teach again. 'Please God, please let it work out this time,' I made a silent plea. I hoped Mr. William Whyte himself stayed out of the day to day running of the school – I didn't need him to deflate my confidence. I peeped into the bags and observed there were too many grammar files. I swung my load every which way trying to make it more comfortable.

I heard footsteps coming up behind me, "Hello there."

I turned to find myself face to face with a girl who seemed to be about my own age. "Hello?"

"I'm Ursula, I'm Irish too. I saw you in the office just now. I teach at Whyte's."

"Oh, what's it like to work there?" I was anxious to get an honest opinion from a fellow Irish woman.

"Odd."

There was that word again, echoing my own initial gut feelings.

I put down my bags and looked at my new acquaintance. She flicked aside a lock of her long, thick, black, wavy hair as her beautiful violet eyes squinted back at me, "Have you time for a beer?"

"Sure," I thought I detected a Dublin accent.

We sat on Rattan chairs on the terrace of the first café along the way, called Café Gavroche. Only a few people sat there, but the waiter rushed in and out wiping tables, moving chairs and apparently ignoring me though I raised my hand and called to him. I tried like this several times to get his attention without success.

"Monsieur," Ursula threw back her hair, smiled broadly and suddenly the waiter was beside us and bending over backwards to serve us. In seconds, we were each sipping a cool Kronenbourg.

I studied the girl sitting opposite me. Ursula's khaki trousers and floating cream and yellow top accentuated her curvaceous and sexy figure. The gold trimming on her heeled sandals added to the effect. I felt very prim and older in my navy skirt and white blouse compared to her youthful attire.

"I have an hour before my next class," Ursula said as her face revealed a pained expression, before lighting up a cigarette.

I didn't comment out loud on the wisdom of her going into her next class smelling of beer and cigarettes.

"What's exactly odd about the school?" I asked.

Ursula held her cigarette with the practiced pose of an actress, "You'll see. Why did you pick Whyte's school anyway?"

"Chance, there was a vacancy, simple as that."

"Yes, but have you heard anything about the school from other people?"

"No, nothing at all. Why, what's wrong with the place?"

"I wouldn't know where to start. Take the name, for instance," Ursula snorted, "it's the most ridiculous name for a school. It's a right mouthful and impossible to even say it without sounding stupid. The whole message is in the name – the school teaches English and then foreign languages. There's segregation right there. Believe me – take one look at the owner and you'll know it's a strange joint."

I didn't reply. My meeting with William Whyte had unnerved me, but I wasn't going to share that information with Ursula.

"Oh come on, you've been inside the door, admit it, it's strange," Ursula examined her ivory painted nails.

"I don't know," I defended, "all schools have a little of that traditional element."

"Did you notice that nobody speaks normally? The teachers are the worst."

"What do you mean?"

"They go around speaking a sterile sort of English. Nobody speaks like that these days."

"I can't say," I thought that Lena hardly fit that category, "I've just been hired, I didn't – I haven't met many members of the school staff so far."

"See, you've even started doing it yourself."

"Doing what?"

"Weighing and measuring your words, afraid that a grammar mistake is going to slip out and shame you."

"Don't jump to conclusions like that, I haven't even given my first class yet." She was right and I knew it, but I wasn't going to give her the satisfaction of knowing it.

"I've been with them almost two years and I'm burnt out already," Ursula followed another line of conversation. "They'll have you working mornings, evenings and weekends without mercy. They're making the money and you're paid pittance to do all the donkey and grunt work. I'm sick of it."

I wasn't interested in her complaints and laments. I'd just arrived and it was only a temporary job until I figured out where to next. I stopped my train of thought as I realised that there was more truth in Lena's words about running and hiding than I cared to admit. I refused to entertain the idea that I was running or trying to escape something. I was just drifting temporarily, I assured myself.

Ursula was warming to her topic and called for another beer, "I need it before I face into my next class."

I felt a pressure against my temples and a warning signal in the pit of my stomach: be careful of this girl. I didn't know Ursula, but I was beginning to realise that she might be a real emotional parasite.

I saw that she was just getting started and looked at the time on my watch. I was already growing tired of her rant. How could she criticize the school on one hand, and on the other, be so unprofessional as to plan to walk into her classes after consuming two beers?

"Judith's a shark, get on her wrong side and you're finished. Lena's cantankerous, she'll bite your head off for nothing, especially in the mornings. She and Judith are like that," Ursula put her fingers together, "peas in a pod."

"Does any of the staff have saving graces?" I quipped.

"Some of the teachers are okay, but a few of them are slippery as eels and they all talk behind your back."

"Sounds like your usual, everyday sort of people to me." I decided that the girl sitting next to me was paranoid. It would have been impolite to refuse to give my mobile telephone number when she asked for it, but I wasn't eager to forge links with her. The day before, I had bought my first mobile phone, a Philips Fizz, telling myself that it would be useful to have it in my potential new job; it was important to be reachable in case of timetable changes. But in reality, I had been itching to get a mobile phone for several months. I planned to keep the expense to the minimum by restricting myself to a pay-as-you-go system and topping up with special cards sold at the Tabac. For a Fifty-Franc card, I got two hours of usage. I noted that Ursula had the more fashionable and lighter Nokia 650 phone.

I understood, because Ursula volunteered the information freely, that she was living with her boyfriend. She'd been in Paris four years and had moved language schools at least three times during that period. I concluded that she were either very experienced or unstable.

"Are you living with anyone?" Ursula bluntly asked me.

"No." What business was it of hers, I angrily thought to myself.

"Ah, do I detect bitterness?" she tossed back her head.

"Not at all."

She smiled smugly, but didn't pursue that line of inquiry. "Anyway, ask others about Whyte. He's the sort of person that might be into a sect or one of those secret societies."

"You shouldn't accuse people like that."

"He already has at least five children, left his wife and is living with a young girl who is expecting a baby – and – "

"Look," I said, "his private life is his own business. If Whyte and his school are that bad, why are you still working there?"

Ursula's eyes filled with tears, "I need the money."

I left her sitting on the terrace. I wasn't sure if Ursula got to her class on time, or if she did what state she was in to teach. The school might be a bit unorthodox, I'd nothing to compare it with; but one thing was sure, Ursula was the oddest specimen I'd met there so far.

I lugged my bags into 9 Rue Montrosier.

"C'est un scandale – incroyable!" Mme Gomes stood before me like a vision.

"What is?"

The concierge gave me the news in a torrent: Room 1 was advertised to be let out again. The dust hadn't settled on the last tragedy and they were inviting in more sorrow, she cried. That sixth-floor family were driven by greed and money. They hadn't found someone yet, but they were seriously looking.

I listened for as long as was polite to do so and soon realised politeness would get me nowhere.

"Bonsoir," I broke away and began the climb to my room.

I wasn't in the mood for more speculation. Nonetheless, I had a morbid curiosity about the identity of my future neighbour.

3

"You've got to help me, the most awful thing has happened," Ursula blubbered down the phone.

"What's the matter, where are you?" I tried to stay calm.

"You have to help me, please," she repeated, sobbing more loudly.

"What's happened?" I made another effort to understand.

Between hysterics and weeping, Ursula explained that she was homeless. She and her boyfriend, Vincent, had been evicted by their landlord. They were thrown out following another noisy argument and break up. Vincent had marched off to a friend's place leaving Ursula to fend for herself. In reality, there was more to the story that Ursula didn't share at first, but which dribbled out by degrees. Ursula was not an official tenant, she had been living in her boyfriend's flat, but he had been in arrears with his rent and the landlord had reached his limit. Furthermore, in France, a landlord was forbidden from evicting a tenant between November and April, so it was likely that this landlord, by giving them notice, was acting within legal limits of time and safeguarding himself from getting trapped into another six months with a non-paying tenant. What did it matter – the fact was that Ursula was now alone and abandoned with a cat.

Some minutes later, I put down the phone, slightly stunned. I closed the English teaching files I'd been studying and kicked some under my bed in anger and frustration. So much for a quiet life. How had I been duped? I barely knew the girl, unreliable was written all over her – one could see from miles off that Ursula was trouble with a capital 'T' – and now I was forced into helping her. I hadn't even started teaching and I was already feeling responsible for a teacher I'd only just met. I had allowed myself to be swayed by the idea that if I refused to help Ursula, I would be the meanest soul on earth. The only thing that pulled that guilt string was the fact that Ursula was Irish. Didn't she have a network of her own, I asked myself over and over? But I had already guessed the answer: Ursula burnt all her bridges and wore people down. It was unkind of me to think it, but she probably held onto boyfriends as long as she kept friends. And now she was inviting herself into my apartment building and my life.

What a fool I was and yet, I brought this on myself. I got the phone number of the landlords of Room 1 from an astonished Mme Gomes and set the inevitable in motion. The landlords, Mme and M. Fleuret, who lived on the sixth floor, were prepared to accept Ursula as a tenant on my recommendation provided Mme Defoe could be my guarantor. So I then had to ring Mme Defoe and explain my predicament to her. She trusted me enough to accept my request and use her name as guarantor for Ursula. I liked to think that it reassured her to know that I would have company of my own age on the seventh floor. I vowed to myself that if there were any problem with Ursula I would do everything in my power to cover the losses without ever involving Mme Defoe.

And so it was that Ursula's crisis was averted. I felt used – it was on my excellent references and my reputation that she'd wormed her way into the room next door. No need to guess who the fool was that took the Metro train to La Bastille at the other side of Paris to retrieve Ursula, the damsel in distress, and who helped cart bags and a crate with one very pissed off cat to the taxi rank. No need to ask either who paid the fare to Rue Montrosier, and who once again made two trips up and down seven flights of stairs to help move her luggage into her new abode.

While the move was taking place, Mme Gomes was stationed at her post at the entrance, a certain gleam of excitement in her eyes. It was easy for me to imagine her thoughts: Room 1 was occupied again, the show would go on and she would have a front row seat to watch. The only question was – what affliction would befall the latest occupant?

Ursula sat on a make-shift mattress in her flowing blue silk nightgown, looking like a tragedy queen. She would have to get up early next morning for classes and was trying to use her recent trauma as an excuse to skip work. She obviously saw me as an answer to her problem and looked at me pleadingly.

"Don't even think of it," I said, "I can't substitute for you; it's your job to teach your classes tomorrow. I'm only starting off myself next Monday and haven't a clue yet how to teach English as a Foreign Language."

"There is nothing to teaching, you just have to speak English with them," Ursula entreated with a smile.

"No, I will not teach your classes. You look in good shape to me; tomorrow is Friday and you'll have the weekend to recover." On that issue I would stand my ground. Enough was enough.

Ursula put a hand to her head and let a tear drop, "I'm so tired."

I refused to be swayed and instead concentrated on the black cat roaming around its new territory, "What's its name?"

"It's a she, her name is Elle."

"Elle?"

"Yes," more tears came, "Elle will suffer in this small space, I'll have to leave the window open to give her the run of the roof. I'm not lucky you know, Vincent, my boyfriend, is a bastard – "

"Ursula, I'm going to bed." I'd had my fill of sob stories for one night and to add to my aggravation, her room looked bigger; I was sure it was eleven metres squared or maybe even twelve.

Ursula didn't get up the next morning to go into the school and give her classes. I don't know how she'd managed to squirm out of teaching, but she had. I suspected that she'd probably put her mobile phone to good use, cancelling and rearranging with her students.

She seemed to have enough energy and enthusiasm for shopping though and tagged along with me on my supermarket visit. Good old Liz; for some reason, I seemed to be carrying one of her bags with tins of cat food up the stairs along with my own shopping. Ursula chirped on about how chic and classy Neuilly was. She was in a much more positive humour than the night before. Things were looking up for her and even her ex-boyfriend seemed to have undergone a change of heart and turned up later that morning with some more of her clothes. He also enlisted some extra hands to help her finish the refurnishing. I was beginning to see a pattern: though Ursula was dumped, she managed somehow to come out on top.

All this activity entailed lots of up-down trips of Everest proportions on the stairs. It wouldn't have bothered me as much if I didn't feel that occupants of the building were watching; it made me cringe. And of course it was no coincidence we seemed to meet Mme Gomes each time, apparently busy cleaning smudges in the mirrored hallway, polishing the brass door handle... The concierge made no effort to hide the fact that she was totally transfixed by Ursula. Her hungry eyes took in the new Irish tenant from head to toe. It was as if she expected to see some deformity appear on Ursula's body, or to hear a story of dark trouble. I had to admit that from what I knew of Ursula to date, the odds were good in that respect for Mme Gomes. If anyone were to have the capacity to draw trouble on herself and others, it would be Ursula. If there were negative energies in Room 1, Ursula would magnetise them. In addition, Ursula exuded external airs of importance; she just couldn't be invisible or blend in with the woodwork as the others on the seventh floor seemed to do. No, she emanated a seductive air that was mastered to perfection. Ursula had a way of taking her time, and her lazy, swinging gait attracted looks whether on the street or the attic floor. The effect was enhanced by her sad violet myopia eyes which reflected like pools of need that unsuspecting people would find irresistible. She rarely wore glasses, opting for Contact lenses or nothing at all. It was clear to me that men had and would continue to fall like tumbleweed around her. She was the 'femme fatale.'

"Liz, come here, have you met M. Jacques?" Ursula called to me from the end of the corridor; she was intent on pulling me into conversation with our neighbour from the opposite corridor.

"No I haven't," nor did I want to; I felt that keeping a polite distance from all my neighbours was a wise course of action.

"He's a scrap collector," Ursula ignored my cool answer and introduced me to M. Jacques anyway.

M. Jacques shook my hand vigorously. He was an awkwardly tall man, wearing ill-fitting jeans with the legs rolled up at the bottom and a large off-white shirt that hung outside his jeans. He had tightly-curling grey hair, sported round-framed glasses and seemed to be somewhere around the age of fifty. M. Jacques communicated with lots of hand gesticulating and for some reason was excited by the fact that Ursula and I were English teachers. He also had a tendency to shout, as if by shouting it we would understand his French better.

"I speak a little English, I would love to learn it," he boomed at us.

I smiled thinly. No way, I thought, I wasn't going to go down that road and offer him free classes.

He told us that he did business with the Irish College on Rue des Irlandais and so was pleased to have two Irish neighbours.

Business, I understood, meant storing junk at the College. The College housed the Polish seminary and the Irish Chaplaincy, as well as providing accommodation for Irish visitors and students. The place also served as a good networking hub for the Irish. It was recommended to attend Sunday mass in Chapelle Saint Patrick inside its grounds and stay on for tea and coffee afterwards in order to meet up with others and make contacts. I was urged by many to go there when Marc-Antoine left me, but had yet to visit inside the centre, purposefully avoiding all things Irish since my arrival in Paris.

Ursula told M. Jacques that we worked at a language school near Rue des Irlandais.

"Not Whyte's?" M. Jacques asked.

His response surprised me: once again another person with a negative reaction to the name Whyte and the school.

"Yes, Whyte's," said Ursula, "do you know it?"

"C'est bizarre, trés bizarre."

"Well, we have to earn our money some way," I dismissed and walked off back to my own corridor. If Ursula wanted to socialise with tenants on the floor that was her business not mine.

I returned to my room, sighed and threw myself on the bed. In a few days, the seventh floor had transformed itself from a small village, with its inconspicuous shadows and hidden lives, to a noisy café or a shady boudoir – I'd yet to decide which. I looked at my watch, almost 11p.m. 'Hey, hang on a minute' – I switched off the light and went to stare out my window, trying to see an illuminated Eiffel Tower. I could see nothing. I stood on the chair, but still saw no lights or sparkles. Mme Misere had lied, there was no view of the Eiffel Tower from this room, I thought despondently.

I turned my back on the window and prepared for bed. I could still hear the loud voice of M. Jacques talking to Ursula; she seemed to be negotiating the purchase of a cupboard or something from him. 'God, that girl!' I huffed in disgust and flopped back on the bed.

But sleep evaded me as a little anxiety began trickling into my mind about William White's School. Why did a scrap collector from the other side of Paris regard it with suspicion? Would I be better off finding another job? I finally stopped worrying, turned over on my stomach, smothering out those pesky thoughts.

'I am running wild, racing bare legged through the meadows. The canvas of greens is dappled with buttercups and daisies, and sand dunes peep over the horizon. The sunlight sprays happiness all around. I am a little girl and can see my mum's smiling face. She is standing on the cliffs, waiting with her arms open wide. I feel the grass whipping off my skin and thorns pricking the soles of my feet as I run towards her. There is a cool breeze on my face – I run faster and faster – I have to get to her. I see a seagull alighting on a rock ledge and everything is so open, I am free – free – '

Bang! "Jesus!" I'd fallen out of bed and my hand had struck the iron bed-frame. I sat on the floor dazed for a while, before scrambling back onto the mattress. What a bad end to a nice dream. I missed Mum, the meadows and the sea so much. It was hard to accept that Mum wasn't there anymore. Of course I could go back to Ireland, but I would never feel at home again. The confinement in this tiny room was making me feel claustrophobic. I envied the freedom of the seagulls, but couldn't understand what brought them away from the sea to the crowded city. Why would they want to leave the openness and wildness of the coast? The city was for pigeons, not seagulls. But I shouldn't complain – the vast woodland of Boulogne was nearby with lots of ponds and lakes. I could run crazy and wild there if I felt the need. Things could be worse, a lot worse. I still had my dreams and could go home in my memories anytime I wished. I just had to close my eyes and I was there.

I realised that it was Sunday. Maybe I should go to mass or say a prayer and thank God for my blessings: I was in Paris, well sort of in Paris; many would kill to visit or live here. Come to think of it, I was in a building where someone had supposedly been murdered. Now, wasn't that thrilling? I had a roof over my head. I was warm and dry, admittedly in a hot and balmy room to be more precise – but autumn had arrived and I would really appreciate that extra heat more when in the throes of winter. I had food in the cupboard, even if it disappeared as quickly as it arrived, and even if I was sharing it with cockroaches. I had a job, even if everyone I met seemed to think the school was odd and that the job itself wasn't the best foundation to build a future on. Teaching English as a Foreign Language was seen by professionals as a temporary side-line, not a real job. At least, there would be some money coming in. On top of everything else, I wasn't totally alone – I had neighbours, lots of them – very friendly neighbours, one of them very Irish.

I listened to the corridor noises, picking up the sound of voices. I heard the toilet door being slammed and it reminded me that I needed to go.

"Liz, Liz."

I didn't need to guess who was hammering at my door.

"What?" I would try to handle this from the bed, "what is it, Ursula?"

"Let me in, can I come in?"

"Why?"

"That toilet is a disgrace; one of those students or Mme Gomes's son was in there. Can you imagine, he didn't have the decency to clean it after himself; I had to use the toilet on the other corridor."

Clumsily, I dragged on a pair of jeans. Ursula seemed intent on announcing our conversation to everybody. All fingers and thumbs, I buckled the belt and put on a T-shirt. I threw open the door and took one look at her, "Good God, get dressed, put on a dressing gown or something." Okay, it was hot, but that light pink slip Ursula was wearing was much too hot, definitely not for public viewing.

Ursula didn't appear to care, "We've got to find out who's messing up the toilet and nip the business in the bud immediately."

"Well it's not Mme Gomes's son as he's been here all along and there have been no problems with the toilet before now," I pointed out.

"It's obviously one of the two students here on this side, Sebastien or Olivier; they arrived yesterday. I already knocked at their doors, but they're either under the covers or have gone out."

"Eh oh," called M. Jacques from across the landing, "is there a problem?"

"No," I shouted back.

"Room 1, it's Room 1, isn't it?" he uttered the words with breathless anticipation.

"What's he talking about?" Ursula steered her mind to the meaning behind his words.

"Nothing, Ursula," I took her arm. "Come inside," I urged. I should have realised, the history of Room 1 was a well recounted story, known to everyone except Ursula. The concierge wasn't the sort to keep information like that to herself.

Ursula and a very sprightly feline Elle paraded, if that were possible, around my room.

"It's small here," Ursula wrinkled her nose.

Her comment didn't warrant a reply.

Elle found the right spot on my bed and settled down.

Nonetheless, given the history of Room 1, I couldn't resist probing a little, "Did you sleep okay last night? You know – it's a change for you, you must be missing your boyfriend."

Ursula pulled out my only chair and perched herself right in the middle of the room, generously leaving me the edge of the bed. "That's another problem. I didn't sleep well at all. My night was disturbed by a very unsettling experience."

"Oh, the bed wasn't comfortable enough?"

"It wasn't the bed, it was my dream; I dreamt of a woman called Eva – it was a strange dream."

"Eva?"

"That's what she called herself, but in fact I think Eva lived here," Ursula said matter-of-factly as if it were the most normal thing in the world.

"I see."

"Liz, you've got to listen to me, it's spooking me out."

I was getting used to the fact that Ursula turned on the 'poor-lonesome-me' act easily.

I made an effort to understand, "So, what you're telling me is that you had a visit from a ghost?"

"That's right, a ghost called Eva. In her life she was an actress, a servant and a prostitute. I'm not sure how she died, but I suspect it was suicide or murder."

"That's – am – those are – very precise details." This was great, just great – Ursula was finally unveiling her madness. Mme Gomes would have a field day – Room 1 still had its powers.

"Believe me, I pick up those sorts of vibes, and that's why I'm shattered this morning and nearly out of my mind," Ursula wrapped up her explanation.

What was clear to me was that Ursula was unhinged. "Look, I'm sure it's just part of being in a strange, new place. Those dreams will go away once you've adjusted."

Ursula peered at me for a long moment and then said, "I'm going for a shower."

"Well, good luck to you on finding a shower; let me know where, if you find one."

****

"I'm off." My wake-up call to Ursula was basically a toe to her door.

A weak moan, lacking any energy, reached me. I didn't lose time ruminating over it. She had asked me to wake her on my way out, but I wasn't about to start feeling responsible for her – if that girl ended up being late, there was nothing I could do about it.

My stomach muscles tightened. I hadn't been able to eat any breakfast because I felt stressed and anxious. I, who had sworn never to enter a classroom again, was returning to teaching. 'But this time will be different,' I told myself, 'I will be teaching adults and not teenagers.' It was ridiculous for me to be so anxious and nervous. But I really felt like an actress getting ready for my debut. I had seven performances to deliver that day: in the company P.A.F.I., I would have a group of five, a group of four, an individual class, a telephone class, and two more groups of four – and then it would be back to the school for the highlight of the evening – a group of sixteen independently registered students preparing for a business diploma. The business class should really have been split into two groups with two teachers, but the school apparently made the most of their metres squared and didn't believe in cutting their profit margin. I now understood better the principle of undersized tables and chairs and of packing people into small spaces. I realised that each of my teaching performances would be different. I would be a one-woman show or stand-up comedienne depending on my audience.

Finding my way around La Défense was trickier than I had anticipated.

Fortunately, I had wisely allowed myself plenty of time to get lost. Patience and that extra half hour were my saviours. I had elected to take the bus rather than the Metro train to get there as it was more calming and pleasant to be above ground than underground. After classes at La Défense, my plan was to take the R.E.R. train back to Paris and walk to the Latin Quarter where the school was located. The R.E.R., Réseau Express Régional, was a different train network to the Metro. Its train carriages were larger and it was the fastest transport system moving commuters between city and suburbs, stopping only at central stations in Paris itself.

I knew from my own research that La Défense was the largest purpose-built business district in Europe and also incorporated a huge commercial centre called Les Quatre Temps. The whole project started in 1958 and replaced old factories, shanties and even two farms that once occupied the area.

La Défense district itself was dominated by a monument-building called La Grande Arche. As I crossed concrete slabs and footpaths and went by several fountains on the 'Esplanade,' La Grande Arche loomed closer and closer. The view back towards the Champs Elysées and L'Arc de Triomphe was very stunning. Indeed, La Grande Arche de La Défense was described as a late 20th-century version of L'Arc de Triomphe. I read a plaque explaining that the project was started in 1985 at the request of the then President Mitterrand and finished in 1989. The result was something that resembled a cube with lots of glass and concrete. The sides housed government offices and the roof was used for exhibitions as well as accommodating an IT museum. It was intended to be a monument to humanity and humanitarian ideals rather than the military victories which were carved in the stone of L'Arc de Triomphe.

My attention, however, was focused on the surrounding tower blocks. Not having been to New York or any high-rise city, La Défense's glass and steel skyscrapers were impressive. I couldn't believe that I was going to enter one of those towers of 260 metres high and that I was going to be teaching on the 57th floor, just a few floors from the top.

I got a security pass at reception and instructions to the right lift. I experienced the altitude effect as the lift took me upwards and then it was just offices and corridors. I was met by the HR assistant, Mme Chabot, a pleasant young lady in a smart grey suit, who led me to a meeting room, wished me luck and I was then on my own. I was disappointed that the room assigned to me was in the middle of the floor and windowless. But the HR assistant did say that I had to check in with her each time as I would be using different rooms, so I hoped one day to have a room with a window and a view.

I set out my teaching materials, took a deep breath and drew together physical and mental forces, waiting until the first head appeared – 'Here it goes,' I thought.

A middle-aged woman came in shyly and we shook hands, "Good – good morning, I am Arlette Frery."

I asked her a few basic questions and her replies came out in broken English. One by one, the other students straggled in and found their place around the table. Ten minutes passed before everyone had arrived. I was learning quickly that for many French people, being on time was an approximate notion, and I would have to accept that or forever be annoyed.

The students sat in front of me: Arlette, Philippe, Joelle, Ghislaine and Laurence. Judith had already filled me in on what I needed to know about these people and the previous teacher had left very good detailed notes and impressions. I knew that their jobs were in jeopardy and the company's policy of outsourcing would mean many of them would have to adapt by converting to a different job in the company, or simply leave. To stay in the company, they needed English. To leave and find another job, they needed English. They weren't here taking my class for the love of it.

"My name is Liz Downey and I am your new teacher," I began, "You can just call me Liz."

They all ploughed through introductions and I had to concentrate hard to understand what any one of them was trying to say. I knew that nobody outside the world of language teaching would have the patience to take several minutes to listen to what should have been said in seconds. From their explanations and body language, I felt strongly that some had given up hope about ever progressing in the language. Others were more hopeful, maybe thinking that this time around would be different and perhaps this teacher had the magic method. These weren't just beginners, they were eternal beginners and desperate language cases. Philippe's look said it all: 'I'm zero at English, I don't want to be here, I'm no good, can't learn it, never could, I'm too old – I want to make it to retirement without ever having to use the language.' Joelle wasn't so defeatist, but she was running out of fresh starts, she told me. Arlette explained in strangled sounds that her boss wanted her to improve her English.

Saying hello was the easy part, but to my surprise, the next steps were not too hard. Conducting the class came more naturally to me than I'd expected; questions and ideas came and flowed. What wasn't natural though was trying to integrate the heavy duty grammar structures and programme that Judith had given me. I could sense the frustration mount in my students as soon as I tried that approach and so I eased off.

I had to pinch myself once or twice during the class; I was actually teaching again, really teaching and the sky hadn't fallen on top of my head yet. The students were looking at me with respect, listening to me and trying to do what I asked them. I was enjoying the good feeling.

I made on-the-spot decisions and changes, the main one being to digress from the curriculum given to me by the school. These people needed the basics so they could easily hook onto the language. I reviewed letters, numbers, time, and dates. At least that way, they would feel they had tools in their language bag. I did a lot of chiselling, chipping, sifting, filtering and ice-breaking with words and phrases. But I also wanted them to enjoy conversation in English and I made them talk or rather try to communicate about family, children and day to day life. I asked dozens of repetitive questions, and by the time the class ended, I had accumulated a sack full of apparently insignificant information about my students. I knew what time they started and finished their work day, every morsel of what they ate for breakfast, their favourite colours, music, sport, and so on. I knew the time and duration of everything in their routine lives. It might be described as useless information, but if I were a detective, I would garner a lot from those scraps of detail about their lives.

From my perspective, I was beginning to appreciate that the whole English teaching experience was stimulating. What I wasn't prepared for was the fact that my personal needs would have to take a back seat as I ignored my hunger pangs and just never seemed to find the right time to go to the toilet.

I made a few simple rules: if I needed to go to the restroom, just go; I was never going to have the time to eat, so I would have to educate my stomach accordingly and invest in small and digestible treats to nibble and stave off hunger. Alternatively, I could get up very early and take time to tuck into a bigger breakfast. It was soon clear that teaching English was going to be demanding on my mental skills, which involved moving up and down the piano of language levels from beginner to advanced. Weaving through the students' fears and complexes was also going to be an athletic défie. A hangover would be hell to pay for and so I would have to practice temperance. I learnt one more important thing: I was going to have to improve my presentation. My clothes were a little faded and shabby, but Mme Defoe, my trusty patron, assured me some help in that department and promised to provide me good second-hand outfits. I had to stop looking like an impoverished student and start looking like a professional.

Judith telephoned to inform me that M. Chevalier had cancelled his individual class. I was happy to have the respite offered by the cancellation, although I would have liked to put a face with M. Chevalier and also experience a one-to-one class.

In the afternoon, I carted myself and lugged my bags back to W.W.S.O.E. & F.L. I exited the R.E.R. station at Jardin du Luxembourg and stood for a moment looking on enviously as some nannies pushing strollers passed through the black and gold wrought-iron gates into the gardens. Some people wandered along the tree-lined promenade that led to the Medici Palace and Senate House, others followed pathways that criss-crossed lush green lawns and flower-beds, skirting the central lake and fountains. I gazed longingly for several minutes, before turning to climb Montagne Saint Genevieve hill to an area overlooking the left bank of the Seine and the 5th district. I reached the Pantheon, a grey mid-18th century building that I had yet to explore. It served as a secular mausoleum for the remains of distinguished French citizens, including Victor Hugo, Emile Zola and Marie Curie. Its Neoclassical-influenced façade was modelled on the Pantheon in Rome and was surmounted by a dome. But my eyes were more drawn to the bell tower of a flamboyant Gothic, Renaissance-style church on the west of the hill. That church I had visited and like most churches in Paris, its origins went back to the early centuries of the city. It had endured wars, rebuilding and renaming often to different saints depending on date and century. What stood on the hill today was dedicated to Saint-Étienne-du-Mont and built in the early 17th century.

I walked on regretfully, crossed the square and traversed a few streets into Rue des Soeurs. I felt the ghosts of the past sticking to the soles of my feet every step of the way. Anywhere one walked in Paris was like browsing back in time. History was my favourite subject – I couldn't get enough of facts and stories about the magnificent sites and buildings. Unfortunately, I needed to work and for now had to leave such historical indulgences.

Evening was peak time for the school and the pace was hectic. The place was filled with students and teachers and many English accents of varying shades. I checked the timetable board to see which room I had been designated – I was in 'London.'

I went to say a diplomatic hello to the staff.

Lena was looking decidedly grouchy.

Judith was getting ready to leave, "Hi Liz, everything go okay?"

"I think so."

"William – Mr. Whyte will see you for a few minutes before your class," Judith gave me a pitying look, almost apologising that I had to endure his presence.

'Damn,' I thought, 'just when I was starting to feel good about things.'

Mr. Whyte looked me up and down making me feel instantly very uncomfortable.

"Miss Downey, I know you have a class to go to, so I won't keep you long. Did your classes go well at P.A.F.I.?"

"Fine, except that M. Chevalier cancelled."

"Yes I heard," his facial twitches got more pronounced. "I want to impress upon you the importance of M. Chevalier. He is a top manager and is seeking promotion to the position of C.F.O., that's Chief Financial Officer. The current C.F.O. is due to retire before the summer of next year."

I barely nodded in acknowledgement of his condescending explanation.

"English is an obstacle and M. Chevalier must absolutely improve his level if he is to succeed."

"I'll do my best with him, but if he keeps cancelling, I won't be able to do much to help."

"It will be your job to motivate him."

Once again, I didn't appreciate his manner of speaking to me. "I'll be late for my class," I stood up.

"I have not finished, please sit down," Mr. Whyte said coldly.

I plopped down again.

"There is competition for this promotion; M. Fabre, Ursula O'Grady's student, is seeking the same position and he too has problems with the language. Therefore, my school and my teachers play a key role. The future C.F.O. will have a great influence over the English language training budget and the service providers they choose."

"So if either M. Fabre or M. Chevalier procures the C.F.O. position, the school benefits."

"But if neither succeeds, an outsider could take the position. That might create great uncertainty for the future of my school."

"I see." Maybe I did, but I didn't see why I should carry that extra responsibility on my shoulders. I'd have to talk to Ursula. If it were that important, why didn't he send a more experienced teacher than me to P.A.F.I.? Then again, I had the distinct impression that reliable teachers were hard to come by, let alone keep in his school.

I got up and grabbed the door handle.

"Remember – I need very regular updates and details of your classes," Mr. Whyte's words sounded menacing to my ears.

God, I wished Judith had never given me M. Chevalier, William Whyte was going to stick to me like a clam.

The sullen faces in 'London' wiped everything off my mind, including the fact that Ursula appeared to be late. I took in the hostile audience in my room with one glance – they were not happy and I had to deal with this. I divined fairly quickly that these people in front of me were feeling abused, misused and ripped off. I realised that teaching in outside companies was one thing, but teaching in the school a different experience altogether. These clients were here to prepare for and earn a business diploma. They had already put in a long, hard work day and their reward was to sit in this hot room, with an electric fan, one whiteboard, a CD player and me. They desired to leave the school feeling richer in the language and receiving value for money and something to forget their sore bottoms and cramped up bodies. These students had been lied to about maximum group class enrolments. The brochures promised a maximum of eight per group and instead I counted a total of sixteen packed into one small room.

I heard Ursula's voice somewhere in the corridor, arguing rather forcefully with Judith. "If I'm late, blame the Metro. It is hardly my fault if somebody decided to jump under the train and finish their days. Suicide is a serious matter, you know. What's being a few minutes late when measured against life?"

It wasn't hard to imagine Judith's face. I could see through the glass panel in the partition wall dividing my room and 'Oxford' the teacher, Michael, already in action. I'd read his full name on one of the lockers, Michael Young – I thought it a nice name. His room had the blue furniture. He gave me a friendly wave and I waved back. It heartened me. On the opposite side, I had a view into 'Cambridge,' the white room, where some agitated students were still awaiting their teacher. Oh, just my luck – Ursula would be next door to me, which meant she would want to go home with me too.

In my red room, I took a yoga-like breath and dug deep into my energy resources. I had three hours of explaining and drilling ahead of me.

Half way through, we took a five-minute break. I went to 'Lindisfarne' for a triple coffee. Ursula was talking to a teacher who resembled a Boy Scout. She introduced him as Richard. He nodded quickly at me, looked at his watch and dashed off. Richard, Ursula told me, was dictated by time. He had a watch and yet for some reason found it necessary to also carry at least two small clocks in his bag. Just another manic teacher, I thought.

"Ursula, I need to talk to you about Mr. Whyte and our students at P.A.F.I."

"I knew it," Ursula said, "Whyte has given you his weird pep talk."

"I've had a double dose of it. Did you get the same? Do you have to write out special detailed reports on your students?"

Ursula made a face, "I hardly get around to doing my usual teacher reports. When I do, I just make up something and drop it in his box. But I don't fill in his stupid questionnaire – it's like an immigration document. I told you he was odd, that or an asshole."

"What about this M. Fabre?"

"What about him?" Ursula appeared to want to change the subject which struck me as unusual.

"You're teaching him, aren't you? I understand that it's vital for the school that either he or M. Chevalier becomes future C.F.O."

"Huh, is that what he told you?"

"Well yes," I said.

"It isn't that simple."

"What are you getting at?" I asked.

"Ask Michael."

"Michael? What's he got to do with it?"

"He's teaching the HR manager at P.A.F.I."

"You're talking in riddles here."

"Oh, forget it," Ursula said crankily.

"Ursula?"

"I'm just saying that there's favouritism; the Human Resources manager and directors have a preference and so does William Whyte."

"I get that much."

"Besides," she added, "if William Whyte's that anxious about a job promotion in P.A.F.I., tells you how bad the finances of his school are, doesn't it?"

"I suppose," I said.

Ursula traced the shadows under her eyes. "I have other things to worry about. It might mean nothing to you, but I'm not getting a wink of sleep – and it's your fault."

"What have I got to do with your sleep or lack of it?" I asked incredulously.

"Room 1 is haunted, that woman, Eva, never leaves me alone."

"For God's sake Ursula, what are you talking about now?"

"If I'd never met you, I'd never have been living in that room," she lobbed her plastic goblet into the dustbin and flounced off.

I wanted to choke someone. Instead, I crumpled my own goblet and threw it towards the bin. 'Bah, missed it.' I picked it up and flung it good and hard. That action didn't calm me so I looked for something else to throw.

4

I locked the school door happy in the knowledge that my Wednesday evening individual class had gone well. Judith had sneakily added the class to my timetable, telling me that it was a very short contract. Mlle Leroy, a young woman who was between jobs and trying to boost her language level to improve her career opportunities, was enthusiastic and motivated to progress. While it was hard finishing yet again at 9p.m., the student's bright cheery personality made it easy on me. It was only a few weeks since giving my first class, but I was beginning to feel like a natural at teaching English as a Foreign Language.

I checked twice that the door was properly locked. It pleased me that Judith had trusted me with a key of my own, but I realised it served her purpose too. Giving me a key meant Judith could go home sooner.

I skipped on to Rue des Soeurs and headed towards the busy and bustling Rue Mouffetard hearing sounds of chatter and banter as I passed every door and terrace. I thought about stopping off at a café and then realised that I had forgotten to bring the big heavy bag Judith had promised to leave on her desk for me in advance of a new Friday class in P.A.F.I. It contained photocopied material to give to the students. I hesitated – perhaps I could take it home after tomorrow morning's class, but then it would hamper my movements all day. No – it was easier to fetch the bag now.

I back-tracked to Rue des Soeurs. Shivers suddenly ran up and down my back. I looked over my shoulder and saw Mr. Whyte in the distance carrying his briefcase. Not wanting to meet him I did a U-turn on to a café terrace where a few people were scattered. I could see that the waiter was already beginning to stack chairs and that the café was winding down for the evening. I wasn't usually cowardly, but avoiding Whyte had been an instinctive move. I thought, what could bring William Whyte back to the school at this hour? He appeared to be by himself. I shrank into a corner as he passed in front of the café and watched him continue towards the school building. He looked behind him and then I realised that he wasn't alone as two other men joined him. Mr. Whyte looked around several times before all three slipped into the yard. What a really strange way to enter your own premises, I thought. Why were they stealing in like thieves or people who did not belong there?

"Mademoiselle," the waiter looked at me grumpily.

I waved my hand, signalling that I didn't need anything and stood up. I could see that the waiter was relieved to clear the terrace and close up.

I scratched my head and looked to the school entrance – dare I go in there after them to pick up the material?

But now the temptation was too strong, not only did I want to get the bag of material, but I was also curious to see what Mr. Whyte was doing.

I found myself imitating Mr. Whyte's manoeuvres, looking around me before pushing in the courtyard door. It was very quiet, although there were lights on in some of the apartments in the surrounding residential buildings. The school door was locked. I peeped in through the barred window, but saw no light on inside. Where were Mr. Whyte and his friends? I glanced back up at the other apartments overlooking the yard – maybe there a logical explanation for all of this and he had a flat up there. In any case, I needed the class material. I took out my keys and opened the door.

Inside, the place was in darkness and there wasn't a sound. Feeling more confident that I was alone, I walked into Judith's office and found the bag on her desk. I decided to take a quick walk down the corridor and noticed that 'St. Alban's' door was open and the light was on. In my short time in the school, I'd observed that Mr. Whyte always locked his precious office, even if he were just going out for a few minutes. I put my head around the door cautiously. Mr. Whyte's briefcase and umbrella were on the table and three coats hung off the coat stand. So they had come in here after all. Where had they gone to? I scanned the room again and realised that the bookcase had been moved to reveal a second door. As I approached it, I heard a sound at the other side and immediately felt scared. I scurried back onto the corridor and left the place as fast as I could, remembering to lock the door after me. I only started breathing again once I got out on the street. It was ridiculous to be so panicky. Ursula had told me her suspicion about Mr. Whyte belonging to a secret society – perhaps he was holding a meeting.

My mobile phone vibrated in my pocket – I let it ring thinking that it was probably Ursula. I walked briskly, taking a diagonal line into a deserted Rue des Irlandais and short-cutting out by the Pantheon. I wasn't going to take time tonight to appreciate the past calling out to me from all those historical sites, but I did take a brief moment to take in the quiet dignity of the Pantheon looking down over Paris from the top of Montagne Sainte-Geneviève.

On Rue Montrosier, my phone vibrated again and this time I answered, surprised when I heard Michael's voice.

"Hello – Michael," a smile spread across my face. I liked his voice – it was a deep baritone. He was calling to invite me to join him and a few of the other teachers for a drink at their favourite café.

I thanked him for his thoughtfulness, but declined his offer. I had an early start in the morning – it was wiser to give it a miss, I told myself.

I put away my phone, a warm, funny feeling stirring inside me. When I didn't answer the first call, Michael had been anxious about me and was making sure I was okay.

I keyed in the code of my building and stepped into the hallway. The sound of television voices resounded from the concierge's lodge – for once, Mme Gomes wasn't on watchdog duty but having a family evening. I had met her husband a few times – a low-sized quiet man who worked with a small electrical company. He appeared to be a hard worker who left early and returned late every day.

I climbed the stairs, stopping to take a breath on the landing – one day, I would get up those steps without feeling like I'd run a race. While there was some chatter and sounds from the other side of the corridor, my own side was very silent. The two students, Olivier and Sebastien, often stayed out very late in the evenings and it was rare to meet them. Apart from Sebastien's brown hair and Olivier's black, they could be identical twins, and I sometimes had a hard time telling them apart at a distance, especially as jeans and T-shirt seemed to be their usual attire. I tip-toed past Madame's room – a nickname I'd given Ursula in my head.

I opened my window wide to cool down my little space, but the night air was heavy and thundery. Putting my head out farther, I saw Ursula's room was in darkness. I was still thinking of Michael's call and thoughtfulness – it had almost taken my mind off William Whyte and the strange scene I had witnessed earlier.

My phone buzzed – I picked it up absently realising that I had dozed off fully dressed on top of my bed.

Ursula's voice whined down the line, "Liz, are you awake?"

"I was sleeping."

"No you weren't."

I sighed, "Why are you ringing me?"

"Liz, I'm afraid to stay alone in my room."

I threw my eyes heavenwards, "What do you want me to do about it?"

"Open your door."

"Are you mad?"

"Just leave it opened for about half an hour to give me a chance to try to sleep; then you can close mine and yours," Ursula pleaded, "I'm too anguished."

"And what about my sleep?"

"You never have problems sleeping. Please, Liz, please," her voice trembled.

I cursed under my breath, got off the bed, unlocked and opened my door very slightly. I believed that this time she was being genuine and if I didn't open the door, I wouldn't get a moment's peace. Ursula had a knack of getting under my skin and making me feel guilty for things that had nothing to do with me. I quickly slipped into a light pair of pyjamas.

I heard Ursula's own door open and she called out, "Thanks, Liz, now I don't feel so alone."

I grunted a reply and lay on my back. With the shy stream of light coming from the corridor and through the window, I watched bugs dancing on the ceiling and listened to the buffered sounds of cars.

"I need a man," Ursula's voice reached me.

Couldn't she stay quiet for one minute? I asked myself. I decided not to respond and mentally started counting the bugs, 'One, two, three – '

"And you?" Ursula was oblivious to my silence.

"I don't need a man," I couldn't help retorting.

"Would you prefer a woman?"

"No."

"You're asexual then."

"I'm just single."

"You are twenty-five."

"No, I'm not, I'm twenty-four and will you please hush up."

I continued counting: seven, eight, nine – nine bugs – no, that last one was just a spot of dirt. The thought came to my mind once more that William Whyte might indeed have been holding a secret society meeting. I didn't know what such societies did, but surely anything that was secret couldn't be good.

"Do you believe in ghosts?"

"Damn it, Ursula! No I don't believe in ghosts."

"Liar."

"Go to blazes and to sleep, I have a group to teach in the morning."

I opened my eyes! Something had disturbed me – I felt somebody had been watching me. Then I held my breath as a shadow moved on the corridor near my open door – I had fallen back to sleep and forgotten to close the door, but now it was wide open. My body broke out in a cold sweat – any crazy person could be out there. I listened for a second, and then bounded from the bed and slammed the door closed, panting in relief. My respite was short-lived as screams filled the corridor. Had somebody attacked Ursula? I was seized by panic – if Ursula's door had been open like mine, then maybe she was being attacked. Everything went quiet again – I listened hard at the door, swallowed several times, and finally opened it a little. It was deadly calm – surely others would have heard the screams? I switched on the corridor light – not a sinner in sight. Puzzled, I looked towards Ursula's room. The door was still slightly open, but she seemed to be sleeping peacefully. I closed her door gently, went back to my own room and feeling totally drained lay down on top of the bed. The noise from the corridor started again – this time there was arguing and lots of weeping. I got out of bed once more and opened the door, but found an empty silent corridor. I shook my head, I must be going crazy, I thought. Tiredness was playing with my mind.

****

I yawned as I entered the school and looked at my watch: 7:45a.m. Everything seemed less shady and mysterious than the previous evening, just as my room and the corridor appeared normal on getting up. I had eventually grabbed a few hours sleep and on waking decided that the voices, screams and weeping had just been my own nightmarish dreams. But my later than usual rise meant skipping breakfast and allowed little time to dawdle and especially to absorb the unfading drama of early morning commuters. There were gurgling coffee machines, tinkling and crashing of crockery and cutlery, and happy and dour faces lining up at café-tabacs for cigarettes, lottery tickets and scratch cards. I took in the cheery salutes and handshakes between owners and delivery people, as well as chipper waiters reorganising tables and chairs and other energetic sounds coming from butchers, bakers and grocers as I hurried to Rue du Soeurs.

I shouted out 'Good morning' to the two open doors at reception and got one raspy reply from Lena who seemed to be in the middle of testing a new student. I looked at the timetable board surprised to see a different teacher's name next to my group.

"Liz," Judith stood at her office door, "I've rearranged your timetable. M. Chevalier wants to take a class in the school this morning, so I've made an exception and put another teacher on your group class to allow you to get started with him. He's in 'St. Thomas's Tower' waiting for you."

Judith's resolved face told me that she was the manager and she decided, even though I felt it wasn't fair to me or my students to be switched like that at the last minute. Surely it was against the rules to allow a client take a class at short notice and mess up scheduling? Here, however, everybody had to jump simply because M. Chevalier and his company were deemed important by William Whyte. Since starting at P.A.F.I., I had not done one class with M. Chevalier as he had been away on business trips. This would be my first chance to meet him in person. I was told that he would do most of his classes in P.A.F.I., but would occasionally come to the school.

Having to do the class in 'St. Thomas's Tower' didn't improve my humour, nor did the bright fluorescent light help. Also, it wasn't yet 8a.m. and I felt rushed and disorganised when my student was in the room before me.

M. Chevalier was sitting on a white tin chair at a white tin table. The scene appeared all wrong to me; Judith could have given him a decent desk and chair if he were that important. Perhaps she'd done it deliberately to give him a subtle message about his last minute arrangement.

M. Chevalier stood up and extended his hand. He was well over six feet tall and towered over me. It was normal to shake hands the first time, but I had discovered that while friends regularly gave one another a peck on either cheek, known as the 'bise,' when saying hello and goodbye, business people did a lot of hand shaking. In my classes, I'd gotten into the habit of giving everybody a big wave and smile. It worked as they saw it as the Irish way.

"M. Chevalier, good morning," I said, trying my best to sound professional and in control. I didn't feel it especially as I had no pre-warning or preparation for this – this was the man who'd complained about a previous teacher and who was relying on me to improve his English to target promotion, but yet who seemed to have little time in his busy schedule for learning English.

His overall air exuded wealth from his well cut navy suit to his gold cufflinks and watch. His black tightly cropped hair, generously sprinkled with silver, made him look older than the forty-two years Judith had told me he was. This effect was added to by his severe grey eyes and intense face that didn't show a hint of a smile.

I dropped my bag and threw out a few files on the table, nervousness making me appear abrupt and awkward. I looked at my watch, it was a few minutes to eight, "Please excuse me a moment, I'm just going to fetch a coffee. Would you like one?"

"No, thank you."

I went straight to the main office to request a decent chair for a man of M. Chevalier's height – surely a chair could be temporarily taken from Mr. Whyte's office?

Lena was still busy talking to a young man whose language level she was assessing. "Monsieur Ragot, you ain't up to taking a business exam course, your level ain't good enough; you gotta do a general revision level first and then target the business diploma."

"But –" the young man stammered.

"No way, Sir." Lena sniffed and tapped a sheet with her pencil, "Your level ain't good enough."

There was a snore from Hamilton, her dog, under the desk.

The potential client nodded, apparently too frightened to argue with her bullying approach. In effect, Lena was successfully selling two courses instead of one.

"Sorry," I backed out of her office. Next door, I heard Judith bellowing down the phone, lambasting a teacher who had just rung in sick – from the few words I gathered, it wasn't the first time for that particular teacher.

I gave up on the chair and made a quick getaway to 'Lindisfarne' where I spooned lots of instant coffee into my cup and added lukewarm water. It made for powerful treacle.

I returned to the 'Tower' to face my student who sat there like a statue. I launched into my first question, "M. Chevalier, can you tell me something about yourself?" 'What a stupid opening question from someone who was supposed to know all about him already,' I thought. 'Cop on, Liz.'

He must have thought so too because his answer ignored the core of my question.

"I am M. Chevalier."

"Right so – ah – can you describe your job?"

"If you want," he sounded bored. "I am an internal auditor, I am the internal auditing manager. My job is to audit."

"How long have you worked in your company?" 'Boy, I was brilliant.'

"I work many years."

'Inspiration please,' I begged in my mind.

I continued with my questions, but after five arduous minutes, I was looking at my materials in desperation. This class was going to drag and M. Chevalier was going to make me work for every second. By now, I wasn't surprised he had difficulties with English, he had difficulties communicating – full stop. I noticed through the partition window a light switching on next door – William Whyte appeared and began rearranging furniture. Did he have to make it so obvious that he was spying on my class? But then as I'd discovered, sneaking around seemed to be normal activity for him.

I continued serving up questions to M. Chevalier who kept returning monosyllabic answers and quenching whatever enthusiasm I might have had.

I felt forced to resort to the CD player for teaching support. "Could you listen to this track and summarise it for me please?" I was ashamed of myself, I knew by relying on the CD, I was opting out and had given up on trying to interact with this student.

"If you want," his granite features gave nothing away and it was impossible to tell what he was thinking.

I don't know why, but his 'If you want' really got on my nerves causing me to blurt out, "It's nicer to say 'if you wish'."

He shrugged, "If you wish, then."

I gripped my pen, 'Control your temper, Liz,' I told myself, 'he's not a teenager, he's a grown man.'

"M. Chevalier, is everything all right? Was there something in particular you wanted to work on in today's class?" I tried to challenge him.

"You are the teacher."

I hit the button on the CD player – going into automatic mode.

Long after M. Chevalier left, I remained slumped on my chair like a rag doll. He'd taken all my energy, extracted everything from me. I eventually mustered up enough courage to move again, even if it was just to close my bag and switch off the light. What a flop that was – my confidence was dented and I needed to get out of the school, teach other students and prove to myself that I could do better.

I got back out on the corridor in time to see M. Chevalier, coffee in hand, go into 'St. Alban's'. I imagined he was going to complain about my teaching skills to William Whyte. It annoyed me that it was the first thought that entered my mind. I'd been mistaken in believing I'd put my bad classroom experiences behind me.

I hesitated on Rue des Soeurs trying to decide between walking back to the Jardin du Luxembourg R.E.R. Station or going to the nearer Place Monge Metro Station. In the centre of Paris, commuters had multiple choices and I usually decided depending on mood and time. The R.E.R. was the sensible, more efficient option at this moment.

"Liz," Michael was standing there with a big smile on his face. I realised that he had been waiting for me. "Liz, if you're taking the Metro, I'll be along with you."

My choice was made. Michael had the magic touch and my mood changed immediately, "Hi, Michael, I am taking the Metro. What company are you heading to now?"

"I have to do a stint up at Cité de la Science-Porte de La Villette, a chap who organises some exhibits on earthquakes or something. He isn't difficult, he just likes to talk and talk." Michael tossed his folder in the air and caught it easily like a circus juggler. He was tall, light on his feet and moved with the suppleness of a dancer, given to grace rather than the power of muscle and bulk. "Oh Champs Elysées, Oh Champs Elysées," he sang a popular tune I'd already heard several times on the radio. I noticed how his brown eyes twinkled. His charming smile could win even M. Chevalier over.

Michael glanced at my bag, "Let me carry that for you, it looks rather heavy. What have you got inside there?"

I frowned, "A lot more than you have in your folder, obviously." But I let him carry the bag; it was thoughtful of him and a touch old-fashioned, which I liked.

In the train carriage, we chatted easily about our classes and schedule until we reached Palais Royale-Musée du Louvre Station where we were both taking different connecting lines. With a little wave goodbye, Michael sauntered off as if he'd all the time in the world. By my watch, he would barely be on time for his class. However, my good humour had been restored. I tried not to dwell too much on the fact that Michael tended to seek me out. It wasn't the first time that he managed to catch me on my own or to hop out from nowhere, just as he'd done this morning, and always when I needed a boost of confidence. I didn't want to read too much into it, but it gave me a pleasant feeling.

5

By early October, after my first six weeks in the school, I had built up more confidence in my teaching skills. I also began staying on later in the school on Saturdays after my classes. It was a good way to catch up on preparation for the following week and easier to do so in the school library than in the confines of my room. I could also avail of the photocopying machine and the computer without being disturbed. I was able to work quickly and it usually didn't take longer than thirty to forty minutes in total. I always made sure, nonetheless, that it was okay with Lena. Today, she was tidying up her desk and as usual in a hurry to get away after the Saturday morning shift.

"Sure, Honey. Got your key?"

"Yes. Oh, Lena, I wanted to ask you something?"

"Yeah?"

"Is the school used for something else besides language teaching?"

"Hell no. Why the question?" Lena fumbled to put the leash on Hamilton.

"You know, Mr. Whyte might let out some of the rooms for other activities. I mean, I heard that he –"

"Sorry gotta go – come on, Hamilton," she yanked the dog after her, blowing me a kiss. "Shall I lock ya in?"

"Yes, I don't want strangers walking in."

Lena had given my question short shrift, but that wasn't unusual as she tended to be abrupt anyway. I was happy that Lena trusted me, although she was hardly taking a risk – apart from the computers there was little of great value to steal, and even those few computers were old.

I went to 'Stratford-upon-Avon' leaving the door ajar. Daytime changed a lot of things and I felt silly about being so afraid the night I'd seen William Whyte and his friends skulking around. I was still curious though and toyed with the idea of checking out 'St. Alban's' and investigating where the second door in his office led to. It was probably just a wine cellar, I reasoned.

I worked efficiently and soon put the last files in my bag with satisfaction. The library door creaked open a little wider. Distracted, I looked up and thought I saw somebody. As I got up from my chair, I heard footsteps across the floor tiles.

I walked down the corridor, blinking several times, but there was no sign of anybody. My mind was playing tricks again, I decided – it wasn't a comfortable feeling knowing that my brain could deceive me like that. This was the same experience as imagining sounds and voices on my attic floor corridor.

"Elizabeth Downey?"

I jumped, "Mr. Whyte, I didn't hear you come in."

"What are you doing here, it's late?" There was no mistaking the angry tone of his voice.

"I was just finishing some class preparation." I zipped up my bag, "I have to go, bye."

"Miss Downey, where is M. Chevalier's report, I haven't received it?" The whites of his eyes held my attention.

I averted my own eyes and kept moving towards the door, "It's too soon, I haven't done enough classes with him. I'll bring it next week."

I didn't wait for his reply and escaped outside.

"Oops, sorry," I skidded to avoid a dark-suited burly man who was just entering.

He brushed past me into the school.

Obviously William Whyte and his cronies were having another get together – that must have been what I had seen and heard from 'Stratford-upon-Avon.'

****

While most teachers disliked evening classes especially as they had to teach again early next morning, it didn't stop a few of the staunch night owls from having a couple of drinks before heading home. Café de la Rose at Place Saint Michel was one of the favourite haunts for the teachers. I didn't want to make a habit of it, but generally relented and joined them on a Thursday or Friday evening. The day had gone very well teaching wise, from my early start at La Défense to the evening business class at the school, and I was happy and still high on adrenaline from putting sixteen students through their paces.

October was spoiling us with mild temperatures and the overhead heaters on the café terrace, while comforting, were hardly necessary. Café de la Rose was fairly busy, but with the main tourist season drawing to a close, the atmosphere was more relaxed than a few weeks earlier and the waiters strutted casually between the tables. I appreciated the view of the River Seine, softly lit by yellow lighting, while directly in front of us the fountain and sculpture dedicated to the Arch Angel Michel provided an interesting distraction.

Some teachers from the evening shift, Michel, Jonathan, Cynthia, Angie, Ursula and myself, sprawled around two tables. Our hands and faces were smudged with marker dust – the cloth dusters in the school were totally ill-adapted for the job of wiping white boards and it was impossible for a teacher not to end up stained one colour or another. Blue seemed to be the favourite colour this evening. Michael sat next to me and I felt myself relax. I was too tired to talk and preferred to listen to the others rattle on about how bad the pay was, how peculiar Mr. Whyte was, and the usual gripes about absenteeism, students who asked awkward questions...

One of the recurring discussions was the growing trend of using mobile phones for sending short written messages, called SMS (short message service) or texts. I, along with most of the younger teachers, was very much in favour of the short text to communicate. It was easy, efficient and fun. However, some of the older teachers found it difficult to come to terms with the speed that the new technology was spreading as a means of communication. They felt the whole text message phenomena was destroying the English language because the acronyms and abbreviated words and phrases ignored good spelling and grammar. But we all did agree on one thing: we should avoid using our mobile phones to conduct telephone classes with students. There were several reports warning people of the dangers of prolonged use of the device. I noticed myself that my cheek got hot if I held a conversation for more than fifteen minutes on my mobile phone.

Ursula examined her blue-tinted hands, "Whatever about mobile phones, I'm fed up of those cloth dusters – I've asked at least ten times for proper dusters, but they're too scrooge to spend the money. I'm like a 'Smurf' with all this blue."

There was a mumble of agreement as Ursula practised a few more pouts and crossed her long legs clad in slightly flared black jeans and an expensive pair of high-heeled black booties.

I noticed that Ursula complained more than anyone about being broke, but she always seemed to wear expensive clothes in vogue with the latest fashion. Her slate blue top was simple, but was obviously well cut and high quality. I wondered where she managed to store all those clothes in her room. I too had on a pair of black jeans, boots and blouse, but my jeans were several years old and straight legged and my boots needed a lot of polish to look good. However, my white cotton blouse and brown leather jacket – although second-hand, were gifts from Mme Defoe, and I was pleased to note they still looked trendy, as was often the case with her clothes.

Cynthia, from Wisconsin, confided in us that she missed living in the States and was making plans to go home permanently after the Christmas holidays. She had completed a year at the Sorbonne University following Civilization Studies. Language teaching had just been a way to make a little extra and allow her to extend her stay by a few months. I doubted if her visa permitted her to work also, but kept those thoughts to myself.

"Judith will have a fit," Ursula said.

"I haven't fully decided yet, so keep it to yourselves," Cynthia pushed back her long blond locks and looked at us pleadingly with innocent blue eyes.

"I'm not coming back either if I can help it," said Jonathan, the Welsh teacher, who was always threatening to leave, but wasn't sure where he was going. He'd managed to stick the school a year and a half. Jonathan looked eighteen although he was closer to thirty and I couldn't help comparing him to a street urchin. His hollow cheeks and thin frame made me want to feed him. His mousy hair was badly cut and fell over his forehead, partially covering his eyes.

Michael who had turned twenty-five wasn't any more certain than the others about staying on at the school. However, he didn't feel up to going back to England, he told us, and hesitated between staying on in Paris or going to India, or maybe somewhere else. I didn't know anything about Michael's family but his mild, easy manners and accent reminded me of someone who grew up in a comfortable middle-class background.

"I'm stuck here," Angie reminded all of us. Angie hailed from Devon or thereabouts. She was the oldest, in her late fifties, divorced with a grown up family, and she needed to work. Her face was quite wrinkled under her honey blond coloured hair because of her heavy smoking.

Despite the beer I sipped, my throat was parched. I had been doing so much talking and forcing my voice all day that I felt if I had to formulate another carefully constructed sentence, I'd crack up. Then I got hold of myself; 'Liz, you are among natives, it should be possible to speak, well at least converse in plain English.'

Here I was in beautiful Paris, lounging on a terrace and too tired to appreciate it. The smells of skewering, grilling and cooking coming from the Latin Quarter's diverse mix of restaurants filled the air. There were dozens of French, Italian, Turkish, North African and Greek restaurants. I was sure I could sniff a fusion of Boeuf Bourguignon, Pizza, Chicken and Lamb Kebabs, and other tasty skewers such as Couscous and Tajine. The smashed plates at the entrances marked out the Greek places, underlining the tradition of customers being allowed to break a plate if they dined there. The restaurant owners, who in August clapped and drummed up business as they tried to herd passers-by into their places, were less vocal now as autumn progressed. Crowds that moved in slow ripples up and down Rue de la Huchette and other narrow streets during peak summer season had thinned out and the quarter was no longer thronged with people. For those of us who lived and worked in Paris and spent a lot of time in the heart of the city, the calmer sensation and feeling that one could breathe and move without fighting for every inch of space among tourists was welcomed this time of the year.

I saw a familiar pair pass in front of the fountain.

"Lena," I called and waved.

Hamilton was pulling ahead as fast as he could go and towing his owner after him. He looked like he was having the time of his life, darting between, around, or just barging into people. It was quite a different dog from the one that usually lay in a lazy ball under Lena's chair in the office.

"Wow, wow, wow," Lena tried to jerk Hamilton to a stop. But Hamilton kept pulling at the leash – he'd gotten a sniff of a river walk and was doing everything to get there in double quick time.

"Can't stop to talk now – bye, guys," Lena was swept off.

'Running from something or someone,' I thought once more of Lena's words spoken the first time we met. I supposed that Lena was no different than the rest of us – she'd probably just been passing through Paris like so many others, and thinking 'One day, I'll move off somewhere else, one day I'll really know what I want to do.' It was also people like Lena who added the diverse mixture and quirky ingredient to the recipe that made the city unique. Then again, Paris had enough exotic tastes of its own without foreigners, I realised on seeing a man laden with bags cross onto Boulevard Saint Michel. I recognised M. Jacques whose scavenging instincts had him furrowing all over the city for bits and pieces of people's junk and leftovers that would probably become once again centrepieces in somebody else's home. I was sure he noticed Ursula and I sitting on the terrace, but deliberately took a different street to avoid meeting us. I could understand his reluctance and his wish to be left alone when out on his rounds foraging.

"So," Michael drew me back into their conversation, "I heard you got the old talk from Mr. Whyte?"

"Yes," I said. "What's behind all that? Is he some sort of spy or is he simply mad?"

Michael laughed, "I try not to take him seriously, but I must say he's an embarrassment to English people. He's just obsessed because he's afraid of losing the P.A.F.I. contract. "

"Is this connected to the so-called competition between Fabre and Chevalier?" I asked.

"That's it, as far as I can make out," said Michael. "And, apparently Chevalier isn't partial to our school."

That was one reason to explain Chevalier's uncooperative attitude in class, I thought.

"Don't see why," Cynthia commented.

"He had a bad teacher," Angie explained.

"That's just an excuse," Ursula yawned.

"Anyway," Michael added, "according to the HR at P.A.F.I, the job might also go to an outsider. But Ursula's student, M. Fabre, is definitely a favourite, and I heard that he really likes our school."

"He must like his teacher too," Angie smiled.

"Huh," Ursula looked away. "English is important for this promotion, that's all – and besides, Fabre is only marginally better than Chevalier at English."

"I can't believe that language is the only criteria for promotion in this deal," Jonathan called for a second beer.

"You have a point," I said, "but it can be a good excuse for eliminating a candidate. Still, I'm inclined to believe that Whyte is just an odd ball."

"Absolutely," Cynthia raised her glass.

"Dead right," Michael nudged me teasingly. "Forget about it, about him; none of us will be here that long." Michael stood up, gathered together some cutlery from the vacated tables nearby and began to juggle forks, knives and spoons for our entertainment. He drew a rowdy applause from us, the waiters and some people going by.

Trust Michael to bring out the sunshine. He had a way of lightening the mood and smoothing over the bumps. At the end of his little performance, he gave an exaggerated bow and sat down again, stretching his long legs in front. His thigh brushed lightly against mine; I wasn't sure if it were deliberate or accidental, but on catching sight of Ursula's narrowing stare, I ignored her and made no effort to move my leg away.

Jonathan examined his half empty glass and brought us back to a favourite theme, "From what I hear, the money's not much better in other schools, so there's no point in moving from Whyte's elsewhere. When I move, it will be to totally change and do something different."

"What about you, Liz, how long are you planning to stay?" Angie accepted one of Ursula's cigarettes.

"I don't know, I'm new to the job – but so far, I like the teaching part." I surprised myself by saying it out loud and it was true: I liked language teaching.

"Liz is perfect," Ursula made a face, "always on time, never late, only thinks of her classes and students. Talking to her is like talking to an encyclopaedia – she can't walk by a monument without giving long descriptions and historical detail about it. She's a real nerd."

Ursula's comments didn't feel like a compliment and stung me. I felt my eyes water. I shouldn't let her get to me that way, but I couldn't help it.

"Unlike a lot of us, Liz knows her stuff and when it comes to teaching, she is a professional," Michael's words made my eyes water even more.

"Yes, she is," Cynthia supported him. "You are so lucky, Liz, I wish I liked my job as much as you do."

Angie inhaled, "I liked it too at the beginning, but you soon grow tired of it."

"Not Liz, she's a saint," Ursula wouldn't let it go.

This time I defended myself, "I'm content with things for now – where's the problem in that?"

"Anyone for another beer?" Jonathan asked.

I shook my head and was beginning to regret making the stop over at Café de la Rose. I wanted to be refreshed for my morning classes, but I wasn't going to say that out loud and provide more fodder for Ursula's sarcasm.

"My eyes are closing with sleep," I lied, "I'll catch up with you guys again."

As I reached the Metro entrance, I heard Ursula call my name, "Hey, Liz, let's drop into the Irish College."

Ursula had been mean to me back at the café and now she wanted me to go along with her on a late evening excursion, just because she felt like it. I didn't want to go, not after her jibes at the café. I was angry at myself for not telling her straight out and for hiding the fact that she'd hurt me. I didn't want to show my feelings. Wasn't that what Marc-Antoine had accused me of – too much control over my emotions and not letting myself go. That had been his excuse for leaving me. But the truth was that he had been two-timing me from the beginning. In my opinion, my main weakness was in wanting to please everyone and that had come from being an only child. I wasn't trying to be the good girl, rather I didn't want to hurt people. In the end, I'd hurt Mum pretty bad.

"You can do whatever you want, Ursula, I'm going home. Besides, the College must be closed by now, it's after ten."

"Don't be that way; I'm sorry I poked fun at you, but you bring it out in me. Don't be so sensitive." Her voice trembled, "Please, Liz, it doesn't close until eleven and I really want to say a prayer in the chapel there."

I wanted to scream. It was totally ridiculous and I was totally ridiculous for not doing what I wanted to do – go home.

The quieter, hushed atmosphere of Rue des Irlandais soothed me. The little street had no cafés or businesses and it was possible to hear our own footsteps echo on the pavement. We pushed in the courtyard door to find ourselves face to face with a large statue of the Virgin Mary as the lighting came on and the yard opened into a wider garden. The main building looked exactly like a college. I picked up a stray pamphlet from outside a closed reception window and scanned it. It described the building as a fifteen-bay, four-storey structure. It was originally a town house that dated from 1765 and was converted after being closed during the French Revolution, 1798. The Irish College itself was founded in the late 16th century and for three centuries was a major Roman Catholic educational establishment that had several different locations in Paris. Today, as well as serving as a religious centre, the current building provided paid accommodation, long and short term, to Irish visitors and students as well as housing the Polish Seminary from 1945. There were plans to renovate the place and turn it into a proper cultural centre.

"Oh, listen to this," I said to Ursula, "this street wasn't called Rue des Irlandais in the past, but Rue du Cheval Vert."

Ursula wasn't listening to me. She spread her arms towards the statue, "I was here before, I know it."

"Probably, when you first came to Paris, a few years ago," I was getting used to her deranged tangents.

"Smart ass – no, in another life."

"If you say so. Let's go into the chapel, that's why you dragged me here isn't it?"

The chapel was small with seminarian choir seats stacked sideways leaving a lot of space in the centre for an uncluttered view of the altar. It was dedicated to Saint Patrick and the initials SP were visibly engraved on the seats and on the floor tiling. There was one stained glass window high over the altar and several statues and pictures honouring Saint Patrick, Saint Brigid, Christ and Our Lady. What piqued my interest was information on the pamphlet which explained that above the chapel was a vaulted library and archive storing 8,000 volumes and at least 19,000 archives, some dating from 1772. I was determined to return there again and explore more when

I could.

Ursula wasn't interested in the historical facts, but feelings. She stood with her hands clasped together, "Can you feel the echo of history in the silence of this space and smell the prayer of hundreds of years?"

"Yes," I admitted.

"But a lot of people were sacrificed and killed here too," Ursula added.

"That applies to anywhere in Paris – there were many wars and plagues," I wasn't going to let her go completely off on her metaphysical tangent.

"You don't understand. What I'm talking about is not something you read about or that any of those pamphlets will tell you. But I sense human pain, the same way I sense it when I wake up at night in Room 1."

"Really?"

"I tell you, Liz, I'm clair-sensitive. Alcohol dulls my senses, but I feel something – it's like electricity current. I feel it in the school, in the room and now here. There is a link between the places, I'm sure of it."

Ursula looked so sincere and serious that I let go any scathing comment I was about to make. "The past is certainly all around us."

Ursula walked down the aisle in front of the altar, "I see Eva here on her hands and knees polishing the floor –"

"Eva?" I was in the right place to pray for patience. "You see also, so you're clairvoyant then as well?"

"Sort of, the image is strong in my mind."

"Whatever you feel, it was long ago and has nothing to do with your room or anything else."

"Maybe so, but some people manage to feed on energy from the past – different times, parallel worlds, same abuses and crimes."

"Oh, Ursula, you're getting carried away. You don't like Mr. Whyte, fair enough – I don't either. You live in a small uncomfortable room – I agree that it isn't easy. We're standing in the Irish College, a place that touches us deeply as Irish people – that's all. It's natural to feel something – a connection."

"Yeah, if it were something good. But it isn't – and Whyte is the seediest man I've ever met."

"So you keep telling me." I hesitated to share about the evening I saw William Whyte and his friends sneak into the school, but decided against it. "Come on, I'm going home, I don't want to have my eyes hanging out of my head tomorrow morning."

To avoid a Metro line change, we zigzagged to Pont Notre Dame and crossed the river, taking a moment to lean over the bridge and admire the floodlit River Seine flowing under the many other bridges that marked its passage: Pont Marie, Pont Neuf, Pont des Arts… We walked on towards Rue Rivoli, casually window shopping en route.

We passed by Hotel de Ville admiring the arresting Renaissance-style town hall. The old-fashioned lamp posts and lighting effects showed off the ceremonial doors, a large clock and lots of sculptures and murals on the facade.

Finally, we hopped onto, as always, a crowded Metro Line 1.

Ursula leaned towards me and whispered in my ear, "Vincent wants to see me again, what should I do?"

I'd need the patience of Job. Why did some people have to share the personal details of their lives?

"I can't say, Ursula, I'm barely acquainted with your ex-boyfriend."

She took the hint, but looked like a crucified Saint Ursula. We clung to the central pole in our section of the carriage, sporting our tired blue marker stained faces, and grasping bags filled with teaching material in our blue hands.

"So what about you, what brought you to Paris?" Ursula asked. "It was a man, wasn't it? You wouldn't have taken the risk of coming on your own." Ursula was intent on driving me to distraction.

"I've no intention of discussing my life with you on this train."

"I'm right then."

I didn't grace her comment with an answer.

"Bonsoir, Mademoiselles," Mme Gomes wheeled out a dustbin, giving Ursula that now familiar startled look, as if puzzled that the girl renting Room 1 was still standing. And no, I mumbled to myself, the blue colour isn't a new type of disease ravaging her face.

M. Jacques was doing sentry at the top of the stairs. He'd apparently been waiting for us girls.

"Bonsoir, Monsieur Jacques," we chimed.

"Bonsoir," he pressed his face close to ours and then redressed himself, straightening his shoulders. It was a habit of his, as if his drooping shoulders needed constant lifting up, like repositioning a coat on a hanger.

He turned to go but seemed to change his mind and once again, he pushed his greying bushy head and round spectacled face this time towards Ursula, "I have the bath and I can set it up for you now."

"You are wonderful, Monsieur Jacques," Ursula flattered him, "it should make my life more civilised. Otherwise, I'll be running back to my ex-boyfriend, just for the luxury of a proper shower."

M. Jacques had managed to put together a shower-come-bath for Ursula. It didn't look much at first glance, but it was a step in the right direction. It was really no more than a giant pink plastic tub which could be filled directly by attaching some tubing to the sink taps. Compared to my chipped basin and basic orange plastic tub, it seemed like luxury. Its unique design feature was a plastic wall that fitted easily to the sides. It gave some privacy while keeping the floor dry.

Soon, a small crowd had gathered around to see it. The Bjania couple admired it, as did Sebastien – the friendlier of the two students. Even M. Brosse raised a head that seemed to be permanently in his chest to look and express a grumpy acknowledgement of 'Well done' to M. Jacques. Elle, the cat, jumped in immediately to explore the new addition to the room. All that was needed was Ursula standing in the tub and giving a demonstration.

Sebastien was a fresh faced, brown haired young man. He was very chatty and expressed his delight at having English teachers as neighbours. I was happy to talk a little with someone normal – that is until he began hinting that English classes would be useful to him and his friend, Olivier, who had yet to return from some party he was attending for the evening. Sebastien explained that getting extra tuition to improve his English was expensive.

I knew where he was going with this and was not going to feel sorry for him and start offering free classes.

"I was wondering –" Sebastien began to broach his main point.

"Do you have Internet?" I interrupted.

"Of course," he was surprised by the question.

"I don't and Ursula doesn't either for the time being."

"So?"

He wasn't getting it and Ursula who had joined us spelled it out more clearly, "We don't have money, we need to work as much as we can for money, so we cannot afford to offer free classes. Do you understand?"

Sebastien looked more confused.

"Look," I said, giving into my gentler nature, "I'm quite happy to help you out from time to time, but I can't give you regular classes. I'm sure there are lots of tutorials online."

"Then again," said Ursula, spotting an opportunity, "if you let us use your computer, we could always do a trade-off. Let's say, an hour on your computer for conversation classes."

"It's not important," Sebastien slipped back to his room – the barter was not what he'd bargained for.

"Please yourself," said Ursula, "amazing how motivation drops when put to the test."

I opened my own door with Ursula and Elle at my heels.

They followed me into my room, "Liz," Ursula whispered.

"What's the matter?"

"M. Jacques told me that there's a catacomb tunnel from the Irish College to Rue des Soeurs and it goes right under our school."

"Really," I cocked my ears.

"He stores junk in the cellars under the Irish College and that's why he knows."

"What else does he say?"

"He won't tell me. He had a drink or two and let that information out. Then he got all funny about it and wouldn't say any more. Strange isn't it?"

"Maybe he's even met Eva, the ghost, wandering around there."

Ursula took her cat in her arms and walked out.

"Ursula?" I called after her.

She didn't reply and banged her room door.

It was cruel of me, but I wasn't going to feel guilty about my harmless joke. I closed my own door with a firm clack.

6

I stood in the school reception area feeling a little dazed and wondering, 'How do I keep doing this?' I had once more been bamboozled by my need to be nice and inability to say no. I scowled at my reflection in the glass door, thinking that I should have seen it coming. It started when I was entrusted with the keys to lock up after my evening classes. It was reinforced by Judith's explanation that it was difficult to find reliable teachers, but I was quickly pin-pointed as one. In the days that followed, I was at the receiving end of little compliments: I was so dependable and trustworthy and a real people person. Then today, the final blow came when Judith offered me the honour of taking over Saturday testing and administration from Lena. They had both been hinting at the possibility strongly from the beginning and as my Saturday morning group course had just finished, it was the perfect opportunity.

I had been hurrying to zip up my bag after a morning class in the school and about to head off to La Défense and the world of P.A.F.I. when Judith called me into her office and sprang the offer on me.

Now, Judith stood there beaming at me while Lena practically hugged me to death. I was her salvation. At last, she'd off-loaded her Saturday morning duties.

"You are so nice," Lena gushed.

"Yes, one of the nicest teachers we have," Judith's smile showed gleaming teeth.

Boy did I hate that word. Nice in my opinion was another way to describe someone as docile and gullible.

Lena gave a chesty cough, "Now, Liz, you come in one of these afternoons and watch how I do it." She was determined to have me, her prodigy, operational as soon as possible.

****

I tried to make the most of my new Saturday morning position. I told myself that while I wasn't ambitious to become a top assistant, I would acquire new office skills – and I set myself one big goal: I was going to perfectly pitch that 'W.W.S.O.E. & F.L., Bonjour,' used to answer the phone, if it killed me.

Part of the job consisted of getting people who rang in for a free test and advice, as offered on the school's brochures, to actually sign up for classes. These potential clients usually completed a written test online or came into the school to do it on the premises. The next step was an oral test on the phone or face to face. It cost nothing to go that far. It was a basic sales tactic and it worked. It was Lena's job to make that free advice pay in every sense of the word.

"That's what marks us out as different from the others," Lena explained to me. "We don't just settle for testing people online, we talk to them and do a real assessment. We give honest advice."

Lena didn't spare her honesty. I'd observed her using a lot of coercion with people based on what could only be described as manipulation of facts. She had the ability to make even potential clients with good English believe that they were well short of the level required by today's standards of professional life.

Judith whispered to me one day, "Lena's great in here. We get so many mavericks coming in looking for personal solutions and paying for courses out of their own pockets. Lena enrols candidates with wonderful efficiency and that's key in filling up our group classes."

I understood that while in-company classes at places like P.A.F.I. were important, group classes at the school, consisting of 12-16 paying individuals, was lucrative business.

I did my required training time sitting with Lena, watching and learning the ropes from an old hand.

"See, I don't trust computers," Lena pulled out several roll-books and notebooks from a drawer in her desk, "I write everything down."

She insisted on taking me slowly and agonizingly through the testing phase. I wasn't a step by step person myself, preferring to get to the crux of the matter immediately. Lena, however, had taken the boat across the Atlantic, and that's the gauge she kept with her for life. Pace yourself slowly was her motto.

Lena had brought many flavours of America with her, the most important being her ability to make a deal. She was a hustler and resolute to pass on her experience.

"Listen to me and take note, Liz. You got different kinds of people coming in. Firstly, there are those who come for the free ride. You've gotta shoot them down at the doorstep – can't have them wasting your time."

"Right you are."

Lena sniffed, "Then, you got those who have money trouble written all over them. They don't have the bucks, but try to nuzzle their way into courses. Show them the door – fast. Others are trouble just because they are trouble wherever they go. They'll get students riled up, start filing complaints about books, materials and teachers. Tag those. If they've got the money, take them, but put everybody on the alert. You got it?"

"Got it, loud and clear," I gave her a military salute.

"Ha ha – don't be too smart," she retorted. "When you've got it narrowed down, it's a question of level and potential. There are those who are a lot stronger than what they think at English – you can get those to sign up for a few contracts. Suggest courses to bring them back up to level and build up their confidence slowly to target an exam class. People like that are good money spinners. Others think they're a lot stronger in the language than what they are really, so you gotta put them in their place – if you know what I mean."

"Oh, I do, I do."

"Lots of people have method fixations. 'What's your method?' they'll ask."

"And what do you reply?" I was curious, having heard the word 'method' so many times since coming to France. To me, sophisticated theoretical methods weren't ideal when it came to learning how to communicate in a language. I believed in an approach that combined listening, speaking, reading and writing in an interesting, lively and painless way.

"Our method is simple," Lena laboured on. "We test and we have a proven programme that works. We give students a grammar base, vocabulary exercises, role-plays and –"

I didn't yawn, but I was ready to fall asleep.

"Liz, are you there?" Lena poked me.

"Yes, yes."

She smiled indulgently.

I didn't trust that smile.

"Would you mind taking Hamilton for a walk – he's gotta get out and I'm tied up here?"

I jumped at it, willing to put up with anything for a few minutes of freedom. "No problem, where will I take him?"

"Just as far as Jardin de Luxembourg – you got the time, the next test isn't for an hour."

"That's a big run."

"You're young."

I took the leash from Lena, hoping I wouldn't end up strangling Hamilton. "Where's Judith?"

"At Cité de la Science – she's supervising one of the classes."

"That's where Michael teaches, isn't it?"

"Sure is."

"Is he having problems? Is she inspecting his teaching?"

"Could say that – Michael can be a bit spaced out, but it's also to give the right signal to the client."

I didn't like the sound of that and hoped Michael's job wasn't in jeopardy.

"That boy is sweet on you," Lena winked.

I was taken aback, "I don't think so – Michael's a sweet guy, he's nice to everybody."

Lena handled her packet of cigarettes and went into the yard with me. She lit up and puffed with pleasure, "I know sweet when I see it and he ain't the same with you as he is with the others."

I held the leash firmly as Hamilton wiggled with excitement. I preferred not to think about Michael in those terms and instead asked, "What about you, Lena, you must have been sweet on someone once?"

"Sweet turns sour with the years."

"You would know."

"What do you mean by that?"

"You're older with more experience of life. Anyway, you've stayed with the school which means you like it. That hasn't turned sour."

"It fills a few gaps in my pension."

"It isn't easy making ends meet," I concurred.

"That's for sure," Lena inhaled smoke.

"There are worse places than Whyte's."

"There's better too. It used to be more fun when Tom ran it – things ain't the same now."

"Tom?"

"William's brother. It was Tom who founded the school and ran it originally."

"What happened?"

"Dropped dead five years ago. Happens the best."

"So things changed after."

"I guess you could say that." The phone rang in the office and Lena crushed her cigarette on the window sill, "Off with you now, Hamilton needs exercising."

I was practically knocked down by Richard, the teacher who reminded me of a Boy Scout, making a very dramatic entrance into the courtyard. He looked closely at his watch, "No time to talk – I'm late – I'm late."

Richard's reputation was to be too inflexible and severe and students constantly complained about him to management. Honestly, I thought, where did these teachers come from and what qualified them to be in a language school, other than their tonic accent? The tonic accent, which meant stressing and accentuating sentences in the right places to give the perfect Received English accent, was something that French people longed to have and valued above all other skills in the language.

****

I hated late evenings as much as Lena hated early mornings. This time it was with M. Chevalier in P.A.F.I., at La Défense. His lesson had been hanging over my head like a shadow all day. How was I to come up with five hundred ideas to help cross that classroom desert with my least communicative student? I found myself checking his balance of hours and ticking off every one with vengeance. But no matter how I counted and recounted it, it looked like I was stuck with him until well into next year. I sighed and began to lay out a folder of newspaper clippings. I plugged in the old CD player, making sure I had many tracks to back me up. I'd invented scores of new questions for this class. All I wanted to do was go home to bed. Of all the rooms in the building, I'd been given one which supplied neither whiteboard nor flipchart. If M. Chevalier were at his uncooperative best this evening, I wasn't sure I'd have the patience to put up with him.

But at least, this room did have windows and I hurried to look out from the tower block. The lights coming from surrounding buildings cheered up the dark November evening. I could see the traffic along the quays of the River Seine, sluggish and congested – but it was the royal view of the Eiffel Tower that lifted my spirits somewhat.

Ten minutes later, I saw a silhouette reflected back from the window pane and turned to face M. Chevalier. His brow was creased and I visualised hundreds of emails and Excel sheets etched out in every furrow.

"Good evening, M. Chevalier."

"Good evening."

"How was your day?" I garnished my words with exaggerated fervour pretending I cared. But somewhere I did – a good day might result in me having an easier class.

He gave me a harassed look communicating that his day was a long ways from being finished and assessing if it were good or not was far too premature.

I looked pointedly at my watch – I wasn't letting him get away with not acknowledging his being late.

"I'm sorry, I had a meeting. It is – was difficult to stop it sooner," he offered an explanation.

He didn't sound at all sorry and wouldn't have said anything if I hadn't drawn his attention to it. That bothered me.

"Did you have many meetings today?" I asked politely.

"The usual, not very interesting."

It was going to be one of those classes. I controlled my rising temper, thinking – 'the point is, interesting or not, you are supposed to talk about them. Talk about something, for God's sake.'

"If I remember, you were to have a conference call with people in

Houston yesterday. You were anxious about understanding their accents. Did you manage it in English?" I tried to open a different avenue of conversation.

"The meeting was cancelled."

"So, did you read the article I gave you?"

"The article? Oh – forget it, no time."

Great, just brilliant, I could already see the headlines: 'TEACHER THROTTLES STUDENT!'

"I suppose you caught the news on the radio or somewhere?" I tried again.

"I do not remember."

"You must have listened to the radio in your car on the way to work?"

"I played the CD you gave me, but it is hard to understand."

Well tough, I thought.

"You have to keep doing it," I insisted, "if you have the channels on T.V. at home, turn on BBC or one of the English radio stations and have some English in the background while you are feeding the cat or something."

That caused a lip to curve upwards, "You have a cat?" he asked.

"No, but my neighbour does." Hurray! He'd asked me one question, which was progress. But he soon lapsed back into apathy again.

"Right," I made a stoic effort to restart the language engine.

"I need more vocabulary," M. Chevalier said.

I took a breath and held onto my sanity, "Sure, but you have to put the work into listening and reading and writing too." Most students believed that learning vocabulary by heart made them more fluent. It was as if acquiring a language was a chemical formula whereby one just had to pour a glossary of terms into the brain and ideas would flow out in beautiful fluent speech.

"I need to speak more."

I folded my arms, "So speak, we've got lots of time, speak."

"It is difficult to find your words when you are tired. I am better in the morning."

I'd been up since half past five, eaten one and a half biscuits since breakfast and would only get home around half past nine tonight, that's if I were lucky and didn't collapse going up the stairs. I'd have to eat tuna out of a tin and share my bread with cockroaches, while listening to Ursula's moaning. I'd then have to try to find a respectable way of using a hole in the ground as a toilet before sleeping on a hard bed. And he was tired!

"Why M. Chevalier, you're breaking my heart. We've done classes in the morning, in the afternoon and evening, and you're always tired. I think you should see a doctor." It was too late to rein my words back in now. I held my breath and waited.

For the first time, M. Chevalier eyed me cautiously. He coughed, "I can try to read the article out loud and you can correct me."

It was a start, but it wasn't my goal. I wanted him to engage, not read a text. Still, I had to be thankful for small blessings.

****

It was past two o'clock by the time I got home tired from another Saturday shift at the school and feeling that the day was practically over. The reduced daylight in November contributed to that feeling. Still, I had to admit that being on office duty for a change rather than teaching required less energy. I was hungry but didn't feel like doing more than boiling some rice in a bag.

Ursula's cat, Elle, padded across the roof and was doing a slow waltz outside my window.

"Hungry, Elle, or are you just being friendly?"

Neither, it seemed – Elle's mistress had company. For an ex-boyfriend, Vincent wasn't good at playing hard to get. I couldn't imagine letting Marc-Antoine back into my life, but it was easy to be strong when temptation was nowhere in sight. I hadn't decided yet where to fit Ursula in my life. She'd passed the acquaintance stage, but wasn't exactly a friend. She was a nuisance, that's what she was.

I opened the window, "Come on then, Elle, you want a bed to yourself and above all peace and quiet. My wee place, that you would normally cock your tail at, is ideal today."

Elle made a few dutiful arches and leaped onto the bed before beginning the arduous task of licking and washing herself.

I picked up one of William Whyte's questionnaire sheets that I was supposed to fill in about M. Chevalier. But I didn't feel up to doing it and let the page slide out of my hand, preferring to look out the window and watch the traffic spewing around Porte Maillot. I closed my eyes and pictured another scene where the waves crashed and the seagulls called, and somewhere, Sally, the dog howled. I remembered the coffin being lowered into the grave and me saying, "Goodbye, Mum – "

BANG! "MERDE – QUEL CON!"

I reopened my eyes to witness the aftermath of another car accident on the roundabout, fortunately not too serious this time.

My mobile practically did a jig on the table.

"Michael!" I didn't try to hide my pleasure. Michael wanted to know my plans for the rest of the day and I made it clear that I had none, immediately forgetting about my intention to go shopping in search of a winter coat. He suggested a picnic in the woods.

A picnic in November was a crazy idea, I thought. But who cared? It was a mild day and the sun was beginning to peep through the clouds – there were no laws about when or how one should picnic. I accepted his invitation with pleasure.

I switched off the hot-plate and removed the saucepan of water I had been heating up. I chucked my phone on the bed and made haste to wash and change. Elle gave me an indifferent look and coiled herself into a ball.

I didn't really fancy Michael, I told myself. He wasn't my type, more like a brother or something. It wasn't a crime to make friends.

I tiptoed away – this was one woodland walk I wasn't interested in sharing with Ursula. I could hear her voice moaning on and on. Poor Vincent was getting an earful.

"GOOD AFTERNOON," M. Jacques was on the corridor at his loudest and best. M. Brosse was with him and he grunted something that resembled a greeting. He was an expert 'grunter'; it was the perfect language, the ideal weapon, especially if you were terrified that someone would launch into a foreign language. The stale smell of exotic cooking stagnated in the air. I still hadn't made up my mind whether I liked the smell or not. I certainly was getting used to it. M. Brosse grunted again and went off to his room. M. Jacques followed me down the stairs, making warrior efforts at speaking English, before switching to French.

"I sometimes see you in the Quartier Latin," he said.

"Yes, like we told you, our school is there. I've seen you too, I heard you store material there."

"I store things in many places."

I didn't doubt him. It would be quite interesting to do a tour of the city following his guide book and directions.

He looked around and then stooped towards me, "I have to tell you that Whyte's –"

Mme Gomes came out her back door and M. Jacques jumped back.

The concierge put her hands on her hips and looked skywards, as if she could see right into Ursula's room. M. Jacques stared up too.

"Ursula is in great shape," I said and left them.

I ambled in the general direction of the Metro entrance.

Michael's head of dark curls appeared as he came up the steps. He waved, "Hey, Liz."

"Hey, you, where's the picnic basket?" I mocked gently.

"It's in my mind's eye. I just wanted to get out of the city and this is an easy solution."

"Teachers have a lot of fanciful ideas."

"Yeah, especially English teachers," he grinned, "but it was also a good excuse to see you."

I blushed and got very busy securing the catch of my bag. I fell easily into his rhythm of walking and we made our entrance to Les Bois de Boulogne. We were soon side stepping roller-bladers, avoiding tripping over dog leashes that stretched for metres, while bicycles swerved round us and joggers wove through. Everything seemed beautiful rinsed in late autumn colours: reds, goldens, yellows and russets of planes, oaks, maple, sycamore and lots of horse chestnuts. Conkers littered the ground. There was also plenty of evergreen spruce and pine. People greeted people, dogs greeted dogs, and a whole mix of friendly sounds congregated along the central pathways. The unusually clement autumn temperatures and slow onset of winter gave a false sense of seasons – even nature was confused. I could see a balloon seller outside the entrance to Jardin d'Acclimatation, blowing, twisting and squeaking balloons into animal shapes. They were much too expensive to buy, but it cost nothing to watch. We savoured the aroma of popcorn tempting us into the small amusement park.

"Ah, Michael, did you say you wanted to get away from people and traffic," I teased.

He took hold of my hand, "It doesn't matter, let's go into the park."

"There's an entrance fee."

"I know a guy working here and he can get us in for free. Leave it to me," he walked nonchalantly to the entrance.

I don't know how, but Michael succeeded – we were in.

"Magic," I said.

"Yes," he took a pack of cards from his pocket, "shuffle those."

I did.

"Now, look through the cards and memorise one."

I complied, then handed back the pack.

He reshuffled them, tapped the deck, "Come up to the top," he ordered.

I waited.

Michael flipped over the top card, "Was your card the seven of spades?"

I nodded, impressed.

He bowed.

"How did you do that? Show me the deck."

He did so willingly.

I went through them, but they seemed like ordinary cards, "Beats me. I know it's done with a slight of the hand, but you caught me this time."

His eyes twinkled, "I have many tricks. Come on, let's visit."

So we did, like a couple of kids. It was really a children's amusement park with a miniature train ride, pony ride and puppet show called 'Guignol'. We visited some monkeys and the bear cave in the little zoo. There was also a tiny farm consisting of some chickens, a cow, a goat, a few sheep and a couple of donkeys. It wasn't much, but it made me feel homesick. Michael rested his arm on my shoulders as if he felt my nostalgia. He spun me around in a little waltz, made me laugh several times by just being silly and swept me off to the magic mirrors. Our picnic ended up with us buying two ham and Cantal cheese baguette sandwiches from a food truck and two small bottles of water. We scoffed the sandwiches down as we strolled through the garden. On passing another food stand, we looked at each other, realising that we both had the same idea: warm waffles topped with Chantilly cream were too enticing to resist. That indulgence cost us more than the entrance fee might have, but who was counting.

Michael kept up his jokes and good humour, but by now I was beginning to appreciate more sides to his personality. I felt that behind all Michael's games, teasing and light-heartedness, he too was a little lost as to his future.

"Did you come to Paris as a student, Michael?"

"Yes and no."

"You really wanted to become a magician, didn't you?"

"Yes, but I'm a dabbler. I do tricks for children's parties, for adults too, birthdays and such. Sometimes, it brings in useful money. I like to see people laugh and smile and watch the children's eyes grow as big as saucers. It's my way of helping people, at least I think so."

"That's wonderful, it really is."

He bit his lower lip, "Unfortunately, it doesn't spell out a career that meets my parents' expectations, especially my father's. The problem is that it is a little of everything and not much of one thing. So I still need to teach to cover my basic expenses, although teaching does bring useful contacts from time to time. My brilliant skills as a magician spread by word of mouth."

"That's a good way of managing," I was determined to be optimistic.

"Being in Paris is a great excuse to keep well away from my family's disapproving eye. But I'm learning new tricks and illusions all the time and getting better." His quirky smile said – 'That's it, not much is it?'

"Well, that's all right too."

Michael was gentle, kind, sad and wishful, all wrapped up together. I understood that he came from a good upstanding family and was running from that. How far would he get? He was so English and I so Irish, the city boy and country girl. I'd built enchanted castles in the sand and run barefooted through the dunes and fields. Michael had grown up in well-to-do suburbs, was sent to private school and expected to become a successful business man.

"And you?" he asked.

'And you,' I thought – it was a throwaway line, lip service to return the favour of listening. I'd gotten some of my students to get as far as making the token 'And you?' question. People liked to talk about themselves, to be at the centre of their own worlds. Having someone listen and focus completely on 'you' was a little special. Were we really interested in what others did? Did we want to know about their dreams, desires and wishes? I wasn't sure. We were concerned, naturally, when they were bound to our own destinies: close friends, family and lovers.

Michael appeared interested and sincere, making me feel like the only other person in the world. It was flattering to be at the receiving end of that attention, yet I recognised that Michael sprinkled the same effect on everyone.

"And me?" I echoed.

"Yes, you."

"I'm just – just taking a breather."

"A breather?"

"Yes, until I decide what to do next. I need the money, but I do like the teaching."

He seemed satisfied with my reply and didn't probe further.

"Michael, I've been meaning to ask you?"

"Yes."

"Mr. Whyte –"

"Ah, I was wondering when the subject would come up."

"What do you mean?"

"It's impossible to hold a conversation with a teacher from W.W.S.O.E. & F.L. without getting into a discussion about William Whyte's oddness or one of his peculiarities."

"Well, don't you think asking for detailed, personalised –"

"Shush," Michael put a finger to my lips. He did a pirouette in front of me, pulled a ribbon from his pocket, then another and another and another. He rolled them into a ball. He tucked the ribbons into my hand, cupped it, blew on it, and then drew the silk back out gradually. And hey presto – it was a long, seemingly endless multi-coloured ribbon.

I laughed, "Are you trying to impress me, because if you are, it's working?"

"Distract you and maybe impress too. Let's not talk shop," he touched his lips to mine softly, barely making contact, a melting snowflake.

"All right, I get the hint, no more talk about Mr. Whyte."

He brushed his lips over mine again, "That's better."

"Hey, are you flirting with me or is this another magic trick?"

"Come to think of it, Liz, now that you bring up the subject, I think I am flirting. Do you mind?"

"Do you take all the girls to the woods?"

"No, you're the first one."

I didn't believe him, but it was nice to hear.

We wandered back out of the park.

"Now, let's shake off these people and really explore the wood." Michael took my hand more firmly this time, "Come with me."

"I hope you have a good sense of direction, because if we're going off the beaten- track –" I didn't put up much resistance.

"We are, come on."

We passed a small lake called Mare de Saint-James and went deeper into the wood. I loved the smell of the earth and pines. "You really do like nature, don't you?" I said.

"Yes, I do. But no matter how far you get from something in this place, you are never far from something else. It doesn't feel like a real wood, but it's enough for today."

We found a refreshing stream and crossed a quaint little stone bridge. Then, as if to confirm his point, we stumbled onto a practical, strategically placed bench.

We sat and did what young couples do when they sit on a bench. For all his talk about fantasy, Michael could fall into routine as easily as anybody else. We became another typical boy and girl embracing and kissing each other; hogging the bench and forcing everybody who happened to wander into that clearing to avert their eyes and hurry on, slightly embarrassed. I had it all then: living and working in Paris, sort of; a romantic walk in the wood, a wood with very tailored trees; an attractive guy kissing me, and he was good at it. I liked it and didn't need to think beyond that.

We parted at the Metro entrance and I returned to my room, still a little hungry but happy. At the top of the stairs, I heard Ursula's loud 'war cry.' She wasn't exactly howling, but her voice sounded near enough to it. Ursula wasn't just in a bad mood, she was on the rampage. I didn't need to be told that she'd had another argument with Vincent who had gone from being her Ex to her Ex-Ex.

Now, to add woe to all her troubles, she'd walked into the Turkish toilet to "That – that – horrible – disgusting sight."

"Pipe down, Ursula," I tried to calm her, "you'll get us both thrown out of here. You've already been ditched out of one place. Control yourself. What are you doing now, where are you going with that?"

Ursula was brandishing the toilet brush. She marched down the corridor and hung it off the handle of Olivier's door. "It's him. I know for sure, because Sebastien is away this weekend." Ursula then went into her room, scribbled on a piece of paper – CLEAN THE TOILET AFTER YOU – and went to great rounds affixing it on to the toilet door. "If he doesn't get the message from that, he'll never get it."

I couldn't really blame Ursula for taking action. The condition of the toilet had become a problem and had to be tackled one way or another. I put Michael momentarily to the back of my mind. I wasn't sure how Ursula would feel about Michael and I, but this certainly wasn't the moment to tell her.

Ursula fingered her phone.

"Who are you calling now?"

"I'm trying to reach Vincent to get him to come back. I'd prefer not to see him, but what choices do I have? He's refusing my calls and texts." 'I am a victim' was written all over her face.

"Ursula, if you don't want Vincent, why do you keep asking him to come here? You're giving him very confused signals."

"I like to keep my options open. It works for me. You can stay in your holy cloister."

I took a deep breath, she was such a frustrating girl, "But I can't see what works for you or how it's working. You don't seem very happy."

"I don't like sleeping alone in that room. It's eerie. I get nightmares and wake up with panic attacks and I can't breathe. I feel like there is this ghostly woman Eva, these departed souls around me."

"I guess it would be different if they were men."

"Oh, you're so funny, I think not."

I tried to be serious, remembering the strange sounds I'd imagined on the corridor, "I'm sorry you feel that way."

"Liz, did you know the person in the room before me? Why did he leave?"

"No, I didn't know him." It was time to give Ursula some honesty, "In fact, he had just died when I got here."

"Oh no," she grabbed me by the shoulders; "he died in the room, didn't he? Why didn't you tell me, why didn't someone say something?"

"I'm sorry, Ursula, I didn't plan on keeping it a secret. Your coming here wasn't exactly planned either. I hardly had a foot in the door when you came crying for help. I didn't know you, the school, this place or anyone."

Ursula released her grip, "How did he die?"

"He was ill, just wasted away, cancer or something. It happens all the time, lots of people die in rooms all over the place. I'm sure someone must have died in my room too sometime. It stands to reason."

"That's it," Ursula was fingering her phone again, "I'm not staying alone."

But for once, Vincent wasn't jumping to her beck and call. Ursula turned to me, "Liz, would you –"

"No way, Ursula, I'm not sleeping in there with you or you here with me. That's physically and psychologically impossible. I need my space, my bed and my sleep."

"We could switch rooms?" she used a softer, silkier tone.

"No," I knew where this was heading.

"Huh, well at least leave your door a little open and I'll do the same with mine."

"I can't keep doing that, anyone could walk in from the corridor."

"Please, please, I've got to sleep."

Why did I feel steamrolled? Oh, why bother asking, I knew the answer.

7

I was enjoying a Saturday off work. Judith had closed the school for the day while the extension roof was being repaired. Lena told me that they couldn't put it off any longer as the rain had started leaking through the ceiling of 'Durham' classroom.

The door burst open!

"Our November pay hasn't been transferred yet and I haven't a penny. I rang Judith, she pretended surprise and then blamed the bank – said the school was not at fault. Feck the lot of them anyway. Can you lend me some money?" Ursula walked into my room bearing the bad news, followed by Elle, the cat, miaowing for extra affection.

I put down the Francoise Sagan novel, *Bonjour Tristesse*, I had been reading and stroked a persistent Elle, "Damn, I haven't a penny either."

"You'll have to ask Mme Defoe to tide us over for the weekend."

I was not going to humiliate myself by begging from Mme Defoe. "Why don't you ask Vincent?"

"No way, I'm not asking him."

"You never think twice about asking me," I accused.

"That's different, you're different."

"Is that so," I opened the cupboard, there were just a few tins. "If they weren't going to get the money into our accounts on time, they should have informed us. What will we do? I want bread." I'd never thought about how vital a plain piece of bread was. Although I loved chocolate, I could live without it, but not bread – bread was essential.

"We scavenge," said Ursula.

"Scavenge?"

"Yes, like pigeons. But seagulls are better at it."

"Who told you that?"

"Read it somewhere."

"I don't see why seagulls would prefer to pick scraps from city bins and dumpsters than catching fresh fish from the sea."

"It's easier to pick bins. So, we scavenge selectively. You get on one train carriage, I get on another. We have to change every few stations and keep our eyes peeled for lost coins."

"Are you serious!"

"Deadly, it works every time, believe me."

I struggled with the idea and concluded that it was less humiliating than asking someone I knew personally for a hand-out.

"Okay, but no begging or sitting on the street with a cardboard that reads, 'A centime please for two hungry Irish girls'."

"I guarantee you, no begging. Seriously, just keep your eyes on the ground, it's surprising what people lose," Ursula sounded very confident.

"Looks like you're an expert."

Metro Line 1 was as good a place to start as any. I sat and watched, changed carriages and continued to watch. Travellers were noisier and more relaxed than on a typical week day. The weekend was a time when Parisians flocked to and from different parts of the city to shop, browse D.I.Y., music and book stores, visit exhibitions and meet up for lunches. Many simply enjoyed ambling and strolling. At this time of the year, they repossessed their own city wearing that 'just-out-of-the-sheets' by day clothes style convincingly. However, there was no mistaking that stylish boots, well cut coats and jackets, and tasteful scarves were more visible than the usual tourist mix and match. I looked on, envying them and wishing that I too could chill out, treat myself to the latest exhibition at the Grand Palais or Museé d'Orsay or wherever, or just splurge out on a new outfit.

I soon realised that scavenging wasn't that easy and one had to be careful not to draw suspicion by staring too much. After an hour, I decided it was completely stupid. I'd have been better off staying in bed and saving my energy. I decided to do exactly that, go back home and live off my canned food. This was not a crisis situation, it was a minor setback, nothing more. Just then, I saw something glint on the floor. It was several seats away, but looked like a 10-Franc coin. That would be enough to buy bread and more. I pinned my eye on the coin – it would be too obvious and embarrassing to pick it up immediately. I kept it in my sights and moved down a few seats at the next stop, and the next again, until finally at Gare de Lyon Station, I was sitting over it. I stretched my leg out and tried to slide the coin towards me. I managed little by little to get it right under my seat. I bent down and clasped it in my hand. It was mine.

I got off, crossed to the opposite platform to change direction and return to base. I sent a text to Ursula, but didn't receive acknowledgement of reception. I suspected she'd probably given up after the first quarter of an hour and gone running off to Vincent. She could at least have sent me news. Well, too bad for her.

I left my tunnel burrowing and went to ED, a low-cost supermarket. After long deliberation, I got a large pan loaf that looked like it might last a month simply because it was full of preservatives. While I would prefer a fresh baguette, I knew it would go hard quickly and my 10 Francs wouldn't last long. From my short experience as an attic tenant, I had learned valuable lessons – and sacrificing something fresh and crispy for long-lasting and bland was one of them, especially given my lack of suitable storage places.

I held the pan tightly in my hand – bread would make the weekend more tolerable. There was no sign of Ursula on the seventh floor – if she wasn't ringing or sending text messages, she wasn't badly off. Feeling no qualms, I tore off a good chunk of bread. I had the essentials and I wouldn't have to beg Michael or Mme Defoe or even Ursula. I beached out on top of the bed munching the dry bread contentedly, allowing Elle a few precious crumbs. My phone flashed with a text message from Ursula, 'With Vincent and won't be back tonight' – I dropped the phone and dozed.

I dreamt of food, sweet and savoury, and woke up hungry next morning. I decided to go out and walk around the Sunday outdoor market. If I couldn't have something nice to eat, at least I could look at it. There were lines of standings with lots of bric à brac, clothes, jewellery, flowers... But I was drawn to the food stalls, a feast of sights and smells, with everything to entice and taunt. They displayed the best from the French regions, including the whole range from fresh fruit and vegetables to soft, hard and blue cheeses: Camembert, Roquefort, Pont l'Evêque, Brie, Cantal... There were seafood, charcuterie, salads, terrines, confectionary and breads. The smells of skewering and roasting were appetising. But the sight of game, ducks, pheasants, rabbits – hanging from hooks – was too sickening to me, so I moved on and passed a cross-cultural mix of pre-prepared cuisines, including North African, Indian and Chinese. But the foreign choice was limited – this was Neuilly-sur-Seine where the palate didn't roam too far from the traditional French base and prices were out of line with the earnings of a seventh-floor language teacher. I could only watch the Neuilly Bourgeoisie with their wicker baskets and caddies, dressed in smart casual navy, white, beige, darker reds and greens, and showing off labels like Lacoste, Carven, Petite Bateau, as they sniffed, prodded and examined products, and discussed the pros and cons of each item with traders. The cafés and bistros surrounding the market place had opened out their heated terraces offering perfect places to sit, view, gossip and grab a light breakfast before returning to cook family lunch. Some people would opt for a stress-free Sunday and instead linger and have a long lazy lunch on one of those terraces.

I sighed, returned to my room, stretching out on the bed with only Elle, the cat, to comfort me. I munched on another piece of long-lasting bread and dreamed of better days ahead.

****

Lena told me that William Whyte lived in the St. Germain des Prés district. It was an expensive upmarket area, and yet the school was barely breaking even, or so the rumour went among teachers. Some said that being slow to pay teachers at the end of the month was an accounting game to take advantage of bank interest rates. A few older and bitter teachers said the rumour of the school's difficulties was a deliberate tactic to evade taxes and also avoid increasing their hourly rate. There was even wild speculation among teachers that there was some connection between the management of the school finances and the introduction of the new Euro currency to

11 countries, including France and Éire, next year, 1999. Although I found it hard to understand that connection, I was excited about changing to the Euro. While some of the English teachers were somewhat sceptical, as Irish people, Ursula and I were looking forward to the change. I think that we both felt that sharing the same currency would make us feel less foreign and part of a wider group of Europeans. But all of that didn't alter the fact that the school was showing worrying signs of financial troubles and that its owner was apparently untrustworthy. Mr. Whyte was reported to have between three and six children from his first wife who were all living somewhere in England, while his girlfriend and mother of his future child was French and living in Paris. He travelled regularly between Paris and London. Angie said he liked to think that he was connected to high society on both sides of the channel and boasted of important friends in political and business circles.

I sat in 'St. Alban's', in front of the very same Mr. Whyte.

His pale, lifeless eyes focused on me, "I have received your report on M. Chevalier. It is short on detail."

I chose my own words carefully, "I explained everything that I have been covering with M. Chevalier in class."

"Has he discussed the job promotion with you?"

"It's only come up indirectly."

"In the satisfaction questionnaire, M. Chevalier has indicated that he is pleased with his teacher – that is a good point for our school," his eyes came alive for a second. He was perspiring heavily and took out a handkerchief from his pocket to wipe his brow several times.

"I do what I can to help him progress."

"Good. This is an excellent school and I hope he has no reason to think differently."

"My discussions with M. Chevalier are purely professional."

"That will be all, keep me informed," he held the handkerchief in a shaky hand and wiped his brow once more.

I left, not sure what to think of this strange encounter. It was hard to understand William Whyte's extreme anxiety unless the school really was in deep financial difficulty. That troubled me. I was not so fond of the school that I imagined working there forever, but I'd only just got started and wasn't ready to pack my bags and move on again.

A freezing gust of winter wind hit me as I left the school premises. I put down my bag to fasten my jacket. Two hands covered my eyes, startling me for a second until I recognized the owner, "Michael, you gave me a fright."

Michael dropped his hands and turned me towards him, "Where have you been hiding out, I left a message on your phone?"

I looked up into his worried dark brown eyes and noted that his beard shadow looked sexy. "Did you? Sorry." I took out my mobile, "It's been off for hours, I didn't have a second to spare between classes."

"Hmm," he tugged gently at my pony tail, the lazy solution to doing my hair today. "Are you sure you aren't avoiding me, it's been difficult to get hold of you since our picnic in the woods – do I detect a cooling off like the weather?"

"No, not at all. But our visit to the woods was not a real picnic, although I did enjoy the waffles."

He played with a stray strand of my hair and dropped a kiss on my forehead, "Is that so, because while the waffles were nice, they didn't satisfy my appetite."

All I could do was smile – he was impossible to resist.

He studied my face, "Is there something troubling you?"

"Michael, tell me exactly how bad the school finances are. Are we likely to lose the contract in P.A.F.I.? What does the HR, your student – what's her name – Mme Michot say?"

"Not that subject again. Is William Whyte on your case?"

"Not really, not like I thought. But is there any future in the school?"

"I can't imagine what the future holds. But I do believe that William Whyte's problems don't have to be ours. So in the meantime, let's take it easy and enjoy the present."

Michael had a point. I'd do well to take a leaf from his book: stand back and let troubles go by.

"Ursula says that he's extreme right-wing and racist," I added.

Michael was practising swallowing small red sponge balls. He did an impressive illusion of swallowing three at once and then of removing them from my jacket pocket. "You see," he said, "nothing is what it seems. That's just what we need in the world, another hypocrite."

Michael repeated his trick and this time fished different coloured balls from my bag.

"Hey, that was even better. I think you have an audience." It was true, some curious people had gathered around us.

"That's how you build your fan base," Michael gave a theatrical bow and moved on.

"May I ask you something, Liz?"

"Yes?"

"Don't misunderstand me, but what do you think of M. Chevalier?"

His question surprised me given our discussion, nevertheless I tried to answer. "He's a workaholic. Maybe that's because he's divorced, although he does have two children. He's ambitious and the promotion is very important to him. His English is rudimentary, but I think he has progressed. I don't know if he'll get the job promotion because when I listen to you and Ursula, it seems more likely that the odds are in favour of M. Fabre or perhaps an outsider. But I do believe that M. Chevalier is not very – very attached to our school."

"I hear in P.A.F.I. that he is attached to his teacher."

"Well it's more than I hear. What exactly are you insinuating, Michael?"

"I'm a little jealous, that's all. Do I have to be William Whyte or one of your students to get you to focus on me?"

"I –" I was lost for words, "I hope that's not the impression I give all the time. I've a lot of time for others, for some teachers especially."

"I'm glad to hear it because you're difficult to read sometimes." He let a host of ribbons float in the air and disappeared with a "See you, Liz."

I looked after him, hands in pockets, easy strides, overtaking other pedestrians effortlessly; he had made his intentions clear. Michael was right, I was playing hard to get. I'd taken some distance with him and my excuse was that I'd won some freedom by moving to the room and was just beginning to enjoy being on my own and counting on myself. Firstly, Ursula had butted her way into my life and now Michael was forcing the door as well. I hadn't been looking for romance and hadn't planned for someone like him. What was I afraid of – taking care of others? I was already doing so with Ursula and I didn't want to start doing it with Michael. I wanted someone strong in my life, someone who wouldn't need that kind of supporting. At least, I thought I did. Why couldn't I just go with the flow? Perhaps the truth was that I was afraid of getting hurt again.

****

Olivier, our student neighbour and accused toilet spoiler, wasn't saluting or acknowledging us. But that did not interfere too much with our daily routines as we seldom met him.

"No skin off my nose," said Ursula. "We're the ones who should be upset having to put up with his bad toilet habits."

Ursula was grasping a rubbish bag and it was no coincidence. Ursula frequently and conveniently found an excuse to appear on the corridor at the very moment that I was leaving my room.

"Oh, you're going downstairs, that's handy. Could you drop this in the bin for me, it's nothing?" Ursula's smile was full of good humoured apology.

I wrinkled my nose, "It's Elle's litter and it's disgusting. It should have been taken down yesterday."

"It's natural and organic. Be a pet, I don't feel very well today," Ursula disappeared into her room, hand to her tummy.

I was going downstairs with my own rubbish bag and couldn't refuse her request. That girl really had a way of driving me nuts. My weakness nettled me. Why couldn't I stand my ground and simply refuse as she would? But it wasn't in me and I also knew that it was Ursula's way of making me pay back for not telling her about the dead man in her room. She was taking advantage of my guilty conscience. But this wasn't the first time she'd taken advantage of my goodwill. I started totting up the favours: I'd found her the room, given her many handouts and small loans, and I ran errands for her. I didn't appreciate being the skivvy, not to mention putting up with her complaining. I had worked up a good temper by the time I got back upstairs again. There was too much time to think and brood while taking all those steps. I decided Ursula was a hussy, a – a – there were so many names for the occupant of Room 1. I made each of my footsteps sound loud and clear on the corridor. Ursula's door was open. It was often open, she just assumed that the corridor was an extension of her own room and didn't seem to care who walked by. Fortunately, Mme Gomes's son just used his room as a basic bedroom and preferred to be with his family the rest of the time – and the students were night owls and daytime sleepy heads.

I closed my door with a small bang and crashed out on the bed to take a well-deserved nap. I was woken by a sound outside the door and on opening was greeted by a pushy Elle. "Just like your mistress, aren't you?" It wasn't difficult to understand the source of the cat's problem. A strong scent of incense reached my nose from the corridor. I went to Ursula's room to investigate and found several candles burning in a circle on the floor and Ursula wrapped in a white veil seated in the middle. Beneath the veil, she seemed to be swaying to a ritual chant.

"Come on, Elle, I understand your feelings perfectly. It's difficult to be loyal to your mistress, especially when she's in her higher meditative state and hunting away evil spirits. I don't think a dog would even put up with that." Elle leaped on my bed. That was another thing I had to add on to Ursula's I.O.U. list: taking care of Elle. Why, that cat was practically my full-time lodger.

I opened my eyes to loud screaming and to Elle miaowing at the door. I leapt off the bed – that was Ursula screaming. I looked at the time – my God, it was after midnight! I must have nodded off. I ran into the corridor and knocked at Ursula's door. She didn't reply, but the screaming continued from inside. I pushed at the door which hadn't been shut properly. As it fully opened, I was hit by a violent gust of wind that flung me back against the wall. Blue smoke billowed from the room and I could just discern Ursula in a state of collapse on the floor – she appeared to have her hands to her throat. I was momentarily paralysed with terror, but forced myself to draw on surplus energies and concentrated on moving towards her. However, my desperation grew as I kept hitting an invisible barrier blocking my way. Then, just as I was on the point of giving in to despair, I felt an energy shift and the strange wind dropped abruptly. I ran directly to Ursula. Her face was turning purple, she was choking herself – I finally managed to pull her hands away from her throat. To my relief she began coughing and her complexion returned slowly to normal.

I fetched a glass of water and watched as she sipped.

"What happened?"

"I remember nothing," gasped Ursula. "I think the incense I was burning while I chanted was too strong and made me faint."

"But you were screaming," I rubbed my forehead trying to make sense of everything.

Ursula shook her head, "I didn't scream, you must have dreamt it. If I had screamed, surely the whole corridor would be here by now."

I was confused. Had I imagined the screams and everything else?

Perhaps all that had happened was that Ursula had absorbed too much of that strange vapour and in panic my mind had conjured up the rest. It was better, I thought, not to tell Ursula what I had experienced a few minutes before.

"So you are okay?" I scrutinised her face.

"Sort of, I'm still not happy sleeping in this room and I know it's not comfortable keeping our doors open, but I have a solution for that."

"You have?"

"Yes, I've asked M. Jacques to put a chain lock on both our doors; that way we can leave them ajar and reassure each other, but at the same time feel protected."

"I see." If it helped Ursula then it helped me.

I returned to my room, instinctively looking behind me. I saw the silhouette of M. Jacques. He seemed to be just standing and staring at me.

"Yes?" I asked inquiringly.

But he didn't reply and backed away to his own side of the corridor as if he had seen a ghost.

****

I trailed along Boulevard Saint Michel under a miserable cold December drizzle, rubbing my right shoulder, sure I was getting lopsided from lugging bags around. I spotted my neighbour again and watched the familiar figure for a while before calling, "M. Jacques – M. Jacques."

He didn't turn.

I caught right up with him until he had to see me and stop. He was carrying a box of what looked like picture frames.

"Your friend is in the café," he nodded to Place Saint Michel. His voice was distant and unfriendly compared to the usual friendlier M. Jacques of the seventh floor.

I got the message and let him walk on, convinced that he must think Ursula and I demented.

I crossed to the café in time to see Ursula leaning into Michael, her hand resting on the back of his chair. I might have been hesitating about going further with him, but I wasn't letting Ursula take my place. I greeted them, took a chair and sat close to Michael who automatically draped his arm across my shoulders. Ursula's mouth opened and closed. She looked accusingly at me while I just sat it out. I carried on conversing as if nothing had changed. Ursula went from sarcasm to silence. I understood that her problem wasn't that Michael and I had started something, it was that she had no tolerance for other couples when she wasn't in a relationship herself. In her books, Vincent didn't count.

Later, on the Metro journey home, Ursula continued to give me the silent treatment and then stomped off to her room, locking it. Sometime later, I heard a knock at her door and recognised the voice of Vincent. My only thought was that at least I was off the hook for the night and could look forward to a good sleep. If Vincent was spending the night with Ursula, the chances were that there would be no strange ghostly visitations.

I wasn't surprised when Ursula came up with a crowd-pulling, spotlight moment some days later.

"Ursula, what is Mr. Bjania doing?" I could hardly believe my eyes as I watched our Indian neighbour turning around in the middle of her room and mumbling strange words.

"Shush," Ursula said.

I waited politely until Mr. Bjania finished his ritual. Finally, he bowed to both of us, whispered something to Ursula and left.

"He's a sort of witch doctor and is putting spells and charms in the place to clear the room of bad energy – he might have more success than I had," Ursula explained as if it were the most normal thing in the world. "And he's just told me that the energy is so bad here that he will have to repeat the process several more times."

"An Indian witch doctor?"

"It was the nearest I could get."

"For an Irish woman, you astonish me. Why don't you just do it in the Irish Catholic way – bring someone from the Irish College to say mass or some prayers or – I don't know, something you can relate to?"

Ursula pushed back her hair, "This is a foreign spirit, not an Irish one. This is major, I got the full story out of Mme Gomes – I'm sure you know all about it. There was a massacre in this room in the past – a woman was murdered here. Apparently, other terrible things happened here. Who knows how many more were murdered. Mme Gomes told me of other tenants who stayed here and who simply disappeared, never seen again, at least two; then there was a pregnant woman who fell down the stairs and lost her baby –"

"Ursula!" I shook her.

She looked at me confused, but it calmed her.

"Listen, Ursula, we don't know that there was any murder – you said that you thought this Eva ghost died by suicide. Besides, Mme Gomes is full of horrific stories – don't listen to her. If you really feel that way about the room, why don't you try looking for somewhere else to live," I suggested weakly.

Ursula dropped her head, "No, the bad spirits will follow me. I told you, Eva is now part of me, she's part of my past. It's no coincidence that I ended up in the school, in this room – I'm possessed."

"Hang on here, let me sort this out in my mind – your ghost, Eva, is from a different century, but somehow you are responsible for her soul or you are the reincarnation of Eva?"

"Bad karma is connected."

"There is no proof of that." I tried to sound convincing, but deep down was ill-at-ease; it was difficult for me to dismiss everything given Ursula's recent near choking drama.

"Eva comes to me in my dreams and tells me her life. She worked as a prostitute in whatever existed before the school on Rue des Soeurs and she died a horrible death here. Then terrible things happened other residents of the room. You cannot deny the death of the previous tenant. Everyone who stays here suffers or dies. The past is stuck to me and I have to deal with it."

"Ursula, the past might be stuck to you, but as far as I can see, you're stuck to me. Why don't you go back to Ireland and find out what's really troubling you – then you'll see that all this talk of possession and being doomed will lift and disappear?"

Ursula's anger escalated, "I'll do what I bloody well like. You don't know who or what I am."

"Fine, fine," I said, "there's no need to shout. If I know nothing about anything, don't keep drawing me into your problems."

"Well, I won't in the future."

I should have known it. That little discussion won me Ursula's stiff back and a closed door.

She could suit herself, I thought, I wasn't going to be a victim of her moods. But of course I was – it was difficult to ignore someone when you encountered them several times a day. My hellos were met by a marble face, the atmosphere was thick and charged with accusation and I became the guilty party. However, it took my mind off Michael and the school. Vincent turned up that night and the next and it wasn't necessary to test the chain locks that M. Brosse put on both our doors in return for a monetary tip. M. Brosse told me that M. Jacques was too busy to do it, but it seemed more likely to me that he was keeping his distance from his strange neighbours.

****

I decided not to waste too much of my Saturday at the school and planned to limit my time in the library preparing classes for next week. I read from Judith's notes that Ursula had signed up to teach on Saturdays in the new wave of courses beginning in a couple of weeks – trust Ursula not to have mentioned anything to me. That would mean my fretting about her time keeping among other things. And Michael? I hadn't seen him for a few days and I missed him – perhaps he too was keeping his distance. But at least some semblance of normality had returned to the seventh floor. After a stand-off that lasted all of three days, Ursula was talking to me again. M. Jacques too was saluting us once more.

I checked my watch – almost two o'clock – time to switch off the photocopier and tidy up.

SMASH!

I jumped up – that sounded like a cup or a plate breaking. Was somebody in the 'Lindisfarne'? Suddenly, a shadow moved past the door, there was a shout and footsteps pattered on the corridor – there was another shout and a banging door. I hurried out, but the corridor was empty and all was silent. There was only the sound of my own footsteps on the tiles.

I looked in 'Lindisfarne', but everything appeared normal. There was no evidence of broken crockery.

I went back down the corridor and listened at 'St. Alban's' door – perhaps William Whyte or his friends had come in. But I could hear nothing and I daren't risk trying the door. Maybe once again I had imagined the whole thing – all this talk about ghosts and murders and Ursula's wild ideas had gotten to me. No, I shook my head, I had definitely heard something and the likely answer was that William Whyte had come in as he had before. I scratched my head, I was sure that both Judith and Lena had said earlier in the week that he was in London and would not be back for ten days. Frustrated, I closed the outside door firmly and locked it – the whole thing was maddening.

8

I was feeling restless. It was official exam day for some of the school's business classes and P.A.F.I. was holding an Employee Motivation Seminar, thereby postponing activities such as English training for the day. I should welcome a Monday and Tuesday morning off and it had been nice to sleep in and laze over my morning coffee with daylight instead of winter darkness. But all that extra rest had left me with too much energy and the only thing that I was in the mood for was walking.

I put on solid boots, buttoned up my new heavy, beige, fleece-lined coat and wrapped Mme Defoe's gift of a cream woollen scarf around my neck. I put on my only pair of gloves, slipped a little guide book in my pocket and set out towards Avenue de Ternes where every window decoration and street garland reminded me of the reason for my restlessness – Christmas. Christmas Day was just one week off and I didn't want to hear about it. While everybody had plans and places to go, I'd decided that on December 24th and 25th I wouldn't put my face outside my room door. At the same time, I just wasn't up to going back to Ireland. If I went back, I'd feel in the way. Relatives and friends would invite me; they meant well and it would give them pleasure to offer me some kinship, but I knew I wouldn't enjoy it. I didn't want to be in other people's houses different to the cottage I had grown up in or to have to fit the routine of other folks, even old friends.

Ursula had lots of plans – she'd put up with family for about two days, she said, and afterwards intended to swing by at least half a dozen places in Ireland and in France. She was going to zip through Christmas and the New Year in her own unique way.

I reached the top of the Avenue, too preoccupied with my thoughts to admire the scenery. I hopped on the Metro at Place de Ternes, got off at Pigalle Station and continued walking. The bold, vulgar posters and crude window displays of the red light district did not interest me and I found myself taking Rue Saint Georges in the direction of the more agreeable Boulevard Haussmann and the Opera Garnier district with its elegant avenues and boulevards. My eyes feasted on the centrepiece, the majestic and opulent Palais Garnier - Opera House. I was aware that the late 19th-century building was a setting for Gaston Leroux's 1910 novel, *The Phantom of the Opera*. I read in the guide book that it represented the best of Neo-Classical architecture, balancing purity and heavy decoration. The book also provided useful detail on the decor and I soon became obsessed with matching its description with what I was looking at for real. The front façade was monumental and lavish with Neo-Baroque decorative elements. I counted five levels under a copper dome that itself was crowned with a golden statue of Apollo, the Greek god. The first level, I observed, consisted of arches embellished with four splendid allegorical groups sculpted by different sculptors. The arches supported seven columns topped by a wide frieze decorated with masks. I went up closer, drawn by a very detailed dancing sculpture.

Out of the corner of my eye, I noticed a curly, black-haired young man waving goodbye to a few unkempt-looking people. For a moment, I was disorientated before realising that I recognised who it was. Michael was sitting on top of the flight of steps that swept up to the Opera House entrance. Below, throngs of shoppers charged by and traffic roared down Avenue de l'Opera and Boulevards Capucines and Italians.

"Michael, who were those guys?"

"Homeless people."

"What were you doing with them?"

"I don't know – trying to help. I don't think I'm very good at it. You know how I sometimes perform magic on the street when I'm short of a penny or just for the pleasure of practicing – well, one day I came across those chaps, I gave them a little money to buy food and I've – we've kept in touch since then."

That did it. Michael sitting on a cold damp step, talking to a few homeless guys to whom he'd probably given what was in his pocket, was my undoing. I was falling hopelessly under his spell. Nothing else he might have said or done to impress me could have had that effect. It was just finding him like that, totally unexpectedly. It was seeing him, son of a well-to-do English family, so innocent in his intention and his desire to help in whatever way possible. Some might say it was completely naive and futile. I didn't care, it touched me. Michael continued to sit there with that slightly embarrassed look simply because I'd discovered him. He'd got me and I knew it, I was in over my head.

"Oh, Michael, that's very kind. That's really giving. I've passed countless homeless, drunks and destitute and never done anything so generous. Sure, I've tossed some coins in their direction, but you're really doing, giving your time."

"I don't know about that. They say helping is just another way to ease our conscience, make us feel less guilty. It's more difficult to give to our own than to strangers."

His confusion about it didn't diminish him in my eyes. He looked lost and vulnerable. I couldn't think of anything else to do except to kiss him.

We ended up taking a Metro together to Place de la République, the crossroads between the 3rd, 10th and 11th districts. We stood in the square looking at a bronze statue in the middle. There stood Marianne, the personification of the French République, holding an olive branch in her right hand and resting her left on a tablet engraved with "Les droits de l'Homme" We walked around it and I saw that it was surrounded by three little statues personifying liberty, equality and fraternity, three medieval theological virtues that represented the values of the French République. At the base was a lion guarding a depiction of a ballot box. It was a plain statue and looked very ordinary, but it was a powerful symbol. The square was an important starting point for protests and marches in Paris. It was usual for demonstrators to gather at Place de la République before marching on to Place de la Concorde and L'Assemblée Nationale, the French Parliament building – and then on to the Champs Elysées and the Elysées Palace, home of the President.

Michael's studio window looked out onto Avenue de la République. In the heat of the summer with open windows, the din would be deafening; one might feel that they were in the middle of traffic lanes. In winter, it was perfect. He hadn't got around to putting up real curtains. Instead, he'd flung up a wicker blind that wasn't hung straight. Neatness wasn't his strong point, but he had a real bath and shower. And God, I was almost in tears, a toilet, a genuine toilet and it was clean. The room smelt of Michael.

He was looking at me with a bemused expression, "Has it passed inspection?"

"Was I that obvious? I like it, you should see my room, it isn't a patch on this."

"This place seems cosier now with you here, less lonely."

"Really?"

"Yes, really."

"Are you lonely?"

"Sometimes."

His honesty was affecting, but I couldn't resist teasing a little. "And now that I'm here, the place is cosier, is that it?"

"It's not what I –"

"Less lonely, are you?"

"Well –"

"Well?"

Michael took my hand, "You know I've liked you from the beginning. I've thought of nothing else except you and getting you here."

I recorded that line in my memory. It wasn't the most romantic thing I'd ever heard, but it was real.

Realising the awkwardness of his words, Michael tried again, "What I wanted to say was that with you here, it's just right."

"Okay, that will do, Michael."

"Will it?"

"I think so. How long have you been living here?" I was stalling, throwing him a typical teacher's question.

He wasn't listening, but leant over me, touched my face with one hand and pressed his lips to mine.

I stopped looking for assurances as he drew me in really, really close. Finally I stopped thinking and started doing, I'd worry, after – about after.

It wasn't slow – it was wild. We didn't waste any time on the finer details.

Everything was a bit of a tangle and a hell of a mess – shirt and top here, shoes and garments there. It wasn't far to get to the bed, but we didn't make it that far. I realised that I'd wanted it like this; no more niceness, no more games, just pure and simple sex. We had all the rest of the evening to go back over things and rediscover what we'd missed out on the first time. I don't know how we managed it, but we did. We did alright; hands, legs, lips and tongues everywhere. We were uncoordinated and clumsy, but it didn't seem to matter – we got there, we both got there and it felt right. It was flesh and bone and pure sensation. Our murmurs and voices were so strange, so familiar – the last of reason slipped away and release came.

We lay there until sounds of traffic drifting from the street were audible again. Michael was sprawled on top of me and I had no desire to move. It felt good.

After a while, I shoved at him gently, "Michael?"

"Hmm."

"Do you think we could move to the bed?"

"Hmm."

I pushed at his shoulders a little more forcefully, "I mean now."

He lifted his head, grinned down at me, "Look at you?"

I felt colour creep into my cheeks and tried to get up.

He eased himself away and took my hand, "Come on, Princess."

'Princess?' I'd been called many things, but it was the first time I'd been called that, I could get used to it.

"I have an idea," I was feeling audacious, "why don't we try out your shower, I've been dying to since I got here?"

"Ah, so getting at my body was a roundabout excuse to use my shower."

"I wouldn't say that exactly."

We didn't quite make it to the shower that time either. But we did the third time and the day stretched ahead.

****

I took the narrow, treacherous flight of stairs in leaps and bounds, two by two. I still had air left in my lungs when I reached the top landing. My room didn't look so gloomy. I spilt my coffee and wiped it up, I bumped against a chair and giggled, knocked over the sweeping brush and picked it up. Nothing annoyed me or made me lose my temper. Nothing would ever bring me down again. There would be no more grumbling or crankiness about getting up too early or coming home too late. I could survive it all now. I danced around my little space, "Hello, cockroaches, come out and have a good time with me." I opened the window and called out, "Hello, Rue Montrosier."

The sun was bright in the sky. It wasn't a day to stay indoors and I decided to go back down again. I'd got shopping to do, lots and lots of it. I changed shoes, grabbed a real handbag and skipped my way to the supermarket admiring the Christmas lighting along Avenue Charles de Gaulle. The supermarket was busy and vibrant. I found myself really noticing faces and people. Some were open, others closed – there were happy eyes and thoughtful ones. I smiled at a woman who looked very sad.

My relationship with Michael changed things. There was no going back now, not that I wanted to. I was going to enjoy things and make the most of the feeling. Keep work out of it was my new decision and, above all, keep Ursula out of it. But that was easier said than done and it wasn't long before my Irish neighbour came inquiring at my door –

"You didn't come back last night," Ursula moaned. "You should have told me. You know how hard it is for me in that room. If I'd known you weren't coming, I could have taken your key and slept in your room."

What had I ever done to deserve Ursula, I asked myself. "I'm sorry, Ursula, but I didn't know that you and I had that kind of arrangement. I don't question your moves or where you are. I refuse to give you a detailed timetable of what I'm doing or what I'm supposed to be doing."

She pouted, "That's selfish, you know the agony of my nights; if you're not sleeping here, you could at least give me your keys."

I counted to ten, tried to bring the blood pressure back down, "I am truly sorry for breaking from my predictable behaviour and routine. You can try whatever tactic you like, Ursula, but you are not sleeping in my room. I've accommodated your cat, Elle, that's already big-hearted of me. I've no intention of adding you to the list."

Ursula was clever enough to change track when she knew she was on a losing one, "Off cavorting with Michael, I suppose. Do you think that's wise, Liz? I mean, Michael is nice, and I'd be all for having a fling with him myself, but he's light – "

"What exactly do you want to say?"

"Michael's weak and is never going to get anywhere by himself. He's a poor little rich boy and will soon go running back to daddy."

I didn't know whether to laugh or scream. I decided to play the part of the highly offended, "You dare to talk like that, you of all people."

"Liz, I'm not saying it to hurt you, honestly. He's a lovely guy. It's just that he's all wrong for you. You're so serious and – in control – no – what I mean is strong. That's it, you're strong, you're a leader. You'll lead and he'll follow, and when he can't follow or live up to your expectations and ambitions, he'll stray."

"Stray?"

"For want of a better word."

"Ursula, you don't know me, even if you think you do, and you don't know Michael. We're not talking permanent, just a –" I should shut up, I was saying too much, "– just a bit of romance."

"That isn't you, Liz."

"Oh, let it drop."

Ursula took another deviation, "You're right. I'm sorry, it's none of my business. I was upset and alone last night and I've no right to take it out on you. Of course, you have your life. I've got to face my demons. I can't keep depending on others to pull me out of trouble."

"Demons! I thought it was the spirit of Eva among others."

"They become demons when they torment you," a tear flowed down Ursula's cheek.

This time I did scream in my head. What was it about me? Was it my face? Did people look at me and say, she's an easy touch? There I was all mad at Ursula, and the girl had just to turn it on and she had my heart bleeding for her. I take one look at Michael giving the time of day to some homeless people, and I go all soft on him, putty in his hands.

I relented, "So what happened last night that got you all upset? Did Eva come back?"

"Eva never leaves me. But no, it was something M. Jacques said."

I bit my tongue. I should have guessed – when an off-the-wall girl gets to talking seriously with a slightly off-centre guy, some rather flaky conclusions are drawn.

"What did M. Jacques say?"

"He said that he'd noticed odd and strange happenings around Rue des

Soeurs. He's talking about our school, even if he didn't name it."

"He's been hinting at that from day one. I don't see why that should bother you, it has nothing to do with us."

"It was the way he said it, the implication behind it."

"Are you sure you're not reading too much into things? M. Jacques can overdo the mysterious part and be a bit farfetched, and you do have a lively imagination."

"Suit yourself, if you don't want to believe me," Ursula huffed and stamped back to her room.

I refused to let her attitude affect me this time, I couldn't solve that girl's problems. I preferred to return to my romantic bubble and think of Michael.

****

Perhaps it was my new-found good humour, but it seemed that M. Chevalier was marginally less hard work than he used to be. I wasn't sure if it was all the ice-breaking we had been doing, or just the simple growing together of teacher and student, like an old couple who finally get used to each other. It might just be that Michael had taken up a large portion of my mind and everything else had dropped back in importance.

That's why when the class opened with M. Chevalier asking me if I was alright, if I felt okay, it went over my head. Coming from him, it was ground-breaking, but it flew right past me. I did, however, notice that he was more attentive and focused. He was looking at me differently, making a special effort. It's about time, I thought.

At the end of the class, M. Chevalier cleared his throat.

I looked up and waited. I could see the wheels turning slowly in his head. He was excavating for the right words and finally, "Do you think I make progress?"

"Yes, of course I do." I didn't believe I was lying by saying that much. But how to measure his progress in concrete terms was another thing. "You listen better and so understand more. You don't put the definite article everywhere as you used to do. Your prepositions are – are – let's say you have widened your range of prepositions. And you are better able to handle a variety of questions."

He took that much in, swallowed it piece by piece.

"And you, M. Chevalier, do you feel some change yourself, do you notice the improvement?"

"Oh, yes, yes – things – I notice things."

"Good, good, so we'll do a test next class and we'll see where to situate your new level."

"A test?" He didn't look very keen.

"A small one."

"You will continue with me after?"

So that was where he was leading to. Was he trying to tell me he wanted to stop or go on, keep me as a teacher or change me?

I threaded my way carefully, "Naturally I want to continue with you after all the work we've put in, we still have lots of hours left on the contract. Do you want to continue with me?"

"Oh, yes, yes, I have told Whyte's school that I want to continue with you."

"You want to work with me, I want to work with you, then we agree."

"Yes."

After a moment of silence, he asked, "Do you like Paris?"

"Yes, love it."

He smiled, it changed him, "I am happy, it is the most beautiful city in the world."

"It is."

"You are new in the school?"

"Relatively." All teachers in Whyte's were supposed to pretend to have at least two years' experience.

"It is okay for you?"

"Yes."

"I see –" I thought he was about to say something else, but he appeared to change his mind.

I reached for my diary, "Can we fix new appointments?"

"Of course."

"I can't get you out of my mind, come away with me?" Michael took my arm as I left P.A.F.I.

I jumped, "You gave me a start. How was your class, how's Mme Michot?"

"Fine, she's a good student. I want to see you now."

I gave him a smouldering kiss. "You are seeing me, I'm going nowhere. Look, there's a bus coming, let's catch it. Come on, run."

We sprinted and made it in seconds. We managed to squash into narrow seats, "You were saying, Michael?"

He pressed his thigh against mine, "You know what I meant."

"You're welcome to come to my room, but remember I don't have a shower or private toilet."

"Oh, no," Michael looked at his watch.

"What?"

"It's the 20th, isn't it, I forgot about my little show. See what you do to me. I must go home and change into my magic gear – I have to ignite a surprise birthday party."

"Feather head, you'll forget your own name soon. Never mind, it's not like we don't know where to find each other," I tried to be blasé about it.

"Yes, but it's been two whole days."

"You'll get over it," I said casually, even if I didn't feel it.

"We'll just have to make do here," his fingers caressed my back and I felt his breath on my neck.

"Not here, Michael," but I wasn't fighting him off very hard.

"It's your perfume, I can't resist it. I love how you smell."

"It's Hermes."

"It's you."

I didn't tell him, it was one of Mme Defoe's unfinished bottles. I owed that lady a lot.

The bus moved slowly, rocking us to its beat.

"Your M. Chevalier is improving his English a lot," Michael had his eyes closed and his head resting against the window.

He had said it in an offhand way, but my antennas were out, "Yes, I know, but so is Ursula's student, Fabre."

"The HR told me that too."

"Mme Michot talks a bit too much, doesn't she?"

"Oh, I don't know. It's a very tough job being a Human Resources Manager, nobody cuts you any slack. You get all the blame and none of the credit."

"If you say so," I didn't like those jealous feelings, just because he was showing sympathy for a student.

"Has Ursula said anything to you about Fabre?" Michael asked.

"No. I get a sense that she doesn't lose a lot of time worrying about such things."

"I think you're right. When I ask her about her students, she confuses names and job titles. I thought I was scatter-brained, but I think I've met my match in Ursula."

I considered it, "I don't think she's as scattered as that. She just doesn't care enough about them or the job to sort and organise the information in her mind."

We were jolted hard, "Wow, that bus driver is heavy on the brakes, isn't he?" Michael tightened his arms protectively around me.

"French drivers," I said, letting myself relax against him.

We went under Neuilly Bridge, through the tunnel, out the other side and rolled along Avenue Charles de Gaulle.

"My stop," I got up. "Don't even think about it." I sensed Michael was going to throw caution to the winds, renege on his magic show and follow me. "Do your party tricks, I'm not planning on doing a disappearing act any time soon."

Ursula fluttered into my room to give her evening report: "Judith blew a fuse today."

"Nothing unusual about that." I'd already seen her run amok for different reasons: a teacher not turning up for a class; a teacher resigning or leaving without informing anyone... There were dozens of ways to spark Judith off. True, Judith was speechless the day the young executive student requested to have Angie replaced by a younger teacher. He claimed that Angie dozed off in class. Later, Angie admitted that it was true. She was going through a difficult time in her life and had accumulated many sleepless nights. She'd darkened the room to show a ten-minute video clip when that fateful catnap crept up on her. It could have happened to anyone. I guessed that Angie was in great need of money and that she had lied about her age to get a job in the school. She wore a lot of heavy makeup and I suspected she must be over sixty. Unfortunately, in our job like in so many other professions, ageism was an obstacle.

"It was about you," Ursula stood brushing her hair and studying her appearance in my mirror.

"Me?"

"I overheard them in 'St. Alban's' – they didn't think anyone was listening. William Whyte was talking about changing Chevalier's teacher. He claimed that Jeffery would be more suitable to continue the next part of the contract."

So now I knew what was bothering M. Chevalier earlier. It was Mr. Whyte who was being sly. He was trying to take me off the contract and M. Chevalier had put a stop to that. Why would William Whyte want to do such a thing? If he were concerned about the future and nurturing M. Chevalier's opinion of the school, surely he would want me to go on teaching him. It made no sense.

"Who is Jeffery?" The anger I felt was hard to hide.

"An oldish, boring blow-in teacher who pretends he has a background in finance and accounting." Ursula put her hands on her hips, "The usual crap. If he's so good, beats me why he wants to teach in Whyte's – must have a charitable heart."

I was getting used to the fact that some of the teachers, and often the male teachers, found the title of English teacher, at least the variety of language teaching that we did, lacking. It didn't measure up to a real job. Hence, they often qualified it with other things and wrapped it in terms that earned more respect: 'I worked in the legal domain, in finance, IT, and whatever.' Teaching lawyers or accountants or computer technicians was enough to justify such labels.

"So what happened?" I was more troubled and bothered than I showed Ursula.

"Judith defended you tooth and nail, and apparently Chevalier too was adamant about not changing you. So you see, after a few short months in the school, you're already in with the right people." Ursula drew an Ursula conclusion.

"Not Whyte obviously."

"Whyte's dim. He thinks that now you've done the ground work, it's a perfect opportunity to introduce a new teacher. By proposing someone with so-called expertise in finance, he wants to show Chevalier how professional the school is. He doesn't understand that it's exactly the opposite of what the student wants. I told you he's an asshole."

She was right, William Whyte was bungling things. If the school had succeeded at all, it was thanks to his brother Tom. Lena had hinted as much. William Whyte was living on his brother's success and burning up his assets quickly.

"What about your student, M. Fabre – is William Whyte pressurising you over him?"

"No, not really."

"That's strange, isn't it?"

"No."

"No?"

"No, Whyte isn't focused on Fabre because they're friends. I told you before."

"But how do you know that?"

"Fabre lets things slip."

"Does he now? You appear to know him well. How long have you been teaching him?"

"It's our second contract."

I might have been wrong, but I was sure she was avoiding my eye, "Ursula?"

Her phone rang, "Oh, Vincent, again. That's the fourth time he's rung. I'd better call him back." She sailed off.

Maddening girl.

****

Christmas in Paris was splendid and harmonised. It was festive and tasteful and it couldn't be more different from my country village. At home, it wasn't just putting a Christmas sheen on things, but layering it on, like a thick coating of makeup. Buckets of baubles and decorations weren't enough, we needed baths-full. People had to hang as many lights as they could, the more the merrier for good measure. In Paris, the feast was celebrated with subtlety and understatement. The neat perfection didn't feel like the Christmas I knew – it was beautiful, but it left me feeling somewhat homesick.

I checked the time. It had been Michael's idea to meet near the Christmas market chalets on the Champs Elysées. I smiled. I was early and he'd be late. That gave me a quarter of an hour to kill. I wove around the wooden stalls. The air was toxic – it was difficult to avoid that syrup-sweet aroma of candy as confectioners rolled out sheets of gluey chewies. There were hot pan-fulls of nuts and chocolate mix. These were stirred together before being removed and cooled, and finally trowelled into plastic bags that cost much too much for far too few. They called such candy making 'artisanal.' For good measure and if still hungry, one could go for the sugared wafers and sweet waffles. There were pancakes ready for all sorts of fillings, but mainly chocolate spread, jam or icing sugar. The roasted chestnuts sellers with their stoves made from half-barrels were also on hand. But they were all over the city. It was difficult not to be drawn by the woodsy-smelling plumes of smoke on street corners where the seller fanned the flames of his makeshift outdoor oven. I kept wandering through the market sniffing rich honey and sweet floss in the air. I watched candle makers use wax of every scent possible. Should I get one for Ursula, I wondered? I decided not. If she got one more candle, she'd burn Rue Montrosier down. I walked past stalls oozing oils, essences and perfumes. I kept going. Maybe I'd get Ursula a bag or something ornamental. I walked by strongly smelling leather goods, knick knacks in wood, glass and metal... Then, another food stall – this time I was swimming in savoury stands. There were hot dogs – French style using the Strasbourg sausage, Greek and Turkish sandwiches, soggy Croque Monsieurs and soggier Croque Madames... I was developing a headache and quickly escaped out of what felt like a poisonous cauldron.

In my Irish memories, Christmas had another smell. It was turkey roasting in the oven, stuffing mix, almond cake and warm conversation; it was damp churches, incense and altar candles. I recalled Christmas Eves full of anticipation as a child sitting in the front pew for midnight mass. I loved listening to the choir and trying to sing along to 'The First Noel' and other hymns and carols, looking at a baby Jesus statue in a manger, spellbound and wrapped up in wonder and anticipation of what Santa might bring.

I spotted Michael. "Over here," I called. I wouldn't be alone this Christmas. The Champs Elysées suddenly shrunk to my size and became more intimate. The daunting waves of people moved back like the tide. It was just the two of us.

"The view is marvellous and it's free," said Michael, gesturing up and down the avenue. He shook the paper cone of chestnuts he was holding, "Only five of them, expensive for that, but well worth it for the hand of the most beautiful girl in Paris."

"Don't overdo the compliments." The roasted chestnuts were tasty.

The first time I'd tried them had been a let-down, they'd tasted dry and bland – but this time they weren't so bad, not bad at all.

Lines of cars raced up and down the lanes. The rows of maple-leaf plane trees bordering either side of the avenue were covered in thousands of Christmas lights glimmering joyfully. The whole scene that had left me unmoved a few minutes before now excited me, raising my adrenaline. It was fun playing the tourist – I could get to like this.

I always enjoyed wandering and didn't mind doing things on my own. You couldn't wander with somebody, it just didn't work, it was much more fun sharing. We left the Champs Elysées and walked for a while towards the Opera Garnier, 9th district. However, on reaching Boulevard Haussmann, it started to get too much for me. The crowds were milling around us. They kept coming and coming and coming from all directions.

I lifted my hands, "Get me out of here, I can't breathe, I need air, I'm gasping for it."

"Let's escape in here," Michael directed me through a door of the department store, Galerie Lafayette. It took less than five seconds for me to back out again. "No way, that's the perfume department, Michael. I'm still trying to 'detox' from my Christmas market experience. I want to stay outdoors and I want to avoid people."

We extricated ourselves from the madness of Boulevard Haussmann's commercial strip and the crush of parents and children. There were lines of them creating a human traffic jam while trying to see the animated window displays.

"Okay then." Michael raised his arms and pointed in two directions, "Which will it be – Avenue de l'Opera or Avenue de la Paix?"

I opened my fingers and made a sign of peace, "Any street with Rolex and diamonds is bound to be empty and gloriously free of crowds."

Avenue de la Paix was exactly that. Luxury never failed to clear the pavements of the masses. While there was no such thing as a cheap shop, some places were really off-limits.

"This is great," I exclaimed, "we have the footpaths to ourselves. We can stand and admire a window display without being moulded into a human Plasticine ball."

"My Dear, shall I buy you a diamond?" Michael pretended to open the door of Cartier's jewellery shop for me.

"That's awfully kind of you, Darling, but rings were never my thing. On second thoughts, an emerald-studded bracelet might do the trick. Oh, isn't Place de la Paix magnificent and so empty?"

"It is. This is part of my Lady Di tour," Michael told me, "I take people right here in front of the Ritz. Then, I cross Rue Saint Honore to Concorde. From there, I go to Pont d'Alma and the golden hand monument, near the tunnel where she met her tragic and final fate."

We did the tour all the way, taking in a little of the fashionable Rue Saint Honore and its generous range of haute couture boutiques. We crossed Place de la Concorde, the Obelisk standing proudly where once a guillotine from the Revolution had stood, but still hovered as a ghostly silent memory. We skirted the Jardin des Tuilleries and kept going until we were leaning over the side of Alma Bridge and looking down at the lanes of traffic along the banks of the Seine at the very point where they disappeared into the underground tunnel.

"And finally," said Michael softly, "I show them the entrance to her tunnel of death."

We finished up by reading the graffiti and messages scrawled on the bridge and around a golden hand, the accidental memorial to a popular princess. Originally the monument commemorated the Battle of Alma, 1854, during the Crimean war, in which the Ottoman, France and British Alliance achieved victory over the Russian army. Today, barely eighteen months after her death, it had become an effigy to a woman called Diana.

"Once upon a time, long, long ago, there lived a fairy princess – and so the story goes –" I broke off my recitation – "cities and monuments are stark and vivid in the way they carry memories of crushed dreams and hopes. It's too much, it tumbles in on top of you. I'd prefer to stand on a mountain top and I don't know, I suppose rise above it all."

Michael ran his fingers through my hair and dropped a kiss on the tip of my nose, "Quite the little philosopher, aren't you? You sound disappointed and disillusioned when you say that. But I think all those monuments don't just carry the bad stuff, they carry good things too, belief in the future, looking ahead."

"Maybe, but in a very materialistic way."

"That's city life for you, great and small, moving and changing."

"Yes, it's never still. I feel the trains vibrating in the deep earth, and below that, I imagine the sewers and deeper again the catacombs and cemeteries of lost generations going back centuries. Listen and you can hear the voices of the past."

"I'm listening."

"Lucky for us, we've only our badly developed senses to tune into a small part of that. Imagine, Michael, imagine if we were opened up and exposed to all the parallel lives and worlds, even just for a second – we'd go bonkers."

"Liz, take it easy."

"I try."

"Put your hand here."

I placed my hand on his chest.

"Can you feel it beating?"

"Yes."

He drew me closer until my ear was pressed to his heart.

"Can you hear it?"

"Yes."

"That's real."

I knew it was.

"Let's pretend, Liz, that we have lots of money, what would you like to do right now?" Michael asked.

"I would go to my favourite café and have a sinful hot chocolate."

"You're on."

An hour later, we both sat on a heated terrace as I drank the nicest chocolate I'd drunk in a long time. It flowed down my throat like silk, rich and smooth. I watched Michael play with his magic ribbons. Pretty soon, a crowd gathered around us, watching until the waiter gave us the hint and put the ticket under our noses. We didn't care. I put my hand in Michael's and we continued our ramble through Paris.

9

We did all the things romantic couples do in the movies. We even tried ice skating in the temporary ice rink that had been set up for the holiday season in front of the Hotel de Ville. How many times growing up had I watched those dreamy American Christmas movies, where somehow somewhere the leading characters end up skating, kissing and promising undying love on frozen lakes.

On Christmas Day, Michael's bed was the centre of our world. I adored how he'd decorated the studio: a tiny Christmas tree on a shelf, a garland reading Happy Christmas over the doorway, sprigs of mistletoe and holly, and the giant Christmas card he presented to me. Michael wanted to surprise me and he succeeded. We didn't lose too much time cooking, and instead pooled our resources for 'amuse-gueules' bought at the local supermarket: canapés of artichokes and pâté, imitation foie gras, smoked salmon, pork rillettes, Brie cheese and tuna mousse terrine. Michael added escargots in sautéed garlic butter and stuffed in mushroom caps. The Irish in me still preferred the turkey slices that we got at a special bargain from a friendly butcher in Michael's neighbourhood. We had tiny chocolate Christmas logs to round off as dessert, and reasonably good wine to accompany all the courses. We got several bottles of Brouilly 1996 which Michael assured me was a solid choice from the Beaujolais region even if it wasn't a vintage year. Michael had also bought one bottle of Champagne.

I enjoyed our leisurely time relaxing in bed, surrounded with remote controls and glasses of wine. We alternated between TV programmes filled with sloppy goodwill and cheerful music.

I forgot about my students and pushed all school affairs to one side. I didn't have a care or a worry about Ursula who I knew was safely out of the way in Dublin. Being in Ireland might encourage her to stay there, though I doubted it. Neither did I lose time fretting over Eva – the ghost of Rue Montrosier. However, Ursula had entrusted me with the responsibility of Elle, her cat. I shared out that duty with the Bjania family who were spending Christmas Day on the seventh floor. I also asked Mme Gomes to check in on the cat when I wasn't there. For the most part though, I managed to make daily trips over the holidays between Michael's studio and Rue Montrosier to ensure that Elle was not neglected.

Michael switched off all devices, "I don't want to be distracted by anyone but you."

"Same here," I snuggled close to him and left myself drift into the Christmas spirit and Michael's loving embrace.

I did eventually ring my uncle in Kerry and my aunt in Galway, and some cousins in Ireland, wishing them Merry Christmas.

I encouraged Michael to ring his family in England. I knew he was thinking of them, he'd already brought up family memories twice.

"Ring them, go on, you'll feel better," I urged. "Do it, if not for your father's, then for your mother's sake. They only want what's best for you. When they're dead and gone, you'll regret lost moments like those. You'll think of all the things you should have said and done, but didn't, because pride got in the way. One day you'll miss them. Believe me, I know." I realised I was bossing and taking command as Ursula might say. But I believed it was for his good.

"You're right, you're right. Hey, you keep saying you want to use the shower – so why don't you take your shower and I'll ring them while you're doing that," he reached for the phone.

Michael hated head-on conflict and I knew he wouldn't start a row. For peace and goodwill, he would pretend to pay lip service to my wishes.

When I came out of the bathroom he was fiddling with the remote control and zapping channels. I knew he had not talked with his parents.

"Is everyone okay back at home?"

"Yeah, everyone and everything's great," he said lightly. "My turn for the shower."

He was a bad liar, but I was good at pretending and didn't ask any more questions. I didn't want to hear a second white lie added to the first one. Two white lies would make for a real one. I chose to preserve our perfect Christmas and gloss over those little lies that might spoil this memory.

****

"You want to go where –" Michael rolled on his side towards me.

"To the school," I repeated.

"To Whyte's school on New Year's Eve? That's an exciting prospect to celebrate in 1999."

Then I told him about the evening I had seen Mr. Whyte and friends do their disappearing act and my curiosity to discover what was under the school.

"I think I know where Judith keeps a duplicate key of 'St. Alban's', I told him excitedly. "We'll never get a better time than this."

"Who do you take yourself for – Miss Marple?"

"Please, Michael, if you're going to compare me with someone, make her sexier."

"My apologies, it's just the Agatha Christie angle."

"I'm no detective, I just want to satisfy my curiosity. Be a sport, it won't take five minutes. Nobody can enter a room and then vanish into thin air."

"Wait a second, maybe I can upgrade your profile, I think I'm dealing with a C.S.I. agent."

"Why don't you upgrade me to a vampire hunter; William Whyte is a notorious vampire and keeps his coffin in the dark dungeons of Rue des Soeurs."

"I'm game then. I've never been one to miss a vampire hunt," Michael laughed.

The school looked like most offices should on such a night – a bit sad and cold, deserted by staff and devoid of all life.

"Lock the door after us, Michael, in case somebody does arrive. You never know," I whispered.

Michael saluted me with an exaggerated gesture.

I was dictating. I couldn't help it, someone had to and it was my investigation after all.

I shone my torch, "The key to 'St. Alban's' is in this drawer, I'm sure. Now, Judith keeps it locked with a key that she puts in the petty cash box, which," I pointed, "is in the little supply cupboard over there. The keys to the box and cupboard are hanging here under her desk."

"You have my admiration so far," Michael gave a low whistle.

"Don't be such a sceptic."

I took the keys and opened the cupboard, grabbed the petty cash box and opened that too. I found the envelope and took out the drawer key triumphantly. So far so good. Then I proceeded to open the drawer and search inside. It was full of files and documents. I searched and searched –

"Nothing. Damn, after all that."

Michael laughed, "I take back everything I said. You're definitely not in line to play Miss Marple, you've quite a ways to go yet to reach her sleuthing standards."

The click-click of the courtyard door caught my attention, "Shush, someone's coming." I shut the drawer quickly and replaced the key.

"It's just residents of the other building, going out or coming in," Michael whispered, but he turned off his torch. I did likewise.

"They're not residents, Michael, it's him."

From Judith's office window, we could see the dim courtyard light outlining the recognizable form, sporting coat, umbrella and winter hat. It had to be William Whyte, and he wasn't alone.

"Let's get out of here and hide, quick," Michael didn't need further proof.

I was already on the corridor, "Come on. We'll hide in 'St. Cuthbert's', that store room or broom cupboard, or whatever."

We forced ourselves inside the cupboard, knocking over several containers. The only way we could fit was if I pressed myself against Michael's chest. The tiny space smelt strongly of detergents, dried out sponges and cloths.

"This is the last place he'll think of checking," Michael spoke in my ear, his voice shook.

I realised he was stifling a laugh. I saw the humour of the situation myself.

"It's the craziest start I've ever had to New Year's Eve and –" he broke off.

There were voices, at least two, maybe more. We listened, but the voices soon faded. I opened the cupboard door slightly – Silence.

I was feeling more courageous, "They've gone into his office. Give it another minute, if it's like the last time, they'll do the disappearing act and we can escape."

We waited several minutes and then made our way carefully down the corridor. At 'St. Alban's', Michael put his hand to the door. It was ajar but the room light was off. There wasn't a sound. He pushed the door open wider – nobody. It was déjà vu all over again, they had disappeared just like before.

Michael switched on his torch, "This is peculiar, Liz, his coat is hanging there with another one. There must be a second door leading to the cellars. If we switch on the lights, we'll probably see, but it's too risky."

"I did the last time, the door is behind the bookcase," I flashed my own torch inside – the bookcase was pushed aside revealing a closed door. It was a plain door and didn't seem to have a lock.

"That's it then – he probably has a wine or Champagne cellars and he's just getting some crates for his midnight party," Michael affirmed.

"Don't you think it's an odd time to come looking for bottles of bubbly?"

"Not really, blokes can be like that. It's still a couple of hours before midnight and a good excuse to get away for a while. I mean, away from family duties before the New Year's Eve feast."

"Hmm, he might of course have his family locked down there or he could be planning a ritualistic ceremony," I wasn't willing to settle for ordinary explanations.

"Lots of imagination, but no proof, my little sleuth."

"He's up to no good, that's for sure."

"It's none of our business." Michael turned back out of the room. "It's his life – if he wants to go to secret dens and run around caverns, that's his choice. Come on, let's get out of here. Time to catch some fireworks."

I didn't argue this time. Although I didn't give in totally to Ursula's stories of ghosts and links between Rue Montrosier and the school, or her obsession with the seediness of William Whyte, I was determined to know what was down in those cellars. I would avail of future opportunities to explore.

"What happened? Place Saint Michel has filled up." I looked at the time, "Goodness, ten o'clock – were we that long inside, over an hour?"

Although cold, the clear starry night was ideal for celebrations. The streets were electric, they had gone from being crowded to totally mobbed. It was going to be a midnight crush to ring in 1999 and our new money, the Euro. It wasn't every day that people got to celebrate entering the last year of a century and converting to a new currency. If all went according to plan, we should be able to use our credit cards just after midnight and withdraw Euros instead of Francs from our accounts. We were thrilled at the prospect. Although many older people were afraid and sceptical about the new money, I felt excited about the fact that in a few hours the money people used in Ireland would be the same as the money in France, Germany and several other countries in the European Union. Michael was disappointed that he would not get to experience exactly the same thing as the UK had opted to stay outside the Eurozone.

"Forget the public transport," said Michael, "and we're not going to get within miles of the Eiffel Tower. I know just the place we can go to view the Eiffel Tower fireworks at a distance. If we walk we can easily get there in time and see the full show."

We crossed Pont Marie, one of the four bridges traversing the Seine at the fork of Isle Saint Louis, and followed an ascent northwards. We got to the 2nd district and hurried past a rather sober, grey-brick building with Grecian-style columns known as Palais Brongniart or the former Stock Exchange of Paris. Then we continued to climb towards the 9th and 18th districts, taking Rue Montmartre right up to Pigalle, the centre of the red light zone. We passed women selling their bodily wares on street corners, doorways and inside the windows of seedy clubs. I had never seen as many graphic sex shops, vulgar neon lights, as well as dozens of brasseries and bars jam-packed with people.

The Moulin Rouge signalled from the top of Boulevard de Clichy. It looked better at night compared to the jaded and faded day-time appearance, but everything was more attractive when lit up. The old windmill cabaret, with its red bronze monument and vanes displaying Belle Époque decoration from the end of the 19th century, was now lost in fumes, smoking exhaust pipes, and visitors who knew little of the cabaret joie de vivre of the old days. In truth, the red light area seemed to me to have the air of a neglected seaside resort with its mix of out-of-datedness and cheekiness. While it hosted the full range of decadent ingredients, its shock value was muted. Perhaps it was linked to the fact that it was overrun with tourists. What intrigued me about Pigalle was that it was also home to Parisians who lived out their day to day routine – sent their children to local schools, went to church and did the shopping. The open-air street markets together with cheese and fish mongers, butchers, bakers and grocers grounded the district in ordinary life.

"A penny for your thoughts," Michael dropped a kiss on my cheek.

"Sorry, I was just thinking of this and that."

"You aren't supposed to be thinking of anything or anyone except me. I'll wager not one of your 'this and that' begins with an 'M'. Remember 'M' is for Michael. It's not good for the ego, especially when the guy you're supposed to be besotted with is right here beside you," he put on a sad clown face.

"You're at the heart of all my thoughts. How could I forget someone as charming as you?"

He lifted me in the air, "I can carry you the rest of the way."

"Don't be silly. Save your energy for the important things later on."

"Wicked lady."

My feet found the ground again, "Show off."

We took Rue Lepic simply because we had covered the distance faster than expected and it was more fun to take the winding narrow street up and up and up into the older and more rustic part of Montmartre.

As we mounted, the illuminated white travertine stone of Sacré-Coeur Basilica, the late 19th-century monument to martyrs, came into view. It stood high and aloof and detached from its surroundings. I gave Michael a history lesson and told him about the Romano-Byzantine features which were said to be a reaction to the neo-Baroque excesses of the Palais Opera Garnier.

Michael listened studiously to my rambling explanation for a minute and then chided, "Ursula is right when she says you are a walking encyclopaedia. But I like it." He took my hand, "Ready for the steps?"

"Nothing to them," I retorted, "I've had lots of training."

We continued upwards, with each step our legs growing heavier, our breaths blowing foggy air.

"I'll tell you," Michael panted, "climbing this must be what making a pilgrimage feels like."

"I understand what they mean by 'ascension into heaven'," I gasped.

Given that it was New Year's Eve, the place was even more crowded than usual at this time of the night, with groups also gathering for a special service in the Basilica. We began to follow a train of tourists right inside Sacré-Coeur, but as they poured down the side aisles, we decided not to go farther. It seemed a pity having gotten that far not to at least pay homage, but it was all a little disrespectful. I looked at the stained glass windows, beautiful painted ceilings and walls, and thought how such a holy space must feel so violated by hoards of gaping visitors oblivious to its spiritual and sacred past. For centuries this place held the prayers of souls now deceased. I hoped the venerated souls eventually found peace, before the dawning of the day.

Outside, a few unimpressive musicians wrapped in blankets sat around on a grassy slope, strumming guitars and drumming djembes. Other music sessions were sprouting up all over the place. Street hawkers covered the territory like ants, with matching arrays of junky souvenirs and plastic curios.

We descended into Place de Tetre, the artists' square, where pigeons and vendors battled for crumbs and sales.

Michael looked mischievous, "Do you want to do the full tourist and get our portraits done?"

"Not on your life. Why don't we get a few cans of beer and a couple of sandwiches, then get out to the spot you want us to go and wait for the fireworks to go off at the Eiffel Tower?"

"There's no romance in you. Monsieur – " Michael signalled to an artist and rode roughshod over my protests of expense and tourist rip-off.

We sat with foolish grins as the artist deftly speed painted our portraits. Michael got very upset when I wanted to pay my share. In the end, I gave in. I had to get used to letting people do things for me. It was his pleasure to treat me, he told me.

I looked at the final masterpiece. "That woman does not look like me. But that handsome hunk is totally you."

"You're right," Michael scratched his chin, "the woman in that painting is not half as pretty as you really are. Still, I'm going to get it framed."

We sat by a beautiful two-storey carousel with its stairs, colourful wooden ponies and carriages and looped circus music. An accordion busker saw his opportunity and made a beeline towards us. He squeezed some wails out of his instrument, drowning out the sound of the carousel.

When he finished, Michael slipped a generous donation in his pocket and a word in his ear. With a gap-toothed grin, the musician broke into a ballad.

"Come dance with me, Liz," Michael held out his hand.

"What, here, in the middle of all these people?"

"Pretend we are the only ones here."

I let go of my self-consciousness and went into his arms. He was right, once I closed my eyes there was just us.

"Que serais-je sans toi," Michael hummed the song in French and in English, 'What would I be without you'.

I recognized the song of Jean Ferrat, a popular French folk singer-songwriter. Even with a rough accordion rendition, it was beautiful.

I closed my eyes. Fireworks and cheers went off all over the city. I made a wish for 1999. Michael's lips were close to mine.

"What did you wish for?" he murmured.

"I wished for –"

"Yes?"

"I wished to be here with you again in one year and –"

His lips found mine and caressed sweetly before deepening as the accordion notes trailed off.

I opened my eyes, "What did you wish for?"

He tightened his hold on me, "I wished to always be this happy."

That was the kindest thing anyone had ever said to me – I found myself go all weepy and pressed my face against the rough wool of his jacket.

"Liz, have I upset you – I didn't mean –"

"No," I shook my head, "I'm happy too, that's all."

We stood together, arm in arm, gazing into the distance at the biggest fireworks display of all at the Tour Eiffel.

****

"Lena?"

"Yeah, Honey?" Lena spread the word 'Honey' on the people she liked, which included those she needed or would need.

"This place's got cellars, hasn't it?"

"Sure has, as far as I know."

"It's an unusual collection of buildings, isn't it? It's full of nooks and crannies, but I suppose cellars are usual."

"You got a thing about cellars. Don't forget the attics. In the good old bad days, people lived up and down. Up under the roof to the servants' rooms, governesses and such folk, and down to the stable lads and street urchins."

"Indeed. But it was a smart move opening a school here," I wasn't very good at winkling out the information I wanted, but did try.

"Tom bought the place and turned it into a business. He added the extension later. They probably couldn't do that today, wouldn't get planning permission. But it was done at a time when it was easier to get around the law, if you had the right connections. The main thing is it has to be safe and certified to prove it isn't a fire hazard."

"Lena, it's only got the one window."

"Fire exit front and back. You don't need a window to be fireproof."

"Huh, I'm not sure how Mr. Whyte convinces the authorities today that it is safe."

Lena didn't answer, only reached for her cigarettes, "You wanna step outside?"

"Why not?"

"Just a second – oui, Monsieur?"

A well-dressed gentleman stood at the doorway and explained he'd come to sit a level test.

"You're late, young man," Lena waved her finger, "I'll let you take the test, but you gotta complete the written part inside twenty minutes, instead of the usual thirty. We'll check out your oral level after. You got it?"

The man took one look at Lena and didn't argue.

Lena bundled him into 'Oxford' and then came outside for her smoke.

"Lena," I reprimanded gently, "I'm sure you get a kick out of frightening people. The poor man is terrorised before starting."

"He was late. I've said it before and I'll say it again, give – "

"I know, I know, give them an inch and they'll take a mile."

"At least."

"What are the school cellars used for?" I decided on the direct approach.

"You're a nosy parker."

"Just curious."

"I wouldn't know, I've never been down there."

"Really?"

"I'm claustrophobic."

I believed her.

All good things come to those who wait, and a few hours later on leaving the school, I couldn't help but overhear Judith speaking on her mobile phone. I dawdled about on purpose while buttoning up my coat, keeping my ears wide open.

"William – you forgot what? Your wallet? I didn't see it lying around here. Do you want me to check your office?" Judith sounded impatient.

The main landline phone rang and it was my cue to enter as Lena had gone home.

"Liz, could you take that call while I go to 'St. Alban's'?" Judith asked.

"Sure," I said willingly.

Judith took up a bunch of keys, picked one out and opened the filing cabinet under her desk. She parted some folders and from beneath a purple file produced the key. Ah, so that was where it was tucked. I was now more than ever determined to discover what was in the cellars.

Judith came back a few minutes later, still talking into her mobile, "Sorry, William, there was nothing at all on your desk. Give me half an hour and I'll look more thoroughly around there.

"Very well then, come and check yourself."

I'd no doubt about it, he would check himself. I wondered about Judith being constantly harried and under pressure. She didn't seem to enjoy herself very much. Maybe she had at one time. She seemed more stressed somehow. Apart from the outdated computers and equipment, there were disquieting financial signals, including paying teachers late and shortages of office stationery. Those in themselves were worrying, but their reoccurrence made them alarming in my opinion.

****

I clenched the key and smiled as it turned sweetly, unlocking 'St. Alban's'. I threw up the light switch – no one would notice at this time of the morning. There wasn't a sinner around. Getting up at the crack of dawn hadn't been difficult, not for Miss Marple on a mission. Besides, I was a pro at greeting the break of day. Even if Michael was probably right in saying that William Whyte stored nothing but wine down there, I was determined to find out for myself.

The mobile bookcase was practically empty and easy to wheel aside to reveal the door. I turned the handle and as hoped it wasn't locked. I couldn't find any light switch and shone my torch on stone steps going down. It was narrow and winding and I descended carefully, thinking William Whyte must be quite nimble.

Finally, I arrived at a small opening. Damn, another door and this one was definitely locked. I'd reached the end of my journey. It had been too easy.

I returned to the main office with a whole hour to spare before opening the doors for the Saturday morning shift teachers. Idle hands and curiosity had me looking through some old school files that sat on shelves. It was amazing what little bits of life people left forgotten in ordinary places, I thought. The envelope was tucked inside a tattered accounting journal and it contained a few photographs. I slid them out. One was of Lena looking every inch Lena, brandishing a cigarette. Her face was less gaunt than today, but overall the years hadn't changed her too much. Judith had changed more. In the faded photo she looked a lot younger, softer and apparently in love. Her smile and face were joyful. The man standing beside Judith wasn't difficult to recognize – he resembled William Whyte, but was taller, and I knew it must be his brother, Tom. Indeed, Judith had changed. The Judith I knew had lost that glow evident in the old photograph. How quickly happiness greyed. I put the photos back.

I opened my bag and took out a few pictures I kept with me. There was me as a baby with Mum and Dad; then me aged eight with Mum and Frisky the cat. I had added one of Michael at the Christmas market. Something about it had an ancient quality, like an old memory.

'WHAM – ' the first teacher had arrived.

"I hate Saturdays, I really do," Cynthia gave another wallop to her locker door and kickstarted the day with gusto and the usual burst of begrudgery and 'painful noise'. Contrary to her promises last year, Cynthia had returned from the States after Christmas, but didn't seem to be appreciating the fact.

I greeted her and braced myself for the arrival of more bad-tempered teachers.

After my morning's work, I strolled towards the Pompidou Centre to meet Michael. I passed in front of the wonderful Notre Dame de Paris. No matter how many times I saw it, the Gothic Catholic cathedral on Île de la Cité never failed to impress me. I crossed Pont de Arcole and Hôtel de Ville and wove my way along Rue de Renard until the coloured tubular Centre Georges Pompidou stood brazenly in front of me. Opened in 1977, it was a project that honoured a former French President. Some people called it, 'love at second sight'. At the time of construction it was a new concept combining culture and art, housing a modern art museum and public library. Architecturally, one had the impression of a building turned inside out with brightly coloured tubes and mechanical systems outside, thus affording maximum space for exhibits and such inside. The tubes had specific coding for what they contained: green for plumbing, blue for climate control, electrical encased in yellow and circulation elements such as fire safety in red.

I sat on the verge of a wall bordering the sloping square that led to the entrance and scanned the area. Some artists were touting their works. I was familiar by sight with many of the street performers: the jugglers, the break dancers; the sword swallower was already in action, while the fire eater was in preparation. A young man played haunting music on an instrument resembling an elongated mandolin. Michael told me that he was a student from the Kabylia region in north Algeria and the instrument was the mandole used for traditional music. I soon found myself blocking my nose; there was a strong stink of urine and bleach and I didn't want to know how many people had hung out here, drinking, getting sick and peeing all over the place the night before. It would have been hosed down by city street cleaners, but the stench was permanent. The wider area, also known as Beaubourg, was close to Châtelet and Forum les Halles which was comprised of a vast underground shopping mall and an overground hub of narrow streets gorged with restaurants and knick-knack shops. It was a hodgepodge, a hang out place for shoppers, tourists, drug dealers, junkies, winos, artists, students... I learned that originally this district had been Paris's central fresh food market and the streets around Châtelet would have been filled with merchant stalls and popular everyman cafés, bars and restaurants serving workers and Parisians haggling, dealing and supping. Some people regretted that everything was demolished in the early 1970s and replaced by what I now saw before me. The fresh food market had relocated to a charmless suburb called Rungis in the south of the city.

I forgot the past and my heart did a little tumble – there he was. I was as proud as if he'd just been voted President instead of Jacques Chirac and had arrived to give his inaugural speech. Michael stood in the middle of the square, tall and straight. True to form, his curly hair was tousled and he had on a red shirt, baggy jeans and yellow braces. He'd finished off the effect with a funny blue hat. It would be clown magic today. I watched him spread out his black and gold cloth and switch on some music. He launched into his comic dance to draw people for the show. It astonished me how much money could be made from some of those brief performances.

I knew I was biased, not a grain of objectivity in my opinion, but he was more than good. I liked Michael best in that role and knew that he too was happiest performing. Since we'd been spending more time together, I witnessed the hours and hours of practice that went into each magic trick. Michael was an artist – teaching English was the last thing on his mind and preparing classes even further. He was on a high out there in the square and spared no effort. He spotted me and waved before going into his rainbow ribbon trick. More people gathered around him.

I thought about how I could help Michael. There were thousands of musicians and performance acts all over the city, in every city, some better and some worse. He was still young, but the clock was ticking. Young potentials quickly became 'never beens', without ever knowing 'has been'. Each year would be harder, even if he made a small-time career out of it. He should be doing more to improve his chances: attach himself to some performing company, join a circus or theatre.

****

My New Year's resolution that I kept up right through January was to take every opportunity to push Michael to focus more on his magic, although I preferred to call it 'encourage him'. I didn't frown if he told me of another messed up English class. I closed my eyes to tales of his forgetting material or walking into a top executive's office with nothing more than the *Financial Times* under his arm and a broad smile on his face. I didn't nag him on those points, but I did on his magic. I tried to convince him that he was getting somewhere and going places in small ways. And it was true – word of mouth helped and demand for his performances was increasing all the time. He told me he liked it, liked my pushing and encouraging. It was the first time someone took his magic seriously, was behind him and believed in him.

I didn't let up and pushed him also to reconnect with his past and not let the month of January pass by without taking some steps in that direction. "You're going to go home, visit your parents, and face your family. Show them. Show your mother and father what you are able to do. Let them see that you're serious about the career path you've chosen. Give them proof and they will help you out, I'm sure."

"Liz, Liz, you are like an army general. I can't say that I'll follow all your advice, but I do need a boss – and I've found one, a female one who's a vamp into the bargain."

"A vamp?"

"Yes, and she drives me crazy. Outside, you are so serious and disciplined, but underneath the General burns the soul of a real vamp and she's all mine – now be careful –" he backed away.

I had him tackled and flattened on his bed in a few seconds.

"Mercy," he begged, "mercy."

"No, no mercy until you take back everything you just said – I am a lady."

"Yes, you are my lady and I don't deserve you," his look was impish.

I made short work of his show of humility.

10

"Ursula, hang on."

"What?"

"Wait for me, we can go home together." What was she doing scurrying away from P.A.F.I?

Ursula kept going, but did slow down a fraction, if grudgingly. What was up with her? We were windswept in the middle of the high rise brick, steel and glass of La Défense. It couldn't have been more manmade, but I found something savage and wild here. Even on this cold and windy Monday in February, it energised me.

"So, how did your class go with Fabre?" I asked.

"Okay."

She was like mining through hard rock for information.

"He's progressing then," I tried to prompt her.

"If you want."

"I bet he's doing a lot better than Chevalier is with me. That will please William Whyte."

Ursula turned on me, "What's that supposed to mean?"

"Ouch, touchy. I'm just saying that if he's promoted, it'll be good for the school. You told me yourself that Whyte and Fabre were friends of sorts."

"Why don't you just leave me? Go and get your bus – isn't that what you prefer? I'm walking."

What did I do to bring that attack upon myself? She was in a dark mood. I was about to make a biting retort when I saw something glisten on her cheeks. "Ursula, are you crying?"

"No, I'm not."

Her denial gave me more concern. Those weren't crocodile tears. "Ursula?"

She strode off.

"Bus is coming," I said, "it would be crazy not to get it."

She relented, got on and ignored me for the short ride home. I stole a few cautious glances, but decided it wasn't worth the risk opening up the conversation here on the bus.

Ursula returned Mme Gomes's greeting with a short good evening and attacked the stairs with fierce determination. By the time I reached the landing, her door was banged shut.

"Boff," I said. It was one of the most useful French words I'd learnt. It expressed everything from 'don't ask me' to 'who cares' and 'no skin off my nose'.

I hated admitting it, but Ursula's abrupt cold shoulder bothered me all the next day. I was used to her complaining, but this time was different. By the time I got to the school in the evening, I felt that Ursula's bad-tempered bug might be catching. I could see that Judith wanted to kill someone and was looking for a target to lop her anger at. I didn't want any of it. I wanted to soak in my dreamy world where everything was Michael shaped, but I'd been summoned to the office.

Judith stared while Lena presented me with the facts of the case. "On Friday evening, there was a new giant jar of instant coffee in 'Lindisfarne'. Judith here opens up the school on Monday morning. At eight forty-five, she goes for a coffee and – it's gone. There ain't no coffee jar, it has disappeared. What do you make of that?"

"I can't say," I replied, "that's the first I've heard of it. I used up the last grains from the old jar on Saturday morning and put out a new one.

Nobody complained about anything, so I can only conclude that it was still there at break time. After, I don't know. I didn't check the cupboards in 'Lindisfarne' before closing up. But I did meet William Whyte when I was leaving. Maybe he went on a coffee binge."

Two sets of eyes bored into me.

"What?" I raised my hands, "I know it wasn't me. What do you want me to do? I'm alone in the office on Saturdays, the appointment book is usually full up and I don't have eyes at the back of my head."

"We're not accusing you, Honey," Lena was clearly enjoying playing her sleuth role, "we just wanted to put you in the picture."

Judith clattered a few cupboard doors closed, "Just keep watch, half an eye will do. If it happens again, there will be no more coffee. Teachers can buy it down the street in the café. Bye, see you tomorrow."

Lena looked disparagingly at the computer, took out her trusty journals and began paring a pencil.

I folded my arms, "So now I'm in the picture, what do you expect me to do?"

"Like Judith said, keep half an eye, that's all. It ain't the end of the world, but a lot of things disappear: books, CDs, pens, any number of things. When your back is turned, teachers will get dozens of pages copied, we're always buying paper, ink and toner for the photocopiers. It adds up and things are damn tight at the moment."

"Are you saying I'm a soft touch on Saturdays?"

"Hell no," said Lena, "this goes on every day. It wasn't any different when I was doing Saturdays. It ain't –"

"It isn't –"

"What?"

"Nothing," I was never sure if Lena was letting her guard down or was just putting on the accent for good measure.

"People ain't honest, that's the all of it."

"Aren't –"

"What?"

"People aren't honest."

"That's what I said."

"You know very well, Lena, that many teachers live on a shoestring budget. Anything that's left lying around will disappear. Why is Judith making such a big deal out of it this time?"

"It takes her mind off the important things. I'm going out for a cigarette," Lena closed the conversation.

By Saturday, even my own good humour was letting me down. Jonathan rang in sick. Somebody had smashed a bottle on his head the night before. He'd spent the night in the hospital emergency room. Though I was concerned and felt sorry for him, it did leave me with the problem of either telling twelve clients to go home or finding a last minute stand-in. I was beginning to understand the behaviour of Judith and Lena. If I were dealing with that every day, I would quickly become a snarky cold-hearted person. I rang everyone looking for a substitute teacher and Richard was the only one willing to come in. Now I could empathise with Judith and understood better why the school kept slightly crazy teachers like Richard on its list – when you were stuck, you accepted whoever you could find. It was a gamble. He might be on an okay day and his classes would go fine, or he might be on a completely daft day and terrify the life out of his students.

Richard arrived like someone on the last spurt of a sprint, face polished with sweat. "I'm on time, aren't I?"

"Yes, yes. I can't thank you enough, Richard, you're a life saver. You're in 'Durham'."

"Ouf," he wiped his brow.

I detected a rhythmic noise like an electricity meter from his bag.

"Richard, how many clocks do you have? Do you need all of them, I mean each and every one of them?"

He looked at me as if it was I who was out of my mind, "We have to watch time. If we don't, it flees us."

"But having half a dozen clocks on you won't change that. You can't capture time."

"Miss Downey," he jutted his chin at me, "you don't know what you're talking about."

"I'm sure I don't." I didn't want to vex him more. I put my hands together and prayed that at least some of the switches in his brain would start firing up before he reached 'Durham'.

Speaking about time, it was nine and where was Ursula? I rang her mobile, "Ursula, where are you exactly?"

The answer came back as cool as a breeze. She was only at Argentine Metro station. Casual as you like, Ursula told me she'd slept it out. I had practically beaten her door down earlier that morning to avoid this very situation occurring. But Ursula was impossible these last days and swang from bitchy to glum to airy indifference. I suspected she was on some medication. There were many boxes of pills and tablets in her room. Ursula told me that she took them to control panic attacks and to help her sleep. I went into the office, closed the door and kept it closed. It was better that way. It was the last line of protection, preventing me from killing Ursula when she did arrive.

At break time, I went to the coffee space, 'Lindisfarne', in trepidation to see if Richard's students had that stunned look or if a revolt was starting. Fortunately, it was the former. By the time they recovered and needed to complain, I'd have the school locked up.

I ran back to answer the phone, "W.W.S.O.E. & F.L., bonjour?" The words came out effortlessly and I realised that somehow, over the past months, I had mastered answering the school phone. I wasn't sure if I should be proud of that fact.

I was kept too busy for the rest of the morning to even think of petty theft, steps of stairs leading somewhere or nowhere under 'St. Alban's', or M. Chevalier's challenge to overcome obstacles in English and get promoted. I did think about Michael and the fact that he would be coming in regularly from next Saturday to teach a new course of Business English. While it pleased me no end, it stressed me too. I already couldn't bear it if Judith or Lena criticised him. How was I going to cope if his students started complaining to me?

At one o'clock there was a rush to exit. I saw Angie slipping away carrying an unusually bulky bag.

"Angie, do you have a minute?"

"Sorry, sorry, Liz, I don't have a second. I have to get to Roissy Charles de Gaulle Airport. My son is coming into Paris for the weekend. Was it important?"

"Oh no, not really." I tried another angle, if not a very subtle one, "That's a heavy bag to be carrying to the airport – do you want to let some things here, I can lock them away until Monday, books or something?"

"That's awfully nice of you, but I'll manage. This old bag looks bulky, but honestly it isn't." Angie pressed it close to her chest, "I'm very fond of it. Though I got it for practically nothing at a car boot sale, it's got sentimental value," she prodded it ferociously.

I spotted William Whyte in the courtyard and decided not to pursue the subject. "Well, don't be late then, and have a nice weekend with your son."

"Thanks, see you next week."

Angie was probably carrying a lot of photocopying work in her bag and maybe some coffee. I made photocopies myself, but only what was required for classes. I knew Angie gave private tuition to students to supplement her income and Whyte's school was probably useful in providing her with extra material and topping up her office supplies. 'Use whatever is lying about under your hands,' I knew was the mantra of some of the teachers. If I went looking for three honest people in the school, I wasn't sure I'd find them. Everyone felt that they were within their rights to steal something.

William Whyte loomed in the hallway and Angie scurried away.

"Miss Downey, would you mind sending that Irish girl – O'Grady – to my office." He walked on.

I rang Ursula's mobile guessing that she must be in 'Lindisfarne', since I hadn't noticed her leave.

"Ursula, William Whyte wants to see you in his office," I spoke into the phone.

"He can feck off."

"Please yourself," I hung up.

I went out on the corridor in time to see Ursula go into 'St. Alban's'. So much for her bravado.

Half an hour later, I wondered what Ursula and William Whyte could be talking about and was about to give up on her and just go home when I heard a locker slam shut.

Ursula sailed right past me, "See you."

Nothing I could do if she insisted on staying in a bad mood, but she pushed my buttons and unnerved me. However, Michael's text changed that –

'Late lunch at La Rose?'

I didn't hesitate and sent – 'Okay – starving.'

I felt obliged to tell Whyte that I was locking up and went to 'St. Alban's'. I could hear him giving instructions to someone inside and the sound of a vacuum cleaner. The cleaners had arrived, although I had seen nobody come in. He couldn't possibly be talking to himself and he'd never do his own cleaning. I was tempted to wait on and see who would come out of his office, but a new text from Michael signalled – and I didn't hang around. Michael was a far more interesting prospect.

****

"Liz," Judith's voice was controlling so much temper and I knew that tint of red on her cheeks had nothing to do with her makeup.

"Liz, where is Ursula?"

It was going to be one of those evenings, I thought. "I don't know. Why are you looking for her?"

"She didn't turn up for her class out at P.A.F.I. with her student, Mme Lemorvan. The HR at P.A.F.I. rang the school to complain. Now it's time for her evening class and we still have no news."

Judith was showing very white gleaming teeth and a highly flustered Lena was ringing to find a stand-in.

Being made feel responsible for Ursula was annoying to me, but I took my phone, "I can ring her. Have you tried her mobile?"

"Lena has left four messages," Judith shifted some files on her desk, took the paper weight in her hand and wisely put it down again.

"Look," I said, "I don't know where Ursula is – she isn't answering her phone for me either."

I took refuge in 'Lindisfarne'. I added rather cloudy water to a dangerous dose of the precious coffee and stirred it vigorously. I thought, 'Oh, Ursula will surely turn up with a good explanation.' I was angry at her. This was Valentine's Day, I was supposed to meet Michael later this evening after a little show he was performing. I should be thinking about that and not about Ursula's problems.

At break time, however, Ursula still hadn't shown up or telephoned and I began to get anxious. Ursula was wilful and unreliable within certain limits. She went far, but never that far – she was still predictable in her unpredictability.

I returned to my class. Two of the students had been difficult from the start of the evening, questioning everything and doubting my answers. I felt that their mood was due to external circumstances beyond my control. In Whyte's school, dissatisfaction was often related to money issues. I knew from Lena that those particular students still hadn't paid all their course instalments and I figured out that they had more than likely been harangued by her earlier. Money discussions were recipe for a rotten atmosphere and when students sat on an uncomfortable chair in a windowless room, they lashed out at the teacher. I worked hard to set things right. The students threw their demands at me: they wanted more and more – more material, more exercises, more computer-based work and more of everything. I tried to give reasonable answers to their demands and did my utmost to sow a few grains of goodwill among them and to stop the bad mood of some from spoiling the class.

I felt the strain on the back of my legs as I climbed to the seventh floor. Ursula's door was unlocked, but she was nowhere to be found. Elle was sitting on her bed and next to her was a note – 'I've had enough of life – I will find peace in the wood.'

"Shit," I'd never imagined anything like that. The worst went through my mind. She hadn't committed suicide, no, it wasn't possible, not Ursula. I looked through her medicine stash. It was impossible to know if she'd taken something or not. If she had gone off to the wood, I couldn't lose another second and must find her. 'Please don't let it be too late, please,' I prayed.

My phone flashed.

It was Michael. I explained about Ursula's disappearance, but left out the part about her note. I didn't want to bother him before his show and at the same time, I wanted to protect Ursula's privacy. He told me that he had seen Ursula that morning at P.A.F.I. where she had two classes scheduled; apparently she gave the first class and was nowhere to be found for the second. Suspicious thoughts started turning in my mind, especially when Michael told me that the first class was with Fabre. I tried to keep my humour upbeat as I wished him luck for his performance and accepted his offer to come to my room later in the evening

I tried Ursula's mobile once again, but in vain. It was ludicrous – I'd been so determined not to have anything to do with Ursula's life, or as little as possible, that I didn't even have the number of Vincent, her Ex. I didn't have her family's numbers, I'd nothing.

I raced to the wood, thinking that I'd scout around for a few minutes and if that didn't produce anything, I would call the police. If Ursula had really done something out of despair, she – I couldn't bear to think about it.

I stood at the opening to the wood. It was dark and felt dangerous and I regretted coming alone. I pulled the hood of my coat more fully over my head and dug my hands deep in my pockets. My eyes began adjusting as the street lamps from the nearby Boulevard Maillot threw some paltry light my way. If Ursula had come here, she wouldn't have gone farther than the first little pond. Even in day time, I'd never known her to walk farther. Ursula and exercise of any name were alien.

I heard a cry and jumped back. What was that? I peered at a semi-naked body near a van. Then I spotted another and another scantily clad individual. There were prostitutes all over the place. I stood still, feeling threatened, and decided to go back to the room and call the police. Disorientated, I moved onto the main pathway.

'Jesus!' My heart almost stopped as something moved in the hedge. I heard voices and murmuring. I hurried to find my way back to Boulevard Maillot and bumped into a bench.

What was that bundled up on the bench – a homeless person? There was something very familiar about the bundle – "Ursula, for God's sake," I cried in relief. "Were you planning to sleep out here for the night? What –"

Ursula was in my arms, sobbing loudly.

Somebody shouted and another voice screamed at us. I heard footsteps coming towards us. An object flew past my head, "What is – let's get going, ouch," I twisted my ankle stumbling over the flying missile, a stiletto.

"Come on, come on," I called Ursula. But Ursula was out of it and had difficulty in standing. I dragged and carried her as I would a drunk.

Eventually, we got to Boulevard Maillot, crossed Avenue Charles de Gaulle and back on to Rue Montrosier. Step by painful step, we made it to the building. I hoped nobody I knew met us with Ursula in this condition. Fortunately, Mme Gomes was preoccupied with family life. The curtains were drawn and there was lots of chatter mixed in with television sounds from inside her lodge.

"Can you make it up the stairs, Ursula?"

Her 'Yes' was weak. She needed a lot of help to get there, flight one, two, three – and at last the landing. The corridor was empty and I dragged Ursula directly to her room.

Elle pranced and danced around us, "Oh, Elle, Elle," cried Ursula, "my darling." She took the cat in her arms.

They both fell on the bed. Elle jumped from her arms and began padding around, purring and meowing, affectionately head-butting and curling herself against her mistress.

"Okay," I said, "while you two get re-acquainted, I'll make tea. How long were you on that bench?"

"I don't know, I don't know how I got there."

"You don't know? You left a note."

"Did I? What did I say?"

I told myself to calm down, this wasn't the moment to get hysterical. On closer examination, I decided that Ursula didn't look too good and appeared to be in shock.

Tea wasn't going to be strong enough, so I went to my room to find a small bottle of whiskey and make a hot toddy.

"This is what you need."

Ursula took it and sipped.

I made a second glass for myself and took a good slug before refilling it generously. I waited for the whiskey to take effect on Ursula, and it did, but not in the way I expected.

"I'm going to be sick," Ursula put her hand to her mouth.

The toilet was too far away. Thank God the bath tub was nearby.

A good hour and a lot of slopping up later, I was glad to see some colour come back into Ursula's cheeks.

"Do you want something to eat?" I offered.

Ursula shook her head – she was still shaking, but more aware. She looked around her and then, "Oh, Liz, Liz, I'm sorry, I'm always in trouble and dragging you into it with me."

"I have free will," I said.

"I'll lose my job and be on the streets, I won't have a thing or a friend left."

That was more like Ursula, whining and complaining. Now I knew my Irish neighbour was getting back to normal.

"What happened?" I asked.

"I don't want to talk about it."

I saw her hands tremble and she pressed them on her lap, "I'm fine, leave me now."

I didn't give in. "It's Fabre, isn't it?"

"Is it that obvious?"

"Not to most people. It's small things that I've noticed."

Ursula sighed and began pacing and talking.

I listened and tried to make sense of everything.

"I was stupid enough to have a one-night stand with him early last year," Ursula blurted out.

I groaned inside.

"It was an office party at P.A.F.I. and the teachers were invited. I had split up with Vincent and was in a bad mood. I had too much to drink. I don't know how exactly, but I finished up with Fabre. I think he'd taken drugs because he was on a high and blabbed a lot about himself, Whyte and some sort of secret society."

I gave Ursula a glass of water.

"He talked about sex orgies and horrible stuff."

"What happened after?"

"Nothing. I just tried to get taken off his course, but he insisted with Whyte that I stay on as his teacher."

"I see."

"I don't think you do. Fabre is afraid. He doesn't know what he told me that night. He's scared shitless for his promotion. Keeping me as his teacher is a way of having a hold over me. He keeps putting pressure on me to sleep with him again."

"You don't have to put up with that."

"It's not that simple. I don't feel in control of the situation. I'm not like you. When I came back this evening, I felt sick, sick in my mind and in my body." She turned sad eyes towards me, "I did have some dark ideas, you know. I've sleeping pills and I thought about – I started taking some."

"Ursula," I put my arms around her to try to offer comfort.

Ursula began sobbing again, "He was really coming on to me. I left P.A.F.I. and came back here. I felt bad and dirty and that I didn't deserve to live. I wasn't thinking straight and didn't want to talk to anyone, not you, nobody. I heard voices like ghosts, like Eva telling me to go to the wood and I can't remember anything after that."

She took the hankies that I handed her, "It's a mess. Fabre has the power. He's already threatened to have me fired from the school, the only thing stopping him is not knowing how much he revealed to me the night we spent together."

I was incensed, "It's you who has the power. You don't have to take that from him, you must make an official complaint."

"I'm a nobody. I wouldn't stand a chance lodging a complaint against him. The school will have no problem getting rid of me."

"Don't underestimate them. If you explain to Judith or even Lena, I'm sure they'll stand by you."

"You must be joking, they're not the people who call the shots. P.A.F.I. is William Whyte's baby. If he loses that contract, he loses the school. There are at least half a dozen teachers fully occupied out there. There are classes practically every day of the year, not to mention all the intensive courses going on. The school has immersion programmes with several of P.A.F.I. executives. That's a lot of money and we've heard that Whyte is up to his neck in personal debt. I don't stand a chance. If Fabre becomes C.F.O., and the rumour is that his chances are getting better, then Whyte's going to be sucking up to him."

"You have to talk to someone, Ursula – a professional who can really help you. I can get a name from Mme Defoe. You know, if it comes down to it, it's easy to get a job in another school. But you won't need to, we'll make up some story for Judith."

Ursula shook her head, "Fabre has a wide network, he could spread rumours and make trouble for me even after. Anyway, when I leave Whyte's, whether I'm fired or I quit, that will be it. I'll be done with teaching. I'm no teacher, I'm not made for it."

"Then for your own sake and for others, report Fabre."

"I have to stand up to him, but reporting is not the way. I can't imagine what I was thinking when I slept with him."

"You were drunk and maybe even drugged. But it's really playing on your mind and what happened tonight is a warning signal. At least see a doctor, see someone, please say you will."

"I've seen shrinks before. It doesn't do any good, not for me. I know my problem, the what and the why. I know it, just as I know there are paranormal forces."

"So you are blaming it on ghosts."

"I'm not, but there's something pulling my energy in this room. The darkest thoughts get into my mind here. I'm reliving the life of Eva in different ways. There's no other explanation for why she should fill my head. I knew nothing about the history of this place or Eva's life when I first came here.

"But you don't know if any of that is true or if this Eva ever existed."

"Eva does exist. She must have gone to that wood many times in despair or to prostitute herself. Then you had the murder in this room. All those souls leave their karma stuff and I just happen to pick it all up."

"Look, Ursula, supposing I accept your supernatural hunches. You told me that you'd started to take the pills when you heard Eva's voice urging you to go to the wood. It sounds to me like she saved you by getting you away from here, away from all that medicine. This Eva is trying to communicate good vibes to you." While I didn't fully embrace Ursula's belief in ghosts, deep inside and from my own unexplained experiences, I knew that something about all of this could not be explained by science and rational thinking.

"Do you think so?"

"I do. Damn that phone – oh no, Michael," I'd forgotten totally about Michael.

Ursula made a 'no–no' sign; the message was clear, I had to say nothing to him about her.

I hated having to hide the truth from Michael. I hurried onto the corridor.

"I'm not staying on my own, Liz, I can't, please," Ursula called after me.

"Alright, alright, Ursula. I'm just going down to talk to Michael. I have to give him some sort of explanation. You won't be on your own tonight, I'll be right back."

Michael was leaning against the wall outside the door, "You could have just given me the new code."

"Michael –"

His face changed, "It's Ursula, isn't it?"

"Yes, I can't explain it all to you or go into details, she doesn't want me to. Trust me when I say that, this time, it's for a genuine reason and I'm worried for her. I can't leave her alone. Sorry – it's complicated, believe me."

He put his hands on my shoulders. I felt the strength of him, "This isn't a tactic because you don't want me to come up – you've had your wicked way with me and now you want to discard me?"

That hurt. "How can you say that? You can come up if you want and see for yourself. I'd really rather spend the night satisfying your desires and mine than playing nanny to Ursula."

His annoyance went as quickly as it had come. "Forgive me, I'm behaving like a child. I can see from your face that you've been through the mill tonight. If I go up, I won't gain a lover, but Ursula will have the benefit of two child-minders. I'm out of line here. On second thoughts, I'm not behaving like a child, but a jealous husband, and I have no right."

"Don't say that, Michael. I sort of like it that you are a bit jealous, I don't think anyone has been like that about me before. But honestly, you have no need to be jealous. If it were just one of Ursula's whims, we would be upstairs now and my door barred and locked against her. It's not the case."

He put his mouth on mine and kissed me possessively, taking his time over it, before letting me go reluctantly, "You have a lot of making up to do, don't forget it."

"I won't forget it, I'm looking forward to it."

Michael took a single red rose from the inside pocket of his jacket, "Happy Valentine's."

I took the rose and smelled it, "Oh, I'm so sorry, Michael, what a way for us to spend Valentine's evening."

He shrugged, "There will be others."

I held the rose, "I'll treasure this."

Michael smiled, "Ring me if you can't sleep."

We kissed again, parting with regret.

I felt guilty sending him away.

M. Jacques was standing on the landing upon my return upstairs.

I nodded and tried to move on.

He stooped towards me, "So she's back."

I realised that Ursula's movements were practically posted up on the wall for everyone to see, but I wasn't sharing with M. Jacques anything about what really happened tonight.

"Ursula was never gone, just a minor misunderstanding. Oh hello, M. Brosse, you here too?"

I made myself as tall as possible and smiled as if I hadn't a care in the world, "See you maybe tomorrow, M. Jacques. Goodnight, M. Brosse."

I returned to find Ursula in my room, sound asleep on top of my bed with Elle snuggled in beside her. I pulled a blanket over both of them and switched off the light. I retreated to Ursula's room and lay on her bed. I was so tired, I didn't care if a thousand ghosts like Eva visited me. But I found it difficult to sleep after the evening's drama. I thought how little I knew Ursula. I really didn't know her at all. She walked around as if her life were an open book, but when we tried to read it, some important chapters were missing. Ursula's true story was well and truly hidden.

11

Dragging myself out of Ursula's bed the morning after her crisis, I found it hard to shake off the awful feeling of how she might have taken her own life. I had little appetite for work, but fortunately it was Saturday and office duty was less stressful and demanding than teaching.

However, as the morning progressed, the tiredness got to me. Thinking about Fabre and Ursula's muddled explanations made me anxious and mad. By midday, I was so nervous that it made me cross and snappy. When Lena dropped by at half past twelve with a panting Hamilton, I practically barked at them. Since Lena had offloaded Saturdays on me, she seemed to take pleasure in dropping by between midday and one. It was probably to remind herself of how fortunate she was to have escaped the Saturday morning shift. Lena recognised bad humour like nobody else.

"You getting on fine, Honey?"

"Just dandy."

"I'll be hopping along then, sure looks like everything is under control."

"Sure does."

I did my best to shoo everybody out the door by five past one. It was an ordeal getting people into the classroom on time, but it was even more difficult getting some of them out.

Michael took my bunch of keys, "You look spent. Let me do a last check of the windows and cupboards."

"Thanks, and see that the photocopiers are off and that the coffee jar is there."

He did a quick inspection and came back dangling my keys, "You're falling asleep on your feet. Go straight home."

"I will. I intend to crawl under the covers and I'm not coming out until Monday morning."

"Can I join you?"

"If you're real nice, I can probably make room for you."

I read Ursula's note, 'Gone shopping'. That was a relief. The pleasant surprise was that, for once, she'd been thoughtful and had changed the sheets on the bed.

Michael filled my room like a giant, "So, are you going to tell me what's up with Ursula?"

I didn't want to lie to him. "Look, I gave Ursula my word, but what I can tell you is that things got a little complicated with Fabre. He's a slime bag. Don't open up the subject more than that. What are you smiling about?"

"It's really endearing how you stand up for people and defend them. There you are, all riled up about Ursula – I like that about you."

"Ursula drives me around the twist at times, she's the most frustrating girl alive. But it's true, she's gotten under my skin. I don't know why she needs so much attention. She's a beautiful girl, very intelligent and yet so hopeless at making herself happy. I suppose I want to help her. It must be my vocation in life."

"You mean helping the Ursulas of the world?"

"I don't know if I'm helping them or if they're helping me. But even as a child, my best friend in school had Ursula's gift of getting into trouble. I thought it my mission to get her out of it. My mother used to say, 'There goes Liz again, she's just taken another bird with a broken wing into her clutch'."

Michael drew me into his arms, "And you think you can fix Ursula's wings?"

"No, I can fix nothing, but I can't ignore her pain."

He brushed back my hair, framed my face in his hands, "And how do you see me, another bird with a broken wing? Do you feel sorry for me?"

"I –" there was a trap, wide open in front of me, "it's different, I find you attractive and you are talented. You can be a little complicated. I think about you, I like thinking about you. You aren't so different to me in wanting to help people, those homeless –"

He traced his finger along my lips, "You think about me a lot, do you?"

"I said, I think about you – that's normal."

"Normal?"

"Of course, we're sleeping together."

"When Ursula doesn't get in the way."

"Or your magic – or our separate rooms."

"We could change that, move in together, get a bigger place."

"We could –" just like that, he'd snared me. But I felt it was too soon to think about moving in together. I'd done the impulsive before and didn't want to be rushed into such a commitment this time. I was just beginning to get into my stride in Paris, gaining confidence and getting to like teaching. Living on my own wasn't too bad. I was actually enjoying myself. Why change it?

"Now what are you thinking about – talk about me being complicated, Liz? But that's okay. I'm partial to that too."

"I'm just like any other girl."

"You're not like any other girl, Liz, not to me," his lips moved down to my neck setting off my senses.

"Do you know what, Michael?"

"What?"

"I think we should spend less time talking and more time doing."

"I'm all for that." His expert fingers had already undone buttons, zips and clasps and just as quickly removed every layer of clothing.

I was still undoing his as we fell on the mattress together.

It was funny how the bed had seemed too small for one, but was just right for two, two people moulded together as one, not caring what creaked or rocked, just seeking satisfaction.

I heard some doors on the corridor, probably the students, Olivier and Sebastien – their steps pounded on the stairs. Another door banged, must be Mme Gomes's son – more steps hit the stairs. Soon I heard nothing except my murmurs, Michael's whispers and both our sighs – and the rest was pure feeling and sensation.

We must have slept for a while. When I awoke, Michael was still holding me. I could tell from his breathing that he was awake.

He yawned and that set me off also.

"What about those homeless people of yours, do you often give them money?" I asked.

"No, not every time, sometimes I give them English classes of a sort. One is a prostitute and not really homeless in the way you imagine."

"What do you – what is she –"

"He – his name is Guy and he wants to learn English."

"For the job?"

"Yes and no. I think he doesn't know himself. Guy has this idea that life would be better in London – picking up some English is a way of hanging on to that dream."

"How did you meet him – same way as the others?"

"More or less, he just turned up at one of my street performances like a stray dog. I'm lucky, rich parents and all that. I've got a safety net. Some would say that's why I'm playing the role of living the poor boy's life. Ursula told me that one day. She's right, but that doesn't stop me from feeling something of others' suffering. I can't live my life and not see how hard it is for some people. Guy is only eighteen and I don't think I can change his situation very much, if at all. I just give him a few books and talk to him. But in the long term, I can do nothing. I certainly can't promise anything."

"You are trying, it's better than nothing. Your parents would be proud of you."

"My parents would nag me to put my time into something more useful."

"Nagging is a form of loving."

"Oh, Liz, I'm sorry, going on about my parents. You must miss yours dreadfully, especially your mum."

"Yes I do. You know, I miss Mum most when I'm happy. There's nobody like family to share your joy."

He kissed my hand, "Friends can help."

I smiled, "Some are helping an awful lot. Tell me more about how you first got interested in magic."

So he did, recounting it like a fairytale, the enchantment of a young boy and the dream of bright lights.

I encouraged Michael to talk. In moments like this, just lying together, I would let his voice ripple over me, close my eyes and wish it could always be so.

****

In the end, Ursula didn't have to give too many explanations to the school management and her wish to be removed from teaching Fabre was accepted. I was surprised but glad that Judith and Lena left Ursula so easily off the hook. They read a lot into the words 'personality clash'. Lena gave me the gist of how the news was being taken from the office side. One of the advantages of working on Saturdays was that it handed me a certificate of approval in Lena's eyes. That also meant that I was privy to insider information. I wouldn't get rich from it, but it was useful from time to time.

"Ursula is under strain and Judith is no monster and we ain't dumb in here either," Lena puffed out smoke and words.

"That's good, but I've heard Judith giving out to teachers so often I was expecting the worst."

"Na, she handled it very smoothly with William. When Judith likes someone, that's it, they can get away with a lot of things – and she likes Ursula."

"Ursula kinda grows on you."

"Sure does. Now was there something else you wanted to add to the tale?"

I laughed, "You're a crafty devil, Lena. No, I have nothing else to add."

"At least you didn't say, 'a crafty old devil'. So?"

"So what?"

"Are you going to tell me what's going on out there in P.A.F.I.?"

I did a French shrug. It sometimes came in useful, all that 'don't ask me' body language.

"You know, Lena, personality clashes do happen."

Lena looked at me dubiously, "Sure."

"So who's going to teach Fabre?"

"Jeffrey, I think."

Huh, it wasn't the first time I'd heard that name.

"Where did this Jeffrey come from? I mean, a short time ago he didn't exist in the school and now his name pops up all over the place, like he's some sort of hero and the best thing since Marie Curie."

"Get over it, Honey. That's how you came along, how practically everyone in Whyte's came. I told you, they come and they go. What Judith expects is that they do the job and the client is happy."

"The client is often not happy."

"I'll say. But I'm sure you've noticed that we have every sort of teacher, from all walks of life. How many do you think work here?"

"I don't know, around thirty."

"At least double, but just a handful of true teachers."

"Double, where do they all hide out?"

"Every darned place you can imagine; but in a few months, some will have moved on and many of the names and faces will have changed."

"It must be very difficult to build a team – where does the job satisfaction come in to all of it?"

"You ask, you seem pretty satisfied."

"Yes, but as a teacher, I have quality contact with the client."

"Saturdays ain't hurting you."

"Okay, there is some pleasure in being at the office side. But I'm not hiring and firing all the time. I don't have to worry about scattering my human resources over city and suburbs."

"It's true that it ain't fun when you have to put out fires, always papering over the cracks. But hey, some people like doing that. Satisfaction is what you make of it."

"That's true too. By the way, Lena, I noticed we're low in photocopying paper."

Lena raised her arms, "Where the heck is all the paper disappearing to, I only re-ordered a new batch the other day?"

I made a cross-eyed expression, but didn't answer.

"Oh by the way," Lena added, "there was a special delivery for William, but the courier didn't heed my instructions and dropped it in the middle of the corridor. It's a large box and very heavy – could you help me push it to the side out of harm's way until William comes to pick it up."

"Sure."

It was a very large box that I guessed was full of brochures or something. The school might be low on funds, but that didn't seem to curtail the boss's expensive deliveries. There could be no doubt but that William Whyte was running his secret society and what not with school money. I glared at the door of 'St. Alban's'. The answer was in there somewhere. In my view, Whyte was the main handicap of the school. He and his activities were bankrupting the place. Like a dog with a bone, I'd made several trips down the back steps from 'St. Alban's', each time getting no farther than the locked door.

Loose ends bothered me and that wasn't the only one. There were many of them with Ursula. She wouldn't have to teach Fabre again, but she could expose him and he knew that. There was no doubt but that Ursula could seriously damage if not ruin his promotion chances in P.A.F.I.

****

"Buck up, we'll be late and I don't want to be rude and stick out like a sore thumb." I pointed to my clock radio and coaxed a sluggish Ursula.

"It's such a waste of a Sunday morning," moaned Ursula. "I know I agreed yesterday, but I'm just not an early morning person."

"That's not news to me, but eleven o'clock mass is hardly early morning. Remember, I promised you a free lunch after."

"So you said."

"And mass might help you on the spiritual side of things."

Ursula puckered her lips in front of my mirror and tied back her thick, wavy hair, "Purifying my soul is the only thing that convinced me. It can help the spirit of Eva and all the others."

I was afraid to inquire more about the 'others'.

I had stupidly managed to lose my passport and needed to replace it. It was ridiculous, but Irish citizens did still need the signature of a pillar of society to confirm their identity for a passport photograph. I'd rung the Irish College Chaplain, Fr. Sheehan. The minimum trade-off was a Sunday mass followed by tea and biscuits for his stamp and initials on the back of my photo.

I was beginning to warm to the idea of going to mass in the Irish College chapel. Going to mass reminded me of home and I welcomed an Irishness other than Ursula's brand sometimes. I'd grown to love this part of the Latin Quarter – Rue Sufflot sweeping down from Montagne Sainte-Geneviéve and the Pantheon to the Luxembourg gardens and the lavish Palais du Luxembourg housing the Sénat. I relished the pleasure of breaking into the sights, sounds and smells of food and market hustle on the popular Rue Moufftard. But I also treasured the calm of Rue des Irlandais and the serenity of the College grounds and chapel. On the last Sunday of a cold but bright February morning, the faintest hint of spring was in the air.

We were ten minutes late. I slid into the first seat I could find and tried to be as inconspicuous as possible. That wasn't easy to achieve when Ursula walked boldly up the central aisle before picking a seat closer to the altar, obliging me to follow her.

She responded to my frown with a throwaway remark, "God never asked us to hide ourselves."

I don't know how she managed it, but before tea was over, Ursula had triggered a search for old maps and plans of the College, and she'd captured the interest of a young Irish seminarian, David Brennan. He was in Paris for the year mainly for research reasons and was working on a doctoral thesis relating to the Irish College. His thesis was under the shared supervision of a Sorbonne professor and a professor in Maynooth University, Kildare, Ireland.

"Ursula," I warned, when I got her by herself for a moment, "be careful, that boy is dedicated to becoming a priest —"

"I know what I'm doing, Liz – you came for your passport, I came for my soul."

It didn't come as a surprise to me that Ursula wouldn't last long without male support, just in case. She was the sort of person who needed to have someone running and racing for her. Ursula had no problem putting into action what most women understood: there was nothing more satisfying for a man's ego than having someone take an interest in his work and in what he did. She had it down to a fine art. I doubted if David would ever get to take his vows. Poor guy, and he seemed genuinely nice.

Ursula was a ray of sunshine all through lunch. That was something at least. When she smiled, she went from pretty to stunning. A happy Ursula made for a very happy life for all on the seventh floor. Rue Moufftard was a messy confusion and full of commotion: traders were taking down street stands after the open-air morning market, street cleaners were sweeping up the leftovers and hosing down the streets – and cafés and bistros were a flurry. We had elected to have lunch in Le Vieux Bistro, attracted by its wooden façade and calm interior. Moreover, a 12-Euro set menu for good traditional French food was a deal breaker. Ursula and I, like others, were still trying to work out if we were better or worse off under the Euro. Many people suspected that lots of businesses were hiking their prices to take advantage of people's confusion between the new and the old money. 1 Euro was the equivalent of 6.5 French Francs, so items seemed cheaper because we were paying fewer Euros. But in reality, the cost of bread and many other staples had risen. A few cents more didn't seem significant, but when one lived on a low salary, it mattered. The Euro notes were colourful and reminded me of Monopoly money. There were greys, reds, blues, browns, greens, yellows and pinks covering the range from 5 Euro to 500 Euro banknotes. But eking out an existence from day to day wasn't a game and made me pay very close attention to spending, right down to the copper-covered steel of 1 Cent or Centime, as we still called it in France. The little coins were so light that some people nicknamed them buttons.

I studied the limited selection on the fixed menu and went for the mixed salad, Coc au Vin and Crême Brûlée.

When dessert arrived, I gently cracked the hard caramel topping, took one spoonful of the tepid vanilla custard base and laid down my spoon. I was full – the Coc au Vin, chicken braised in red wine with lardons and mushrooms, had more than satisfied my appetite.

Ursula eyed my Crême Brûlée. She had made short work of her own Alsatian bacon and onion pie, known as Tarte Flambée, and her Chocolate Mousse had disappeared in minutes.

"Go ahead, it's yours, I can't eat another thing," I pushed the dish in her direction.

She savoured it, "Something is bothering you, Liz. It isn't good, you've lost weight. You're supposed to be in love and blooming."

In love? I hadn't allowed myself to analyse my feelings in that way. In a short time, I'd gotten used to Michael, couldn't imagine being without him. But I'd been in love before, or thought I had. Ursula was right, something was bothering me. I was of course fixated on William Whyte and the idea that the school was in financial trouble. I might be soon looking for a new job and I wasn't ready to change again, not just yet. But I couldn't explain to Ursula that she was one of my biggest worries. I didn't want to upset her by telling her that. However, I knew that since her adventure in the woods, I'd been monitoring her fragile emotions for any sudden changes.

"Ursula, I didn't want to stymie your style at the Irish College, but the next time you get into conversation with David, ask him about M. Jacques. I'd love to know if they really let him store his things in the College cellars and if there actually is a tunnel underground that goes all the way to our school." I decided to be practical about the friendship Ursula was striking up.

Ursula was concentrated on getting the waiter's attention, "Monsieur, un peut avoir une deuxième carafe d'eau si vous plait?"

The waiter was delighted to bring more water. Ursula had him dancing attendance to her needs.

"I'm not going to waste time asking David stuff like that. M. Jacques told me and I believe him. David's historical knowledge is much more fascinating. He's access to lots of old documents. Do you know that he has a chapter in his thesis dedicated to brothels?"

"No, how exactly is he working that in?"

Ursula released her hair from the red band that was holding it together and swept it back, "Well, he's analysing the historical relationship between the brothel and the Church, and in particular the uneasy relations between the Irish College and one or two brothels in this district."

"You don't say – when finished, that should make for fascinating reading."

"Yes, I mean, there are all sorts of historical leads he could take. I feel he should zoom in on the life stories of individuals. There must have been many women like Eva, knocking at the College door for help, perhaps working for them, as well as for the brothels and some of the hotels around here. It's a shame he isn't inclined to follow that line. In my opinion, he just isn't going deeply enough into those aspects. He's taking a factual, chronological approach, instead of having an insider point of view. On top, he plans only one chapter on the theme. What a disappointment," she yawned, "fortunately, I caught up with him in time and might get him to change his mind."

"Ursula, it's his thesis, not yours."

"I know, but I'm just trying to help," she gave a saintly smile.

We walked off lunch, strolling as far as La Conciergerie on the Seine. The long building with pointy towers set back from the banks of the river always struck me as ominous. Its sombre Gothic style combining religious and secular architecture of high and late Medieval times was highlighted by the dark waters flowing by. It was one of the first buildings I visited when I came to Paris and the only place where I'd taken an official guided tour. Its towers reminded me of the castle in the German fairytale where Rapunzel was imprisoned by the wicked witch. The guide told us that its origins went back to the 10th century when it was the seat of the Medieval Kings of France and the royal palace. Today, it was used as Palais de Justice for law courts as well as housing a museum. It still had the Great Hall of Soldiers, once a banquet hall and now used for hosting events, as well as the Sainte-Chapelle, a place of worship and a venue for special concerts. The most impressive part of the building for me was the former prison whose origins went back to the 14th century. This was where Marie Antoinette and other nobles were imprisoned during the 1798 Revolution before being taken to the guillotine. I learned about the different categories of prisoners: the wealthier paid for rooms with writing tables and places to exercise. The very poor were dumped in vermin-infested cells, and the wretched were thrown in the dungeons to be forgotten and eaten by rats. The surviving three towers had different functions in Medieval times. The Caesar Tower was named in honour of the Roman Emperors. The Silver Tower was named for its alleged use as a store for royal treasure. The third was called Bonbec, good beak, and was used for torture; here, prisoners were encouraged to sing while being tortured. How I loved history and how I loved revisiting those details, however ghoulish, every time I walked by.

The squawking over our heads distracted us. We watched the acrobats of the sky in their motionless, graceful float. Others seemed to be nesting on the roof of the Conciergerie. The high decibel cry was distinctive – Iyo-Iyo-Iyo – GA GA GA GA GA –

"Those seagulls make me sad," said Ursula, "when I hear them, I feel like crying."

"It is a poignant call," I agreed. "They always remind me of home. I like to think that my mother sent them to protect me. But that can't be, I'm just superstitious."

"If you believe it, that's all that counts. I've heard that those birds live for many years, more than twenty, some even up to forty. They know about equality and both the male and female share the tasks of feeding the fledglings."

"Interesting," I said, "but I still wonder why they roost so far inland."

"I looked into it." Ursula elaborated, "there are different sorts. There's a black-headed gull that over-winters in Paris before heading home to eastern Europe in March. But those we see on the Conciergerie with the white head and body, grey wings and yellow beaks are called herring gulls and stay in Paris the year round; they reside and nest in the city. They aren't really seagulls anymore and have become Parisian birds."

I watched a gull swoop off and thought, 'We have a lot to learn from them. With our wings of clay trapped by our own fears, we cannot fly. But we can dream and in our flights of fancy, we can take to the sky and lighten our hearts'.

12

J udith's face appeared thundery, "William wants to see you, Liz."

"Judith, do I have to? I don't want to speak to him, I've nothing to say to him."

She picked up the phone, plastered a smile on her face, and that was it. It annoyed me that Whyte always caught me just when I had a few minutes to myself.

I knocked, waited for his "Yes" and entered the dimly lit office. He sat behind the desk in his three-piece suit. I wouldn't have been surprised to have seen moths flying out. I glanced at the bookcase and saw that some shelves were no longer empty. They were stacked with several packages.

"I've been looking over this," he held my latest report on M. Chevalier in his hands. He focused on one line: 'Progress is slow'.

Surely that wasn't why I had been summoned? He must be in a pretty sorry state if he was drilling for bits of information like that.

"Slow but sure," I said.

"M. Chevalier is planning an internal audit in some departments of P.A.F.I, I hear." I thought his voice sounded panicky.

"Yes, he mentioned it." He was, after all, Internal Audit Manager, that's what auditors did.

"In which departments?"

"In Legal and Insurance," I felt very uncomfortable.

William Whyte's face relaxed. He returned to my report.

I had heard that M. Chevalier's audits were feared. His reputation was that of a rigorous manager and strict task master. M. Fabre was by far more popular among staff, seen to be friendly and genial. It just goes to show, I thought, never take people at face value.

William Whyte swelled himself up with importance, "M. Chevalier must progress more. The standard of English required for C.F.O. is very high. The successful candidate will need to meet the Press and do some interviews in English. He will have international events to host."

"That's true. But the classes have helped as I'm sure they have helped M. Fabre. M. Chevalier has improved on many points."

"You write here that he is – introverted and not a communicator – " he put his finger on some line of the report.

"I didn't say that, I just said that he needed to come out of himself a little."

William Whyte's acid eyes burnt into me, "It's written here."

Had I said all that? I'd hinted at some of it. It had been at the beginning when our classes had been heavy going. "Those were first impressions. He's much better today."

"We shall see," he closed my report and stapled the pages.

I noticed again a shake in his hand.

"You just wanted to see me for that or was there something else, Mr. Whyte?" I was dismayed that my report seemed to give away so much information on the personality of M. Chevalier. Those were my views and by consequence subjective. I vowed, in future, to stick strictly to more boring, pedagogical information.

He put the file in his briefcase, "There is one more thing – Jeffrey will be going to P.A.F.I. in the coming weeks to test M. Chevalier's English level. It's routine for an important client such as he is. We must have an objective view on his real level. Judith's rather busy and Jeffrey has the necessary skills for that. I would undertake to do it myself, but the student knows me and it is not my defined role here."

"That's not usual practice," I wasn't going to take that lying down.

"There will be no argument. You lack the experience and the background to teach a student with a profile like that. While he might be making some progress and I thank you for your contribution, I need a second opinion. Furthermore, it makes for a good impression," he closed his case with satisfaction.

"M. Chevalier is the person best placed to have an opinion about his own progress and about my teaching. He's told me himself that he's very happy with our classes."

"This discussion is finished. What we need is a regular update on your timetable to allow Jeffrey to plan a visit to one of your classes with M. Chevalier. Jeffrey will firstly observe you teaching the student. He will then take the relay for an hour or so to allow for a comprehensive assessment. Jeffrey has well-prepared role plays around financial case studies."

No shit, I thought – wasn't Jeffrey wonderful. I preferred not to say anything else. Silence was the best answer to this situation. It wasn't right – none of the others had that type of treatment. It wasn't necessary and was completely stupid.

Still, I couldn't resist asking my next question, "Who will test M. Fabre?"

"That's not your concern," he shuffled some papers again, his signal for me to leave, "just keep your reports coming in on time."

I couldn't refuse to give basic reports. If Whyte and Fabre were friends, it was very likely that every useful piece of information about M. Chevalier was being passed on. I'd already chosen my preferred candidate. Whatever the consequences for the school, I didn't want Fabre to reach the top spot.

****

As March advanced, the stretch in the evening was evident in the light coming through the windows of the meeting room at P.A.F.I. I noticed that recently I was often given one of the nicer meeting rooms and it pleased me. I guessed it had something to do with M. Chevalier.

He came in the door carrying an open laptop which he held towards me.

"What do you want me to see?" I asked. "Oh, isn't that nice, you've put photos of your children up on the screen."

"You like to see more?" M.Chevalier asked.

"Yes, I'd love to."

"I have these from a trip to Dublin. You are from there and I thought you would like them."

I looked at his children photographed on the streets of Dublin. I didn't have the heart to tell him that my only trip to the grand capital had been to Dublin Zoo when I was around ten years old. I concentrated and tried to give the pictures a respectful amount of attention.

"What did you think of Dublin yourself, M. Chevalier?"

"It's nice, the people are sympathetic, I drank a Guinness."

"Did you like it?"

"It is different," he was too polite to say otherwise.

I decided to shift gears in the class. "M. Chevalier, we're going to have to begin practising for the real interview situations. You'll have to field all sorts of questions."

"I know, I know, my strong and weak points."

"For instance, tell me about your previous work experience."

He read out two very well prepared paragraphs.

"You're not going to read that in the actual interview, are you?"

"No, I will learn it and use it if I need it."

"I see."

I tried a new question, "Are you a team player?"

"A company's most valuable assets are invariably team players. They work for the common good and look for solutions instead of people to blame –"

"Really?"

"Yes."

"Do you consider yourself a natural leader?"

"Leadership requires, first of all, charisma and vision; then it is a lifetime learning process. But the essential qualities should include a commitment to excellence – a leader should be strong and equipped with good people intelligence – "

"I think the word is 'emotional' intelligence."

"I took it from a book."

"That's exactly the problem. M. Chevalier, can I say something here?"

"If you want."

I put down my paper, "Your answers are too sterile."

"What?"

"You're not natural."

"What do you mean?"

"The picture is too artificial. It gives a very bad impression of your personality."

"It is not possible, I know about team spirit and leadership."

"I'm sure you do, but put it in your own words. It's better to make some grammar mistakes than to do what you're trying and not succeeding to do."

He made no reply.

"Look, you have just taken readymade expressions. You know you can't just learn expressions off and regurgitate them. Nobody is going to believe you."

He frowned.

"I understand that you have to use some quotations and expressions, but you must be careful not to overdo it."

I took a marker and stood up, nothing like taking the teaching floor to drive home a point. I turned over to a fresh page on the flipchart.

"Instead of saying things as you just did, put your ideas into everyday words: 'From my experience' – or 'I encourage team spirit by' – 'I've had to use leadership skills in'."

I scribbled several ideas to highlight my point. "Try to deal with the human points like that. Give examples from your job. If you continue to copy–paste sentences, you'll fail the interview from the word go. Do you understand what I mean?"

"Perhaps."

I didn't like the sound of that tight reply. I was treating him like a child. I tried to rebalance the scales, "You have lots of qualities of course – quick analytical mind and such."

He had wound down to silence and it seemed he really had taken my earlier comments badly.

"I presume you have ideas on the whole company strategy, from a financial point of view, budget control and things like that?"

I waited, but he uttered nothing.

"I mean, you really are the expert in that domain, I'd be completely lost myself."

More silence.

I put the top back on the marker. "M. Chevalier, are you okay, is there a problem?"

Still nothing, except a glower.

"Are you sulking?"

"I do not understand."

"Sulk means 'boude'."

He looked at his watch and got to his feet, "I have an important phone call to make. Sorry, if you will excuse me," he walked out.

That was one way of dealing with it. I couldn't decide if his leaving had been rude or not. What I did know was that I'd made 'a right balls' of that class and while it was too easy to walk out as he'd done, I probably deserved some of his reaction.

"Good afternoon."

I turned. The man standing there was so thin and pale, he'd fade into the background if he weren't in the middle of the doorway.

"Good afternoon," he repeated. "You must be Miss Downey – I'm Jeffrey Peterson, I teach M. Fabre," he held out his hand.

Well, if he were an English teacher, he should know that teachers didn't usually shake hands with each other. I recognised him as he'd passed me out often enough coming and going from the school but had never felt the necessity to formally introduce himself.

"Hello," I said, and subjected myself to the handshake.

He looked back towards the corridor, "Is that the chap I'll be testing?"

"Yes, that's M. Chevalier, a brilliant manager," I was surprised at how protective I suddenly felt. I tried to study Jeffrey: mid-forties, shabby and a bit odd looking, but that wasn't uncharacteristic in the business I was in.

"M. Fabre has many qualities of his own," he said like a challenge.

"Good luck to him too. They'll both probably get outdone by an outsider anyway," I zipped up the front pocket of my bag.

Jeffrey put a hand to his thinning hair, "I don't think so – talk of an outside competitor is just a rumour put out by management. They have to pretend the position is open, but everybody knows they would rather give it to an insider. Oh by the way, I'll be expecting to get a list of your class times with M. Chevalier?"

"Sure. No point in doing it this week. I'll leave next week's times in for you at the school. M. Chevalier hasn't confirmed all the classes yet. So Jeffrey, where did you work before W.W.S.O.E. & F. L.?"

"Oh, I freelanced a lot. I've worked all over, had my own consultancy service."

"Is that so, but who were your clients?"

"You wouldn't know them, mostly financial companies. I was in Japan,

Spain, Germany —"

"You must speak a lot of languages then," I feigned admiration.

He made a sound in his throat, "Naturally, one picks up a lot of things."

Just as I'd thought, he was lying through his teeth.

"What do you work on with M. Fabre?"

"We do serious work, macroeconomics, negotiation and hard-nosed bargaining." He lowered his voice, "Between you and me, I don't think his last teacher was very good, just a flirt."

I was enraged. Even if I'd thought and called Ursula that myself many times, I wasn't going to let this pale-faced glop, with a comb-over across his egg head, degrade her character.

"Who told you that?"

"Come on, you only have to see her once to read between the lines."

"Is that right? You know what, I think you need glasses," I made it to the door in two strides.

He appeared affronted, "Why are you being so aggressive?"

"Work it out. Ursula's my friend, I don't stand by and listen to anyone spread false stories," I walked off.

That was not very clever, showing my colours and making enemies, I thought. The corridor lit up automatically as I moved along, passing open plan, more open plan, and a few individual offices reserved for the privileged.

M. Chevalier's office door was open. The soft glow of a table lamp contrasted with the whiter glare of the computer screen on his impassive face. I regretted my earlier words. He'd worked on those expressions for his interview, collaged his efforts from books and dictionaries, and I'd rejected all his hard work. I paused at his door. I was about to put my bags down, then changed my mind. I'd done enough damage.

He swivelled around in his chair; "Oui? Est qu'il y a quelque chose? Vous avez un problème avec le planning?"

His use of the 'Vous' clearly set the distance. The roles were reversed — this was his office and speaking French was his way of making a statement. I couldn't really see his eyes in the low light. I constructed my answer carefully in French: "No, M. Chevalier. There isn't a problem with the schedule. You just have to confirm next week's class times. There's no hurry, you can ring the school tomorrow."

"Mon assistante le fera."

It was difficult, but I had to do it. I continued in French, "I wanted to say also that I'm sorry for pushing you so hard in class. I can be a little too direct sometimes." Tiredness was making my accent stronger.

I saw amusement cross his face. He inclined his head, indicating that he'd heard me, then switched to English, the ultimate put-down, "That's all right, see you on Thursday."

He turned back to the screen.

I bent to pick up my heavy bag. My head started spinning and I focused hard trying not to show that I didn't feel well. I hadn't eaten since six in the morning, hence the dizzy attack – but I wasn't going to fall down in front of him. It would take very little to start crying now. On top, it was definitely the wrong time of the month. I knew the weepy feeling. I had to get out fast, "Goodbye then."

I took a few shaky steps.

He turned. I saw surprise on his face and he bolted out of his chair, "Are you okay, can I get you a glass of water?"

"I'm fine."

"No, you are not, sit here."

"I'm perfectly okay, I just need to eat, that's all."

"To eat! You do not eat today?" He sounded quite angry.

"I did," I wasn't admitting that it was two squares of chocolate.

"How many classes do you do for your school?" He was beginning to look fierce.

"I do the same as the other teachers. Honestly, I'm fine, M. Chevalier. I'll go home now."

"I will drive you."

"No thank you." I picked up my bags and held onto them like armour, "Good evening."

I didn't give him a chance to react and quickened my steps to get as far away as possible. I was going to have to be more guarded with weak moments like these.

I went directly to Au Petit Théâtre du Bonheur in Montmartre where Michael was performing. I was so happy to see him and wanted to jump into his arms and hug him, but had to restrain myself while he was on the little café theatre stage. He just had fifteen minutes between two musical acts to perform his magic, but the capacity crowd of twenty people applauded warmly. I could see that his performance had improved a lot – it was more polished. I sat back and shed the problems of the day.

After his act, Michael sought me out immediately with the good news that he had been asked by a troupe to perform during the interval at Théâtre des Abbesses for one month solid. That theatre had a capacity of 420 people, so it was a step in the right direction for his career. Next step – his own show. I let go of my worries and we celebrated with a good, cheap Chow Mein in the Chinese Quarter of Bellville.

We giggled all the ways up the stairs. I didn't care if Mme Gomes was peeping out, if M. Brosse's head had fallen off from bobbing, or if M. Jacques was up and down the corridor like a restless hound. I did check on Ursula. She wasn't at home, but had left a note under my door saying she'd a rendezvous. I presumed she was exploring the library vault of the Irish College with David. Elle was not visible and I hoped was sound asleep in Ursula's room.

We were like giddy children as we attempted to have a bath. There wasn't enough hot water in the immersion tank so we filled the tub with kettle after kettle of heated water. Michael made light of my embarrassment and the impossibility of two people trying to stand together in an orange plastic tub. We didn't even bother to dry ourselves properly, before falling on my narrow bed. That was when I knew I was in deep. Until then, nobody had made me feel so wanted or needed. Nobody had made me really feel like a woman.

We lay in a tangled knot, Michael spoke somewhere into my hair, "We're going to have to move in together."

"Isn't this fun, we are living like we were still students."

If he'd noticed that I'd dodged his statement, he didn't show it. "I don't see why we can't be students forever. Why does growing up mean that we become all serious and wear pin-striped suits?" he grumbled.

"I'm not sure it does, but life does move on and we can't stand still. We get older and want different things. I don't think a few years from now I'd be happy to climb those stairs and say, 'Yippee, my beautiful room'. If you want to do something with your magic, you will have to set yourself standards, raise the bar, become professional – and that means changing."

"YES, MAM."

"I am sorry, I'm doing it again, telling you how to live your life."

We faced each other in the bed and then just laughed.

"It doesn't stop us living out the last of our student days for a while longer," Michael closed in on me.

****

I feared that my next class with M. Chevalier was going to be a strained affair. I discussed my worries with Ursula over a few cans of Guinness that we shared to mark Saint Patrick's Day, March 17th. We bemoaned the fact that Ireland's national holiday barely got a mention in France. It was a Wednesday and we were both so tired that we didn't even feel like going out. Ursula advised me that the best course of action during my next class with M. Chevalier would be to take a step back, work on the technical points of the language and stay well away from commenting on his approach. She suggested I shouldn't try to teach him how to be a good interviewee. I agreed with her – from now on, he could go to the HR for that sort of advice or he could pay a consultant.

M. Chevalier strode in and put a package on the table, "Here –"

I looked at it.

"For you," he said.

"For me?" I wasn't sure I should accept this.

"It is not dangerous."

I laughed in spite of myself – so he could make a joke.

"Well, thanks," I said, "it's not called for – why?"

"Why? I was at the airport, I thought at you – "

"Of –"

"All right, I thought of you."

"Thanks for the gift," I went back to the lesson.

He was disappointed, "You may open it."

"Okay." There was no point in telling him that I already knew it was a box of chocolates.

It was a box of – not chocolates, but marzipan sweets. They were from Aix-en-Provence.

He was pleased with himself, "It is a speciality of the region."

Everything in France was a speciality of one region or another. In fact, France was full of specialities. There were so many that I wondered if the word generalisation existed.

"Thank you very much, but you shouldn't have." I then spoilt the atmosphere by informing him about Jeffrey and the forthcoming English test which should be scheduled before the end of March. He wasn't pleased.

"It was decided by Mr. Whyte," I explained, "if you don't want to be tested like that, you must speak directly to him." I was relinquishing all responsibility. "Personally, I know your English level and you are best able to measure your own progress. But it might be a good idea to have an outsider's opinion."

"We will see."

13

I paced the coffee space at P.A.F.I. I didn't need another shot of caffeine, but I got one anyway. It was just after seven in the evening and Jeffrey and M. Chevalier had been in the room almost an hour.

I wasn't surprised when Jeffrey walked into our class in his badly cut suit, sporting a superior look. I knew this was the inspector's visit. It was the last week of March and Mr. Whyte had warned me that Jeffrey's visit would take place before the end of the month. I'd immediately guided M. Chevalier through predictable exercises to highlight his progress, before turning him over to Jeffrey.

"Bonjour, Madame." A blond woman approached the coffee machine. She was maybe thirty-one or -two, stylish and very attractive.

"Bonjour, Mme Michot," I shook her outstretched hand.

"You are from the same school as Michael, aren't you?" the HR's smile was very tense – she looked at her watch and tapped the machine nervously while waiting for her cup to fill.

"That's right, I'm here for M. Chevalier."

"Oh yes, of course. Is he making progress?" she continued to tap the machine.

"I believe so."

"Good, good," she checked the time again, took her coffee, then nodded to me and exited the space.

What a harried lady, I thought. I'd gathered from Michael that, as HR Manager, Mme Michot was under enormous pressure with a very heavy workload. The fact that she was still at work after seven in the evening was proof of that. She seemed too young for the responsibility. But apparently, she was the shining example of a top potential in the company. That category of employee got fast-tracked up the career ladder.

I decided it was time to rejoin M. Chevalier and Jeffrey in the meeting room.

I listened for a moment outside the door, before knocking and entering. "Testing finished?"

"Yes," Jeffrey spoke with satisfaction as he exited the room with a stiff goodbye.

M. Chevalier didn't appear overly disturbed.

"So, what did he do with you?" I asked.

"Nothing. We talked. I had a phone call and I went outside to speak for ten minutes. I came back. We talked again. He is easy to understand. I felt confident."

I piled my teaching materials into my bag.

M. Chevalier was checking a file on his laptop, "Excuse me a moment." He keyed in something, "Ah, yes."

He was quite deft at typing, not the two- or three-fingered effort.

He finished what he was doing, "Sorry, it was urgent. You asked about the test? I think I make progress."

"Yes, I believe so." I watched him clipping his laptop shut. He seemed content. Apparently, Jeffrey's grilling hadn't bothered him too much. Yet, Jeffrey had left with the look of someone who'd gotten what he'd come for.

I pondered over the whole event. Both parties had appeared pleased and I couldn't figure out why. It was probably just me trying to over-analyse their meeting.

"They say that under Paris you have another city, 400 miles of tunnels going down at least seven levels, that's 300 feet deep," Ursula declared on walking into my room later that evening. She was fast becoming a connoisseur and full of knowledge.

"Who says?" I asked.

"M. Jacques for one, David for another."

"Soon to be Fr. David."

"That's a long ways off. M. Jacques is king of the other Paris. He told us that though he lives in 11 meters squared, he has hundreds of square meters underground spread over many districts."

"I wonder what he pays for his eleven meters."

"Ask him?"

"I will," I suspected it was a lot less than what I was paying for my room. "Those tunnels of his must stink."

"No, some of them are completely dry. You have to distinguish between the city's arteries: Metro and transport system; the intestines: sewers, canals, cellars and caves; and the morgues: quarries, catacombs…"

"When did he tell you all that?"

"I gave him a few cans and he started blabbing and boasting."

"You mean you gave him my beer?"

"It was the only thing I could find. Those limestone quarry tunnels seem to be way-out. Just imagine it – the city was built from those stone quarries back in the 5th century and then later they became the cemetery for over six million people."

"I read something about that but have forgotten all the details."

"Well, until the early 1700s, the poor buried their dead in unofficial cemeteries – there was one known as the 'Cemetery of the Innocents' around Les Halles in the centre of Paris. But due to lots of cave-ins and the danger of overflowing corpses et cetera, the authorities opened up official cemeteries outside the city boundaries, now inside since Paris expanded."

"Yes, like Montparnasse, Montmartre, Passy and Pére Lachaise."

"But every night over a couple of years, government officials moved the bones from the 'Cemetery of the Innocents' in covered wagons to the catacombs in the south of the city where they had reinforced the quarries."

"We can visit if you want, I heard there's about a mile of catacombs open for official tourist visits," I suggested.

"Ah, but it would be much more fun to visit the unofficial ones. If M. Jacques is right, then there are underground tunnels under Rue des Soeurs and Rue des Irlandais."

"So finally you did ask him about it?"

"Yes, even if he's very secret about it. The direct way to get to our school underground from the Irish College is blocked off by a cavity brick wall. I think M. Jacques knows other ways of going through, but he doesn't want to tell me, just yet."

"A cavity brick wall? Just how do you say 'a cavity brick wall' in French? Where did you pick up all that vocabulary?"

"From men, they talk of nothing else."

"Well, excuse me, I don't ever recall hearing about cavity walls in my conversations with men, bar a discussion with a dentist about the cavities in my teeth."

Ursula wasn't listening, "It's amazing to think of that maze of tunnels. The Latin Quarter is riddled with them, like the veins of a leaf spiralling in all directions. David has some old documents and maps, really ancient ones."

"One moment here, Ursula, are you interested because you are passionate about sewers or about David?"

Ursula examined her red painted nails, "It's linked to past lives and so perfectly normal that I'd take an interest. Besides, David is not just a historian but also a cataphile. With the information he's collected, the whole project should be fascinating to anyone."

The possibility of the underground world had Ursula all excited. It was as if getting down there would bring her closer to centuries before and help her to exorcise Eva and the cobwebs of her past. But I had to admit, since meeting David, she'd complained less about our attic ghost and of not sleeping well.

"To be honest, I'd be very keen in having a look down there myself. If David's doing any excursions, let me know. Careful though, we mustn't ruffle M. Jacques's feathers. He might go crazy if we infringe on his territory."

"Oh," Ursula brushed it off, "I'll handle him."

"What about this famous cavity wall that's blocking off one of the tunnels under the school?"

"What indeed," Ursula took on a conspiratorial voice, "if we're to go by M. Jacques, it isn't there by accident, and we'd be better off not knowing."

****

"I miss you, Liz. I want to come back right now."

Michael had taken advantage of the Easter break to finally visit his family. I'd been pushing him a bit – no, a lot. Above all, he had to talk to his mum and dad – he couldn't run from what was so essentially part of him.

"You're exaggerating, Michael, you've only been gone two days. But I can't say I mind if you miss me a little. I miss you tons."

"It seems like a month."

It was a special feeling to count for someone, to know that you really mattered.

"Liz."

"Yes?"

"I love you."

Funny feelings fluttered inside and brought to the surface what I'd felt deep down, but had been afraid to let him see. I'd avoided using words of love. Now, he'd made it easier for me.

"Liz, are you there?"

"I love you too, Michael."

There was silence –

"Goodnight, my love."

"Goodnight."

A few minutes later, my phone flashed with a text message – 'I meant it – I LOVE YOU'.

I pressed 'save'.

****

The evening designated to visit the tunnel under the Irish College with David was the same day that Michael was to return from England. I hurried to close up the school, quickly making sure that cupboards and doors were properly shut. Suddenly, I felt a blast of cold air and heard a door slap. William Whyte was standing before me. There was panic in his eyes and sweat trickled down his face. He took his handkerchief to wipe it, but it kept trickling.

"Mr. Whyte, what's wrong?"

He didn't answer and walked up and down the corridor as if he were searching for something or someone.

"What's the matter?" I asked again.

He wiped his face again.

"Shall I finish locking up or leave it to you?" I clanked the keys to exact some kind of reply.

"You will excuse me," he went back inside his office.

It was very cold, but he'd been sweating heavily. Maybe he had a fever. I thought it better to double check before leaving. I knocked on 'St. Alban's', but nobody answered. I turned the handle and put my head inside. He was sitting behind the bare table. In the poor lighting, I could see that he'd taken off his jacket and his shirt was sticking to him. The bookcase was pushed aside and the door to the back stairway was wide open.

I approached, "Mr. Whyte, are you all right? Do you want me to call a doctor, or shall I fetch you a glass of water?"

He stood up, "Everything is perfectly fine. I've just been lifting some heavy boxes and putting them in the cellars. I'm not used to that sort of exercise."

"Okay then, I'll let the outside door unlocked. I presume you have your own keys."

"Yes," he looked at me hard – "oh, by the way, Miss Downey, have you seen the cleaners this evening?"

"No, I haven't. In fact, I've never seen any cleaners here."

"Good," he closed his door.

I stepped into the courtyard baffled by what had just taken place. Someone came out of the shadows, "Ursula, is that you moving around there?" Ursula was at the far corner of the yard dancing in circles. She had told me previously that it was her way of making waves and breaking the bad vibes she sensed in some places.

"Liz," she called, "Liz, what on earth kept you? I was going to bring a search party. David has everything organized for our underground adventure?"

"William Whyte is in there acting weird."

"Who cares about him, come on."

"Give me a minute." I buttoned up, put on my gloves and pulled the hood of my coat over my head. "It's freezing – so much for it being April, it's like the middle of winter." I was having second thoughts about underground explorations. I'd really have preferred to go home, snuggle under warm blankets with my beloved. But when Michael had rung me from Roissy Charles de Gaulle Airport, he was all for joining us.

"It will be worth it," Ursula said, "you know the old proverb about

April: 'a cold April the barn will fill'."

"Huh, when did you get to be so wise? Anyway, you never told me how David first got interested in exploring underground?"

"Pure accident. He just came across these documents and old maps in the library vault. People in the Irish College have always been aware of catacombs underneath but not of the extent of them – David's the only one with the guts to explore down there. I told you, it's for his thesis"

"Everything is justified by his thesis."

"Sure, why not."

"You know it's illegal to do what we are planning to do."

"Yes, I know," the idea seemed to please Ursula.

When we reached the Pantheon, it got even colder. We were completely exposed in the wide open square. A bitter wind swept right across us and we had to battle our way to Rue des Irlandais.

Someone poked both of us in the back, "Jesus!" said Ursula.

"Michael, you frightened us," I cheered up on seeing him.

"You girls were so engrossed, nattering, you wouldn't have seen a dozen thieves following you."

"There wasn't a dozen," said Ursula caustically, "there were just four or five."

"Welcome back to Paris, Michael," I felt awkward around him. Those words, 'love you', sat silently between us. Everything had changed. The next time he spoke those words, I wanted to look him in the eyes and to see what was there. He didn't make a fuss about meeting me, just kissed me lightly. I knew it was because Ursula was there. I treasured that sensitivity about him. He wouldn't make Ursula feel like an outsider.

I'd met David a few times. Given his label of researcher and future priest, one might expect him to be a puny sort of intellectual. He couldn't have been further from that stereotype. On the one hand, he was an ordinary down to earth guy; on the other hand, he wasn't ordinary to look at – he was tall and athletic, and his tightly cropped, fair hair contoured an attractive craggy face. He had kindly light brown eyes. He was a girl's dream.

He wanted to work in Asia and do real missionary work, but felt that he would have to serve a few years in Ireland first.

"You don't have to become a priest to do all that, you could go as a lay missionary," I had suggested in one of my first meetings with him.

"Yes, Liz, I could." He hadn't said or explained more than that. He must have been subjected to the same remarks so many times. I felt bad, but his gentle eyes had told me it was okay.

Michael and David nodded to each other in mutual respect.

We were like a gang from a teenage novel going off on an adventure. It was very generous of David to take us with him. The plan was to lead us to a part he'd already visited many times and could guarantee was safe. He showed us some of his maps and sketches enthusiastically and it was difficult not to be affected by his passion. One sketch looked like a labyrinth consisting of a dense network of tunnels – then there was a whole area blackened out.

"What is that?" Michael asked.

David grinned slyly, "I have my suspicions, but I'm not saying for now – I think you can guess anyway. We know that people built many worlds, centres and hubs underground. During World War II, French Resisters had lots of hiding places under Paris and ironically the Nazis too had bunkers beneath the city. Some years back, a secret group of movie lovers even ran a cinema underground."

"A cinema!" the three of us exclaimed.

"Yes, it held around 30 people. There were rock benches covered in wood for comfort – there was a bar, restaurant and annex rooms. It was near the Eiffel Tower. For a toilet, they used water from Trocadero garden where there was a permanent leak and they siphoned electricity by wrapping wires around a state-owned power company's cables."

"Wow," Michael said.

"That's just the tip of the iceberg," David continued. "I mean there is graffiti on tunnel walls from the period of the French Revolution, 1798, and the months of terror that followed. And then all the bones." He warned, "You have to be prepared for that – heaps of bones, hundreds of thousands of them. They are not as neatly piled and stacked up to form walls as those you can see when you visit the official part of the catacombs open to tourists. In the part I'm about to show you, you sometimes end up walking on top of layers of bone."

"Sounds wonderful," Ursula lit up a cigarette.

David laughed, "There are many entrances, known, secret, and still to be discovered. Some entrances are manholes on the street. Or you can have something like we have here, a cellar door in a building and the long spiral staircase." .

"Just like in the school," I said. I had already filled them in on my botched efforts at going down to the school cellars.

David looked at me, "That's what intrigues me. The blackened out part of the maps can be accessed from tunnels leading from under your school on one side and the Irish College on the other." He clapped his hands, "So, are you folks ready to see how far I've gone?"

"Yes," we chorused.

He held three sets of garments in front of us.

Ursula twitched her nose, "What are those?"

"Boiler suits, and I got a few pairs of Wellington boots, you will need them."

We made faces.

"There will be no arguments. Even if it's mostly dry, it's dirty and dusty and will destroy your clothes."

We didn't argue and pulled on the gear.

"Now," David held out helmets with headlamps, "these are good for miners and they're perfect for us – and take these torches too, we'll need all the light we can get."

"I'll say," Michael looked at David admiringly, "if you aren't prepared."

We followed David like cat burglars from his rooms down to the courtyard and into the chapel.

"What if somebody sees us?" I whispered.

"No problem," said David, "Fr. Sheehan has given me permission to visit the tunnels. It's part of my research. As long as I don't make a big deal about it and use discretion, it's okay."

"Is this the same way M. Jacques takes to go down?" asked Ursula.

David shook his head, "No, he uses the entrance under that shelter by the dustbins. It has a wider stairway and is a lot easier to manage. He just needs to go as far as the main cellars to store his bric-a-brac. But I understand that he has done a lot of explorations of his own in other parts of the Latin Quarter."

David opened what looked like a cupboard door at the front of the chapel. But it was a false cupboard and behind it was a second door. He turned the key and that was it. It looked almost like an ordinary cellar door entrance.

David noticed our disappointment, "What were you expecting, secret panels and codes? It's a typical door, just like in your school. Now, everybody queue up for our descent into the belly of another world," he announced hauntingly.

"Stop it, David," Ursula squeaked.

"Sorry, but seeing your faces, I couldn't resist."

I watched David and Ursula closely. Somehow, Ursula seemed much more normal around David. It was as if in his company she became the real Ursula. At the same time, nothing in David's behaviour hinted that he'd fallen for her or that he was under her guile. He treated her like one of the gang.

We began the descent – David led, Ursula followed, then me, with Michael making up the tail. The space was tight and I wondered how David squeezed his way, being so much bigger. Michael was less of a surprise; I'd seen him twist in and out of vents and little openings in his famous magic boxes. He had to be mobile and elastic. Then again, William Whyte managed it.

The flights of stone steps seemed daunting and never-ending.

"How many levels down is it?" Ursula sounded a little desperate, "I was thinking about the coming up, it will kill us."

David stopped, "It's way below cellar level. Have you ever gone up or down the stairs at Abbesses Metro in the Montmartre district rather than take the lift? Well, that's what we're doing. Only, we are walking it, all 118 feet. Come on, courage, some descents are up to 300 feet."

We kept going.

After a while, "Are you sure the sewers are no longer in use and have dried out, and that there are no rats, vermin, snails and things like that?" Ursula aired my sentiments exactly.

"Don't worry," David assured. "It's safe, I've been down several times and I have never seen any rats. Why would rats hang around old bones, there is no food here for them?"

"Nothing is impossible," said Ursula.

"Okay, Liz?" David called.

"Yes," I replied.

"Michael?" David called again.

"Yes," came Michael's rejoinder.

I felt his hand touch my shoulder reassuringly.

Finally, we weren't taking steps anymore, but had to bow our heads to follow a low narrow tunnel. Nobody spoke. I shut out all thoughts, not wanting to think about where I was, or how much ground was above me. We were surrounded by rock. My skin felt clammy and I tried to breathe air that smelt of dust, almost incense-infused. It was what old church stone would smell like, but with earthy odours in the mix. Unwelcome images of the tunnel collapsing and the four of us left to suffocate to death came to mind. Maybe a torrent of water would come gushing towards us and we'd drown and float along with all the other dead creatures for ever and ever and ever.

"Don't be afraid," David called out to us, "the ground under our feet is going to change from a hard surface to layers of bones."

There was a group intake of breath and an even slower pace as we walked hesitantly on what felt like shingle, moving and shifting under our feet. The sensation was horrible.

Just when I could take no more, we came out of the tunnel into an opening with entrances to other tunnels all around – it was like a crossroads.

"At last – space – and a strange smell," Ursula stood straight.

"Just what I was thinking," said Michael.

"I can't decide if we're entering the stomach of the Latin Quarter or the heart," I said.

"The heart is more romantic," said David. "You've got the arteries and veins, everything's connected."

Then we saw them –

"Jesus," said Ursula, 'Jesus – Jesus – Jesus' echoed through the air.

"Those aren't tunnel walls," I said in awe, "those are stacks of bones."

It was unbelievable; there must have been thousands and thousands. We stood speechless.

After a few seconds, David spoke, "The emotion hits me every time."

"Never seen anything like it," said Michael.

"Makes you wonder about life, death, souls and all that, doesn't it?" Ursula whispered. "Is this it – is this the end facing every one of us?"

"Don't get morbid," said David. "But you're right, these were mass burial places following war, plagues and epidemics. Come on, let's go – this way."

David led us through another tunnel that sloped downwards. "I'll keep my torch on, but you switch off yours," he ordered, "it isn't a good idea to use up all the batteries. Your head lamps are enough."

We switched off our torches immediately. From David's torch and the illumination thrown out from our head lamps, we could see it was a real maze. While skeletal remains continued to be scattered on the ground and piled up on either side, there were also enclaves and what appeared to be caves or caverns. Some looked like they had been artificially closed or walled off, others had deep holes on the floors that would be certain death to anyone who fell through. Fortunately, David knew his way by heart and led us along sure and safe territory.

David talked as if to set his and our minds at rest and to stop us thinking too much. "Just imagine that the Metro is running over us. Do you realise we have descended another 50 feet or so and are now directly under Rue de la Huchette?

"I really feel like I've got the whole weight of Paris on my back," said Ursula, her voice no longer echoing, but sounding flat in the thick air.

For once, I didn't think the statement too exaggerated.

"Amen to that," added Michael.

"We're here," announced David, "just near your school. That wall is modern and is sealing off the tunnel that led into what is represented by the blackened area of the map."

"Ah," Ursula said, "the ancient brothel."

"Yes," David admitted.

"Are you sure about the brothel?" I asked.

"As sure as I can be, I found documents and letters about it in the old College archives. There was a town house where your school is today. In fact, there were two town houses side by side. Later on, they got split into flats and shops and things like that. One of the town houses was a gentleman's club. Over ground, the activity was what you'd expect: billiards room, lounge, dining room, cigar room, gambling tables and such. Under ground, however, was designed for other activities. Some people called it a 'hell'."

We drew nearer the wall, "So who built this?" Michael tapped it.

"I think there are different periods to that wall," said David. "The seminarians and staff in the Irish College closed it off firstly around the mid-19th century. That's what I read in letters in the archives. They didn't ask permission, they just did it. Then the wall was added on to and patched up from time to time. But here," he kicked at a part, "the brick work was done more recently, probably the seventies. Maybe the original work was crumbling. What do you think?"

"I know very little about things like that," said Michael, "but my guess is the same as yours."

"I wouldn't be surprised if it were done by William Whyte or his brother when they started the language school," I volunteered.

"M. Jacques says he hears unusual noises underground and has seen strange things, but he won't tell me what," said Ursula. "I'm sure he has explored the other side of that wall, but accessed it from a different tunnel."

"That has been bothering me for a while," said David. "I daren't try to knock this wall down, but if M. Jacques knows another way through, it could be really interesting. I have to talk to him."

I put my ear to the stone, "Shush, I can hear something at the other side."

We all glued our ears to the wall and listened. There seemed to be some muffled sounds. It was probably the grumbling and settling of stones and earth that was creating that sensation. We gave up after a few minutes.

"We should be getting back," said David, "it isn't that far, but everything seems farther down here. The trick is to take our time, step by step, and not to panic."

We respected his advice and concentrated on nothing else except putting one foot in front of the other and keeping our eyes fixed on the light from our lamps and torches.

Going back up the last steps was punishing. After what seemed like an eternity, we panted our way to the top, arriving into the sanctity of the church sacristy.

I looked at my watch, it was just past midnight. Then I saw that our boots and boiler suits were stained with light brown mud. Thankfully, David had been sensible about protecting our clothes.

"Out into the yard," David directed, "we must not dirty inside here."

We went outside, pulled off our Wellingtons and got out of the suits. The freezing night air made us shiver.

"Now, back inside the chapel again or you'll get your death of cold."

"Yes, Fr. David," said Ursula.

We obeyed meekly, returning to a warm and comforting chapel.

I saw David smile at Ursula and she smiled back at him. It was obvious to me that Ursula had confided a lot more in David than I first thought.

I realised that Ursula was infatuated with him, maybe even for the first time in her life a little in love. A man, seemingly immune to her seductive charms and not afraid of her, was a totally new experience for Ursula.

I let out a loud sigh of relief, "I'll tell you this much, given the choice of living under an attic roof or underground, I won't leave you guessing which I'd choose."

"You can say that again," agreed Michael, he swaddled me in his arms, "feeling better."

"A lot, but don't tickle," I felt his fingers tease.

David clapped his hands to warm them, "I want to see the other side of that wall. It might not turn out to be the crowning glory of my research, but I've got to know."

"There have been some books done about brothels" said Ursula, "perhaps you could get an idea from them, you know, the décor and such. Then you just use your imagination for the rest. You can speak of the two sides – from the College to the Brothel – the ritual of the tabernacle to the virgin sacrifice, or something like that"

David grinned, "You can compose that thesis, Ursula, I'm sticking to the facts."

"Well," I took her defence, "it looks like Ursula's definition isn't too far removed from the facts to me."

David thought about it, "I could ask Whyte to let me go down from the school side."

"I wouldn't be so quick about doing that," I cautioned.

"I understand you think he's odd and unpleasant, but he doesn't know we're friends," David reasoned. "I can in all innocence and in the interest of my research ask his permission. If he says no, then okay, I won't push the issue."

"Look, I have my reasons," I updated them on William Whyte's recent behaviour.

Ursula's eyes opened wide, "You never told me all those details before."

"I didn't want to bother you. Anyway, what I know amounts to very little. Michael thinks I have, to say the least, a creative mind and there is perhaps some simple explanation behind it all."

"Still, I'm glad you told me," David said, "that puts another slant on things. I think I'll have to approach it differently. I might, after all, just get a professional opinion about making a small opening in the wall and justify it by using a heritage argument. Under those circumstances, they might be persuaded to let me conduct an excavation." He scratched his chin, "Of course that could take months, even years."

"Oh," said Ursula, "you church people have influence everywhere, you just need to knock on the right doors and pull a few strings."

"You might be right," he acknowledged, "but when you take that direction you don't always end up with what you asked for. It's evident from my documents that the real entrance to that place is directly under your school. So, if I ask permission, I might in any case have to go via Mr. Whyte. He could halt that procedure for years."

I agreed, "I can imagine all the tactics he would use: attention to the place would damage and disrupt business, and so on."

"What other options are there?" asked Michael.

"We're back to M. Jacques and his claim to know a different way," said David. "But, he isn't the easiest to deal with – he can be such a wild creature."

"There are ways to get around M. Jacques," Ursula said, "it's all about timing with him. He is beginning to trust me and has already told me little secrets related to other things. I'll keep working on him."

"Alright, my clever girl, you do that," David smiled.

Ursula radiated under his compliment.

"Whatever we decide, I'll have to be careful," David said.

"You're already that," said Ursula, "at least for research," she added, in case people thought she'd gone completely soft in the brain over him.

Oh dear, I thought, I hope one of them isn't going to end up with a broken heart. I looked at Michael, I'd found him quiet, too quiet and pensive. Something had happened in England, I was sure.

****

It wasn't two different Michaels, but I was wondering if I'd missed something. He had spoken very little about his trip home. When I thought about it, he'd hardly spoken of it at all. I didn't mind that, it was his private business. But I felt it had gone well. I sensed a new hope in him and there were positive signs such as his calling home more often and easily. That door had been reopened and I was glad. However, something else had changed. If I were pushed to find words to describe it, I would say that somehow he had made a growing up step, was more of a man. But that was ridiculous. How could a week spent at home with his family be so significant?

A few days after our visit with David and Ursula underground, Michael and I walked along the left bank of the River Seine. The sky was an icy blue, triggering a yearning for warmer weather and a real taste of spring. But the 'Bouquinistes' were open and braving the cold weather – the dealers in used and antiquarian books plied their trade along large sections of the banks, from Pont Marie to the Quai du Louvre on the right bank, and from Quai de la Tournelle to Quai Voltaire on the left bank. We ambled by the recognisable permanent bottle green boxes which both stored and displayed books, posters and other wares.

I took out my little guide book and read from it, "Sir, do you know that the tradition of second-hand booksellers began around the 16th century and was legalised some fifty years afterwards."

Michael looked at me bemused and shook his head.

"I thought so," I continued in a grand voice. "Now, the term 'bouquiniste' appeared first in 1789 in the dictionary of the Académie française. Their emblem was a lizard looking at a sword. The rules rewritten by the City of Paris in 1859 allowed the book traders to be established at fixed points, each one entitled to 10 metres of railing for an annual fee of 26.35 Old Francs and a licence of 25 Old Francs. Imagine, roughly the size of my room. Their openings for business were from sunrise to sunset.

"Today," I waved my hand, "the 240 'bouquinistes' here make use of 900 green boxes to house something like 300,000 old books, as well as journals, stamps and trading cards. But unfortunately, although forbidden, more and more supplement this with tourist trinkets."

"Same old story," Michael said, "money wins out in the end."

I sighed and put the book back in my bag.

With a lonesome call, a seagull flew out over Place du Châtelet on the right bank. A second seagull followed. Even though Ursula had explained that they were called herring gulls, to me they were still seagulls. I remembered how at first I thought they were out of place in Paris, but gradually realised that those birds were more at home than I was.

"Do you like the call of the gulls?" I asked Michael.

"Yes," was all he replied, sounding so far away.

I took his arm, closed my eyes and allowed myself to be transported back to my seaside village. It was my way when I needed reassurance and that touch of home. In my mind, I could hear the waves crashing and see the seabirds soaring skywards, while gannets and cormorants plunged and dived, and puffins nested in their thousands along the rock edges.

I imagined walking with Mum.

'Keep your scarf on, Liz, you'll catch cold,' Mum scolds me.

'Mum, where are you?' I ask silently.

'I'm by your side.' I hear her reply.

I came back to the present where the city voices and sounds around me were very different.

"Michael?"

"Yes?"

"You've been quiet since you came back from England."

"Have I?"

"Yes, is there something on your mind?"

"I've been thinking about an offer I've had."

"Is it very important?"

"It could be, for me anyway, yes."

"Do you want to tell me about it – it can help to discuss things?"

"No."

It was a definite 'No'. I wondered if he realised how abrupt and short his answer had come out and how excluded I felt. Michael's reply hurt, though I tried not to show it. It wasn't hard to figure out that his mother and father had clearly put some choices and options his way. They had probably suggested helping him set up his own show, or had given him pointers in the right direction. That's what parents did, they offered what they could, and rich parents could offer more. I was sure Michael's dilemma was that eternal struggle between proving he could do it alone on his own terms, while at the same time admitting that some help was necessary. Help wasn't all bad. Of course, there would be strings attached – there were always strings, and more so between parents and children.

Making a living out of magic was Michael's dream. Even if he didn't spell it out clearly, it was obvious to anyone who knew him. He had a lot of talent and could work at improving that. But he needed to find resources to build some type of a structure around that talent. The best way was sponsorship and his parents were offering to do it. They weren't just throwing him a line, but a big rope. It was an opportunity to turn his passion into reality, his magic and illusions into something real. I could decipher all that, but Michael wouldn't tell me. I had pushed him to see his parents and now he was locking me out.

Funny, one whole week and the word 'love' hadn't re-appeared. I'd been too unsure to bring it up again. How easily I lost assurance.

We made our way to Pont des Arts. The chilly sun dipped and conjured silver sparkles on the dark water. Cheers rose up from a fly-boat that passed under the bridge, carrying some tourists who dared the cool temperatures. What was it about people in tours? Why did a whole group of strangers feel the need to raise a rousing cheer as they went under a bridge and came out the other side, and why did I and others instinctively wave back? We were easily pleased, simple things made us happy if only we realised it.

We crossed the wooden boards of the bridge. A few padlocks had been attached to the side trellis, with names, hearts and words of love scratched out on them.

"Did you ever carve your love for a girl on a tree trunk, Michael?"

Michael had walked ahead. He stopped and looked around impatiently, "What? Oh, that's trite for children and teenagers."

I tried not to take his reaction personally and was determined to keep the embers of my heartfelt feelings stoked up, "It can be romantic. I'm sure you wrote the name of your sweetheart on something somewhere when you were a child?"

"I don't remember."

Michael was walking with me, but his mind was elsewhere rolling out his future and I wasn't in there. Did I want to be? If he made it, really made it in his chosen career path, the Michael I knew today might be a very interesting Michael in ten or fifteen years. Who could tell?

We descended into the Metro Palais Royal-Musée du Louvre. At a junction of tunnels, I turned to take my direction home.

Michael seemed to wake up then and to come back to me, "Liz, where are you off to?"

"I'm going to Porte Maillot."

He was confused, didn't understand the gap he had created between us, hadn't seen it widening. "I'm not letting you out of my sight, the night isn't over yet," he stood and waited for me to take a few steps towards him.

I hesitated, not sure it was a good idea. Something was coming undone and fraying – I could feel it.

He gave me a winning smile. I melted a little, finally relented. I shouldn't take it so hard that he didn't want to share those thoughts and let me into one of the most important decisions of his life. I could share his bed, he mine, make love and feel totally one with him, but be shut out from something so vital. Then, didn't I do the same? I hadn't exactly explained all my thoughts, wishes and dreams. But I believed that if the roles were reversed, I would tell him if I were on the brink of making an important decision in my life, one that might change things for both of us. I would, wouldn't I?

I found myself doing exactly what I'd promised myself never to do, finding excuses for him, justifying his behaviour.

"Come with me, come home with me," he gave me his hand. I took it, let the warmth pass between us and pretended the rest didn't matter.

14

I lay in my bed and saw the clock radio flash six o'clock. At first, I panicked and then relaxed as I realised it was Sunday morning and I could enjoy a lie-in. Elle jumped off the bed and I stretched my legs gratefully. I thought about my unofficial job of managing the people around me. Directing Michael wasn't easy. I would push him out of bed and on to the floor, "Time for you to get up." Or if we didn't sleep together, I'd ring and ring until his groggy voice came over the phone. I also kept up my routine of kicking Ursula's door in the mornings to wake her up – and following that up with reminders during the day. I could manage that much, but I couldn't manage everything. What they did in their classes – I shook my head. I had seen enough through the window divides in the school classrooms to know that it wasn't that easy being a student of Ursula's. But more recently her overall sense of humour was better and it seemed her students suffered less. As for Michael, he wouldn't win medals for professionalism. He was too easy going, too light, and too inconsistent – and despite my best efforts to help him, Lena told me that there were often complaints about him bungling appointments. I hoped his second career would take off soon. If it didn't, he'd be taking off out of the school whether he wanted to or not.

Elle squeezed her feline bottom on a ledge by the hot-plate and sat looking out the window. The street lamps went off and the luminosity gave way to natural light. I pulled myself up on the bed and put my hands behind my head. Michael hadn't come to my room last night because his show finished too late, but he'd sent a string of texts before morning, telling me of famous people he'd met. I knew little about the world of magicians and the names meant nothing to me, but apparently they were important to him. It still hurt to know that he hadn't shared more with me about his visit home to England and the offer he was considering with respect to his future. But I had come to terms with his not wanting to share everything and realised that I was probably being too possessive.

"What are you looking at, Elle? Can you see things that I cannot? Maybe you can see the enigmatic Eiffel Tower that justified my landlady wringing extra rent out of me."

Elle didn't spare me a blink.

"No, Elle, you're probably trying to stare down a bird somewhere – poor dreamer."

There was something comforting about the cat and the shy April sunlight stealing through the window panes. I closed my eyes and let the rays caress my face. I needed that consoling warmth and gentle healing. Maybe, I'd been so absorbed taking care of everything and everybody else that I was lacking a little loving care myself. Michael and I certainly hadn't got tired of each other so far. Creeping into my fairytale tower, as he called his visits to my room, at midnight, still gave me a thrill. Lounging around his larger place on a Saturday or a Sunday was heavenly to me. But lately I noticed I needed more time for me. I'd all sorts of ideas in my head about what I wanted to do professionally. For now, I kept them in my head. Ursula accused me of being too self-sufficient. I recalled her saying, "We'd like to help you Liz, but you're the kind who doesn't need help. You've got it all worked out."

Was that how I came across – Miss Independent, needing nobody? It made me understand that I wasn't exactly the best example of revealing my own thoughts. Perhaps, it shut out people in ways I didn't intend. Well, I hadn't the answers to everything, but I couldn't deny that these moments on my own were precious to me. My little room was now a retreat where I could turn my back on the rest of mankind.

The sun shone more strongly through the window and I had no desire to stay longer in bed. The prospect of a fine day changed everything.

Spring was definitely in the air. Mme Gomes was busier with her broom and duster on the stairways, in the hallway and in the courtyard. People climbed the stairs with a greater oomph. There was much more industrious action on the top floor. Although nobody had exactly been hibernating, it had felt like that. We started living differently, like insects coming out from under the stones, shaking off crusty earth. The blue sky gave us new hope and that changed everyone's outlook. Work we'd avoided during winter suddenly became joyous spring-cleaning chores – dusty corners became visible, window panes cried out to be cleaned. While it had been okay to roll in old blankets and quilts during the hard weather, they now smelt stale and needed airing, lots of airing. We opened our windows wide. Fresh energy flowed into the body and head and we all wanted to be outdoors enjoying the longer late April evenings.

I thought about investing in a new hairstyle. Spring fever was getting to me too – change was in the air.

Ursula and I made a pact: we would combine efforts, get internet and a laptop which we would share. I knew exactly where the laptop would be stored and used and I wasn't wrong in that – we shared it fifty–fifty, meaning that Ursula had it ninety percent of the time. I'd almost convinced myself that it was Ursula's and that she was granting me a favour every time I went to borrow my percentage of time on the computer. I'd gone into it with my eyes wide open.

The longer, warmer days and happier mood of people didn't extend as far as Whyte's school. The atmosphere was tense all week. It was hard to ignore the intense discussions that Judith and Lena seemed to be having behind closed office doors. It caused a gossip mill among teachers and we discussed the new tensions in our favourite cafés or in 'Lindisfarne'.

"Serious shit," Ursula commented, as soon as we were alone together. "Believe me, when those office doors are closed, keep out and stay well away from Judith and Lena afterwards, they'll be like wasps."

"Since when did you get to be so insightful about their behaviour?" I asked.

"It doesn't take much skill or observation techniques to second guess their actions. Judith and Lena are so totally disciples of routine. The last time they were huddled in there, we got paid late. It usually means financial trouble. It happens when the big boss hasn't transferred the funds."

"It could be that Whyte has got to them so much that they need to let off steam, tear him to pieces for an hour or so, and then go back to work."

"They do that all the time. No, they've shut the doors because it's more important than that – it isn't just a crisis of nerves. They're regrouping their energies in there, building up strength, calling in some forces. A couple of old hags getting together can hatch up a lot of things."

Ursula was right about the sting part. I got a pinch of it at break time and couldn't decide which of them was carrying the most poison. Judith looked fierce and examined her nails as if she wanted to scratch somebody's eyes out. Lena sat turning pages of her journal carefully and deliberately, her breath coming out like a slow-burning furnace.

"Lena," I ventured, it wasn't a very brave move on my part.

The head over the journal didn't rise.

"Lena," I tried again, now that did require more guts.

"Yes," she snapped.

I didn't smart, but I might have.

"I was wondering if you had anything to brief me on before Saturday. It's the end of the month and a lot of the teachers ring in or come in with questions and that." I didn't want to say what I really meant – if April pay hadn't arrived in our bank accounts by Saturday, I'd be besieged by angry teachers and demands for cheques or cash to tide people over. If military protection were required, I'd prefer to know now and be prepared.

"I'm busy here."

"Well, okay –" She was about as busy as an old hen picking aimlessly at the same piece of ground. "If you're busy then, I'll leave you to it."

I returned to my class, but kept one ear to the corridor for the rest of the evening. Apart from banging doors, there were no other foreboding signals.

I dared to put my head into the office once more before leaving, "I'll be going then – time for a cigarette, Lena, while I'm finishing this coffee?"

"Nope."

Great start to the week, I thought.

****

My classes with M. Chevalier had gone from something I hated to something

I liked doing, so much so that they no longer needed much preparation on my side. Today's class had been a little different. I found M. Chevalier somewhat preoccupied and from time to time caught him looking at me oddly. The large meeting room with little more than flipchart, table and chairs appeared bare and impersonal. P.A.F.I. Company didn't go in for lots of posters and branding. As a financial investment company, its logo lit up the outside of the tower making a statement of its own on the business landscape of La Défense.

M. Chevalier was looking right at me, quizzically.

"Do you have something you want to ask me, M. Chevalier?"

He didn't answer immediately.

I watched him piecing his sentence together in his head.

"If you're anxious about the big interview, we can fit in an extra class or two," I volunteered. "We could even do some practice over the phone if your timetable allows." I wanted him to succeed. Sometimes, when I was in a more optimistic frame of mind, I was sure that his English was improving. I believed that he could manage structured presentations and handle predictable English language challenges around his job much better. Other times, I was not so sure.

"I am enough confident," he passed over my offer and suggestion.

"Confident enough."

"I do not understand the difference."

"Adjective versus adverb," I said. "So?"

I waited and he slowly formulated his intended question, "Are you going on with your school – are you in your school long?"

"Which do you mean: do I plan to go on working at Whyte's school or how long have I been working there?"

"The first."

I wasn't expecting that type of question, "I like what I do, so I certainly plan to go on teaching English. Staying or not at W.W.S.O.E. & F.L. depends on different things, I haven't thought about it much."

"Ah, you could work in another school?"

"Yes, I could." What was he getting at, I wondered.

"Are you happy in Whyte's?"

"I – happy is a big word, I'm happy teaching, I – we can always look to improve conditions."

"Why did your colleague stop to teach M. Fabre?"

"You mean stop teaching – I don't know," I feigned ignorance, "I don't wish to –"

"I understand – and the man who tested me?"

"Jeffrey?"

"Yes, does he work long in your school?"

"I don't really know. What about you?"

"Me?"

"Yes, you – how well do you know M. Fabre? He's your direct competitor for the job, isn't he?"

"You think?"

"I thought he was."

"P.A.F.I. is a big company. Top management take their decisions using many elements. The interview is important, but not the only thing. I am ready now in English thanks to you."

God, I thought, I hope he's ready.

"That boy, Michael, he is your friend?"

I wasn't sure I wanted to answer that. Just where was M. Chevalier going with his questions and what right had he to ask me something so personal?

I led the conversation in a different way. "You must know more about my school than I do, M. Chevalier. I understand that Whyte's and P.A.F.I. have been doing business together for several years and many of your people have been trained by my school. You yourself had –"

"I begin – began classes last year with a different teacher."

"Can you remember the name of the teacher before me?"

"No."

No, but he'd sent him back, I knew that much. I knew also that the replacement had lasted only two classes.

"Isn't that terrible and when you finish your training with me, you'll forget my name too."

"Maybe, I don't know."

He could be a little kinder. He could at least say, 'Of course I'll remember your name'.

I caught the hint of a smile in the slight curl of his lips and realised I needed to lighten up.

I took on my prissy voice, "Now let's have a look at some points of structure."

"Mince alors!"

It was good enough for him. In the classroom, I was still the boss.
M. Chevalier didn't hurry out at the end of the class as he was used to doing. I noted that instead of leaving the room directly, he waited. He walked me down the corridor and then gave me a heftier and, if I were not mistaken, a more knuckle-cracking handshake than usual.

I bumped straight into Jeffrey with a burly man that I recognised as M. Fabre.

I tacked a smile on my face. As Fabre worked on a different floor, I had only spotted him a few times in P.A.F.I. I'd never actually formally met him up close. It struck me that he resembled one of the men I had seen coming to visit Whyte at the school one Saturday afternoon.

I got a commercial hello from Fabre and a stuffy look from Jeffrey who quickly led his student away.

Well, suit yourself, I thought.

I passed Mme Michot's office. I knew Michael was in class with her. He'd told me not to wait as he was rushing off to do a birthday party just after. I heard the HR manager's voice inside; she was certainly speaking a lot. I decided to follow Michael's advice and go home.

What a difference it made to have daylight in the evening. My building seemed friendlier. Mme Gomes, however, was in a little bit of a temper because people weren't sealing their bin bags correctly and insisted on overloading the bins. I sympathised with her. For once, I made an effort to understand the trials and tribulations of being a concierge and she did have a list. There were dozens of smudged hall mirrors, not to mention dogs with dirty paws. The entrance needed constant mopping up and if it weren't perfect, there were many residents who would complain about it. Things were forever breaking down and out of order. Between electrical faults and leaks, her husband couldn't rest – he was always on call to fix and mend. Residents also held her responsible for non-civic behaviour, street noise at night, bad parking, disrespectful neighbours and lost letters. The same residents wanted her to run errands and they weren't happy when she turned down their offers of cleaning and ironing work. Others complained that she was paid to be on duty as guardian and not earning extra on the side. And all that, for her family and herself to be hemmed in to a small lodge, like ducks in a pen. And those were just her woes with the residents in the main apartments, she hadn't even begun to itemise the problems on the seventh floor, mostly relating to the Bjania family's steady stream of relatives, a never-ending line of girlfriends staying over with Sebastien and Olivier – her son was constantly disturbed at night by noises on the corridor. On top, M. Jacques's junk, often stored in the courtyard, and M. Brosse's rudeness were constant nuisances.

I did my best to make the right sounds and gestures while at the same time not expressing my opinion on anything. I could only imagine what she was saying about Ursula and me behind our backs.

"And your neighbour, your friend?" Mme Gomes asked.

"My friend is in tip top shape and so is the room, everyone couldn't be better." I finally detached myself and began the long climb with Mme Gomes looking wistfully after me. What she needed was some real excitement in her life, something to take her away from the mundane chores of her day. A murder or dramatic accident would serve perfectly for that purpose, I thought wryly to myself.

I climbed to the seventh floor, my mind full of plans about ways to brighten up my room. I might consider painting the walls –

Ursula practically pounced on me at the top of the stairs.

"Don't do that, you frightened the life out of me – oh hello, David." Now, that was news. What was an Irish seminarian doing on our floor, alone with Ursula?

"Hi, Liz," David didn't appear in the least embarrassed.

"M. Jacques agrees," said Ursula, "M. Jacques agrees."

"Agrees to what?"

"To take David underground and to show him another way from Rue des Irlandais to Rue des Soeurs," Ursula spoke as if I should know exactly what she was talking about. What else would she be talking about? Still, if it made them happy.

"That's great for your thesis, David."

"Yes," David acknowledged. "M. Jacques has a wealth of knowledge. He's quite willing to show us how to access other tunnels that might take us right under the school."

The excitement of the pair of them was so infectious that I had to laugh. It was as if they were on the brink of making the greatest archaeological find of the century.

"How did you persuade M. Jacques, Ursula?"

"It was easy. I told you it's all about timing with him. I simply explained who David was, his research, what he'd already discovered on his own. That did the trick – M. Jacques agreed."

"And what –"

"I know what you're going to ask," said Ursula, "what does he want in exchange?

I can answer that, he doesn't want anything."

"Except my beer."

"No, this time I only gave him a small measure of whiskey."

"Mine too. Okay then, when are you going to do this expedition?"

"Soon," said David. "But first, I have to fit in a few short trips away – to Rome, and to Dublin. So the expedition will have to be postponed until after."

Ursula's eyes glazed over, "I am now sure of the connection between my room here, Rue des Soeurs and Eva. I believe also that Eva's looking for freedom. She wants me to help free her spirit and that of the others."

I was lost for words to reply. But Ursula turned to David for backing and he seemed unfazed. I thought, either he's going along with Ursula's outrageous theory to humour her, or he's deranged too.

David saw my reaction, "Never dismiss what people say, especially when they persist with what they say. In fact, I did a little research. A business man named Francois de la Perriere was the original owner of your building here on Rue Montrosier. He also owned buildings on Rue des Soeurs, including your school. He is the person who ran the famous gentleman's club and brothel that I suspect to have existed underground in the blacked out area of my map. And that's just the beginning, I intend to research it further."

"Well, well," Ursula had definitely found her knight. "I have always genuinely believed that Ursula was picking up some sort of energy or memory. I just didn't want her suffering because of it. If you tell me you've researched it, then I'm ready to believe the historical facts."

"Liz is afraid of being labelled crazy like me," said Ursula. "She has this need to put everything in a logical box."

"I just like to keep my options open and maintain a balanced view on things."

"Huh," Ursula folded her arms.

I mimicked her gesture.

"Is this an argument starting between you two," said David, standing back, "because if that's the case, I want no part of it. Getting in the middle of a sparring match between a couple of women, above all Irish women, isn't something I dream about – I run miles in the opposite direction."

"Don't be such a coward," I said, "Ursula and I do this all the time."

"David isn't a coward," Ursula was quick to defend, "but it's true we're used to harping off each other like sisters do."

Sisters, I thought, why not. It fit, one didn't choose family. "I feel very much the older sister."

"She could be my mother the way she gives out to me," Ursula was never one to let things rest.

"Your mother, I'm not. I'd hope to have a better behaved child who didn't give back chat and who looked up to me as the voice of wisdom on everything."

"You're in for a big disappointment if you expect any of your children to grow up according to your model," Ursula pushed in her room door, "but I like you all the same, God knows why. Do you and Michael want to join us for – supper?" There was something devious in her invitation.

"You mean the last supper, why not."

"M. Jacques is eating with us too," said David, "we've invited him along."

I helped with preparations for supper. Michael arrived and fell right in with our plans. He wore his new preoccupied look on his face. He wasn't the Michael I met a few months before – he still went off on airy flights, but they were now connected to real concrete plans about the future.

Of course, Ursula could never do things by halves and suggested we should set up our feast on the corridor. David and Michael got a long plank of wood from M. Jacques and created a makeshift table. Ursula then sent the men off to the shops to pick up some vital ingredients: wine, fresh baguettes, a roast chicken, tabouli salad, celery and carrot salad, and some Cantal and Brie cheese, because they were not smelly and wouldn't stink the corridor.

M. Jacques came to dinner, bringing M. Brosse for moral support. The six of us around the table made for a rather unique picture – seekers and wanderers. It was fun sharing a meal and speaking about catacombs, underground tunnels, caverns and brothels.

I watched Michael, darling Michael, who had taken up such an important place in my life. He fit in so easily everywhere. Mum would never know Michael. I wished I could share my thoughts and feelings with her. I really missed not being able to – Mum would have enjoyed meeting these people. Mme Defoe had told me that it was time for me to make a visit back to Ireland. Family was family, home was home, and I should keep in touch with my cousins and old friends. She was right. I'd prescribed it for Michael and it worked for him. I needed to try a taste of my own medicine. Everyone needed a native cure. It would help lay some memories to rest.

"What are you thinking about?" Ursula butted into my thoughts.

"Liz often goes off to her own cosmos," said Michael.

It surprised me when Michael said that. He was after all the one who spent most of his time on the moon.

"I was in fact thinking of Mme Defoe and considering some good advice that she gave me," I topped up my wine.

"The famous Mme Defoe," explained Ursula to the questioning faces. "I'm convinced that Liz has invented this private student in the same way a little girl invents an imaginary friend."

"She does exist," I defended. "Ursula's just jealous because Mme Defoe is from the top echelons of society and I won't introduce her."

M. Jacques emerged as my unexpected defender affirming that Mme Defoe did indeed exist – in fact, he knew her and she often gave him useful jumble and even quality secondhand clothes from her husband. He assured an open-mouthed Ursula that Mme Defoe was a real lady who appreciated discretion. He had no intention of saying more than that about her.

That settled that.

I looked up – M. Bjania? "Oops," I said, "are we making too much noise and disturbing the seventh floor?"

"Please join us with your wife and kids," invited Michael.

And so the group of six became a group of ten. It soon became twelve, when a rather bewildered Sebastien and Olivier came home later. They thawed out quickly enough after a few glasses of wine. Arguments about previous dirty toilets were soon forgotten in view of good food and wine.

"Now, we do have the last supper," Ursula counted out loud.

Hopefully, there is no Judas, the traitor, among us, I surmised to myself.

15

I browsed idly through some of Michael's books. Many were on magic, but there was also a Tibetan travel book. There were lots of novels, including authors like Stephen King, Jack London and Ernest Hemmingway. As I reached for one of several decks of cards, a key fell off the shelf to the ground with a thud.

I picked it up. "What do you use this key for?" It was very large and chunky, similar to the one I had for the main school door.

Michael glanced at it and shook his head, "No idea."

I took the school key from my own set and compared them. The ridges seemed exactly the same. The only difference was that mine carried the name of the locksmith and had a code number. "It's for the school, isn't it?"

Michael looked at it, "Gosh, you're right. I can't remember how I came to have it, but it must have been Lena or Judith who gave it to me. Now that I think about it, I did have an evening replacement class a while back – you weren't in that particular day and they must have asked me to lock up."

"It looks like an illegal copy."

Michael shrugged, "Perhaps a former teacher got a copy made on the sly and just decided to turn it in to the school on leaving."

"Why did you hang on to it?" I tried not to sound accusing.

Michael got busy straightening books on the shelf, "Just never got around to it – you know me. Lena and Judith must have forgotten about it too because I sure did."

Why wasn't he facing me directly, why was he speaking with his back to me? I thought – Michael hasn't done any late evening classes, at least not recently. Michael was forgetful, but it was unlike Judith or Lena to have forgotten about the key. Keys like that were expensive. I wanted to believe him, but the key didn't have a code or the locksmith's name. That meant it was an illegal replica. That suggested underhand behaviour and sneaking around, and I didn't want to associate him with that.

He turned towards me then, "I used the key to let my street pals stay overnight in the school a few times."

"What! Supposing William Whyte walked in on top of you, you know how he drops in there at all hours?" Now I was anxious about him getting caught.

"It was during that freezing cold period – Whyte was back in England for a visit. We brought in food. I could have taken them to a café, but it seemed less trouble to use the school than to sit on some hostile terrace where we were asked to move along. It was too cold to go to a park or some other haunt of theirs."

"The coffee – have they been taking it?"

"Not at all, absolutely not. That's awful stuff. We bought and brought everything we used. They might have messed the place a little, but we always cleaned up."

"That's it – you went in there, sat around, washed up and cleaned up?"

"Yes, it was just those nights when it was really cold."

I couldn't criticize him for being big-hearted. But why couldn't he have told me straight out the real reason for keeping the duplicate key, why pretend he had forgotten about it? Using the school to give some homeless people shelter wasn't the crime of the century. Didn't he realise that I wouldn't have minded? I'd even have helped him. Did he trust me so little? I couldn't understand it. It made no sense or maybe I'd never understood him. He was either very calculating, which I preferred not to consider, or still just a boy. Not long ago, we were sharing supper on the seventh floor with the others and I felt I had known him forever. We were lovers, I thought, friends. Sure, people kept secrets from one another, but these were basic things that he held back from me. I tried to push my thoughts away, but the words of Marc-Antoine calling me self-righteous came back. Marc-Antoine said so many things, but the one that stuck with me was saying that my judgemental behaviour encouraged people to become deceitful. Rather than admit to something, they preferred to hide the truth from me.

"Michael, I think I'll go back to my room tonight, if I stay here I'll have to be up at six to get out on time to La Défense. It's easier to go from Montrosier."

He looked puzzled, but didn't argue, "It's late, let me go with you or call a taxi."

"No, stay here. It isn't that late, the trains are still running, I'll be home in no time."

"Okay, go home if that's what you want, but I'm still calling for a taxi."

"Oh, alright."

I could see that he was upset, but was glad he didn't insist on my staying. I couldn't have pretended or been able to reach deep enough to find the right feeling, not with the confused emotions churning inside me. I wouldn't ask, didn't want to ask Michael directly for the truth, it would be stupid over a key – that would be doubting him. I wasn't going to ask Lena either if he had done any late classes recently. I had to pretend though when he kissed me goodnight. I was angrier with myself than with Michael for allowing those stupid jealous thoughts destroy our evening.

Ursula wasn't sound asleep, as I'd been hoping. No sooner had I closed my door than the footsteps pattered up, followed by the knock, which accepted no refusal.

"Didn't expect you back or alone," Ursula pushed the door in. "Is something wrong?"

"No, I'm all done in, that's all, and I have to be up very early."

"You're not good at it, Liz."

"At what?"

"At lying."

I hated that word, "I see."

"Yes, and I see a lot on your face. I see that something is up and it has to do with Michael."

"It's nothing that I want to talk about, I'm just a little peed off about some trivial things. It isn't important."

"That may be the case. But you've helped me out, listened to me. I can listen, I am able to." Ursula took my only chair and sat in front of me. There was nowhere else to sit. It was practically her chair anyway, her spot, her room. I didn't know when or how it had happened, but I'd lost ground to her. Why, the girl even had some of her clothes hanging from my rails.

Ursula put her hand to her ear, "I'm ready."

I made an effort at being civil, "I know, but it's really nothing important and I do need to go to bed. Ursula wasn't budging immediately, she stretched her hand back to open the door again and let in Elle. The tabby claimed her usual spot, the biggest spot ever, right in the middle of the bed. I had to shift to give her space.

"Really, Ursula, I am okay, there is no need to sit up with me."

"I know, but just making sure. Guess what?" Ursula changed the subject. She knew when I wouldn't be persuaded.

"What?"

"I've been counting the days that the toilet has stayed clean. We've passed into the seventh and I'm beginning to get used to it. I think Olivier has finally got the message. I suspect that he'd a change of attitude after we shared the midnight meal with him."

"It's possible."

Ursula stood up, "Do you mind if I keep Elle tonight?"

"No, she is your cat."

"Elle is a comfort to me, she hunts away my awful dreams – cats must have the power to absorb bad vibes. I've noticed also since we started investigating the brothels that I've been tormented less by ghosts. So between that and Elle, it's all helping."

"David's helping a lot too, no?"

"Of course."

"See David this evening?" I couldn't resist probing.

"Unfortunately not, he was tied up with religious stuff."

"That's what he does."

"Sure, I'm not complaining. It's clear in my mind, I'm not mixing things up like you seem to suspect."

"I don't suspect anything," I assured Ursula. "David's a nice guy, but he is also attractive and if I may say so myself, it's a terrible waste to see him lost to the Church. I wouldn't blame you if you'd other ideas."

"Well, I don't, it's just friendship."

Perhaps I was misunderstanding Ursula. She was working real hard at this friendship with David and wasn't going to encourage him to abandon his spiritual ideals for a few nights of passion. At least, Ursula wasn't going to do that consciously, but God help the unconscious side. How blind people could be, I thought. How perceptive we were when it came to seeing things in other people's lives but not our own. Ursula had probably noticed a hundred and one things in Michael that I refused to see. We all harboured our own illusions.

****

"I reckon you would need at least two thousand hours to go from elementary level to post-elementary level."

I'd reached 'Oxford' when I fully registered what I'd just heard Lena tell a potential client. 'Lena has flipped,' I said to myself, 'she's finally completely flipped.' I dropped my bags and went back down the corridor just in time to see a stunned-looking man reeling out into the yard. He stood disorientated for a few seconds, looked back at the school and bolted.

"Lena, have you lost it?"

"Why are you staring at me like that, is there something on my face?" Lena touched her forehead.

"No, but I can't believe you slammed the door so hard on a potential client. I've never seen you do something like that before, not so heartlessly."

Lena frowned at me, "I've got a big heart and I'm charitable, but ain't no point in selling hope when there's none. That guy ain't ever going to progress. Nothing, not even a trip to Lourdes, will help him."

"But I thought you believed no-hopers were vital money spinners for the school. You said they were ideal for multiple contracts. You could have had at least three contracts out of that guy."

"Likely I might, but no law against rewriting company rules. From time to time, you've gotta give the poor sucker sitting in front of you some honesty. That guy's already tried everything to improve his English level and it ain't working. He should invest his hard-earned money on something else."

"Couldn't you have given him the bottom line a little more softly and saved his pride?"

"I tried. I spent a half hour dropping little hints, then bigger and bigger hints. But he didn't want to hear. So in the end, I had to give it to him straight."

Lena was good at hiding her thoughts and diverting people from the real situation. But I was beginning to see through her.

"You've gone through a lot of cigarettes today."

"Now, how do you make that out? How do you know what I have or haven't smoked?"

"I don't have to be very clever to see that you've made in-roads into a second box," I pointed to the bin and to the open pack on her desk. "Where is Judith?"

"In 'St. Alban's' in conference with Mr. Whyte."

"Oh, is there a problem?"

"Don't see why a Friday debriefing should be a problem."

"So was it boredom that made you plough through all those cigarettes. I'm surprised Hamilton isn't smouldering with ash."

"Don't exaggerate, I'm no volcano. Hamilton is happy to make jaunts in and out to the yard, keeps him toned up. And I only tip my cigarette on him from time to time."

"You'll have to try harder, Lena."

Lena picked up her pack, "Which reminds me, time for another."

Hamilton followed dutifully without yanking at the leash. He understood the difference between Lena's cigarette exits and real walking.

I looked at the clock and followed her. I had a few minutes to spare. Lena was in that sort of strange humour where she could let a few secrets slip out. It might be worthwhile being there if and when that happened. Something was amiss and I was willing to rake up what snippets of information were going.

Lena cupped her two hands around the cigarette in a practiced gesture, "I'd offer you one, but they're bad for you." She narrowed her eyes and inhaled, long and deep, "Any plans for the weekend?"

"I'd like to go to a museum or the cinema – go to the forest and fill my lungs with fresh air. But I mightn't do any of that, it all depends."

"On what?"

"Things"

"On Michael?"

"It depends on money."

Lena took a few more drags, "Everything depends on money, but no harm in making plans."

"No, but I like to keep them too. Anyway, I don't like planning, I prefer to take things as they come."

Lena flicked her cigarette, "Used to think that, not sure anymore. The older you get the more you plan, but you plan smaller and in greater detail."

"Have you thought of what you'll do when you really retire?"

"I might not have that choice, or it might be a lot sooner than I think, than we all think."

"What are you saying, Lena – that you're leaving?"

She looked at me through a haze of smoke, "Did I say that? I don't recall saying it. I'm just rambling on, talking to myself, I do that a lot. Man, sometimes thinking around here ain't advisable."

Lena was definitely out of tune today. I didn't know if it were a little bout of the blues or if this conference between Judith and Mr. Whyte had something to do with it. The courtyard doors clicked. I wasn't going to find out now, the first of my students was arriving.

16

It was not the best way to start a Saturday. I paced around the office muttering out loud, "Lena, I'll kill you. If you were to walk in here right now, I'd have your bones for soup – no matter a miserable watery broth, you're for it. I knew there was something bothering you yesterday. Why couldn't you have been frank and saved me all this trouble today? Damn it, you and Judith have dropped me in it."

I wanted to scream and throw something, anything. Ursula had already rung the first alarm bells late yesterday evening on her return from the bank machine, "No bloody transfer!" she shouted to anyone who cared to listen on the corridor before slamming her door. Then a text arrived from Michael at half past midnight to inform me that his new trick – I scratched my head trying to remember which one it was – had gone down well with a bunch of slightly drunk adults, in a club I'd never heard of. Fortunately he'd been paid cash in hand, as his bank account had shown no money transfer from the school. I'd checked my own account at the back machine on my way to Rue des Soeurs this morning – just in case of a miracle – but not a Euro had been transferred. I knew that all or most of W.W.S.O.E. & F.L. teachers would have discovered the same thing. That meant at least fifty of them.

It was seven o'clock. I'd come to the school two hours before the first classes – it was stupid really, as if being there early was going to help me solve the issue. But I thought maybe Lena or Judith might have left a word. They surely would have written a note or something, seeing as they had lacked the courage to tell me to my face. But there was nothing. The only useful thing I did was to look in the petty cash box which contained 500 Euros and 30 Cents.

I sat down, sipped a coarse coffee and waited, calculating how to split the petty cash if necessary. I placed two phone numbers in front of me. I'd respect the fact it was the weekend and that perhaps Judith and Lena slept in. I could be polite. However, at one second past nine, each of those numbers would be rung. I wasn't sure that management would be in a hurry to answer, but I intended to leave stiff messages. If I had William Whyte's number, I'd ring it too. I didn't. Only Judith had that privilege.

I imagined how wretched the morning was going to be. Teachers would be catty and nasty. I'd have bad-tempered visits and threatening calls. It baffled me that though I just sat in the office, testing and manning the place, it qualified me in the eyes of other teachers as responsible for something. An office position, however lowly, was fair game as far as teachers were concerned.

I heard the door –

"Michael, what are you doing here? Your class doesn't start until ten and with your late night show –" I thought first that he had confused his time. While most group classes started at 9am, Michael's class was an exception. It was a course Lena had added on to catch some additional clients.

He took me in his arms and gave me a great bear hug.

"Shush, Liz, I didn't want to leave you alone to face the music. You being you will take it personally that we have not been paid. It was unbearable imagining you sitting here on your own trying to handle it. I told you that I got paid in cash last night for my magic, so I can tide you over and Ursula too, if needs be. It's your rent weekend and you are still paying back for that computer. I know the score – you're skint."

It cheered my heart so much. His thoughtfulness of coming in earlier for me wiped out all his little flaws. Even if I got stoned and slain by the others, Michael being there for me changed everything. If they put me in front of the firing squad, I'd die happy now.

"You're a treasure, Michael, I feel better already. I'd been thinking of how, for the first time, I would have to ask Mme Defoe to bail me out. I'd hate to have to do that. I'm supposed to drop the rent envelope to Mme Misere, my landlady, sometime today."

"Put your mind at ease. I'm here, you're covered now."

Feeling fortified, I went to open all doors.

I watched several teachers arrive together. Coming as a group was ominous, they'd probably been at a café shaking fists and rebel rousing. Ursula would be here just in time or a few minutes after it. A threat of being homeless or risk of starvation weren't enough to have her change routine by getting out of bed extra early.

I saw mutiny on teachers' faces.

"Where's our money?" demanded Jonathan, his eyes still stuck together from late night drinking.

Banging her locker like a drum, Cynthia snarled at me, "Liz, why didn't we get paid?"

"We aren't a charity," Angie swung her bag dangerously.

Charles, a small blocky, bespectacled teacher, who had recently been recruited, stood before me looking ominous, "I'm new here – if this is usual practice, I'm quitting."

"Hello, Richard, who are you replacing?" I gave him a sunny smile.

"I'm teaching the Elementary Business class," he huffed as he gripped his clock. He was counting the seconds down to blast off. "But," he continued, "I refuse to teach if I'm not paid."

"Listen, all of you," I reasoned, aware that students were beginning to stream in and that the phone had started ringing, "please start your classes. I'll ring Judith and try to get some answers – okay? Please."

Michael stood protectively near me, "Come on guys, Liz is in exactly the same predicament as you. If you want to take it out on someone, take it out on the management Monday."

The teachers went to their rooms reluctantly, the last traces of professionalism getting them that far at least. But it had only just begun, there followed lots of banging doors, scraping chairs and generous helpings of coffee. If the school had more windows, they'd have been shattered by now.

There was Ursula's delayed arrival, "I'm right aren't I – the bastards haven't paid us?"

"Ursula, just get started with your class and we'll talk about that after. The good news is that Michael will help us out over the weekend."

"It shouldn't be that way."

"Just get the class going."

Neither Lena nor Judith was answering her phone. But I was surprised that my ears weren't on fire as storms and fury came through the lines from other teachers. I tried to smile diplomatically at the unsuspecting potential students I tested. The words rolled off my tongue, "Yes, Whyte's is a great school, all our teachers are certified. You won't find a better place to help you improve your level." I mustered up all the fervour I had as I ushered each hopeful to the door.

The phone clients were easier. I could listen and reply coolly, "That's right, our teachers are very involved. Not only do they have the skills and competence, but they love their job."

I left additional cries for help on the answer machines of Judith and Lena.

I braced myself at break time.

Richard was the first to re-appear. He walked into the office and sat down solemnly at my desk. He then removed his wrist watch and laid it in front of me, "I'm not going back to the classroom."

"You're on strike," I feared the worst.

"I am not on strike, I'm simply not going back."

Cynthia and Angie walked in, pulled up chairs noisily and sat down.

Jonathan and Charles squeezed inside and leaned against the wall, "We," announced Jonathan, "are going to the pub. Give us the money from the petty cash or we're going to take it ourselves. It shouldn't be difficult to crack open the box."

The group had become a mutinous mob and I'd be lynched. I was feeling faint, the best solution would be to just pass out and let the rest up to fate.

There were curious onlookers as students stood helpless and lost in the corridor.

"Close the door, would you?" I spoke to Charles.

He didn't move.

Michael arrived and found a place among us, "No need to worry," he appealed to everyone; "after class this morning, we'll all get something to eat, I'll cover it."

I raised my hand, "No Michael, you can't pay for everyone. I can give out the petty cash. I'll just leave a message on Judith's phone asking for permission in these emergency circumstances."

Ursula came through the office next door. "We can't go on like this. We're giving our best and this is how we're treated. What's happening here, we need answers? Is this place going down the drain or what?"

Trust Ursula to calm the waters. I braved the very unhappy campers, "Look, this isn't the time to discuss the problem," I felt Michael's arm come around my shoulder. That sealed it, I had fallen in love with him again if that were possible.

The phone rang, I ignored it.

Ursula grabbed the line from the neighbouring desk, "William Whyte's School of Edjets, Fools and Losers, Bon-feckin-jour."

"Ursula! Don't do that," I took the phone line back, "Bonjour?" Silence – what did I expect, another potential customer scared away.

I painted a pained smile for a perplexed student standing at the other side of the glass door. Then I turned to the teachers and addressed them, "I can't force you one way or another. I'm as broke as you are, but I'll finish out the morning and come back on Monday with my grievance. This isn't the time or place for it. You make up your own minds. If you aren't going to teach your classes, tell me and I will inform your students right now. What's it to be – teach or not?"

"I'm with Liz," Michael said, "we owe it to our students at least. I'm not sending those people home. I intend to finish the class today and wait until next week to challenge Judith."

Richard took out a small clock from his pocket and studied its flashing digits. He compared those to the hands on his watch and then to the clock on the wall, "I'll teach for another hour and a quarter and that's it."

"Not without some compensation," said Jonathan.

"He's right," Cynthia was in fighting form.

"Okay, okay, I'll divide the petty cash and whatever else."

"I need envelopes and paper?" Angie was driving a hard bargain.

"Fine, the office supplies can spare a few."

"And some highlighter pens," Cynthia added.

"It's a deal."

That settled it. The mutiny was temporarily contained and the teachers trudged to the classrooms to resume their lessons.

Michael bounced back in to give me a little kiss, "That's my girl."

He hadn't put a foot wrong, he'd been everything I'd hoped for, with me every step of the way. I might have succeeded without him, but it sure felt better with him.

As for the others, I didn't care. If they wanted to ransack the school for all the valuables they could find, then let them. I was pretty confident that apart from already depleted stocks of stationery, there wasn't much else up for grabs. But how many more times was this going to happen? I pulled out Lena's large calendar and looked to see what day the end of May was falling on. I breathed a sigh of relief – it wasn't going to fall on a weekend. That was something, anyway.

At half past midday, I heard a familiar bark – Lena, at last. If she'd the neck to come in and say hello, the situation might not be as bad as that.

I practically ambushed her, "Lena, Lena, nobody's been paid and we're all flat broke. We've had no notice or warning. It isn't fair. You know how people count on their pay being transferred, we've all got bills to meet."

"Hey," Lena braked and reversed, almost trampling Hamilton, "hey, cool it now, I don't know anything."

I wrestled with my emotions. I was making the same mistake with Lena as the other teachers had with me. I was assuming that she knew something. Lena wasn't a full insider. She wasn't invited to every management meeting. Still, she was friendly with Judith.

"Look, Lena, this is happening too often. It just isn't acceptable."

"Honey, what are you talking about, what do you mean not paid?" Lena seemed genuinely bewildered.

"Didn't you check your own account?" I asked.

"No, not yet."

"Well, I don't know about you, but none of the teachers have been paid."

"You're kidding me."

"Look, Lena, I'm going to have to give what's in the petty cash to a few teachers to help tide them over. Do you agree?"

"Sure, if they give it back."

"I can't guarantee that. But I'm giving it and anything else people might need: coffee, tea, or whatever is in the cupboards, right."

"I guess so, but I ain't the boss here."

"Where's Judith, I've left several messages on her phone and yours too?"

"Ah, I'm no good at technology, those answer machines and gadgets –"

"That I can believe – and Judith?"

"Judith's away for the weekend –"

"Convenient, isn't it?"

"I don't think she planned it that way."

"Oh, come on, Lena, don't play that tune with me!"

"Heck, Liz, I wouldn't do that to you or any of the teachers. I'm sure things will be sorted out Monday."

She sounded so genuine, I even felt sorry for her and was mad at myself for having such feelings. I was an easy touch, one doleful doggy look from Lena and I was on the retreat.

I looked at the wall clock and said calmly, "Lena, do you see the time, it's five to one."

She was gone in two seconds flat. I watched the back of Hamilton scamper through the courtyard doors. Lena wouldn't stand a chance against a mob of teachers. Sometimes it pays to know when to cut one's losses.

****

After a weekend of lying low and minimum spending, I sought out Judith for explanations and excuses before my Monday evening classes at the school.

"It's nothing," said Judith, all big smiles and white teeth, "there's nothing to be worried about. You can't trust banks these days. Everything is fine, we've never had more demand for our classes in school. Mr. Whyte and I have just signed some new company contracts. The future is secure."

I didn't blame Judith, but I didn't believe a word. Why should I? I'd observed her in action and I'd had first-hand experience with angry teachers and students myself. I did exactly what I'd seen Judith do and what she was now doing: improvised, pulled out every argument in the book and dragged my lips upwards, wading through it all. It was as natural as sunshine and rain. But I couldn't help pointing out the obvious, "P.A.F.I. is still, despite all that, your biggest client."

"Yes," said Judith, "but our margins are better with our smaller clients."

I dropped the subject. I'd heard it all before, margins and waffle. I didn't have the financial details nor was I a whiz like M. Chevalier, but I did know one thing: when people started feeding you facts about margins and using jargon like that, it was a sure sign they were fencing.

I compared notes with Ursula and Michael during coffee break in 'Lindisfarne'. Ursula picked up gossip from P.A.F.I., we all did. But Michael had the inside story through Mme Michot.

"It's now official. The tender to select the future supplier of language training in P.A.F.I. has been opened," Ursula poured herself some water.

"Has our school been invited to make a bid?" I asked.

"Yes," said Michael, "along with three other schools. The final decision will be made after they appoint the C.F.O., or so the HR says."

Something in how Michael mentioned the HR irritated me, "Your Mme Michot talks a lot. I'm not sure that I would trust her. A HR isn't supposed to blab like that, above all to someone from the school."

Michael made a nervous movement, "The point is, if Whyte loses the tender, it will spell the end of the line for the school and us."

He was right. The longer I worked in Whyte's the more obvious it became. The school wasn't prospering as Judith liked to point out. The place wasn't coping so well with the technological revolution. It wasn't changing fast enough with the times. It was obvious that under William Whyte's outdated style of management, the school was stagnating. To make matters worse, he was milking off all the profits to support his personal life. Judith didn't have the power or the means to change things. She was trying to develop the online side to the language programme, but she needed experts and experts cost money. Judith didn't have it. So it was secondhand everything, botching with old computers and patching things up.

The school had to polish up its image, add a veneer of modernity to the traditional approach. It was true, people wanted and needed 'the genuine teacher' to motivate them, make them speak and react in real time. That was something no online technology could match. Apart from living in a native English-speaking country, a real teacher was still the best way to practice conversation with learners and to help them to commit to regular work. Unfortunately, teachers were variable in quality and W.W.S.O.E. & F.L. paid a heavy price to provide the real thing. Social contributions and taxes in France were crippling. As Lena frequently pointed out – serious teaching was as much a vocation as it was a business. One would never be rich from it, but they could be reasonably comfortable, if they didn't get too greedy.

"That's the trouble," Ursula said, "William Whyte has got too greedy and he's pulling everyone down with him. If you get a chance this Saturday, Liz, see if you can find anything in Judith's office on the school accounts."

"No guarantees – that's easier said than done."

The following Saturday was a much quieter affair. Teachers had been paid and all threats of riots were temporarily suspended. I stayed on after everybody had left and deliberated about snooping around or not. I had been thinking about Ursula's suggestion and wondered if Judith did keep some files on school finances in her office. In the end, I decided against poking around – I would just lock up and be on my way.

Suddenly my skin felt prickly all over. I heard steps on the corridor. Who was it this time – the invisible cleaners, another hallucination of mine…?

Jeffrey walked straight into Judith's office, "Excuse me, Mr. Whyte asked me to do a few things for him." He switched on the computer.

"Be my guest, I'm out of here." Cheek of him, I thought. I took my bag as my mobile phone began ringing, "Yes, Ursula, I'll be with you in a tick, order the usual for me."

William Whyte appeared before me. "I want to see you," he looked at me stonily.

"Will it take long, Mr. Whyte? I'm in a hurry and should have left more than half an hour ago. I'm really on overtime."

"It will only take a few minutes."

I followed him, even if I hated doing it, especially when I noticed a smirk on Jeffrey's conceited face.

I looked at my watch and sat down in 'Saint Alban's'.

Mr. Whyte clasped his hands, "I've had several complaints from students – clients of W.W.S.O.E. & F.L. about the conduct of teachers last Saturday. In addition, items and money disappeared from the premises. You are incompetent at running the office."

I was flabbergasted and struggled to keep a rein on my temper, "I am not running the office on Saturdays. My job is to test potential clients. The teachers, including me, weren't paid on time, this is not a new occurrence.

Contrary to what you say, I've been very competent. Last Saturday I went beyond the realms of duty to save a very desperate situation. I got the teachers to return to their classrooms when the mood was to quit there and then. Moreover, the petty cash and items taken were done so with the knowledge of management. I informed Judith and Lena. It isn't my job to stop a stampede of angry teachers. But I did. I think you should thank me for it."

My angry counterattack destabilised him. He leaned back in his chair and studied me, "My concern is to maintain order in the school and to keep the client happy. I'll discuss the matter with Judith. If I'm mistaken, then we will leave the matter rest there."

It was something I suppose, William Whyte admitting that he might be making a mistake. I prepared to leave.

"There is a second problem, if you don't mind bearing with me a few minutes more," he tapped the desk.

I sat again.

He examined his pen, "There has been too much loitering on these premises."

"I'm not sure I fully get your point, Mr. Whyte."

"If classes are over at one o'clock, then the school should be vacated and locked by a quarter past."

So that's what was bothering him. "I don't loiter, I sometimes stay on later to do class preparation."

"I fully appreciate that, Miss Downey, but rules are rules. You do understand that this is a matter of insurance. We cannot risk an accident outside normal work hours."

"I see."

"Naturally," he became more conciliatory, "if you wish to stay later for preparation, I would be willing to facilitate that. You must simply inform me the day before of your intention. Do you understand?"

"Yes, I understand very well."

He smiled, though I wish he hadn't. "I must congratulate you on M. Chevalier's progress. But I hear that M. Fabre has a slight edge over him. That is understandable given Jeffrey's experience."

"M. Chevalier only started serious training last autumn. M. Fabre has done previous courses."

"It isn't a competition. We're a team and what counts is the name of this school. If either candidate succeeds, our contribution, however great or small, will be noted. Everything will help our bid for future training contracts."

I let him have the last word. I'd stood my ground and that was enough for me. I wondered why the conscientious behaviour of a teacher staying on later to prepare classes would bother him. I certainly didn't believe his explanation and decided that he must be using illegal immigrants as cleaners and that's why it was all hush hush and why he didn't want me staying on without informing him.

17

At P.A.F.I. M. Chevalier had a new demand: "I want to work on presentation vocabulary?"

I felt like pointing out that we'd already covered presentation vocabulary dozens of times. In fact, he could open up a chapter or section of one of the many books I'd given him and find enough expressions to make presentations for the rest of his working life and after. Instead, I said, "Sure, we can revise presentation vocabulary, why not. I could give you a little test on it next class."

"The interview and assessment is tomorrow, I will be asked to present my strategy," he said calmly.

"What! The assessment is tomorrow? I thought you told me it was a week off!"

"The date was changed, it's now May 10th."

"Do you feel ready?"

"We have prepared."

"You must be a bit nervous about it though?"

"Nervous?" he inspected the word as if he were conducting an internal audit.

"You know, butterflies in your stomach, anxious."

"Butterflies? Anxious?" he inspected those words also and didn't seem to find them to his liking either.

"It's important, you've been thinking about it for months."

"I cannot allow myself to be worried. It will be a full day. There are several interviews and evaluation exercises in English. Members of the international board will participate."

"If you don't succeed, what will you do?"

"You have prepared me well and I will succeed."

Oh, dear, I thought, already beginning to feel the pressure.

The following evening, not even Michael was enough to distract me. I had no feedback about how the interviews and assessment had gone and it was driving me demented.

I climbed back into Michael's bed and rearranged the blankets.

"Liz."

"Hmm."

"That's the third time you've gotten out of bed."

"Is it?"

"You shouldn't get so involved with your students' problems."

"I can't help it, Michael."

"You did your best. If M. Chevalier doesn't succeed, it won't reflect on you."

"It's not that, I – he's grown on me, I kinda like him and I want him to do well."

"I hope he realises how involved you are, how much of yourself you've put into helping him."

"That isn't important."

"It is for me."

"Michael?"

"Yes."

"Has Mme Michot given any hints about how the assessments went?"

He burst out laughing.

"What's so funny?"

"I'm telling you nothing. If I do, you'll accuse the HR of talking too much. So forget it."

"But the next time you have a class you could just mention to her that you heard Fabre was a slime bag and that they would be out of their minds to give him the job."

"You're a conniving fairy. Do you really think they would listen to the opinion of an English teacher?"

"I don't see why not," I started to get out of bed again.

"No you don't," Michael pinned me down, "there's only one solution to us getting a good night's sleep –"

"Hey, let me get up, I must have a glass of water."

"You're not moving, it's all in your head."

I found the ideal place to nip him.

"You little vampire, for that you're going to pay. You're playing with fire," he began tickling me.

"Stop, please, people die from tickles."

We struggled playfully with each other until the play turned to passion and I thought only of Michael.

****

Laundry day usually put us in a bad mood. Ursula and I tried to avoid doing it on a Saturday or Sunday, but it often ended up being done on a Saturday or a Sunday. This time it was Saturday and having already worked the morning in the school, it felt terrible to waste another hour of the day on laundry. The nearest laundrette was on Rue de Chartier, about two minutes from Rue Montrosier, but the inconvenience of the stairs made the task harder.

"Boring, boring," said Ursula, "what a waste of a life watching and waiting for that dryer."

"Are you talking about your life or mine," I sat down with resignation on one of the benches in the launderette.

"All the lives in all the launderettes in the whole wide world. I can't wait for the day that I'll have a flat of my own. I wish and wish and wish, but I don't see it coming."

"Oh," I said, "I don't care about owning a flat, I just want my own toilet. The day I have a proper toilet is the day I'll consider myself rich. "

"Some people have limited ambitions."

"So be it, I'm a limited woman and right now having that toilet is my horizon. I see it there in front of me. It will have a wooden seat, a little silver handle and a cistern. It's my dream, my beautiful dream."

Ursula ignored my dream, and returned to planning the essential things she needed in her life. "You could ask Mme Defoe to let us use her washing machine. I don't see why not. She puts so much stuff your way, what's one more gesture?"

"No, she is kind to me because I don't abuse it. I don't bother her for things that we can get by without. Besides, going to this launderette is more convenient than going to her place, full stop."

"Don't you understand," Ursula argued, "it's not the inconvenience, but the image. It's our dignity. We're mixing with all the riff-raff – at the lowest level of society."

"Nonsense, I didn't think you were such a snob. The people who come in here aren't especially from any level, they're just like us. In fact, all those people are the true backbone of society."

"If you say so, have it your own way," Ursula took her bag and gestured that she was going outside to smoke.

I watched the water swirling in the machines. Ursula was edgier these days, but that was easily explained by David's two-week retreat in Rome. All plans to go underground with M. Jacques had been put on the back burner for a while. I'd been on tenterhooks myself – the rumour was that both M. Chevalier and M. Fabre had done well in the interviews and now everybody was waiting for the final decision. In the meantime, M. Chevalier had taken a few days off. I hated uncertainty.

I saw Ursula take her phone and move away from the window. It was difficult to make out if she were answering a call, making one, or checking her messages. She had yet to light a cigarette so I concluded that going outside was an excuse to check her messages and I was immediately suspicious. Ursula had become more secretive about consulting her phone or simply handling calls which was unusual for her. She loved an audience and suffered no qualms whatsoever about carrying on a personal conversation within earshot of others. Her approach was usually to live her life in public or at least blur the lines between public and private – although, I had to admit that more recently I was discovering that Ursula had a very private and secret side.

I suspected that Fabre was still harassing her. What bothered me was that Ursula didn't appear to be doing a thing about it. She was just taking it and yet for other things, she fought like a wild cat.

We carried our bags of laundry back to the rooms, complaining and grumbling all the ways to the seventh floor. The task of finding space and the best way to hang them to air was even more challenging and kept us busy for the next hour.

"Nearly finished," called Ursula from her room.

I went to see how she was getting on – very well apparently, "You're a born home organiser – whatever the situation, you manage to find a solution." It was true – she had hangers and hooks for everything.

"I don't consider hanging clothes a necessary skill in life." Ursula moved around the room adjusting and readjusting garments.

I let a moment of silence between us before asking, "Fabre keeps ringing you doesn't he?"

Ursula repositioned some socks on a clothes-horse, "Yes."

"Why don't you change your phone number?"

"I could, but it would be running away and giving into him in a certain way. He will give up in time."

"He's really two-faced but seems a lot more popular than Chevalier in P.A.F.I."

"Oh yes, he can be real charming. At the beginning, I have to say, I fell completely for it. Then we spent that stupid night together when he became weird and spoke of the other stuff."

"About prostitutes and rituals?"

"Yes, he has very extreme views. It's difficult to explain – I once had a friend who got into a type of sect or cult of sorts and Fabre reminded me of him. Would you believe it, this friend tried to save me, told me I was a sinner and I had to follow him, follow the way of the truth."

"Sounds like some born again Christian talk to me."

"Sort of. I could have put up with that part, even if it were heavier than the usual fare. But my friend's other side was ice cold – it was the closest I got to being near someone almost evil. I didn't stick around to discover just what he was capable of doing and cut him out of my life." Ursula sat on the bed and stroked Elle.

"Was Fabre violent?"

"No, but I sensed he could be. It's all foggy in my mind – I just knew when I woke up that I had to get out of there. So you see, I don't have much to hold against him. I was doped myself."

"You really have damning information about him."

"If he and his pals want to use the services of prostitutes and make up their own religion, dance around naked and drink altar wine, while also being respectable members of society, who gives a rat's ass?"

"He obviously does care. You still have group classes out there – is it a problem coming across him on the corridors?"

"I'm coping. But I'll tell you this, Liz, I think it's a problem for him. He knows you and I live near each other –"

"Near – we're clapped up to each other."

"He knows we're friends and with you being M. Chevalier's teacher and then Michael, it's too close for comfort."

"Michael – what's he got to do with it?"

"He's your lover and he's been giving classes to the HR, Mme Michot, for a long time and –" Ursula looked at me.

"And what?" I prompted.

I thought I noticed something pass in her eyes, but she pulled the veil quickly, maybe I'd imagined it.

"And so you get to notice many things. Michael looks so innocent, Mme Michot probably shares many pieces of information with him. Don't forget he's the one who told us Fabre was favourite for this promotion."

I didn't like the direction Ursula was taking this conversation and returned to the more pressing subject, "Are you afraid of Fabre?"

"No – I don't know, I can take care of myself." Ursula's mobile rang and a smile broke out on her face, "Hey, David, how are things? I'm great, so when – "

I went back to my room feeling uneasy. I wished I could be sure that Ursula was able to take care of herself.

****

"A friend of mine is going to the States for two years. It's a work transfer. He's offered to sub-let his flat to me – to us –?" Michael was very concentrated on juggling large silver balls in the centre of his studio room, but the question was there, loud and clear.

"When would it be available?" I asked.

"From the end of August. It's 42m squared and very nice. It would be perfect for us. He is more interested in having someone he can trust take it than making a profit."

226

"Have I met him?"

"No, he's been travelling a lot and preparing for this job change. His name's Chris, Chris Hall."

"How did you do that?"

"Do what?" Michael returned.

"Change those silver balls into silver daggers."

"Shush, if I don't concentrate, one of the blades can cut me badly."

"Oh, sorry," I hushed up immediately, the blades looked shiny and sharp.

Suddenly Michael shouted, "Don't move, don't move one inch," he juggled the daggers in different directions around me, right, left, over my head –

"Michael, what are you doing?" My voice cracked, I felt my mouth go dry – "Michael, stop!"

Michael smiled and let the daggers drop back into his hands, bringing them together with flair, like an experienced card player would shuffle the deck. "It worked, you believed it."

He placed a knife carefully in my hand, "Feel it."

"It's plastic, they weren't real at all."

He took the knife from me, put it back with the bunch, then did a hand wave and fanned the knives out. They clinked, making a distinct metallic sound. "Now I will invite a member of the audience to examine these blades." He handed me one, "Careful."

"How did you do that?" I was impressed. "This one is really sharp. That's a fantastic trick, though I wish you hadn't frightened me like that. Do it slowly for me, so that I can see how you did it."

He shook his head, "If you know how, then it isn't magic anymore. I'm bound to secrecy. But forgive me for frightening you." He bent and kissed me, "Does that make it better?"

"Sort of," I kissed him back, "but as I've said many times already to you and to just about everyone, I'm a very forgiving person."

"Yes, you are." He took up one of the daggers and studied the blade, rubbing his finger gently along the edge, "So was that a yes, you will move in with me?"

"Yes." The ease with which my answer came surprised me.

"You are sure?"

He genuinely sounded relieved. Did he think I would refuse? It was my own fault, I was too used to keeping things to myself and assuming that others understood. I needed to spell things out more clearly. I said, "Yes, Michael, I really do want us to live together and sub-renting that place seems an excellent opportunity."

He put his hands around my waist and waltzed, "You, Liz, are the real magician. You've made so much of a difference to my life in a short time. You've opened me up, made me see things differently – and I love you."

I had that feeling of walking on air. His eyes were serious, this was for real.

"Michael, I do love you too, you know that – "

"Liz, I wasn't sure anymore. You're very hard to make out – I can't always read into what you mean or feel."

"I'm better at showing it in actions than saying it in words."

"I know, but you help out so many people – there's Ursula, many of the teachers in the school –"

"Ursula barged her way into my life. As for the others, I don't sleep with them either."

"I see what you mean. It's just that when we have this need to please people and help them, we can confuse our feelings. We can find ourselves going along with things just because we don't want to hurt someone."

He seemed to really need reassurance. "Listen, I can't speak for you, but I'm not confused or mixing up friends and lovers. I like many, help some, but you are the only one that I love in this way."

He changed the rhythm of the dance and swung me around, "That's what you do in Irish ceilis, isn't it, can we go to an Irish ceili?"

"If we can find one in Paris. Hey careful, you don't have much room in this studio to fling us both into the dizzy heights."

"I don't care, I'm on top of the world and I want to celebrate. Then again we can do that in the old-fashioned way."

"We sure can."

We tumbled onto the bed.

I woke up, still in his arms. My eye fell on the clock radio, "Is that ten o'clock Sunday morning or Monday – because if it's the second, I'll have a fit?"

"Tuesday," yawned Michael, "it's Tuesday actually."

I punched him playfully, "I can tell with my ears. It doesn't sound like Monday or any weekday noise out on that street to me." I turned into him, "I can sleep on."

"You will continue teaching, won't you?" he asked.

"I think so. I do like it, I just have to make it pay a bit more – and – and you?"

Michael didn't reply immediately. After a while, I nudged him, "So?"

He sighed, "I'm no teacher, you know that."

"You're a magician, that's something else. You're a magician and an illusion artist; you bring something special to people's lives."

"Special, I don't know – but that's what I want to do and to be, only better and better. It gives me a high to see the reaction on people's faces and to be able to entertain adults and children alike – there's nothing more rewarding. Unfortunately, as I told you before, that's not enough to live on."

I waited, then asked, "What would make it enough?"

"I could do some corporate events. I've been thinking about that, but to compete in that domain I would need to become much more professional and develop a real business –"

"Like an entertainment company?"

"Yes, and for that, I would have to enlist help. It takes money to set up an entertainment company. I'm afraid I would become a businessman then, rather than a magician."

"And your father is pushing you that way, offering you backing to set up the company?"

"How did you guess?"

"It wasn't difficult."

"You guessed right."

"Maybe you don't have to make the choice. You could get the right people working with you, a partner or partners – find people who have the specialised skills to deal with the business end of things, while you concentrate on your magic. Then you'd please yourself without upsetting your parents."

"That's true."

"It's not easy finding people you can trust. But if you start small, take it slowly, the rest will follow. Don't worry too much – take it one day at a time, each thing in its turn."

He sat up, "Seems so clear and simple when you put it like that. With you I think I can take on the world, my little sorcerer."

"I don't have a magic wand. But I told you I don't mind listening and it helps to share these things."

"Liz, I'm sorry, I'm sorry for keeping you out of my plans. I didn't mean to, I just needed to sort things out in my head before I could talk about them. I wasn't sure how you really felt about me."

"It's okay, no need to explain." And there wasn't. I'd been upset at the time, but it didn't seem important anymore.

"My father is such a domineering man that I need distance from him. He turns me up-side-down each time I have a discussion with him. Afterwards, I'm spinning and it takes me a while to get my bearings again."

"I understand, Michael. He just wants the best for you."

Michael kissed me.

After a while, I asked, "But you didn't tell me where the flat is – where will our first home together be?"

"In Saint Germain des Prés on Rue de Rennes."

"That's an expensive part of Paris, how much is your friend asking?"

"Not too much, I think around 1,200 Euros between us."

It was possible, I could manage that. "There has to be a hitch somewhere."

"It's an old building, so there's no lift."

"Hmm, we're young, we can cope with that. What floor is it on?"

"The seventh."

I jumped up, "It's another room."

"No, it's a converted attic space, like a loft."

"Well, okay," I slipped down under the sheets again.

"There's a nice bedroom and living room; the kitchen is American style and new."

I jumped up again, "You said nothing about the bathroom or toilet. That's it, isn't it – there is no real bathroom or toilet?"

Michael hooted, "I love to tease you – I was waiting for that. There is a toilet and bathroom, with bath and shower, but –"

"But what –?"

"That part hasn't been renovated fully –"

"Huh –"

"– yet, but it will be finished by the end of August."

"You hope. Tell me, does it work now, does the old toilet work?"

"Yes."

"That's alright then," I smiled contentedly and thought, I'll really be in Paris then, actually living in Paris and not hanging off the end of it.

"I've got to get up," Michael groaned, "got to get into routine for my show tonight."

"What is it?"

"An 18th birthday party."

Michael took his shower. I listened to him splash while whistling a tune. I heard him take his shaving gear as he went from whistling to singing, and back to whistling. He emerged, shiny as a new pin.

I stayed in bed watching him indulgently. For the first time, I felt we were a real couple.

"Pity you have to go." I eyed him seductively, "I think you should get dressed, the people in the flats across the street are getting value for money."

Michael took his sleek black outfit with glittery stars – his star suit, he called it.

"What's up with Ursula and Dave?" he asked.

"Nothing, I think. I believe her when she says there isn't anything between them except a sort of friendship."

Michael shook his head doubtfully.

"That's the situation for the moment. I'm not saying that David isn't playing with fire – the fires of hell and all the demons and ghosts from the other side. But they are consenting adults and I'm sure God will get over it if David digresses from his spiritual path. I can't see what harm it will do to anyone."

Michael pulled me up, "Lazy bones, enjoy my place, bye my love."

I nodded off again into a pleasant slumber, the word 'love' ringing sweetly in my ears.

It was getting late, time to move. I got out of bed, showered, got dressed and gathered my things. I should get going – tomorrow I would be facing a new teaching experience: telephone classes, in fact a string of telephone classes on the trot. I'd accepted the deal because the classes could be taken from home, but thinking about it now – eight thirty-minute telephone classes seemed a lot.

'Oh, damn,' my foot struck a pile of papers on the floor, over it went. I knelt and began to put everything back in order. The pile consisted of class notes and files. It amazed me that his teaching folders were so slim. Guys were like that, they didn't accumulate pages and pages of notes. My eye caught a name on one of the files: Mme Anicee Michot – P.A.F.I. Human Resources Manager. The urge to open it was stronger than me – I scanned the dates on the cover and noted that he had been teaching her for over two years. I hadn't fully realised it was that long. A progress report fell out and I couldn't help glancing over it.

'Anicee is a wonderful, talented student and truly a pleasure to teach. She has mastered many of the basic structures and taken on board lots of new vocabulary. Anicee is very hard working and open to doing lots of homework – excellent example to team and colleagues. Despite a busy timetable, she keeps and respects her class times…'

He had written a lot of drivel and it went on. It certainly was full of glowing compliments. Although I too tended to be positive and constructive in my notes, I didn't put on so much gloss. I tried to remember what I'd noticed from my few brief encounters with the HR. While the woman did have a reasonably good level in English, she wasn't brilliant. So perhaps Michael was trying to boost her confidence. Oh well, I concluded, everyone had their own style and ways of doing things and Michael did say that he wasn't planning a career in teaching. I looked at another page that was just full of doodles – that must have been a class when Mme Michot had talked non-stop. I tended to do that myself – scribble and sketch. I studied his doodles, groups of stars and smiling faces. There was another page of doodles with lots of flowers, cute rabbits and hearts. I grew uncomfortable as I realised they weren't Michael's doodles but hers. I put the documents back in their file and dropped it on the pile.

18

It was Ascension Thursday and one of the many Public Holidays in France during the month of May. Ursula had been lying low all week, which made me ill-at-ease. I would have expected her to be out and about, especially on such a sunny day. I decided to look into things by carrying out an experiment. I took a plastic bag, shook and crinkled it good and loud to give the impression I was taking something to the rubbish bins in the courtyard. However, it didn't produce the desired result of making my neighbour appear at the door with a request for me to take her rubbish bag too.

Elle wasn't coming to my room either and seemed to be keeping vigil next door. That decided it for me, something was definitely up.

I knocked, "Ursula – Ursula?"

There was no answer, but I was sure she was in there.

I tried again, "Ursula?" Louder, "Ursula?"

Finally I heard the bed creaking and the door opened slowly. A pale-faced Ursula stood before me.

"Are you all right, are you sick?"

"I was asleep, I don't feel great – something I ate. I'm just going to lie down again." Ursula retreated inside and lay on her bed.

"Do you want me to fetch you something from the pharmacy or

supermarket?"

"No, that's okay." She pulled a rug around her, while Elle curled up near her mistress.

"Shall I get a doctor?"

"No, it will pass, just indigestion."

"You've complained of that before. You should really check it out."

"I'm already getting better; I've just got a delicate stomach."

I looked for other clues, "Is David okay?"

"David is wonderful, the best thing that ever happened me since I came to Paris.

Imagine, I have to find the most fantastic Irishman here and not at home."

"Is something going on between you?"

"No," said Ursula plaintively, with a quaver in her voice, enough to convince me that David was still hanging on to his celibate status.

"Is there something else, has Fabre contacted you?"

"No, he just stopped and I think I know why."

"Enlighten me."

"Probably because the decision for the promotion at P.A.F.I. has been taken."

"It has! How come I heard nothing about it? Who did they choose – tell me, don't keep me in suspense?"

"I'm sorry, Liz, I heard about it late yesterday and didn't want to spoil your night. The rumour is that Fabre got the promotion."

"Fabre! They're giving the job to Fabre. I don't believe it." The disappointment was overwhelming.

"Apparently, Fabre told Jeffrey, who ran straight off to tell Whyte. It hasn't been officially announced, but that's the rumour."

I was as much distraught for M. Chevalier as I was for myself. I'd always thought deep down that he'd get the promotion. I'd hung on to the idea that good wins out, but nobody ever said that life was fair.

****

Across the bare meeting room table at P.A.F.I. M. Chevalier had assumed his granite face.

"I'm sorry, M. Chevalier, I really am. I think you would have made a great C.F.O." I didn't know what else to say.

"Thank you. That's life – I think the expression works well in both languages. I have often heard you say that."

I felt that his making the effort to take things philosophically was courageous and mature.

"Oh, that old expression – saying it is easier than swallowing it," I said.

"I will have other opportunities."

"I hope so. Will you go on working in P.A.F.I. as Internal Audit Manager?"

"For now, yes. But some things may change, I cannot say for sure yet."

"I see," I looked at my documents. It seemed pointless to even try to carry on a normal class.

"Do you have a particular exercise you would like me to do?" His voice was wooden.

I opened my file, "Yes, there are still a lot of things to work on."

He dutifully took out a writing pad and pen, meticulously dated the page and waited for my next instructions.

I flicked the pages of a book, "So – M. Chevalier –"

"I'm listening."

"Look, about your classes – what do you really want to do? What are your plans? Do you want to continue English training?"

He coughed, "It's true that I will be busy, very, very busy for some time –"

"Yes?"

"So maybe I should suspend my training for now."

"I see. We can stop the classes from today if you wish." I spoke reasonably, but inside I felt let down. Yet, I knew he was right, it was better to stop now, rather than end up with him postponing and cancelling. The goal was behind us. The race was run and he'd come away with the silver medal.

"Only if it does not disturb you."

"No, I agree. It's a good idea to stop."

"I will renew my classes later. I promise I will re-contact you as soon as things have – have been clarified."

"Sure." He would never contact me again, I thought. This was it. He had to find some way of finishing and was trying to do it softly. Of course he would need to do training again in the future, but it wouldn't be with me. It was bye-bye without saying goodbye.

"I have made a lot of progress in English and it is all thanks to you," he sounded like he meant it.

"I did what I could."

He stood up, "Would you mind if I – if you would excuse me –"

"Good English," I complimented him on his use of part of a polite expression.

"I got it from my teacher." He held out his hand, "Thank you."

I shook it, "Goodbye then."

"Goodbye."

M. Chevalier left. Fabre would soon be C.F.O. I was sure P.A.F.I. hadn't made the right choice. Their finances would be in a lot safer hands with M. Chevalier. If it came to honesty, there was no match, as far as I was concerned. Then again, company directors didn't ask the opinion of English teachers, nor were English teachers the most objective or qualified group of people.

I was completely dejected. I packed up my things one by one: CDs, books, markers, and pens. I had too many pens – I wanted to throw them at the wall.

****

"Are you so disappointed that M. Chevalier stopped classes with you?" Ursula glanced at me from my wardrobe mirror as she experimented with different shades of eye shadow. "There was a time I remember that you couldn't wait to finish with him, you were practically driving nails into his coffin after each class."

I pushed my teaching bag under the bed. "I won't deny that he wasn't a bag of fun at the beginning. But I changed my mind. He reminds me of you – a pebble in my shoe that I've gotten so used to. I wouldn't know anymore how to live without the discomfort."

"Thanks for the wonderful compliment."

"You're a regular pain in the ass and well you know it. But you do have some saving graces."

Ursula appeared to prosper under my compliments.

"It isn't so much finishing with M. Chevalier," I explained, "it's finishing on a losing note."

"But, Liz, there are positives. William Whyte will have the result he wanted, so the school will bumble along for a while longer."

"I suppose, but I think I'll find another school to work in. I'll start looking for something else after my move with Michael."

"Me too, I'm going to take up evening classes as well."

"Really, what are you going to study?"

"History and Civilisation in the Sorbonne. David thinks it is a very good idea."

"I do too."

"Liz, it's all sorted, the date is fixed."

"For the History and Civilisation course?" I asked.

"No, to go underground with M. Jacques."

"Oh." I had been so preoccupied with other things that finding out what was under the school was the last thing on my mind at the moment.

"Well, are you interested?"

"Sure, can Michael come too?"

"I don't see why not, I'll ask M. Jacques. But you might want to get in a few more beers, just in case he needs persuading."

****

Mr. Whyte had not shown himself for at least a week. In fact I hadn't laid eyes on him since the announcement of Fabre's promotion. Curiosity got the better of me and when Lena dropped into the school to say hello on Saturday, I inquired from her.

"I don't know," Lena said, "I ain't his assistant. He doesn't have to report his movements to me."

"I was only asking."

"Ask away, but I can't answer," Lena wound Hamilton's leash around her hand and put an unlit cigarette in her mouth with the other.

"Judith must be happy for the school. I'm sure she's relieved to know that Mr. Whyte's friend is to be the new C.F.O. and will probably confirm our school as the main service provider of English language training to P.A.F.I."

"Don't know."

"You don't know? Of course it will be good for our school."

"I guess."

"Lena, is something else bothering you? You seem really out of sorts, not your usual ill-tempered, cranky self."

"No, Honey, what Lena needs to do right now is to think. I need to do a lot of thinking and you can't help me with that." She sloped off, cigarette dangling, dog circling around her.

I went back in to the office. There was a lull in Saturday testing and new business in general was slackening off. There was nothing unusual about that – summer was just around the corner and it was time to spend money on clothes and planning holidays rather than English training. Fortunately, not all our students thought that way, because teachers had to earn money.

I looked at the clock – just one o'clock. I waited for it. A door swung open, followed by a sprint on the corridor –

Clock out of the pocket, back in the pocket, "Bye, got to go, can't be late."

"Bye, Richard, enjoy the rest of the weekend," but he was already almost out on the street.

The place emptied at faster speed than usual. A sunny day was very effective in moving teachers and students.

Angie's bag was looking less bulky today, lighter somehow.

"See you in a while," Ursula was off to intellectualise with David.

"Don't get too carried away about underground brothels."

"Exploring tunnels involves a lot of advance research and planning," Ursula retorted.

"Sure."

I should be excited about exploring M. Jacques's secret catacomb, but I had lost enthusiasm for the project. It was like I had already decided that the school was part of my past and I didn't care anymore about Mr. Whyte, his school or underground tunnels.

****

I put my teaching material slowly back in my bag. My P.A.F.I. Intermediate group class had gone well. A spell of very hot weather at the beginning of June meant the students were more relaxed. I was feeling nostalgic. This summer had a different meaning for me – holidays wouldn't really be holidays this year. Gone were the days of two-month stretches when I was in school myself and when I had little responsibility other than to help out my mother at home. Back then, I would give her a hand to clean windows and do some painting around the cottage. We would also collect seaweed and periwinkles for sale to local shops who in turn sold them to seaside tourists and holidaymakers. Summer used to be a time to fill my mind with dreams. I would stretch out in a cool, grassy corner of a field with a book – do the same on the sand under the shadow of the cliffs. I could walk the coast, lose myself in reverie and play games of pretence. I could be who I wanted to be. And if the skies opened, I would lounge in an armchair and continue reading and dreaming. I'd always known someone was there for me, someone I could count on. Even when Mum and I had the falling out, she'd never been far away. A parent's love was special.

This summer would be a period of change for me. I'd put off going back to Ireland and decided that I would need to do all the teaching possible if I wanted to have enough money to make the move with Michael at the end of August. I wanted to pay my part. My new life was before me – with Michael, I'd found a different kind of love.

Summer in Paris could be fun too, especially sitting on terraces enjoying a glass of Rosé or a cool beer during the long balmy evenings. I noticed how the city was filling up once again with crowds of excited tourists. Though I was working, it was difficult not to catch the infectious exuberance of holidaymakers. The fly-boats chugged up and down the Seine in greater numbers and frequency, each one laden with cheering and waving sightseers. The centre of Paris was chock-a-block as tourists began to invade and take over every popular monument. Everywhere one looked, there were endless lines. I admired the patience of people waiting to get into the Louvre, go up the Eiffel Tower, view the inside of Notre Dame… I felt privileged to live in a place that the world wanted to visit. We were showered with dozens of different nationalities and accents. I likened the change in the city to the canvas of an artist suddenly seized with a frenzy of painting, his brush moving faster and faster, adding, dabbing, stroking in colour, movement and people. Parisians liked balance, sleek and elegant, toned down hues and nuances. Black was always in fashion. Other colours were discretely added – a little hint and tint of suggestion. Locals strutted their style and attitude for most of autumn, winter and spring. But from late May through to late September, the influx of tourists changed the artist's palette. A gaudy stream of colours and shades poured pell-mell across the canvas. After July 14th, many natives withdrew and went away on their own holidays. They vacated their streets for the enthusiastic technicoloured invaders who crammed and jammed the veins of the city.

I was in no hurry to leave the P.A.F.I. building. I picked up the *France U.S.A. Contacts*, a magazine invaluable to the Anglo Saxon community, I'd been browsing – there were dozens of language school names in the training section. I could stick a pin anywhere, pick any place and check it out. I'd have to get at the computer – our computer, the one that Ursula was hogging, and tackle redoing my C.V. Even if I knew I was procrastinating, just thinking about doing something made me feel better. I would quit W.W.S.O.E. & F.L. at the first possible opportunity. When the time came, I knew I would feel a little sad about leaving Lena and the other teachers. But with Michael, I could handle whatever got thrown at me. I'd consciously played down my happiness about our future plans together. I hadn't wanted to make too much of a fuss in front of Ursula. My displays of joy were reserved for solitary moments in my room when my face broke into a smile at the smallest excuse.

I folded the magazine and put it in my bag. It took several efforts, but I finally forced the clasp of my overflowing bag to shut. One day it would snap. I went out on the corridor. It seemed to have gotten very dark all of a sudden. I heard a loud clatter of thunder and another and another – it was as if all hell and damnation had started pounding the roof. An electric storm had broken out. I went into the first open office and ran to the window to watch it. "Wow," I exclaimed out loud – the sky was alive and angry clouds were swirling in agitation. If I made a dash for it now, I'd probably get to the bus stop before the rain started coming down in buckets – or I could stay here and wait it out. I looked around and realised that I'd come into the President's Office. The place seemed deserted. I looked at my watch in surprise, it was after seven. How long had I been moping after my last class?

It was pitch-dark, like it was already the middle of the night. All the street lamps had come on automatically. Streaks of lightning blazed across the city of Paris as the storm raged. I could see the Eiffel Tower to the south and L'Arc de Triomphe directly east brazing the elements. The lightning flashed whiter across a sky that morphed from black to blue to purple, while the thunder walloped and crashed angrily. I drew closer to the window deciding that I wasn't going home now – I'd stay and watch the greatest light show on earth. There was another blinding whip of lightning and roar of thunder. More flashes and claps came, and for a moment the sky appeared to split in two –

"You like that?"

I hadn't noticed M. Chevalier enter. He had a way of walking silently. For such a tall man, well over six feet, he didn't make a sound. But this evening it was easy as the storm drowned out all other sounds.

"Hi there. Yes it's fantastic." I was surprised at how casual I was with him – the fact that he was no longer my student lifted the formal barriers that were usually between us.

I fingered the rich leather of the President's chair, "I shouldn't be in here."

"It is not important, our President travels all the time."

"I don't think I've ever seen him. I only know what he looks like from your booklets and catalogues and –"

My words were lost – the sky was alight and a cacophony drowned our voices for some seconds. During a split-second lull, screams arose from the street where some people were dashing to take shelter from the storm, while others were exhilarated, loving the ecstasy like it were a funfair ride.

M. Chevalier stood still beside me, watching the spectacle.

I turned to him in wonder, "It's hard to image that a few minutes ago it was daylight, and now it's night."

He was staring at me, his face suddenly shadowed, his eyes brooding, "You aren't afraid, Elizabeth?"

"No," my voice was a whisper, "I'm not afraid." His use of my full first name seemed very personal to me for some reason.

He turned back to the window, "See, it is not black anymore, it is grey."

"Yes, it's brightening up and the rain's lightening off."

"It is not over yet," he was in a sombre mood.

I should go. I gestured to the chair and desk, "Would you like to become President some day?"

"I am not ambitious for that."

"No?"

"No. I think I should be C.F.O. first."

"You will one day. You work very hard, too hard."

"Work is the better friend."

"I presume you mean, 'work is one's best friend.' But you have children."

"The children are not my friend, they are my responsibility, my proud. They are me."

"'Pride.' You do have friends though?"

"You ask many questions."

"The folly of youth."

His smile was almost sad, "There are no friends in business, you cannot trust anybody."

"We need some trust, we have to trust."

"In business, no."

"You are better qualified than me to know. I'd better get going now."

"Your boyfriend is still here, I think. You may want to wait for him."

I wasn't sure I'd understood him right.

"He isn't here, that's impossible. I mean, Michael shouldn't be here, he doesn't have a class here this evening."

"I saw him on the floor below. Maybe, he has come for you. I can call somebody to send him up," he reached for the phone.

"No, that won't be necessary. He must just have had a change to his timetable." What was I doing here talking to M. Chevalier as if he were one of my mates? And what was Michael doing in P.A.F.I.?

"Good evening, M. Chevalier," I reached for my bag.

"Bonsoir."

I made my way down the corridor. Practically everybody had gone home, the lights in all the offices were off, though my movements triggered some of them back on. A couple of computer screens blinked in the open space. I took the lift. Something passed through my mind, something in M. Chevalier's words. I shook my head and hurried on to the exit doors, badging my way through bars and barricades and all sorts of security systems.

I was mistaken in thinking the storm had cleared. The sky was darkening again and the rain was now a heavy drizzle. I didn't have a coat and was too encumbered to take out my little umbrella. The street lights were still on and storm episode two was beginning. I quickened my steps to the bus stop.

Something made me turn around for an instant – a feeling. Then I saw him, it wasn't difficult to recognise the familiar stance and black curly hair. He wasn't alone – he was bending towards somebody, and that somebody was holding his hand and her second hand was caressing his cheek.

I stood still. Michael must have sensed something – he lifted his head and saw me. Dismay and another emotion I couldn't catch crossed his face.

He dropped Mme Michot's hand and called to me, "Liz – " a flash of lightning scorched the ground in front of him. For a second we were both stunned. I stood frozen and afraid. The moment passed and the thunder growled.

Michael moved again, "Liz – wait–"

A bus pulled up and I scrambled on. I didn't want to know or didn't want to hear. Somebody had dug a deep pit inside me and filled it with pain. There had been a warning note in M. Chevalier's voice. He had been trying to tell me something, but it was too subtle. I took the first vacant seat on the bus, refusing to look out the window. I stared ahead seeing nothing and noticing nothing. I didn't want to see Michael standing out there and I didn't want to think.

After two stops, I changed my mind. I couldn't stay on the bus, I had to get off, walk, move and do something. I found myself on the footpath bewildered, not knowing what I was doing or thinking. It was raining heavily, but I kept walking, I just wanted to go back to my room and never leave it again. I wouldn't cry, refused to cry. Michael told me he was finishing early, that he had a show to put on this evening, another birthday party. It had been too good to be true, things never – God – the tears were welling up and coursing down my face, and I couldn't stop them. I hadn't realised how deep I'd gotten in or how vulnerable I'd become to being hurt again. I thought Michael was different. How could I have been so blind?

I reached another bus stop. I wasn't able to keep going, my bag almost trailed the ground and a blister had developed on my heel. I sat down heavily on the shelter bench. I would wait for the next bus. I was soaked and my hair was plastered to my head, but I didn't care. Five minutes passed and the bus arrived. I struggled on once more.

I greeted Mme Gomes, trying to pretend everything was fine, holding on to my pride, but knowing that my eyes were red and raw. I stumbled up the seven flights of stairs, hurried to my room and locked the door. Thankfully Ursula wasn't at home. I stripped, didn't bother to wash and just crawled under the covers. I turned off my phone, ignoring the texts and missed calls. I didn't want to face reading them, listening to him, or to anybody.

Something like half an hour later, there was a knocking at the door, "Liz, Liz, open up, please – Liz?" Michael called from outside.

I stayed in mute silence.

The knocking persisted, "Liz, please, let me explain."

I buried my head under the pillow, I didn't want to hear. When I resurfaced, he was still outside calling my name. I thought, 'Just go away, you can't make things right Michael, leave me alone.'

He continued to stand outside the door for several more minutes. I thought he wasn't going to give up, but finally I heard the footsteps go slowly down the corridor and take the stairs.

I fell into an uneasy sleep and woke up an hour later, starving. I heard music coming from the room next door – Ursula was back. Elle meowed at my door. If I got up, Ursula would know that I was home and would want to talk to me. I was sick with heartache, but the hunger gnawed. I had to attempt to eat something, bread, anything. I tried to get out of bed without making noise – too late –

"Liz," Ursula called, "Liz, are you home?"

I didn't reply.

"Come on, Liz, I know you're there, Elle gave the game away."

"I'm sleeping."

"Fat chance, open up, something is the matter, I know it."

I never thought Ursula could offer comfort or that she could be there as a real friend. But for once, she had the right words – no put on, no questions, just understanding. Her sincerity touched me and my defences caved in. I finally let go of the last of my pride and allowed myself to go to pieces and become a snivelling mess.

Ursula helped me to pick the pieces up, offering consoling words, hankies, something to drink, something to eat… "Some men are fools," she fumed, "coming from me, it might not mean much. But I'll say it anyway – you can't depend on men."

"Thanks, Ursula, I'm okay now," I tried to pull myself together, but failed.

"No, you're not. I know you, staunch and strong, but sometimes you have to let it out. I feel awful for you. Sure I was sceptical at the beginning, but seeing how you and Michael were together, I really started to believe that you were right for each other. I was more and more convinced as time went on. I thought it was just a fling with the HR lady, that there was nothing much between them. When you came along, it was – oops."

"What are you talking about, Ursula, what fling?"

"Look, before you arrived in the school, I think, I can't be sure, but I think Michael and that Mme Michot had some brief affair."

"She's married."

Ursula looked at me like I had said something ridiculously naive.

"Why didn't you tell me? Was I the only dumbo who didn't know that?" I asked.

"No reason to, it was finished, over. I honestly didn't think it was very important. You didn't have to know. Would you have told me?"

I shook my head, knowing she was right.

Ursula stayed with me. She pampered me, offering to go to the shop if I needed something. She even proposed to stand in for my classes.

That's where I drew the line, I wasn't going to let Ursula wreak havoc in my classroom. Besides, I had been lumped with eight telephone classes the next morning. At least, I wouldn't have to show my face to anyone. I would manage somehow.

19

I sat on the edge of the hard bed resolutely. My plans for the future would change – I would still leave Whyte's, that much I was sure of, but I wouldn't be giving notice on my room just yet. No, I was destined to stay here longer. Mme Defoe was right when she said that such places were hard to come by and I shouldn't give it up easily.

The iron bed-frame dug into my thighs. I didn't want to move and I didn't want to stay on in bed. But it was too much trouble to dress or to eat, so I sat there, slightly hunched, hands on my knees. My head felt heavy, too heavy to allow me to stand up. A grey light petered into the room and the timid beginnings of street life reached the open window. It wasn't cold, but I felt chilly – and although ravenous, I didn't want to do anything about it.

In the end, I had no choice but to shift, so I forced myself. It wasn't so funny or romantic washing in the plastic tub this morning. I filled a big saucepan and put it on the hot ring and also filled and plugged in the electric kettle. I went out on the corridor to the toilet wearing just a long T-shirt – I was not up to bothering with propriety today. On top, I seemed to have caught a cold and had to blow my nose several times before the first phone class. Eight people in a row on the telephone would be murder. Then again, I wouldn't have to think of Michael, of us, or anything else.

I sat by the phone with a large pot of coffee near me. The phone rang.

I resented the sound – it was like an invasion of my right to be miserable. I spoke to my first student, Marie, about her previous weekend and waxed enthusiastic about her cleaning and ironing, before discussing the latest problems in her Accounts Payable Service, and finally launching a verb check. Next, Guillaume rang and was reluctant to speak about his job, but was happy to speak about his rugby match – I commiserated with him over his sprained ankle. Ursula wasn't the only good actress on the floor, I thought. Bruno had a lot to say about tiling his kitchen. Marie-France talked non-stop about her grandchild, and the pain behind my eyes grew stronger as I tried to steer her towards using the past tense instead of remaining permanently suspended in the infinitive. Albert didn't have a lot to say about anything, so it was a sluggish discussion about his business agenda for the day. Benoît understood nothing I said and forced me to repeat the same thing in five different ways. Sylvie needed to practice understanding numbers and letters and I stretched my acting abilities to a little role playing. Fortunately, Veronique had prepared an article and had lots of opinions about it. Franck had few opinions about his job or the world at large and every second of his half hour class was like extracting teeth with pliers.

Several hours later, my ear felt swollen. I didn't know how other teachers managed to do telephone classes all the time.

I had to get fully dressed and get ready to go to Aubervilliers, a northern suburb. It was to be my first class with a family in the rag trade. Their offices were in the middle of a park of warehouses.

I didn't have it in me today to sparkle and shine and battled to rustle up positive energy. I threw myself back on the bed. Tears came again. 'Stop it, stop it,' I told myself, 'you are not the first to be deceived. You crossed that path before. Anyway, you have only known Michael a few months. Cop on, there's no reason to behave as if your heart is broken, even if it is.' I scrolled my phone and forced myself to go through his messages; "It's not what you think – please call back and let me explain – Liz, call me –"

****

I walked into the school carrying my heart like a ton of bricks. Judith was angry and nobody knew why, who with, or what about. I detected undertones of panic in her way of being. I began to realise that Judith used that outer dark mood to hide anxiety. I didn't understand why though – with William Whyte's friend, Fabre, getting the C.F.O. job, things should be looking up for the school.

Lena was affected by Judith's mood and didn't seem to know whether to look cross or guilty. The teachers too appeared to be impacted by the charged atmosphere around the place. Some took sarcasm to great heights, while others suffered bouts of ill temper. I felt like head-banging a few lockers myself, but knew if I gave into that feeling, a few seconds after, I'd burst into tears.

I paused at the office doorway after my class and forced myself to be civil and say good evening to Lena.

"Darn it," Lena stooped down under the table to pick up her pencil, "that's the third time that's happened me."

"I'm tired, I'm going home," I was not in the mood for a testy Lena.

"You're off today," Lena looked at me sharply.

"No, Lena, I'm not off, I've been working all day."

"Either you're trying and failing to amuse me, or you're really off form?"

"We all have our good and bad days," I knew I sounded defensive.

"Yeah, but you don't, at least not like the others."

"I suppose," I gave a false smile.

"Saw Michael earlier today, he looked pitiful, hadn't even shaved."

My smile dropped, "If you're fishing, Lena, you won't have to try very hard. It's over between Michael and me – that's all."

Lena put down her pen, "Oh, Honey, I'm sorry. I truly am because I like you both and I thought you made a good couple. I really believe that some people are made for each other."

"Is that so?"

"Now, I don't want to tell you how to run your life or your relationships, but it seems to me that you should give that boy an ear."

"Lena, who have you been talking to?"

"Me," Lena looked wide-eyed, "why nobody, just doing my own sums and adding things up."

I didn't believe her – Ursula must have discussed it with her. What did I care anyhow?

Lena stiffened –

I glanced at the door –

"Ladies," William Whyte stood in the hallway with three serious-looking businessmen. A bead of sweat trickled down Whyte's face, "Lena, I have some business to discuss with these gentlemen and will need to use the main offices. You can go home now, I'll lock up the premises." He looked unnerved as he led the grey suits down the corridor to 'Lindisfarne' for a coffee.

I stood with Lena and Hamilton in the yard, "Who were those people?"

"Financial guys – auditors or accountants, or something," Lena drew on her cigarette.

"Lena, be straight with me. Who are they really? Is this a routine visit, are we being inspected?"

"I don't know, Liz, and that's the God's honest truth. They were here yesterday too."

"Then it's a fiscal control and that's why Judith is fuming. Whyte has been fiddling the books, hasn't he?"

"Don't know a thing about anything."

"If there's an inspection and things aren't above board, we're all in trouble. Why, it would seriously damage our business relationship with P.A.F.I."

"Heck, Liz, you gotta keep your feet on the ground – there is no financial scandal. It's usual for the 'Fisc.' to carry out checks and even if there are one or two irregularities, they just ask you to fix them. That's all. They ain't going to shut the place down. They can't do that, we gotta live."

I regretted upsetting Lena. She needed to hang on to her job more than the rest of us. Sixty-something-year-old women didn't find work easily.

"Don't listen to me, Lena, I can see that you're anxious."

"I'm doing okay."

"Poor Lena and there was I thinking only of myself."

"Don't worry about me, I ain't the worst off here. I'll get by, always have, always will."

I decided not to crack that shell of pride. "What's Judith's position?"

"I don't know."

"Does she keep an eye on the school's accounts?"

"Nope, she lost interest in that end after Tom died. Then William took over and preferred to manage it himself. Now she just manages the operational expenses," Lena tipped a long line of ash.

"She has to know some things."

"What are you getting at, Liz?" Lena looked at me through the smoke.

The yard door was pushed in.

"We've got company, see you around," I turned on my heel.

"Hi, Jeffrey," said Lena, "Mr. Whyte's inside."

Far from the self-satisfied look I'd expected, Jeffrey's face was tense. He went straight in.

I left Lena in the yard, staring into space with a subdued Hamilton beside her.

****

"You've got to talk to him, Liz, you have to," Ursula stood at my door and repeated what had become her non-stop recitation. "He keeps ringing me because you won't answer your phone."

"I know, you don't have to say it again." This time I didn't protest. One way or another, I'd have to see Michael and let him talk. I was afraid – afraid that he'd get around me, find a way to convince me that I'd misjudged him, and that my defences would crumble and I'd end up running back into his arms, simply because it would be easier.

Ursula's phone rang again and she held it out to me, "It's him – do you want to take it?"

What choice did I have? I relented and took it. I listened as Michael explained quietly that he was downstairs and wanted to see me. There was no point in putting it off any longer, so I just replied yes to his request to come up. It was better to get it over with.

Ursula gave me the okay sign, "You won't regret it, Liz. You have to give him an ear. I'm sure it's best that way for both of you."

"I'm not going back with Michael. I'll just listen to him because I have to. If I don't, I'll feel bad and guilty and all those things that I suffer from more than others seem to."

The stairs creaked, Ursula disappeared. I would have liked to hide myself away, but there was nowhere to go, so I went back inside my room, leaving the door ajar.

Michael paused at the threshold. His appearance shocked me – it was not just the shadows under his eyes, the drawn features and unkempt hair, but the pain in his expression. It stopped me from saying whatever I might have said.

"Liz," he came in and stood in front of me.

I didn't move, just waited.

"Liz, I was worried sick about you," Michael reached for me.

I stepped aside and went to stand by the window, turning my back to him. Seeing his face made it too difficult. "So how long ago did you start an affair with the HR lady?"

"Liz, I didn't start, I mean it was over. I knew her before you came along. Once I'd met you, that was it, my relationship with – with her was in the past. I didn't mention it because it was over."

"What I saw didn't look over to me."

"For me it was. What you saw the last evening was nothing."

"You were holding hands," I accused.

"I felt sorry for her. Anicee has difficulty moving on and wanted to see me in private. I couldn't – I didn't want to – I couldn't find an excuse not to. I was just comforting her, but nothing happened. I know it looked bad, but I was trying not to hurt her feelings. She's in the process of getting a divorce and – it's just a bad time for her."

I turned then to look at him. I had to see his eyes, to know if he was telling the truth. It was possible I'd jumped to all the wrong conclusions. I wanted to believe that. He held my look, beseeching me to believe him.

"But you were going somewhere, you were going to her apartment?"

"Yes."

"So nothing happened."

"No."

"But it was going to –"

"No – I don't –"

"Why were you going to her apartment?"

"There was a storm remember, it was the easiest place to talk. Anicee – she lives near the office."

"You told me you had a show that evening."

"Liz."

"You didn't have a show, did you?"

"No – no, there was no show."

Honesty, at last. He stood there looking dishevelled, handsome and miserable, all in one. "Why Michael, why did you lie to me?"

"It was a mistake, I can see that now. I was only trying to protect you."

"Despite breaking up, you kept teaching her."

"It was difficult to do otherwise without making a fuss and bringing the school into it." He pushed back his mop of unruly curly hair, his dark brown eyes looking so sad.

"Is she divorcing for you?"

He shook his head, "No, no, she was already separated when we – we – " he let his arms hang.

'I have no right,' I thought. 'I shouldn't charge and condemn him on what might have happened.' It was just his sly ways of hiding things from me that were difficult to ignore.

"Liz, you do believe me don't you?"

"Nothing is clear in my mind."

"I've told you the honest truth."

I relented, "I think I do believe you, Michael. But something has changed and I don't know what. Seeing you and Mme Michot together set off emotions I didn't want to ever feel again."

"If you believe me, then I don't understand."

I was at a loss to explain. When I saw them together, my self-belief evaporated – in a few seconds, I'd lost all that I thought I'd rebuilt. But how could I rationalise that a few days after that, I'd gone from a broken heart to something else? What I did understand was that I'd been throwing everything into our couple, leaning on Michael too much. I'd been depending on him to fill the emotional vacuum left by all that had happened in my life before meeting him.

He stood looking confused.

"I'm sorry, Michael, I don't know what I feel."

"What can I do to make it okay between us?"

"Be clear with yourself about your relationship with this woman. You must have unresolved feelings for her. You still had things to work out with her when I arrived on the scene, and instead of working those things out, you turned to me."

"Don't put words in my mouth. My decision to break up with her was made before I met you. The moment I met you, I knew that you were different. You're the one for me, the only one," he seemed surprised by his own words, as if he'd only just fully comprehended them himself.

"You told me you loved me."

"I meant it, Liz."

I hated myself for putting him in the chair of the accused. It was his life. He was entitled to his past. Relationships burned and fizzled every day, his – hers – ours. His secret garden was his own, just as mine was.

"We, we haven't known each other that long," I knew my excuse was weak.

"It's long enough for me to know what I feel."

"I don't –"

"Please understand, Liz –"

"I need space. Why don't we take a little while apart and see how things go."

"I'm not sure that it's a good idea."

"Michael, I need some time."

"How long?" he asked, resigned.

"I don't know."

"You will move in with me after that?"

"Just give me time and we'll see."

"We were good together, perfect," he put his arms around me.

I wanted his lips on mine, but try as I might I couldn't find that special feeling. Comfort didn't ignite passion.

Michael felt the difference and released me. There was silence. He didn't know what to say.

"Give it time, Michael."

He nodded, accepting reluctantly.

"Tell me about your magic show last night, please do, I'd love to know," I urged.

So he did.

"Is everything okay between you two again," Ursula pressed me for information as soon as Michael had left.

"Yes."

"That's great."

"But we're no longer a couple."

"What? How can that be okay?"

"Because we are friends and not lovers, that's all."

"Huh, that's all."

"Yes, at least for now."

"Hah," Ursula jumped at those words, "I know all about that," she paraded down the corridor, sure of her own conclusions.

Annoying girl, Ursula was too smart for her own good. The only thing I was certain about right now was that it would be wise to take a short break. I decided it was time to go back to Ireland for a little holiday.

****

I pushed back the hood of my wind breaker wanting to feel the wind fully in my face and the sea spray on my skin. A rainbow arched across the Irish sky. Shrieks and squalls rose high above the blustering breeze and the splash of waves on the rocks. The sea rolled to nature's beat. I watched the seagulls like gladiators show off their soars and glides, capturing the centre stage. I walked on, impressing every footprint on the sand. After a healthy dose of salt and sea, I climbed a pathway that meandered to the top of some cliffs where the old graveyard was. I felt free and glad I had escaped a crowded Paris for a few days.

I knelt by my parents' grave and pulled at some coarse grass that was threatening to take over the white chipping and marble stone. When I finished, it looked neat and simple. I rubbed a cloth across the tombstone inscription. It didn't need it, but it made me feel better. Then I placed two little potted plants in the middle. They'd get blown away eventually, but the next time I came back, I'd plant some flowers.

"Well – Mum, Dad, here I am. Mum, do you remember the line in that book I got in the school library, 'If they come back they're yours, and if they don't they were never yours.' I never went, you know that. I've been here every day in my mind. You've been with me all the time. You've never left my side – I sense you and I hear you. I know you're guiding me, every step of the way." I put my fingers to my lips and caressed the marble stone, "Love you, Mum. Love you too, Dad, although I never really knew you – I know Mum loved you and you must be together now – kisses forever."

I went to the cottage where I had grown up and stood for a long time looking over the garden fence.

"Hello," a woman with a kindly face came across the lawn towards me. She was holding a trowel and there was a smudge of soil on her cheek.

"Hello," I said.

"Are you lost, can I give you directions?" the woman asked.

"No, that's kind of you, but I know the area very well. I used to live in this cottage and have a lot of great memories from growing up here."

"Oh, you came from here. It's a lovely home."

"Yes it is."

"They told me about you at the agency. Both your parents have passed on. Sorry for your trouble."

"That's alright."

"It must be very upsetting for you. I've been through it myself – life doesn't spare us."

"No it doesn't."

"It must be strange for you coming back here."

"A little," I admitted. A lot, I thought. Mum hadn't owned the cottage and I could never have afforded to go on paying the rent. So I'd let it go after her death, but it had been like cutting off a piece of myself.

"Would you like to come in and look around?" the woman offered.

I knew my eyes were ready to spill over, "No, no thank you."

"I understand that you're out of the country now."

"That's right, I live in France."

"Where exactly?" she asked.

"In Paris."

"Isn't that wonderful. I visited it once, it's a beautiful city."

"That's true."

Her eyes were dreamy, "I envy you, if I were twenty again, I'd travel the world and live in places like Paris. It's a very romantic city."

"Yes, yes."

"I'm sure you must have fallen in love with one of those handsome French men," she laughed.

I laughed with her.

"Are you staying around for long?"

"Just a few days, I'm at the B&B on Cliff Road. Do you live here full time?" I asked.

"Not permanently, it's a holiday home for us. My husband and I are still working. I wouldn't mind retiring here."

"I couldn't think of a better spot to spend my retirement."

When I left the woman I was feeling less lonely somehow. There was a joy about the place – the cottage wasn't empty and lonesome, it was alive. I remembered another saying Mum was fond of: 'You cannot prevent the birds of sadness from flying over your head, but you can prevent them from nesting in your hair.' 'Brush them away, Liz, get on with your life.'

20

"Liz, you're back." Ursula was on the landing.

"As you can see." I hauled my travel bag up the last step, "I told you that I'd be back today."

"I know, but I was afraid you might take it into your head to stay in Ireland."

"Were you? Would you have missed me?"

"Like a pebble in my shoe. You should have told me the arrival times. David or one of us would have met you at the airport, at least gone as far as the Air France bus stop."

"Ursula, the bus stop is at Porte Maillot."

"So what, it's always nice to be met."

"You're right," I gave her a kiss on the cheek and was surprised when she hugged me. It felt good to be missed.

"We're going tomorrow night."

"Where, and who is we?"

"M. Jacques, David and I, Michael, and I suppose you. You forgot didn't you? The date to re-explore the underground was arranged before you went, remember, June 25th?"

"Yes, now I do." I wanted to see Michael before. I needed to talk to him. Damn, he was doing a late show. It would be the early hours before he'd finish up and I would be stuck in class all day tomorrow.

"M. Jacques is fixed on tomorrow night," Ursula explained. "He would take it badly if we changed the date. I knew you didn't want to be bothered by calls and messages of that nature while in Ireland; otherwise, I would have reminded you."

"You did well. Catacombs and Whyte's school were very far from my mind."

"You look rested."

"I am. Somebody's been using my room, it's tidied differently."

"I slept here – you can't complain, I left everything in order."

"I told you it was okay to use it, and I meant it."

"David stayed in my room."

"David, in your room, alone?"

"Yes alone. It was very nice of him. I was afraid so he came to keep me company for a couple of nights."

"That's nice."

"You're sceptical – believe me, it was strictly separate rooms. He's started some new lines of research on the woman, Eva."

"You mean the ghost, Eva."

"I prefer to imagine her as a real woman who lived, had a life before tragedy befell her. I think her family name was Fenoglio – I heard it in my dreams. David's trying to put together a portrait from clues I can give him. With that, he might find some documents to prove she existed and is not a figment of my imagination."

"I think it's worth trying."

"It is, it is."

"He should check out Mme Gomes's story about the murder she pretends took place here in the past."

"I suggested it to him. He will try, but promises nothing."

"You look peaky. Are you feeling okay?" It was true, Ursula was quite pale.

"I'm just about as well as usual," Ursula shrugged off my question too quickly.

"Has Fabre been bothering you?" I pressed her for more information.

"No. By the way, P.A.F.I. still hasn't renewed any new contracts with our school, so as we are just finishing the old ones, business will really dry up."

"That's probably because they have to wait for Fabre to officially take up his role as C.F.O. and then they have to renew their service provider contracts following the language teaching tender they put out. Fabre can't make it too obvious that he's showing favouritism," I reasoned.

"Maybe, but the inspectors were in the school again, all day Wednesday. They were looking at invoices, student attendance sheets and documents of every sort. It doesn't look good."

"Was Whyte there?" I asked.

"He was everywhere, shouting orders at Judith and Lena. I hate the atmosphere there, things have gotten very sour."

"I hope for Lena's sake that it will work out okay. I couldn't care less about Whyte and I think Judith knows the score, I'm sure she's looking for an opportunity to get out." I had suspected Whyte of so many things that nothing would surprise me. But yet, I'd never been able to pin anything on him – I'd more or less given up looking and had accepted that, apart from bad management, there was nothing untoward going on.

"So did it work, did it help going back to home?" Ursula asked.

"Yes, it helped a lot to put the past into perspective. I realise that after my mum died, I didn't give myself time to grieve. I'd shut out the memories and had all this guilt. That's begun to lift." And it had, just as the morning haze promises a sunny day.

"I was hoping it would do you good. Did you sort out in your mind about Michael?"

"I tried to."

"If you ring him, he'll come running up those stairs in two seconds."

"He's doing a show this evening."

"Anyway, I'm very happy that you got some answers by going back," Ursula said.

"If you're happy, why the sad face? You look like the world has ended."

"You asked if I was okay, well I'm not. I've a pain here," she put a hand to her heart. "It's awful, Liz, but I think I'm in love with David – and it's hopeless because he's in love with God."

"Oh dear," I looked at Elle for inspiration.

****

"Lena, I can't hang on this evening, I've got to meet up with friends and I don't want to be late." I was lying a little. I was meeting Michael before joining the others for M. Jacques's expedition. I'd so much to talk out with him. We wouldn't have much time, but it would be enough.

"I ain't delaying," Lena was dangling her keys, "I'm out of here. It's wonderful finishing at eight o'clock, just like a holiday. That's one thing I like about the summer season."

Politeness kept me waiting while she locked the door. I thought she'd aged; her movements were slow and clumsy. I'd grown attached to Lena, wished there was something I could do to help. Hope arising from winning the P.A.F.I. tender and the prospect of lots of new contracts no longer seemed to be the answer. If the school had serious difficulties, it would hit her hard.

"Ursula was sick last Monday evening," Lena said.

"Was she, she didn't say anything to me about it."

"Some sort of food poisoning – man, she got a bad dose."

"She was a little pale when I saw her last night." I'd rationalised Ursula's appearance to being lovesick. She was pining for David and couldn't have him – it was hard to compete with God.

"Michael covered for her. He's such a nice boy."

"Yes, Lena, he is."

"We were counting on Ursula to lock up that evening. Judith was away and I was in Normandy. As luck would have it, Michael had his own key and the students weren't inconvenienced in any way."

"Lucky he had that key."

"Yeah, Judith gave it to him some time last year. I can't remember why, but he still had it."

"That was handy," I smiled and looked up as a city gull shrieked. "Cheerio, Lena," I gave Hamilton a big pat, "lovely laddie, the most beautiful doggie in the world."

"I'm glad you finally admit it."

I danced all the way to the Metro, feeling better and better by the second. I had to wedge myself onto a carriage crammed with tourists, party goers, beggars and vagrants. There was neither sea, salt nor sand – there wasn't a ripple of water lapping on the shore, or a glimpse of a cloudy sky above. There were waves though, but not fresh foamy ones – instead, train noises and voices surged up at me. It was hot and sweaty. Whichever way I turned,

I had somebody in my face. I should feel suffocated, especially having just returned from the wilds of the Atlantic coast, but I didn't. I'd figured out how the herring gulls did it: when you knew who you were, then there was nothing to it, you just fit right in. You could get on anywhere and still be yourself. The philosophy was basic, but it worked.

I burrowed inside my bag deciding it timely to send Ursula a text. Oh no, where was my phone? It should be just there, in that pocket. I searched every pocket of my bag. I got off at the next stop, George V, sat on a bench and searched thoroughly. It was either lost or stolen, or I'd left it in the school. I had to go back and check. Damn, damn, damn, I hoped it was there. Having a philosophy of life didn't mean crap didn't happen.

I ran across the school courtyard, unlocked the doors and was half way down the corridor when I saw the black plastic bin liner. The cleaners were here. There was a mop and bucket of soapy water by the wall. Whyte wouldn't be happy about my coming in – what did he call it, 'loitering'. Well I'd be fast. I went directly to 'Oxford', where I'd given my class, and skidded to a halt –

An Indian girl who looked no more than fifteen or sixteen stood there holding a cloth in one hand and my phone in the other. She'd been washing the white board.

"Hi, oh there it is, you've found my phone," I addressed her.

The girl didn't move to give it back and just stood there looking at me silently.

"That's mine, sorry for disturbing you, I'll just take the phone back," I walked slowly towards her.

The girl didn't hand it to me, but she didn't stop me from taking it out of her hand. She continued to stand and stare at me.

"Do you speak English? What's your name?" I asked.

She didn't reply.

"French?"

Silence.

"Where do you –"

She didn't wait for me to finish, just grabbed my arm and pulled me, pointing to the door and my phone.

"What do you want, what are you trying to tell me? You want me to take you outside, is that it?"

She tugged at my sleeve.

I let her lead me a little and I realised that in fact she did want me to take her outside.

"Are you afraid, are you in trouble, do you want me to help you?"

Her nails dug into my skin, her grip was vice-like.

"Alright, we'll go into the yard – I'll telephone for someone –"

I felt a sharp pain at the back of my head. Everything started spinning and went dark.

I woke up with my head pounding. Where was I? I was going to be sick. It was cold, the ground was damp and I could see nothing.

I tried to stand, but my head struck a rock or stone that was sticking out. I tried standing again, feeling my way. It was a very small tunnel or cavern, but there was hardly room to kneel. I put out my hands and tried to feel my way – it was damp and wet and I found myself sinking into slush and mud.

Realisation came quickly as a strong putrid odour reached my nostrils. I was in some sort of pit, at the bottom of a stinking hole. This wasn't like the tunnels we'd walked with David. I must be under the school at the other side of William Whyte's padlocked door.

Something slick touched my arm and I shrieked. Was it a rat or another rodent? My head was clearing, but panic was rising up inside, paralysing me. I couldn't move and my body started shaking. My breath came in gasps.

I tried to get my mind to think, I had to get out. I managed to get onto my knees and stretched out my hand once more. My chest tightened, consuming me with pain. Fear was gripping me. 'Keep crawling,' I urged, 'keep moving and crawling.'

Oh no, the space was getting smaller and smaller. I couldn't wriggle any farther and seemed to be at a dead end. I slid and slipped backwards, my face was wet with tears. It was impossible, I was lost. Another creature slithered past and I screamed louder. I was going to die here in this cave of vermin – if I didn't escape, I'd be bitten, chewed and eaten alive by rats and other creatures.

I clambered around. My foot found more room in what felt like a different little capillary. "Keep going," I spoke out loud, "there has to be a way out." I inched my body forward in a new direction, but it seemed impossible. I stopped, wheezing for air. This was worse, I would die of asphyxiation. I let my head rest on my hands and tried to take breaths. It made me dizzy.

Hysteria enveloped me as I felt like I was going to explode. I lost all control and started striking out with my arms and legs at something, nothing – everything. Gulping and panting, I attempted to go forward – changed my mind, then backward. It was stupid and I was stupid for using up all my energy. But I didn't know another way. I flayed, rolled and turned. I was going to die, but I wouldn't do it calmly. "Help, help," I called to myself, to somebody, to nobody. I prayed.

The atmosphere changed suddenly and my lungs were taking in more air. What was nearby? I pushed my body ahead and found myself sliding into a wider burrow. Miraculously, I could stand up. My elbow hit off a barrier. It was a gate and opened into another passage. This passage was drier. I began to walk, my legs numbed and like lead. My clothes and hair were soaked and caked in mud and sludge.

I continued for what seemed like several minutes until the path forked off. I took what I thought was the main way, simply because it was wider. The surroundings changed and I felt that I'd entered another world. There was some light coming from wall lanterns that were hung here and there and smelt of paraffin. I moved very carefully as I began to comprehend that this could be Whyte's den. He must be around somewhere. Someone had struck me at the back of the head and thrown me into some side tunnel. Had they left me for dead? Did they intend to come back for me?

It was difficult to make out all the surroundings; the detail was lost in the dim light. Gradually, my vision adjusted. There were rows of white columns that looked like they were set in marble. I touched one, it was marble. I passed between two larger and grander columns and found myself in what felt and looked like a building rather than a cavern. There was moulded plaster work and ebony board on the walls and ceiling – it was a real ceiling. There were mirrors everywhere – though tarnished and stained I could catch my own reflection in them. It was weird.

The ground was even and smooth – it seemed to be a proper tiled floor. There was door, after door, after door… I tried one and it opened. Inside, there was a four-poster bed that began to crumble at my touch. It was still covered in disintegrating bed linen. Part of a quilt decomposed under my fingers. I began coughing; there was so much dust everywhere that it was choking me up. It was an underground hotel, abandoned from another century.

I went through a new set of columns into a large hall. Here, there were traces of tapestry on the walls. There were more mirrors and an enormous chandelier overhead.

Everything was old and dusty, but somebody had lit the lanterns, so evidently Whyte or somebody must come through here. I squinted, there seemed to be paintings hanging on the opposite wall. I approached and tried to see what they represented, but they were very faded. As I moved around the room, I realised that everywhere I turned there were sculptures. This must have been a museum of sorts. Some works were still covered, while the covers had fallen off others. I walked around them. God, what the hell were these? These weren't ordinary sculptures. I saw a woman's face, her expression was somewhere between pain and delirium. She was held in the clutches of a man. His features were ugly and furious. It looked like a violent act. I turned to the other sculptures. The theme was the same – they all represented various states of demented and ecstatic passion, graphic portrayals of men and women performing lewd sexual acts. Some scenes were sadistic and brutal, others highly erotic. I'd seen enough. I'd read about these artistic brothel pseudo museums in one of Ursula's books.

I came to large double doors. I listened for a while, but could hear nothing. I opened the doors, cursing the creaking sound.

This place was different. It was more ordinary and modern. I'd walked into somebody's living quarters. Was this where the girl was kept? There was a small bed and locker and even a little kitchen. There was also a large metallic machine. I deduced that it was an electricity generator, having seen one before on a farm. There were also gas bottles and several lamps that one could hand-carry. This must be where Whyte brought all the boxes from upstairs. What was he doing with the girl? What was going on here?

There were a few storage rooms. I went into a larger one to discover more boxes, shelves of documents and stacks of paper. In the middle were some computers and monitors. Other enclaves were filled with crates. It looked like he was preparing to move things out.

I walked under an arch into a room with armchairs and sofas. These quarters were very lived in. I couldn't stay here – I would be discovered in no time. I looked around – he might have a phone wired down here. I could hear some clicking coming from behind a door. Was somebody there or was it just a meter? I backed away from the door – if somebody came through here I was done for. I stood still, trying to think – the air was dusty, but at least I could breathe. I had to escape, alert someone and bring help to the girl. I noticed a second door, this one was padded. It was like the door that led to the stairs under the school, but it was locked.

I moved around quickly exploring the room for other exits. I saw that there were two smaller doors leading off the parlour. I checked each one – locked.

I froze for a moment, I could hear voices growing louder.

I hurried to get out of sight, squeezing behind a large cumbersome armchair that was pushed against one corner.

A door opened –

"We have time, William, I've dealt with all the details. Don't worry." The voice was familiar, but my mind was so muddled that I couldn't place it.

"Are you sure that it's the best way?" Whyte spoke.

"Yes, the inspectors haven't proven anything so far, have they? That means my documents are getting past them. You won't be caught, but we can't take risks. We have to clear all this area. There's too much evidence here. Leave it to me, I'll get it done in a week." I identified the voice this time as Jeffrey's.

"And Nisha? Can you take her back? She's too much trouble, like the last one. It's not worth it." Whyte sounded panicky.

"You'll have to hang on to her until I find a solution. Keep her in one of your flats." Yes, it was definitely Jeffrey.

"You can take her back to London, find some use for her," Whyte suggested.

"Too late for that, it's too risky," Jeffrey sounded calm.

"I shouldn't have listened to you and agreed to hide another girl. She tried to run away several times. She's more trouble than I bargained for." Whyte seemed to be pacing around the room.

"Don't panic," Jeffrey reassured, "we have to get the inspectors off our backs first, which we will – then I'll take care of the girl and the rest of that business. Just keep her out of sight for a few more days and, trust me, I'll find a solution for her. There are many places of employment for pretty girls. You didn't come too badly out of it the last time."

"If you're sure, because I have had enough." Whyte opened a door.

"Have I been wrong so far?" The snide voice of Jeffrey faded away as the door was closed.

I waited, thinking the door they used probably led back upstairs. Going by the direction of the voices it was the padded door. I didn't fully understand what was going on. Whyte had said nothing about me. Was he aware of what had happened to me? I crept fully out from behind the armchair. It would be better if I returned to the old brothel and museum part and waited until I was sure of being alone. There would be some indication of time on one of those computers or pieces of equipment. If it was night time or early morning, surely Whyte and Jeffrey would go home. Maybe then I could try looking for another exit.

The lights brightened suddenly. I halted and stared into the glare.

"You couldn't leave things alone, could you? You had to make trouble." Jeffrey emerged from the other side of the room, "You couldn't mind your own business."

I'd been tricked – he must have suspected my presence while talking to Whyte.

Jeffrey stood still, holding something in my direction.

I saw then that he'd a gun in his hand.

I found my voice, "You're mad, what do you think you're doing!"

He sneered, "Your body will be found eventually, one day if somebody bothers to explore those other tunnels. The next time I dump you in a pit, you won't crawl out of it."

"They'll look for answers, my friends will," my words sounded empty, useless.

He laughed, "Friends? If you call those teachers you go around with friends, you're deluded. It's easy to shut people up. Besides, it won't be necessary. If you're stupid enough to go down into the catacombs, you pay the price for it – just another poor fool who got lost. Why should they believe differently?"

"They will."

"Enough talk –"

Jeffrey walked slowly towards me, directing the gun to my head.

"You stink," he approached, "that's how I knew you were here."

I saw he had a syringe in his other hand.

I tried speaking again, my voice was small and distant, "Many people know that this place exists, they'll look for me."

He kept coming towards me, sniggering, "Where you are going won't make any difference." The gun was pressed to my temple, "Now don't move, I'll just give you a little prick. If you as much as twitch, this gun will go off."

I bit my lip as I felt the needle go into my arm. My eyes darted round – there had to be a way, something. Then I noticed that the padded door was slightly open and kept it in my focus. It was my only hope. If I ran for it, would he shoot? Shooting me would destroy his alibi of me getting lost and perishing underground, that's if my body were ever found. Jeffrey looked furious and might do anything. But either way I'd nothing to lose.

I lunged to the side – the syringe fell to the ground. Jeffrey made a grab for me, but I ducked and ran. I had to get to that door. Why did it seem so far? At last – stone steps. Jeffrey was after me, I could hear his swearing. I stumbled, climbed, fell, got up again and kept going. There were so many steps, many, many, more steps, even more – he was closer – I wasn't going to make it. 'Keep going – keep going – ' I urged myself on.

A hand caught my ankle – I tripped. I looked up and saw Whyte – I fell back down.

There were voices, lots of voices – a group of people. Everything was fuzzy and distorted. There were faces looking down at me: Lena, M. Jacques, the police…

"What, what happened?" Someone knelt by me.

"Michael?"

"Don't talk, Liz, time for explanations later. We have to get you to the hospital."

"Hospital?" My body felt like jelly.

"We have to be sure that you're okay, Honey," it was Lena.

"Lena, what are you doing here?"

"Not now, Honey, don't worry about that," she looked haggard.

"Where's Ursula? Where's David?"

"David is at the hospital – he's with Ursula," Michael put a hand to my forehead.

"What!"

"She's okay," he reassured, "but it was a close call. If it weren't for M.

Jacques, she might not have made it. She collapsed in her room – a burst appendix. Don't worry, she's going to be okay."

"How did you know, M. Jacques, did Ursula shout out for help?"

M. Jacques shook his head and looked to Michael.

Michael coughed, "M. Jacques was walking in the wood. He swears he heard a voice call out his name and saw a young woman that he claims was a ghost. She led him back to the seventh floor of the building right down the corridor to Room 1. He found Ursula sprawled on the bed. He raised the alarm, alerted Mme Gomes and – "

I didn't have the energy for more, I closed my eyes again.

I woke up later in a very quiet room on what seemed more like a long trolley than a bed. The drug effects had worn off and a nurse told me I was in the outpatients' section of Hôpital Hôtel-Dieu on Île Saint Louis, Notre Dame De Paris. Apart from a low-grade headache and nausea, I was okay and quickly on my feet. After I cleaned up, the doctors ran some scans. I had a few nasty bumps and bruises, but they were satisfied that I didn't need to stay there longer. Thankfully, Lena had the foresight to get me spare clothes to change into.

I was well enough to marvel that I was in the oldest hospital in Paris according to the nurse. With some pride she told me that it was founded in 651, as a centre of charity and hospitality.

"Really – that old?" I looked around me curiously – the inside was very modern.

She laughed and explained that naturally it wasn't the same building. The current building stood exactly in the original place and was built in 1877.

I looked out from a window as my Social Security information was being processed and saw that some of the hospital exteriors really appeared ancient and imposing, but there was also a square, gardens and fountains at the centre of the sprawling structure.

Michael sat in the waiting room and there was nothing more healing than taking his arm, stepping outside and looking up at Notre Dame Cathedral.

But there were more important issues to deal with, "Michael, we have to see Ursula. Where is she?"

"She's at the American Hospital in Neuilly. It's eleven in the morning and visiting hours aren't until this afternoon." Michael held my arm firmly. "We're not using the Metro, I've called a taxi."

"Oh – okay, I'm totally disorientated."

"Are you strong enough to talk to the police, I think they have many questions?"

"I'd rather do it today, get it out of the way. But, Michael, I really owe you, I was doomed to die down there. Thanks for coming to my rescue."

Something changed in his face, "You could have lost your life – Jeffrey had a gun."

"And the girl, what about the girl, did they find her?"

"Yes, she was locked in another room. She's as well as can be expected."

"They were – Whyte and Jeffrey –"

"No need to explain, Liz. The girl is traumatised, but I – they think she hasn't been harmed physically – at least that's the news after initial examination. She's undergoing other tests. We have to wait though to find out the full story."

"You saved me, Michael, you saved all of us."

"Liz, don't thank me, it was Lena who got onto the police. She was walking Hamilton, and for some reason she had this idea to look in on the school. Apparently, she does so from time to time to be sure that none of us have forgotten to lock up. She saw lights on inside the school and thinking it was burglars called for help immediately."

"Good timing. So how did you and M. Jacques arrive on the scene?"

"You didn't turn up at the café where we were supposed to meet, so I rang everybody. M. Jacques had already telephoned David about Ursula's collapse. I went to Rue Montrosier, thinking maybe you had heard about Ursula and had gone back. Mme Gomes was quite in charge there. You have an excellent concierge."

"That we do, a dramatic one."

"Mme Gomes is rather special, she spoke a lot about the curse of Room 1. In any case, Ursula kept mumbling that she'd left a voice message on your phone and sent you a text."

"I didn't get to check them – I forgot my phone at the school."

"Ursula insisted that we had to contact you. She spoke of someone called Eva and said that you were in danger and that we had to go to the school."

"So you came to Rue des Soeurs."

"Yes. I left David to accompany Ursula. Then I jumped in a taxi with M. Jacques and went straight to the school. The place was empty and at first I thought Ursula had been raving."

"So what changed your mind?"

"I found your phone case on the ground in 'Oxford'."

"That was lucky."

"I knew from you how to get the key for 'St. Alban's'. We went into Whyte's office and opened the door behind the shelves. We went downstairs but couldn't go farther because there was another locked door. But I wasn't going to give up. M. Jacques knew a manhole on the street from which we could enter without having to break the door. So we ended up using one of his famous tunnels. It was faster. The tunnel forks off. If you take one way, it leads under the school and there's no cavity wall blocking the passage like there is in the tunnel from the Irish College. The second fork takes you to the underground brothel that David's researching."

"You saw the brothel then?"

"We didn't hang around to look. But – amm – it's rather well preserved. I'm sure David will find it fascinating."

"You can say that again."

"That wasn't my concern, you were. I found them – that – Jeffrey with you – and Whyte –"

"Jeffrey's bad, they both are."

Michael took my hand, "You know the rest. In the meantime, Lena came along and the police came. Both Jeffrey and Whyte have been taken into custody and there is a big exploration going on in Whyte's cellars."

The next hour and a half was spent at the police station where I sat in a quiet room describing everything to a young policeman who typed it out. I persuaded Michael to meet me later at Rue Montrosier, promising him that I would take a taxi back there after I'd finished with the police. He accepted reluctantly, only when I told him that it would be good too for him to clean up before visiting Ursula.

As soon as I entered the building at Montrosier, I was greeted by a Mme

Gomes high as a kite. 'Room 1 had struck again –' Ursula was lying in a hospital bed. She gushed out the story to anyone who cared to listen to her. By now, it had become a thriller. Mme Gomes seemed to regret that the drama had only produced a near-death experience and not the full thing, no offence meant to Ursula.

"Perhaps, the power of the curse has been broken forever, by Ursula," I suggested. "She survived, after all."

I left the concierge pondering that.

I went wearily upstairs. M. Jacques was hovering along the corridor.

I thanked him and invited him to come with Michael and me to the hospital to visit Ursula.

"No, no, it is not my place," he waved a hand bashfully.

"Ursula would like you to," I insisted. "Please come with us."

"No, no."

"You helped save both our lives. You were magnificent."

"It was nothing," M. Jacques dismissed, but he looked grateful and proud.

I accepted finally that he preferred to stay away from all the hospital fuss and left him in peace.

"I will take care of the cat," he offered.

Elle came prancing down the corridor. I took her up in my arms, "Thank you, M. Jacques. It will be an ease to Ursula to know that her cat is in safe hands. We can share the cat-sitting duties between us."

Elle purred and meowed.

I went to my room. My body was aching all over. I then made a long telephone call to Mme Defoe.

21

It was no secret that Ursula was an attention seeker and this time she had it all. There were visits and calls from relatives and friends. As soon as Ursula got back her strength, she cashed in on it and languished on the hospital bed, surrounded by flowers and cards. I spent many hours with her and the hospital room became like a new living room. It certainly felt like that with Michael and David often joining us.

Information about Whyte's school and his criminal activities dribbled in little by little. We learned that all sorts of forged documents and false invoices were found in the cellars under the school. It appeared that Whyte was drawing off funds to finance his way of life and cover debts. In addition, he did have a secret society – some sort of sham organisation that was also mixed up in the corruption. He seemed to have gone to a lot of extremes to get around the fiscal system. Unfortunately, we were told little about the Indian girl except that she was physically okay and would be an important link to finding out about other possible victims. We understood that the trafficking of some girls was managed by Jeffrey and it involved selling them as servants or prostitutes to a network of nasty individuals. Whyte was in so much trouble financially that he was prepared to do anything to cover his debts.

I watched out for Michael each day and tried to read his face for signs. Since the different events, we hadn't shared a really private moment together. I felt it was deliberate on his side. He was considerate and friendly, but guarded. It wasn't easy getting him on his own. He had little shows and performances here and there. He'd been to London and back on at least two weekends. He was never free and appeared to have the agenda of a director. I'd asked for space in our relationship, but these weren't ordinary times – we'd been through a lot these past weeks. Michael, however, preferred to meet me at the hospital when I visited Ursula. It was a good way to eschew a face to face meeting alone with me. Although frustrated, I decided that perhaps it was best for now. On my side, I tried to concentrate on finalising my updated C.V. and on fine tuning a list of language schools I could apply to.

****

"You'll never guess the latest," was Ursula's greeting as I walked into her hospital room. David and Michael were by her bed and from what I could see pampering her.

"I'm all ears," I said.

"There is proof that links Fabre to Whyte's financial corruption," Ursula said. "There was lots of funny business going on between the school and P.A.F.I."

"How did they eventually find that out – was it through tax inspections carried out at the school?" I asked.

David moved a trolley from beside Ursula's bed to make more space. It was littered with the remains of her lunch – clearly, not hospital food, but all sorts of goodies brought by the guys. "It's quite a story," he said.

"M. Chevalier exposed them," Michael explained. "In a nutshell: he became suspicious from audits he conducted in P.A.F.I. He worked out that Fabre had been tampering with some files and it was his inquiries that originally led the inspectors to the school and Whyte."

Good on M. Chevalier, I thought, one up for him. "Did Lena or Judith tell you all that?"

"No," Michael's reply was curt.

"Oh, do you still have classes with – amm – your Mme Michot – the HR?"

Michael turned away, but I'd already seen his anger flare up.

It had popped out in spite of me. Or maybe, unconsciously it hadn't been by accident – I'd wanted to break through his seeming indifference this past while and to provoke some reaction. I regretted my question immediately.

Ursula hastened to cover the moment, "Michael, would you open that bottle of water for me?"

"Sure – there you are."

"Thanks, Darling," said Ursula. "Now tell me, Michael, what exactly are people saying about P.A.F.I. and Whyte's school?"

"Whyte cracked," said Michael, "he told everything to the police. The rumour I've heard is that Whyte and Fabre were creaming money through sham service provider contracts. Jeffrey was the whiz doing the computer side and they were all drawing profit from it. There were teachers who didn't exist giving classes that never took place. Until recently, Jeffrey was operating behind the scenes. Then, suddenly, as you know he was introduced as a teacher in the school. Going to P.A.F.I. to pretend to check Chevalier's English level was not a clever move. But they must have panicked and I think Jeffrey was looking for some way to help Fabre cover his tracks and hide their corruption."

"What about Judith?" Ursula asked.

"Lena says Judith didn't have anything to do with the corrupt business and knew nothing about it," said Michael. "But she is responsible for negligence and I imagine she won't want to stay on much longer at the helm of the school."

"Is the school going to close soon then?" asked Ursula.

David patted her on the shoulder, "Try not to get anxious about that."

"Surely not right away," I said, "classes and contracts already underway will continue for the time being. At least, that's what Lena told me. The investigation is still in the early stages, I cannot imagine what else they'll uncover. I think there must be enough evidence in that underground place to condemn William Whyte, Fabre, Jeffrey and all their buddies for a long time."

"Criminal bastards," said Ursula.

"It's a mess, a horrible story whatever way you look at it," said Michael.

"It's awful," said Ursula, "that poor Indian girl. David," Ursula put out her hand to him, "I have a request for you."

"Yes," he drew closer to her bedside.

"You have to say many, many masses in the future for the Indian girl and all the girls. Pray also for Eva's soul and the souls of those who suffered the same fate as her, past and present. Will you do that?"

David smiled, "I will and I'll make special mention of all the victims in my thesis, the known and unknown. If I publish some of it in journals, I'll make sure those people are remembered."

"Thanks so much," Ursula leaned back on her pristine pillows. "You know, the one advantage to being stuck in this hospital is having a toilet and bathroom. Can you believe it, I have to get violently ill to deserve that. But now that I have it, I'd give anything to be able to go back to my room for some freedom and independence."

"I get that totally," I said.

****

I caught up with Michael in mid performance in front of The Pompidou Centre. Although not yet eleven in the morning, the air was hot and humid and the weather forecasters had warned that the heatwave would last all July. I waited for him to finish his grand finale of juggling tricks. He bowed to a burst of clapping, while coins jingled and jangled into his hat – and with them, a few lucrative rolled up paper bills fell silently. He took a towel and wiped the perspiration from his face.

"Michael."

"Hi, Liz."

"Where have you been, I've been trying to reach you all morning?"

"Sorry, I was practising with some others in the Magician's Association. While there we have orders to shut down all phones."

I refused to be put off. There had been so much happening recently that he probably didn't know where I was at emotionally or what I felt. I wouldn't let pride get in my way, it was too important for that.

"Are you doing a show tonight?" I asked.

"I'm doing an act in a theatre with a capacity of around one hundred places."

"Where?"

"Théâtre Montmartre-Galabru."

"That's great."

"Yes."

"Yes?" Damn, this was hard, he wasn't very forthcoming.

"It's a small theatre, but yes, it's a big deal for me."

He pulled a ribbon from his pocket and switched on some music, "Come if you want."

"Do you want me to?"

"Up to you," he raised the volume, pulled out some ribbons from his pocket and went into his next act.

My mind was made up – I wanted to see Michael that evening. As soon as I got back from classes, I got ready. I decided on a colourful gypsy skirt and light silvery top.

I went to Ursula's room, "Will you be okay on your own?" While anxious to see Michael, I didn't want to leave Ursula by herself. She had been released from hospital two days earlier and was now back in her room. Although almost her usual self, she was thinner and paler.

"I'll try to manage," Ursula was squatting on her bed, glued to the computer.

"Good, because I'm going out tonight."

"With Michael?"

"Just going to see him perform – I saw that look, I'm talking about his magic act."

"Whatever you say. You go and enjoy yourself, don't worry about me. I wouldn't want to spoil your night."

I was going to give a smart retort, but restrained myself. Ursula had given me enough scares, and although much recovered, she was still weak. I wanted to be sure she was okay. Then I thought of something, "Maybe I could ring David just to keep an eye on you."

Ursula looked contented with herself, too contented, "David is coming, he wants to see for himself that I'm okay." She sighed, lay back on the bed, "I only wish I was feeling stronger – still it will be nice to have him drop by."

"I hope he doesn't have to give Absolution." I left Ursula laid out on her bed, awaiting David's visit.

It was an evening of magic and illusion. The whole show at Théâtre Montmartre-Galabru was very entertaining. Michael was one of several acts, but his stood out, at least in my eyes. The small mid-19th century theatre was full. Michael managed to win over his audience and it hadn't been a foregone conclusion. The applause received wasn't just polite, but genuinely appreciative. 'Michael, you've spent your last days teaching,' I thought. 'Of that I'm sure.'

Afterwards, I went backstage. Michael was surrounded by show business people. He wasn't the star, but he was beginning to shine. He was looking around and found me. Then he continued to look directly at me for a long moment. Eventually, he freed himself from his new fans and made his way towards me.

"Thanks, Liz, for coming. I knew you were in the audience somewhere, I just knew it. I felt it. It gave me confidence and strength, you cannot imagine how much."

"You were wonderful, Michael. I think you're on the road to becoming a real professional –"

He waited –

I went on my toes and kissed him, "Congratulations."

He looked into my eyes, "Liz –?"

"Yes."

"Will you wait for me to finish here, I need to talk to a few more people and –"

"You take your time, Michael. I'll wait, I'm going nowhere."

He took in my words, turned to go and then turned back: "I want to be alone with you to share this little success. But for now, I need you to stay by my side – don't stand here in the corner."

He brought me back into the little group in the protection of his arm. He introduced me and I found it easy to fit in. I enjoyed mixing with people who would become part of his future.

It was a balmy First of July night. We walked towards the Metro station at Place Pigalle. The red light district was humming with visitors and locals, and bars and clubs – there were dozens and dozens of buses parked along the boulevard.

I stopped, "Michael, I promised Ursula that I wouldn't leave her alone.

I'm going back to Montrosier tonight."

"Of course, if that's what you want," his voice was cool.

"You're welcome to come with me, that's if you don't mind making do, once again, with a single bed for two."

"Liz, do you mean that, you have forgiven me?"

"There was nothing to forgive."

"But every time her name comes up, I see suspicion on your face."

"You explained and I believe you. Let's not go back over that. I trust you and don't expect you to have to justify every time you come across her. So did you say you were coming to Montrosier?"

He grinned, "Did I ever. By the way, as you already know, I'm a contortionist artist as well as an illusion guy."

"So?"

"So getting into a small single bed with you is hardly a challenge."

I laughed, "Don't I know it. You'll really be lost when I'm very rich and have a king-sized bed."

He took me in his arms, "The Metro can wait."

After a while he spoke, "It's sealed on Pont des Arts."

"What is?"

"Our love, my love for you. I went back and put a special padlock on the bridge railing. It's black and silver with a little red heart which has the initials M and L scratched on it. I attached it just at the start of the bridge from the Left Bank – the beginning of our journey through life together."

"Michael, I don't know what to say," my eyes filled. It was silly to put locks on bridges, somebody would probably take it off again.

"Here," he pressed a tiny key into the palm of my hand and closed it. "I didn't want to throw it into the Seine – you now hold the key to my heart."

"What's that noise? It's your phone, Michael."

"Always at the wrong moment," he took it out, "Hello, oui, Monsieur, oui –"

I knew from his voice that the caller was important.

"Liz," he whispered, "it's a big promoter. This could be my break – this guy was at the show tonight and really liked what I did."

I looked on as he took the call and saw sheer delight on his face. He moved from one foot to the other, unable to hide his excitement.

He finished the call.

"Michael, it's the breakthrough, isn't it?"

"It's a start. He wants to meet me – we have an appointment Friday morning. I'm going to have to cancel a few classes. That's not hard to do," he leaped high and punched the air.

"That's brilliant, this could be it for you," I jumped into his arms. He whirled me around until we were both out of breath and I was completely dizzy.

"Come on," he grabbed my hand, "let's hop on that merry-go-round." He dragged me towards the carrousel on the island in the middle of Boulevard de Clichy."

"You know, I've been wanting to get on one of those. I haven't been on one since I was a child," I followed him laughing.

He ran, "Look at me," he did a spin and a twirl.

"Michael, careful – watch out!"

I saw it – he didn't. The motorbike had overtaken a parked bus and was coming too fast.

I cried out, "Michael! No!" he'd lost his balance, it was too late to – I screamed his name over and over.

I heard the brakes screeching. There was a thud and a crash – Michael was flung like a rag doll.

I was on my knees beside him. Blood trickled down his face –

"Don't touch him – don't touch him," a woman's voice said, "don't move him, wait for the ambulance."

Somebody pulled me away. People were milling around – a crowd had gathered and formed a circle. I tried to reach out to Michael, but felt arms holding me back. There were fire trucks, Gendarmes and noise everywhere. I put my hands to my ears and tried to block out the sounds of sirens, shouted instructions, mechanical carrousel organ music –

People asked me questions – I don't know what I said or what answers I gave. I remember sitting at the back of a police car and the bright lights of Pigalle burning.

In the hours that followed, I was completely numb, going through the motions, wishing for the nightmare to go away. But it didn't go away. My phone never stopped ringing. There were calls from teachers offering to help or to listen. They were just being kind, being there for me. There were messages from people I didn't know but who knew Michael. They were looking for information, asking me what happened and what his chances were.

****

Michael was in a coma in Hôpital Hôtel-Dieu. I couldn't have imagined being back there in those circumstances. The doctors decided to keep him in an artificial coma for longer rather than risk the damage that an abrupt return to consciousness might cause. But they would not be able to fully determine if there was any brain damage until they brought him out of that coma. The unknown was unbearable.

Michael's family took over. There were trips, endless trips going to and from the hospital, grabbing seconds to be near him. I wanted to sit by him day and night, but I knew his family came first. Ursula and David were never far away. They insisted on preparing meals that I barely touched.

Ursula sat with me for hours every night. The whole seventh floor rallied around. Even Mme Gomes tried to help. It was people's sincerity, the way they were there for me that helped me get through each day. I received dozens of offers to bring something from the shop: cakes, biscuits… People always think you need to eat. But it was the simple gestures that counted.

Lena arrived at my door, short of breath, clutching a bag of food, "You gotta eat and Ursula tells me that you ain't eating."

"Lena, it's nice of you, but I don't feel like eating. I want to be alone."

"Sorry, Honey, I'm winded after your stairs, so I'm gonna have to sit here a while."

She fussed around my little room and managed to produce something decent from a saucepan and hot plate.

So I ate it to please her and because I knew I had to.

"Where's Hamilton?"

"With a friend. Don't worry about him, Hamilton ain't waiting desperately for Lena."

I watched from the window as the stooped Lena tottered in the direction of the Metro. The sunlight danced on the lush green of horse chestnuts and some maple-sycamores. I heard cars growl and grumble on the avenue and roundabout. And somewhere, soaring high above it all, I heard and saw the seagulls. I stared angrily at them and shouted in my head, 'Where were you when I needed you, you were supposed to be guiding and watching out for me?'

And the tears poured down my face again. My eyes were raw and sore from crying. I was empty and lifeless and could only collapse on the bed where I lay for hours. Everyone complained about the drought this summer, but I'd cried enough to water the whole city.

****

"Well?" Ursula came into the room.

Shaking my head, I tossed my mobile on the bed and rested my elbows on the window sill. "No news. I'm okay, Ursula, just let me be."

"No, you aren't okay; you're suffering and you don't know what to do, how to help."

"I feel so useless in this room. I want to be there for Michael, by his bed. Being his ex-girlfriend doesn't qualify me for anything. A few months of knowing him doesn't give me the legal right to barge in as I want. His family have that right. Oh, Ursula, what if they wake Michael up and there is brain damage – it's been seven days?"

"We don't know, we can't know until they do bring him out of the artificial coma. Don't lock yourself in here. It's better to talk to people, even if it's just me."

"Ursula, what do you mean – 'just me'? I don't know what I'd do without you."

"I haven't been an easy neighbour or friend," she stood beside me, leaning out the window – more paint cracked, while white flakes sprinkled on the floor.

"You've been a rock," I said.

Ursula shrugged. "Isn't that sky the bluest you've ever seen," she marvelled.

"It's blue all right," I agreed.

"Did I tell you I had a twin brother?"

"No, you never said," I looked at her in surprise.

"He died at the age of twelve by suicide," Ursula explained. "I think I've spent my life since then feeling guilty over it. It gutted me. I had so many questions, but no answers. Being the surviving twin, I blamed myself even more. Why him, why should I be alive? You made me realize, Liz, that I didn't have to go on punishing myself."

"Me? How did I do that?"

"I think by sticking with me, putting up with me longer than most people have, until I finally had to look at myself in the mirror. David has helped me to see that too. When I got into that mess with Fabre, I realised how far I'd fallen. I'd suicidal thoughts – they were more than thoughts. I didn't like myself and hated who I'd become. I've left all that behind me, I hope. That doesn't mean that I won't fall by the wayside, from time to time. But I think I'm beginning to learn how to treat myself better."

"What about you and David?"

"David and I will never be."

"You're still in love with him?"

"Yes, a little – ok a lot. But I don't want to hurt him, and I would if I tried to tempt him from his ideals. He needs to follow his vocation. I'd never forgive myself if I tried to make him give that up."

"That's a very mature Ursula talking. You could have a fling and he could still become a priest."

"No, because I don't see him as just a fling, I couldn't cope with that. It doesn't mean that we both won't give into temptation, but I'm respecting the rules, his rules. You and Michael are a real couple and you'll have your chance together, I'm sure of it."

I squeezed her hand tightly and prayed with all my heart it would be so, "I just want him to be okay."

22

The news came a few days later. It was July 15th, the day after Bastille
Day, France's National Holiday. Fireworks went off all night long, but
I wasn't in the mood for celebrations. The phone call from Michael's father
in the morning changed all of that.

"I knew it, I knew Michael was going to be okay," said Ursula as she
came rushing into my room.

I cried again, but these tears didn't burn. They fell softly.

They let me sit with Michael and encouraged me to talk to him. It was
important to get him to recognize people and to remember. The doctors
said the early signs were positive. Nonetheless, they had to be careful in
the coming days, weeks and months. They would need to keep him under
close observation.

"Liz," he said my name.

Michael was very bruised and looked in pain. He complained of being
sore everywhere and of the discomfort from all the tubes attached to him.
He grasped the morphine feeder.

I held his hand, stroked his face and spoke to him. I told him about
what had happened, what was happening. I told him many stories about

the school, the teachers and whatever came to my mind. I made up tales to cheer him up.

He couldn't hold the phone for long, his hands trembled. He left me messages that made no sense, just a jumble of words. There was still a hard road ahead for Michael's recovery to full health.

Lena and Ursula urged me to go back teaching. I did. I couldn't live on air. The investigation into Whyte's affairs continued. I still had work, but classes were getting scarce and hard to come by. Contracts weren't renewed. Teachers were laid off one by one. Judith wound things down. Lena told me that Judith planned to return to England. It looked like she would be cleared of wrongdoing in this whole scandalous mess.

****

Michael's progress was a yo-yo. Sometimes he was sleeping and I daren't disturb him. Sometimes he was down in himself, other times grumpy. Some days, he didn't remember the conversations of the day before. I met his parents several times. They were very kind and welcoming – and strong.

Towards the end of August, I saw real improvement. Michael's eyes were brighter and his hand was firmer. He began looking out for me and telephoning me to come. He was well enough to begin physiotherapy and rehabilitation.

It was September 10th and Michael's 26th birthday. His parents brought a cake to the hospital to mark the occasion. Michael was proud to show that he was walking on crutches, even if he did tire easily. Although he tried to hide it, I could see his disappointment when he learned that he would have to stay in hospital another week. After his parents left, I sat with him.

He began shuffling cards impatiently, "I'm fed up of this hospital, I've got to get out of here, Liz."

I looked at him tenderly, "It's just one more week. Your getting bored is the best news I've had in a long while. If they're keeping you here, it's for your own good. It's exactly to stop you from running and racing before you're really ready."

"That's what Mum and Dad keep telling me. Aren't my parents really something?"

"They are. I like your parents and I'm not just saying that – they're very special people."

He lay back on the pillows, "I shouldn't complain, I'm very lucky. I will have to stay quiet at least into early October. First, Dad's going to rent a place in Deauville where I can have fresh sea air for a couple of weeks. Deauville is lovely in September, especially as we appear to be getting something of an Indian summer. While in Deauville, my parents will hire someone to help me to do the day to day things. You know I'd prefer to be in your room with you taking care of me. I remember it all – I remember clearly where we were going to before the accident. I intend to get there, that's if you haven't changed your mind."

He couldn't have said anything else to convince me that he was on the road to full recovery. "The offer still stands, Michael. But if you've got ideas like that in your head, there can't be much wrong with you."

"My mind seems to be just fine where you are concerned. Unfortunately, for the moment, my fantasies will have to be lived out in my head."

"Don't worry, we have time, I'm not running anywhere. You just concentrate on getting fully back on your feet. You're very like your father, you know."

"Is that so," he gave me a crooked smile, "do you think you could tolerate an older Michael?"

"Oh, I could tolerate him very well."

"Michael, careful – it's not good for you to get excited."

Michael was on his feet without the crutches, "You see, I can walk," he crushed me to him.

"Hey, take it easy, you're putting bruises on me." But I put as many on him, I clung to him, "I came so close to losing you."

"Don't cry," he buried his face in my hair.

"You'd better sit, Michael," hugging him like that made me realise how thin and frail he still was.

He obeyed reluctantly.

"When you go to Deauville, I'll miss not being able to see you every day."

"Here," he fumbled in his locker and pulled out an envelope. He stood up again and put it in my hand.

"What is it?"

"Train tickets to Deauville. Dad got them for me."

"Tickets?"

"You're booked for the first weekend – the school can manage without you for one Saturday."

"I can't accept those, Michael, I'll buy my own."

"Shush," he silenced me with his lips, "please accept them, I insist. I don't want you starving yourself just in order to pay for those tickets."

"No, Michael."

"Please, accept them as a gift. It's for my own selfish reasons – I want to be sure to see you. I promise, it's not a bribe. I know how proud you are, but just this time."

"Okay," I relented, only because he was making himself upset. "I won't argue this time."

"Good."

"Where are your parents staying, are they using your studio?"

"Ah, no, they're in Hotel de Crillon."

"I see," I suddenly felt shy. I went to look out the window, I'd a view into a back yard of the hospital – bins and trolleys, I could identify with that.

"Liz?"

"Yes."

"Is something the matter?"

"Your family are very rich, aren't they?"

"My mother and father have done well. Does that bother you?"

"No, I don't know, a little maybe."

"Liz, come here."

I looked at him, his smile was teasing, "Magicians generally don't become very rich, not unless they are hugely successful and lucky."

I relaxed, "You disappoint me – where's your ambition?"

"I'm counting on you for that."

"Pity you're so delicate, we could have made use of that bed."

"I knew it," said Michael, "you're just after my body."

"I do seem to have a one-track mind where you are concerned. But it's not recommended for now."

"There are all sorts of possibilities."

"What exactly do you have in mind?"

"I seem to recall some images from a certain museum."

"Oh, are you suggesting – "

"I'm not suggesting, I'm saying that when I'm better we could go back and study some sculptures, take some notes."

"You mean to help David in his studies?"

"Exactly."

"I've always been a good student."

****

By late September, the official news was that all teaching contracts had to finish before the end of the year. On December 31st, Whyte's school would shut down for good. Judith continued to come to the office, but just for a couple of hours each day, and Lena stayed on to help her to tie up some administrative loose ends.

Lena stood in the courtyard despondently smoking over Hamilton, "I guess it's time for me to retire. Hell, we're all responsible – not you teachers, but the rest of us. We let him bully his way and never challenged him. We preferred to keep our heads in the sand. You had the guts, Liz, to stand up to William Whyte and fight."

"I was new here and had nothing to lose. But remember, I gave up too. In the end, I started to take everything for granted – I let myself be fooled into believing that it wasn't my business."

"Sure, but it don't excuse me."

I looked on as a few of the remaining teachers trailed out, "See you, Angie, nice bag. Is it new?"

"Yeah, isn't it lovely, it was a present."

"It is lovely and spacious."

"Bye," said Jonathan, making a drinking sign with his hand.

I shook my head, "Another time."

Lena seemed fixed on watching a wisp of smoke whorl upwards. "I'm glad Michael is recovering fast. I'm happy also for Ursula. I got attached to that girl, got attached to you too."

"Same here," I touched her hand. I knew how difficult it was for Lena to show her feelings. "It wasn't all bad at W.W.S.O.E. & F.L, there were good things too. I have a lot of happy memories."

"And sad ones," Lena sniffed. "Are you sure that you're holding up okay? You've been through a lot between Michael and Ursula."

"I'm fine, I just wish I'd been quicker to help the Indian girl. Does she have a family somewhere?"

Lena shook her head, "None that have been found – she's in the hands of special services."

"Were there more girls – I heard them speak about at least one more?"

"They've picked up information about a second girl and they're continuing their investigation. Whyte is co-operating fully."

"That's small consolation. I wish I had acted on my gut instinct sooner."

Lena stubbed out her cigarette, "You did what you could. It's a regret I'll have to live with. It makes me sick to the core."

****

A phone call from M. Chevalier's assistant was the last thing I was expecting. She wanted to arrange a meeting with her boss. She told me M. Chevalier wished to discuss a business matter with me.

It was strange going back to P.A.F.I. to meet M. Chevalier again.

He stood by his office desk and held out his hand, "I am sorry, so sorry, for all the difficulties you have had, I – "

"That's okay, M. Chevalier, thank you for your understanding," I didn't want to go into the bad, sad story of my school or other things.

He followed my lead and gestured to a chair, "Please sit down, make yourself at home."

I lifted my brows, another one of my expressions put to use correctly.

He inclined his head, "I use it a lot."

I waited while he smoothed out a page, "Amm – in the interest of good service here in P.A.F.I. – and given the difficulties with your former school –"

"M. Chevalier, are you reading that?"

"Yes. I wanted to use good English."

"Oh, okay," he would never change, "carry on, sorry for interrupting."

He concentrated and continued reading, "As you know, we have decided to give our future contracts of English training to several different suppliers. If you opened your own school or worked as a freelancer, P.A.F.I. would be happy to put some contracts your way. I can recommend people to advise you on the best way to go about that."

M. Chevalier did have a way of surprising me. It had crossed my mind to try going into business for myself – I'd discussed it with Mme Defoe. But having contracts handed on a plate to me like that – well that was a real start.

"Why are you doing this?" I asked him.

"I like to encourage young entrepreneurs and you are a good teacher."

I knew my eyes were moist, but I also knew that tears would embarrass him. I wanted to hug him, but didn't think it was a good idea.

I ran things over in my mind. I couldn't afford to lease school premises – that would be too costly and too crippling at the beginning. I could, however, operate from my room, while giving classes in-company. Even if I moved in with Michael, it might be good to keep business separate and hang on to my room. Besides, with Michael's future career taking off, it was no longer sure where his living base would be. I just needed a good computer and printer for myself. I could start small and gradually add things on. If I did grow the business, I'd only take on quality teachers; then again, I'd need some fillers-in and – well, I had time to work it out.

"I take that as a 'Yes'?" M. Chevalier smiled.

I wanted to say many things, but I simply said, "Yes, I will accept the challenge and the contracts."

"Then it's settled."

We shook hands.

"M. Chevalier, could I ask you something?"

"Yes."

"You knew, didn't you?"

He looked uncomfortable, "About what?"

"About the corruption in the school and all the mishandling of money between Fabre and William Whyte. You knew that they were gleaning money from P.A.F.I. through Fabre and that Jeffrey was interfering with the accounts system somehow?"

M. Chevalier looked blankly at me – he wasn't going to tell me.

"I know you can't speak while the investigation is ongoing. But at least tell me how you knew?" I asked.

He sighed, "I had suspicion, but no proof. Then that man, Jeffrey, interfered with my computer the day he came to test me."

"You set it up, didn't you – you went out of the room, pretending to make a phone call, and left your computer open – Jeffrey walked right into it?"

"I am not so clever, but the opportunity presented itself. I suspected William Whyte for a while – he sent me a strange teacher last year."

"There are a lot of strange teachers in the school. I suppose you suspected me for a while too."

"I did not know you, but I could not trust anyone."

"So will you be the new C.F.O.?"

"Yes."

"You have my congratulations then. I'm sure you'll do a good job."

"I would prefer different circumstances and –" he paused and looked at me. "Ah – Elizabeth?"

"Just call me Liz. What did you want to ask me?"

"So, Liz –" he began and then seemed to change his mind.

"Yes?" I asked, now really curious.

He shook his head, "Another time, perhaps – maybe."

We talked a little while longer. By the time I was ready to leave, my head was full of ideas.

We shook hands again, "I can't thank you enough for your confidence in me, M. Chevalier."

"It is nothing," he walked me to the door and returned to his desk and his spreadsheets.

****

"Can I come in?" Ursula called from outside my door.

"Yes." I dried my eyes.

Ursula walked in, followed by Elle, "Liz, are you crying?"

"I'm crying because I am happy and sad at the same time. Oh, Ursula, I still can't believe how close I came to losing Michael. Then I keep thinking of that Indian girl, how she must have suffered, how she is still suffering. I've no right to complain. I should count my lucky stars."

"You have every right to complain. That's my philosophy – complain as much as you want, feel as sorry for yourself as you wish, nobody else can do it for you."

"I think I like your philosophy. I can see from your face that you have news."

"David visited the underground brothel – hotel. He's very excited."

"Is he – did he tell you about the sculptures?" I queried.

"Sculptures – they're worth nothing," Ursula waved her hand. "It's the paintings – they're the work of Henri de Toulouse Lautrec."

"Is he important?"

"Important, of course he is. You've no culture at all."

"I admit I know nothing about famous brothel artists and I'm not sure I want to know."

"Stay ignorant then," Ursula made a face.

"But – I have a certain knowledge of brothel sculptures."

"I'm going down with David to see exactly what you're talking about. I've been listening to you go on about those sculptures for weeks."

"Do go down, but it might be advisable not to bring David."

"Huh. Liz, there's something else. I hope you don't mind, but I have planned a little dinner here tomorrow evening for the seventh floor. People have been kind and helped me – us, in many ways, and I want to thank them."

"You don't have to ask my permission."

"I wasn't asking, I was just informing you. I was going to go ahead with it anyway."

"Don't I know it, but it's a good idea. Maybe Lena would like to come, I think she's a bit lost and lonely."

"You're right. Liz, I was wondering –"

"Yes, Ursula," I saw it coming, but waited.

"In this new school venture you'll be starting, you won't be able to do all the teaching yourself, will you?"

"In the early stages, yes."

"Oh – but you will let me know if you need help, won't you? I mean, once the business starts coming in, you'll surely need reinforcements."

I closed my eyes and said a silent prayer, 'Lord, help me to never have to count on the wonderful teaching talents of my friend, Ursula.'

****

It was October 3rd and we should all have been feeling a little down that the summer was well and truly over, but quite the contrary, the atmosphere was festive and high spirited. Everybody chipped in to help make Ursula's celebratory meal a success. M. Jacques helped David put together once more our makeshift, long corridor table. Michael was ordered to sit and not exert himself. Ursula didn't need any orders of that kind. Hamilton and Elle eyed each other suspiciously – there followed a lot of sniffing and final acceptance. The group was smaller than the last time – Olivier and Sebastien wouldn't be back until mid October and the Bjania family were visiting relatives.

Mme Gomes declined our invitation initially, but curiosity brought her upstairs with a cake she'd made. She took a good look inside Room 1. As nothing jumped back out at her, she relaxed a little.

Ursula poured her some wine, "Let's drink to the spirits past and present and to happier times in Room 1. And," Ursula added, "to the birthdays gone and forgotten in all the drama. Liz was twenty-five July 17th and I was twenty-six August 8th."

So we raised our glasses. After a quick gulp, Mme Gomes was happy to return downstairs, shaking her head in disbelief.

It got quite noisy and boisterous. M. Brosse, we discovered, could tell a good story when he occasionally abandoned his head bobbing and monosyllabic grunts. M. Jacques was on top form and told us in his booming voice about a few more secret tunnels.

David tapped his glass with a spoon.

"Speech, speech," we called.

"Eva –" he began.

"Eva," Ursula repeated the name reverently.

"Her name was Eva Lavalliere and her stage name was Eugénie Fenoglia. She was born in Toulon in April 1866."

"So she did exist," I said.

"Told you so," Ursula eyed me over her glass.

"She had a hard life," said David. "Her father was violent. He shot her mother in front of her and then shot himself. Eva came to Paris at the age of fourteen to be an actress. It didn't work out obviously and from what I can piece together, she fell into a lower form of acting, erotic theatre, pornographic shows in brothels, and into the darker world of prostitution. A 'chambre de bonne' at 9 Rue Montrosier was her official residence for a while. She was probably used as a servant by the landlord and forced to work at his clubs. If you recall, the owner of this building also owned some buildings where your school premises are."

"What happened in the end?" asked Michael.

"Suicide," said David. "She ended her life in 1901 by jumping from a window on the seventh floor of this building. There is a little cross in Montmartre cemetery marking her grave."

"That's right," said Ursula, "David and I visited it. It's so sad, it just has the lines – 'If the Devil exists, then so too does God – Thou who didst create me, have pity on me'."

"If you don't mind," said David, "I'll say a little prayer for her."

So we joined him in his blessing for Eva.

There was silence for a moment as we all pondered David's words and the past.

"Did you find out anything about a murder in this building?" I asked after a while.

David shook his head, "I did a little research, but found nothing. But perhaps one day, I'll learn more."

I saw Lena reach for her packet, "Now, Lena, if you want to smoke, do it out my room window."

"Thanks, Honey, it's my last packet, I'm gonna give them up."

"That's good news."

"When I see how close you young folk came to losing your lives, figured it ain't right me playing with my health. I said to myself, 'Lena, you gotta wise up'."

"It's a good decision." I opened my room door for her, "You can count on us to support you."

Lena inhaled and leaned her cigarette hand out my window, "You know, Liz, with this new venture of yours, you might need someone to help you out from time to time and rustle up business – we could negotiate according to how you were doing."

"Oh, Lena," I clapped my hands, "you're one hell of a lady."

"What," she chortled, took a puff and blew more smoke out the window.

"Always the business woman. Sure you can help out – in time I might need someone to deal with appointments and cancellations. But you're going to have to learn to type decently and how to manage the basic functions of a computer."

"I ain't promising, but I'll work around it."

"I've no doubt you will."

I was doing it again, giving in to that soft spot, feeling sorry for Lena.

What the heck, it wasn't as if I could afford a top-notch assistant.

"Ain't that view fantastic and look you can just catch the Eiffel Tower shimmering. It must be midnight," Lena said.

"You're joking, you can see the Eiffel Tower." I leaned over Lena's head, "Where?"

"Right there."

I followed the line of her cigarette. There it was, just enough to tease, peeping over the top of the horizon.

"That's crazy, I have never managed to spot it before," I exclaimed.

"They have been replacing all the standard lights with a new system, so it has not been sparkling regularly. They are running tests for a special show that they are preparing for the year 2000. It's going to be a big deal at the end of this year on New Year's Eve when the world rings in the new millennium. The Mayor of Paris, Bertrand Delanoë, wants to have the best show and the authorities plan to have special shimmering lights. I guess you just weren't looking out the window at the right time. But I reckon we are getting a little preview right now."

Lena was right. In fact, after my early days in the room, I more or less gave up looking for the tower out my window. "Hey," I called, "hey everybody, I can see it – I can see the Eiffel Tower."

The room crowded up and we took turns to watch until the shimmering quenched and the tip of the tower faded and was once more invisible to the eye.

"Magic," said Michael and he looked into my eyes, "a touch of illusion."

"Yes," I put my hand to the key that hung from my neck chain. I had gone to Pont des Arts while he was still in a coma and found the lock. There were only a handful of padlocks on the bridge, so it hadn't been hard to find.

"We're like a clutch of chickens in here," said Ursula.

"We are, but I prefer to soar like the seagulls," I corrected, "those birds are able to live on the coast or inland. They can nest on the cliff edge or the chimney pot. They make Paris as much their home as any native. That's what I call strength. They roost wherever they want and learn how to survive."

"I hadn't thought about them like that," said Michael. "But I know that when you've got good roots in one place, you can always face the storms and stand strong wherever you go."

293

"And never be alone," said Ursula, "birds understand the power of being in a flock."

I was no longer alone. I took Michael's hand and fixed my gaze on the rooftops of Paris. One could settle anywhere if they had friends, true friends – that's what made a place a home.

BIOGRAPHY

KATHLEEN CURTIN Was born in Ireland in 1964. She grew up on a small farm in County Limerick. Later she attended University College Cork, where she graduated with a Ph.D in Geography.

At the age of twenty-three, having been awarded a scholarship by the National University of Ireland, she went to Paris to continue her studies at the Sorbonne. Paris has become her adopted home. Writing is her passion and she cannot imagine a day without putting words to work.

Email: kurtin@orange.fr
Twitter: kathleen curtin@kitybern
Facebook: Why Seagulls Roost in Paris-Kathleen Curtin

Previous publications:
Madame Lune (June 2015 by Open Books Publications)
Patching Time (June 2016 by Kathleen Curtin/Spleodrach)

22964366R00178

Printed in Great Britain
by Amazon